Fearless

MARIANNE CURLEY

BLOOMSBURY
LONDON NEW DELHI NEW YORK SYDNEY

Bloomsbury Publishing, London, New Delhi, New York and Sydney

First published in Great Britain in July 2015 by Bloomsbury Publishing Plc
50 Bedford Square, London WC1B 3DP

www.bloomsbury.com

Bloomsbury is a registered trademark of Bloomsbury Publishing Plc

A CIP catalogue record for this book is available from the British Library

ISBN 978 1 4088 2264 7

Typeset by Deanta Global Publishing Services, Chennai, India
Printed in Great Britain by CPI Group (UK) Ltd, Croydon CR0 4YY

1 3 5 7 9 10 8 6 4 2

For John
For thirty-five years of knowing when to crack
a joke and when to say nothing.
Where would I be without you bringing
the sun into my mornings and
closing the cold out at night?
To the next thirty-five years, my love,
wherever they may take us.

1

Nathaneal

He steals her straight from my wings. He takes my love from me right before my eyes.

For three thousand years her spirit and mine lived together in Peridis and, knowing the day would come when we would be together in our angelic-physical forms, we loved each other as if there were no tomorrows. We knew our destiny: that we would be together for eternity, and we swore to find each other no matter how long it took.

We've already been through so much. But we had not counted on the Dark Prince, his hunger for power, his need to destroy and his desire for Ebony.

With my brothers Gabriel and Jerome scrambling over bodies on my right, Michael clearing his own path to my left and Isaac, Sol and Uri close behind, we storm after the enemy, prepared to follow the Dark Throne soldiers into the darkest depths of Skade, if that's where they take her.

I must get Ebony back.

I underestimated Prince Luca. And this mistake – *my* mistake – will have catastrophic effects if we don't stop him. Luca's plans to create Soul Readers by blending Ebony's bloodline with his could threaten the survival and freedom of all humankind.

At the tunnel's edge I see her twisting her upper body to peer over the shoulder of the enemy carrying her off. She sees me. Our eyes connect. Hope reaches across the space between us like a rainbow after a storm. I nod, letting her know I'm coming, that I'm right behind her. Rich violet colour drenches her eyes and she gives me a ghost of a smile.

Then the gates of Skade slam down between us.

The shudder of all twelve gates smashing into the bridge propels everyone backwards into a high arc. Shockwaves pummel us, keeping us airborne, shoving us further back into the tunnel. We struggle to find our balance, our wings tangling with each other's. As we start to drop, hundreds of angels, light and dark, collide. It's a nightmare. My sister-in-law Sami sideswipes me when forces drive her horizontally across the bridge. I try to catch her but she's moving too fast. I look for her husband, Jerome. Soaring in, he hits Michael, their wings becoming so tangled they fall to the ground in a heap. A Dark Throne comes from nowhere. His snapped wing-joint lodges like an arrow into my throat. I yank it out. Blood spurts over both of us.

There's mass hysteria as injuries take hold and pain sets in.

As I lie on the bridge with my hand clasped around my throat, all I can think about is Ebony. And that I've lost her.

'No!'

Still clasping my throat, I stagger to my feet and climb over bodies to get near the gates. A dragging noise makes me look down. My right wing is broken in three places and trailing. When I lower my hand to gather it off the ground, I'm relieved to find only a trickle of blood seeps from my neck wound. At least I'm healing fast.

Finally I'm standing before twelve shimmering gates in perfect condition.

Ebony. E-b-on-ee!

Rage, unparalleled by anything I've felt before, fills me with such force my powers threaten to burst through my veins and cause more injuries to friend and enemy alike. It builds, expands and stretches my muscles and skin.

'Michael. Isaac. Clear the area.'

And as they do as I instruct, I draw my power up, thrust my hands at the portion of gate directly in front of me and blast my energies into it.

Even before the smoke and gasses clear away, I can tell that nothing happened. The gate stands firm. I draw my power up again, holding it and building it until the pressure against my skin is unbearable. 'Stand back!'

I inhale deeply and I expel my power with all the force I can draw in one blast.

This time the bridge rumbles, but when the tremors settle and dust clears, the shimmering white gates still remain standing, intact.

'It's true then.' Michael shakes his head while staring at the gates. 'The High King made them impregnable purposely so nothing – not even *he* – could open them. It was his way to protect us from each other after the rebellion.'

'There has to be a way to rupture one.'

Jerome puts a hand on my shoulder. 'It could be danger-ous to open what you might not be able to close again.'

'There is always a way to achieve the unthinkable.'

And though she will probably not hear me, I forge a mind-link: *Ebony! Ebony, I swear, with the stars as my witness, I will come for you as soon as I can. I will bring you home.*

Michael glances down the bridge to where the blue light reveals the entrance to the Crossing, the dimension that separates the worlds, with portals to Earth, Avena and Skade. The entire length is a battlefield where both sides appear to have annihilated each other. 'You are right, cousin. There is always a way, and we will find it.'

More reinforcements for our side arrive. 'Uri, they wear your colours.'

'Yes, they're from my division.' His tone is disheartening as he comes over and explains. 'Before we left I put a brigade of five thousand on alert. I had hoped they would arrive before we lost …'

My heart skips a beat when he almost says … *Ebony.*

'I'm sorry, my prince.'

Finding a way through the gates and killing any angel that tries to prevent me reaching Ebony feels more important than spending even a second making my friend feel better, but I'm grateful for Uri's support and he needs to know this. 'Thank you, Uri. I certainly could use them.'

He lifts his head, his light yellow eyes suddenly alight. He places his right arm diagonally across his chest. 'My prince, I give you command of my battalion of one hundred thousand soldiers.'

'That's very generous of you, Uri, but I've never led an army.'

'I would be honoured to be your lieutenant.'

I put my hand on his left shoulder and rush to get my thoughts together. 'I accept, Uri. Thank you.'

'Wait.' Gabriel steps over ailing bodies to reach us. 'You can have my troops too.'

My eyebrows lift. '*Yours*, brother?'

'For only as long as you need them to retrieve my future sister-in-law. And I must be your *first* lieutenant.' He passes Uri a friendly smirk. 'You understand, don't you, Uri?' He swings his head back without waiting for Uri's response. 'Deal, brother?'

I look at Uri and wait.

Clearly Uri has something to say but refrains. 'As you wish, my prince.'

I nod, letting him know my appreciation. 'Then let us put these troops to good use. Gabe, Uri, secure the exit. No dark angel gets away today. Send teams after the cowards fleeing through the Crossing. Bring them all to me.'

Michael's hand comes down on my shoulder and I drop my guard for a moment. 'How did this happen, Michael?'

'I've known Luca from the beginning. We played, trained and fought battles side by side, but I didn't see this coming either, so don't be too hard on yourself. Luca has changed so much this last century his actions are harder to predict.'

'She warned me, you know.'

'It happened too fast,' Isaac says, coming over with Jerome and Sol and leading a dozen captured enemy angels. 'You can never fathom how the mind of such deep evil works.'

'That is something I'm going to have to learn, and fast.'

Gabe and Uri return with a large contingent of prisoners; most are healed enough to walk, but some with more severe injuries need assistance.

As I glance over the rows, a female soldier's neck wound catches my eye. She's losing blood faster than her self-healing can replace it. She's not complaining even though her injury must be causing acute pain. I point her out to Uri. 'Bring me that one.'

When he reaches the soldier, he lifts her into his arms and hurries back, laying her on the ground before me. I get down beside her and see that this dark angel is underage. That explains her slow self-healing. That, and the fact that she has a severed carotid artery. I gently replace the hand she holds against her wound, trying to keep the pressure on it. Maintaining eye contact so not to frighten the child, I begin healing her. 'What is your name, soldier?'

'Dajanie,' she murmurs, her eyes wide and fixed on mine as if I were a monster from her nightmares.

I keep talking to distract her while I try to locate the other half of her artery, which appears to have retracted deep inside her ribcage, flooding it with her own blood and slowly suffocating her. 'How old are you, Dajanie?'

'Fifteen, my lord.'

I hear Michael and the others huff around me.

'Have you been a soldier long?'

'Three years.'

This is such disturbing news that my power surges. I use the added energy to assist in removing her pooled blood, locate the other half of her severed artery and rejoin the two ends.

She inhales deeply and smiles, her eyes beginning to fill with tears, tears I have no time for today.

'Uri.'

'On it,' he says, and immediately guides the young soldier back to her position.

My gaze roams over the rest of the prisoners. 'How many, Gabe?'

'Nine hundred and more coming.'

Uri indicates the blue light. 'Here come a further five hundred. We caught fifty escaping through the Crossing. Where do you want us to put them all?'

'Here for now. Gabe, can you find me a Gatekeeper amongst this lot?'

'Gladly!' Gabe plucks five out, dragging three males and two females out in front of me, before he stands beside me and glowers at them. 'Which of you is the most senior?'

No one volunteers. They keep their eyes staring straight ahead, not even a flicker between them that might give one away. Luca has trained them well.

I walk past them slowly, stopping to stare into each pair of silver eyes, so similar and yet each so individual. Something about the last one, the taller female with brown hair slicked to her scalp, draws my attention. It's just a microscopic tightening of her chin, which she lifts slightly while under my inspection. It's enough to make me look deeper into her eyes. She doesn't flinch, but her pride gives her away.

'You,' I say, curling a finger at her to make her look at me. 'Step forward.'

Soundlessly she moves a foot-length.

'What is your name?'

She continues to stare straight ahead. 'Lailah.'

Her raspy voice sparks a memory. *Ah, yes.* On our way into Skade to rescue Ebony's parents, she was the senior Gatekeeper on duty. Though our passage had been court-sanctioned, she waved us through only once Uriel handed her a small bag of sparkling rocks. 'Well, Head Gatekeeper, I don't carry pink diamonds on me today, but under the circumstances —' I drop my eyes to her shackled hands and feet — 'I'm sure you understand.' Lifting them again, I order, 'Open a gate. I don't care which one.'

Despite her confinement, she can barely conceal her smirk. The sight fills me with rage. I barely contain the urge to wipe the expression off her face with my fist. I need her expertise.

Her eyes slide to mine. 'I cannot do as you command, my lord.'

'Why not?'

'The gates have been sealed.'

Heat spreads out in waves from the centre of my chest. 'Sealed? For how long?'

She looks directly into my eyes and smiles. 'A hundred years.'

2

Ebony

Luca grips me with iron strength as he carries me towards Odisha, the capital city of Skade. Wings, black as his heart, beat with deliberate, unfaltering synergy as beautiful as it is ugly. His heart – if that's what I'm feeling hammering against my ribs, thumps away at a dangerously fast pace.

Oh. No, that's *my* heart.

Maybe I'm not hearing his because he doesn't have one. I wouldn't be surprised if that were true. But no, there it is, thudding away in a steady, regular beat.

Surrounding us in the shape of a seven-pointed star, Dark Throne soldiers form our escort. Their silver eyes, glimpsed through narrow slits in their black armour, gleam with pride. They were successful today and it shows in the smug, arrogant looks they send one another.

We fly over farmland where silos, cement barns and stone castles emerge from barren hillsides. And as we draw nearer the capital, the buildings are higher as streets run closer together, and fill with curious onlookers pointing to the sky.

Is this really happening to me?

If only this was one of those dreaded nightmares where

Luca slips inside my mind and takes me on a journey through his realm. From the safety of my own bed, I could handle those, knowing I would soon wake and Nathaneal would hold me and chase away any lingering memories.

But this?

'Turn your face away,' Luca suddenly snaps.

This is no dream. This monster's voice is real. The heat his body emits is burning through my clothes. The powerful flapping of the Thrones' metallic blue wings is moving the air like the slipstream of an aeroplane. And then there's the air, with the pungent odour of sulphur dioxide, the sewer smell of hydrogen sulphide and the unmistakable stench of decaying flesh. I smell it, I taste it, and I have no choice but to breathe it in.

'Cover your face!'

'Tell me why and I might consider it.'

'What are you rambling about?'

'It's your vanity, isn't it? You don't want your people to see me all messed up. Is there a smudge of your angels' blood on my face?'

He looks at my face, scrutinising it with such intensity that I quickly regret my words. The unnatural vividness of his green eyes is mesmerising. I look away but he's inside my head now, picking through my brain as if with an iron poker. I throw up a mind-block. Out of necessity this is something I'm fast becoming proficient at doing. His voice softens. 'Turn your head, my lady, before it is scorched by the volcanic vents.'

Bursts of red steam erupt with a roar from the landscape below. The geysers shoot high into the atmosphere. One narrowly misses us, and only because Luca veers sharply. As he swings back into formation I glance down at a swampland of steaming red mud bubbling just under the surface.

Crap. He was protecting me.

Well, I wouldn't need protecting if he hadn't brought me here in the first place. I don't want anything from him. I certainly don't want him to care about me.

Shivers pass through me in shuddering tremors. I force my heart to slow down, willing it to be calm, not to show fear – or panic – or go into shock. Reality is starting to kick in, a reality I'm not yet ready for. I might never be. But to have a chance to make it through this, I need to give my brain time to catch up.

OK, so Luca has my physical body, and maybe that's something I can't change for now, but it doesn't mean he has to have all of me.

He will never have my soul.

After years of my parents drilling into me that I don't have one, that *no one* does, I finally know the truth. There is a heaven and it's called Peridis. There's a hell called Skade, and a world where angels live, called Avena. That's where I'm supposed to be, where I was supposed to grow up and attend school, learn to fly and use my powers without exhausting myself.

The reality is I'm a real angel, which means I'm immortal. And if I don't get out of here, that means I'm going to live forever in hell.

If my uncle, Zavier, hadn't killed off my memories within hours of my birth, that instinctive sense of who I am would have kicked in sooner. He helped engineer my abduction and hid me on Earth so my real angel family and my true love, Nathaneal, wouldn't find me. And when Nathaneal did, Zavier plotted with my best friend to make me doubt him, to trick me into a trap Luca had set. Eventually Zavier tried to make amends. But it was too little, too late.

I close my eyes and visualise Nathaneal carrying me to Avena. But it doesn't work. The arms around me are not Nathaneal's. Everything about Luca is different, from his overheated, hard-boned body to his slick, polished voice. Even his scent is sharper, woodier, not sweet and crisp and evocative.

As if my yearning conjures him, Nathaneal's blue eyes, as penetrating as ever, appear as if he were standing in front of me. My heart slows and a sigh escapes as his voice forms words in my mind: *Ebony. Ebony, I swear, with the stars as my witness, I will come for you as soon as I can. I will bring you home.* Tears ooze out. I squeeze my eyes shut to stop them, replying in my thoughts, *I believe you!*

Consumed by thoughts of Nathaneal, I do not notice our descent. It comes as a shock when Luca sets me down on my feet. I lose my balance a little and his fingers steady my hips. It feels like a caress. Instinctively I spin around and slap him across the face.

He grabs my upper arms and yanks me in close. Too close. His eyes flash, a fire igniting like autumn leaves caught alight. He stands over me and pushes an image into my mind.

I shut my eyes and try to block him, but it does nothing to stop the beast appearing in my head. The creature is at least four metres tall, with yellow glowing eyes. It has the body of a slender, well-formed man but a bull's head and long horns curving upwards. He sits in a chair made of twisting gold vines with flames licking up the sides. Around him flames burn in shiny black pots.

His arrogance is overwhelming. It pours out of his skin. He knows this but uses it as one of his strengths. He is all-powerful and rules this world. Lounging in his flaming chair of vines, fires burning around him, he is the almighty ruler here, the one, the only one that matters.

Luca is showing me that this beast is the true King of Skade.

And that the beast is him.

3

Nathaneal

Word spreads quickly, causing outrage, shock and panic amongst us all, even the prisoners who have been locked out of their own world. The impact of the Gatekeeper's words is not lost on me either. I will myself to remain calm.

I look into the Gatekeeper's eyes. 'A hundred years? *A hundred years?*'

'Yes, my lord.'

'Since King Luca sealed the gates, I'm sure he can open them again, especially when he learns how many of his soldiers I have captured.'

'Even if he could unseal the gates, my lord, he will not barter for us.'

'Really? So none of you is worth anything to him? Not even *one* of you?'

She flinches. Pain, fleeting and sharp, appears in her eyes but is quickly gone. 'Even if he would agree to such an arrangement, his highness sealed the gates so *no one* can open them, not even *he*, my lord, not for a hundred years.'

'You're lying!'

'No, my lord, I am not.'

14

I see that this soldier has already resigned herself to death. She has accepted the fate of a martyr.

But killing an unarmed soldier, a prisoner, is a line in the sand that I will not cross. All the prisoners before me now are simply soldiers obeying commands. They trust their king, and even though he has effectively abandoned them, they're still willing to die for him.

What will Ebony think when she hears this news? Will she give up hope that I will find a way?

Breathe, cousin. Michael lays his hand on my shoulder. Always beside me when I need him, I do what he advises and somehow the urge to explode remains contained, at least for now.

I survey the large number of prisoners Gabe and Uri's soldiers have gathered; more are descending through the blue light. Since dark angels are forbidden to enter Avena, and to hold them in the Crossing would be impossible due to the way the landscape changes, there is only one place we can take them until ... until what? Surely Luca will negotiate for their return *one* day, even if it is a hundred years from now.

'Gabe, Uri, secure the prisoners for transportation. We're taking them to Earth.'

Gabe blinks hard, but wisely doesn't question my command. 'Destination, brother?'

'Select three of your best to go on ahead and warn the Brothers of the Holy Cross Monastery. They are to inform Monsignor Lawrence of our need to access the underground facility. Those rooms should contain the prisoners until we can expand it.'

'Understood,' Gabe says. 'You know, it's a large number of prisoners we'll be taking to Earth. You've done well today, brother.'

'If I had done well today, Ebony would not be …' I pause to gather my thoughts. 'Ebony would be standing beside me now, preparing to go home to meet her real parents for the first time. That would have been a job well done.'

'Of course,' Gabe says. Swearing under his breath he murmurs, 'I'm sorry, Thane, I didn't mean anything by that. We're all shaken by her loss.'

Jerome nudges him with his elbow, hissing under his breath, '*Loss*, brother?'

'*Ah, shit!*' Gabe looks straight at me. It's the first time I have seen fear in my eldest brother's eyes. 'Thane, forgive me, I …'

I shake my head. There's no time for apologies, no time for *anything* except figuring out how to get Ebony back. 'Forget it. Forget it!'

Solomon arrives, adding several more hundred prisoners to the tally. I call him over. 'Have you spoken with your informant since the gates came down?'

'I've tried over and over, but there's no response.'

'Keep trying, Sol. I want to know where Luca has taken Ebony, and … how she's coping.'

'I'm on it, my prince.'

I watch him fly into the blue light of the Crossing, my mind whirling with what I need to do next. 'Isaac, what are your interrogation techniques like these days?'

'Excellent. I'm glad you asked. Do I have permission to

use them?' His eyes roam purposefully over the rows of prisoners. 'Any prisoner in particular, my prince?'

'All of them.'

For a moment there is utter silence.

'I want them talking. I want to know everything there is to know about Skade's defences. I want information on all Luca's residences, from his city palace to his secret mountain hideaway. I want to know exit and entry points. The prisoners must give me maps, floor plans, drawings, schedules, secret tunnels. I want servants' names, routines, what uniforms they wear, their daily habits and who sleeps where.'

As I reel off my list I walk between the rows, peering into prisoners' eyes. 'I want to know which passages the servants take when they move between rooms and don't want to be seen. And I want information on the beasts. Where they're kept, when they're fed, who is in charge. Use your *techniques* to ensure they're not lying. Each one must give you something every day, or they go without water for forty-eight hours.'

Michael nods. *Now you are thinking as a king.*

I give him a withering look. *What do I care about being a king? Without Ebony …* My powers surge through me again as I imagine where she is right now. While I bring this negative energy under control, Michael takes over instructing our soldiers on how to begin the arduous task of herding the prisoners to Earth.

I remember Ebony telling me Michael's voice reminds her of chiming church bells, and I find myself moving towards the shimmering gates wondering what she thinks

17

Luca's voice sounds like.

Michael places the palm of his hand on my shoulder. 'We will bring her back, Nathaneal.'

'I know that, Michael, because I will not stop until I do. But it's not going to be today. And that's killing me.'

4

Ebony

When Luca finally releases me, I fall backwards a few steps and draw some much-needed air into my lungs.

He stares at me, his lips pressed together, breathing in deeply through flaring nostrils. It's as if the appearance of that creature were as much a shock to him as it was to me.

I really, REALLY have to get out of here. Nathaneal, where are you?

Eventually I am calm enough to take in my surroundings. Only then do I notice the Thrones are gone. They're such quiet-moving goliaths, but being unaware for even a second while I'm in this place will not do.

One way or another I will get out of here.

But where is Nathaneal? The last thing I saw were the gates crashing down between us, but he would have found a way to open them again, surely. Did Luca's soldiers do something to stop him? Is he injured?

Breathe …

OK. So for now it's just Luca – *or that creature, or whatever he really is* – and me. We're standing inside a domed court-yard, lush with tropical trees and flowering plants. On either side of me, two long corridors face each other, with arches, white columns, and a brick wall behind them.

I take a few steps to distance myself from Luca's over-powering presence. He doesn't stop me walking away, just folds his arms over his chest and leans his hips against a brick garden wall. I take this to mean there's no easy way out. 'How did we get in here?'

'You missed the entrance when you had your face turned into my shoulder.'

I glance up at the dome that stretches from one end to the other. 'I'll find it.'

'And then what? You'll fly away?'

I want to slap the arrogant smirk off his face. He knows my wings haven't appeared yet. Instead I squeeze my hands into fists, digging my nails into my palms. The way he watches me is unnerving, like he's an artist who's sketching me naked. And his eyes are the same as that creature's but green. *Down*, I tell myself. *Look down.*

Large square tiles with mirror shine reflect blood on my shoes. I try to ignore the fact that the blood doesn't all belong to dark angels. Nathaneal's blood is on my hands. I shudder at the memory of Luca's highest-ranking officer, General Ithran, pushing his sword into Nathaneal's throat. I turn and walk in another direction.

This path leads to a fountain where three larger-than-life sculptures of Luca's first demons, the shape-shifting blue-eyed Aracals, seem to hover, suspended on the brink of flight. With their wingtips touching, their feathers shiny black, they look almost alive. I walk around them, staring at their eyes, and am shocked to realise that their eyes *are* real. 'That's gross,' I mutter to myself, spinning around quickly at the sound of Luca's snigger and his hot breath on the back of my neck.

Oh, crap!

I fight the urge to run. But really there's no point. As he pointed out, it's not as if I can fly – yet.

I reach inside for my powers and feel them simmering. It's a comfort to know they're still there.

Luca points to the bench. 'Shall we?'

I stare at him with my eyebrows raised. He holds my gaze before belatedly stepping back. I sit by the tree. He sits next to me, so close his thigh brushes against mine. I inch away. His body heat is ridiculous! 'Why are you so *hot*?'

Oh, no, I didn't just call him … ?

He tilts his head to the side, looking amused. 'So, Princess, what do you think?'

His casual tone stuns me. Does he think I'm OK with this? That I'll simply fall in with his plans now that he finally has me here?

He indicates the courtyard.

'OK, well, it's … ah … not horrible.' Not by a long shot, but I don't have to tell him that. 'What do you care whether or not I like your courtyard?'

His green eyes flash to black. I don't care what colour they turn as long as it's not that glowing yellow of the beast's. 'It would make things easier if we could at least be civil.'

'Easier for whom?'

He's silent a moment, watching my face. 'Both of us.'

'Nothing will ever be easier for me as long as I'm here.'

'Everything I have done concerning you has a purpose.'

21

'What does that mean? Have you read some prophecy scratched by the hand of God that declares I have to be the one to bear your children?'

'Something like that.'

'*What?' I wasn't being serious.*

I shake my head, growing angrier by the second. I notice him studying my face, my neck, my shoulders, then brazenly drawing his gaze slowly, frame by frame, back up, where he spends the longest time scrutinising my mouth. I get up and throw my hands on my hips. 'Stop stripping me with your eyes!'

'Do you have any idea how beautiful you are?'

'Stop it, Luca. I'm sixteen, and I'll be long gone from here by the time I'm old enough to have your kids.'

'You were not meant to be here until the eve of your eighteenth birthday, but events turned out differently. No matter. You're here now and you will learn to love it. You will learn to love me.'

What I would give to stretch my hands around his neck and strangle him.

He cackles at the image.

I dropped my guard. I can't let that happen or he'll know everything I'm thinking. I school my expression to look bored, a mask that conceals the fire raging inside me. The red haze encircles my vision and I wonder if he can see it too, or somehow tell when I'm angry no matter how I mask my features to appear calm.

The sound of someone knocking draws my attention to a blue door with a gold handle beneath one of the centre arches.

'Enter,' Luca says.

A woman of about thirty years, near my height, with dark brown hair and dark blue eyes, makes a beeline for Luca while shooting inquisitive little glances at me. Her tight-fitting blue dress to her calves and elbows reveals a thin but shapely figure.

She waits for Luca's nod, then bows low in front of me.

'This is Mela. She will be your handmaiden,' he says. 'Mela will show you to your apartment and provide whatever you need.'

'I need to leave. Can she help me with that?'

Mela looks straight up at me. Our eyes meet. There's so much she wants to say but her lips don't move. Something about her seems familiar. This is the woman my uncle, Zavier, mentioned briefly as he carried me through the Crossing to the Gates of Skade. He told me Mela was intuitive, that she would know the kinds of things I like and I'd be safe in her hands. I try to read her eyes, but she shifts them back to Luca and I lose the sense. He sighs. The sound tells me how fed up he is with my whining already. Good.

'Did you bring the cloak?'

'Yes, my lord,' Mela says. She unfolds a long velvet cloak the same colour as her dress from her arm. She goes to put it around my shoulders, but Luca takes it from her, doing the job himself.

'You will adjust in time.' His mouth at my ear burns my skin.

I jerk my head and step away from both of them. 'It will take me forever to get used this place.'

'Well, Princess, that happens to be the one thing you get

23

for free around here.'

'I don't want forever, if it means I'm stuck here with you.'

Mela frowns and gives me a minuscule shake of her head. She makes as if to move towards me, but I step further away. 'I don't want her either.'

She exchanges a glance with Luca I don't quite catch. He exhales, revealing his impatience with me is growing. I'm glad.

'Ebony, you need to sleep. You won't make any sense until you have rested. In your room you will find wine and sleeping pills.' He glances at Mela. 'A bath first, then give her as many pills as she wants.'

'*What?*' At first I don't understand, but the reality of my immortality sinks inside me like a brick dropped into water.

5

Ebony

I'm in a daze, barely following where Mela leads, but I force my heavy lids to remain open and my mind focused in case I see something that will help me escape. The corridor we're walking through seems endless. There are closed doors on both sides, indistinct sounds of activity coming from behind them.

'Offices.' Mela answers the question in my eyes. 'Skade is run from the palace. There is a division for everything.'

'You mean like war, and kidnapping?'

She gives me the same warning look she did in the courtyard. 'There is a war division where *kidnapping* –' she says the word softly – 'has been a source of discussion for many years.'

'You mean kidnapping *me*.'

'Yes, my lady, along with defence, environment, mining, agriculture, schools, prisons, slaves, to name a few.'

'Really? Skade is *that* organised?' Who would have thought? Apparently they even have a division for … 'Did you say "slaves"?'

'Humans who have passed away and whose souls end up here.'

'I didn't know.'

'I doubt anyone outside of Skade's perimeters would know what really goes on here, my lady.'

'Don't call me that. I'm, like, half your age. It makes me want to squirm. Call me Ebony, please.'

'As you wish … *Ebony*.' She smiles. 'It's beautiful.'

'It's not my real name.'

I ignore her curious frown to concentrate on identifying anything that could help me escape. We come to an enormous room, larger than a football field. Marble columns support a high ceiling and arches define smaller intimate spaces where a few carefully placed screens, armchairs and low tables accentuate privacy although there is none.

The walls have paintings and huge photographic art hanging all over them. It's like a gallery showing a mix of olden styles with modern.

I look for an exit, but the room is so big I can't tell where it begins or ends. 'Where are we?'

'Ground-floor reception area.'

'Like a hotel foyer.'

'It is a hotel at times. Angels from all over Skade often stay at the palace when they have business in the capital or they're attending a function here in one of the ballrooms. The palace has hundreds of guest suites, more than a thousand rooms in total.'

Six angels in dark fitted coats walk in, revealing the position of the entrance doors in the very long wall opposite. I slot it into my memory. Mela moves to shield me from their view. 'Keep your eyes down and continue walking.'

'Who are they?'

'Dignitaries from Zurat.'

I glance around her as two angels, one male and one female, of a kind I don't recognise though similar to Seraphim, step out from behind a desk to greet them. Their uniforms are all black, and while they're clearly not soldiers, not wearing armour, their manner has an air of superiority and their neat, sleek style makes them almost as intimidating.

'What order are those two?'

She doesn't need to look to know whom I mean. 'Virtues,' she says. 'They have superior intellect and organisational skills. Skade runs smoothly because of the Order of Virtues.'

'And those dignitaries from Zurat – what are they doing here?'

'They're asking for assistance with a rebel uprising.'

'Oh.' *Skade has rebels?* Now *that's* interesting.

We arrive at a set of white double doors with gold handles. Mela grips both handles firmly in her hands and opens the doors wide, revealing a stained-glass window directly opposite with a set of stairs going up on the left, another set of stairs going down and a glass lift between them. Two Throne soldiers are standing on the landing, fully armoured and with weapons at their sides. As we pass them, Mela nods, motioning towards the lift. We get in and she selects the eighth floor, the top button. As we rise, I make a mental note of the pair of soldiers I see through the lift's glass walls standing guard at each floor.

From the lift we enter a long corridor where the entire left side is glass. Down the right are closed doors with gold handles, spaced evenly.

'Apartments,' Mela says, noticing where I'm looking.

I move closer to the window. A grey sky is no surprise. In my dreams Luca showed me parts of this world. Volcanoes are erupting all the time, creating chaotic weather patterns, cold temperatures, toxic air and a darkened sky caused by gases in the upper stratosphere reflecting more sunlight than they should.

Far below is the massive white brick wall that surrounds the entire palace grounds, while further out are tidy streets with houses, apartment buildings and stores. And just beyond the housing area are skyscrapers in more densely packed streets, the river with paths alongside it, and angels rushing around, doing their business, whatever that entails here in Skade's capital, along with the much smaller souls scurrying behind them with their heads lowered.

Mela indicates a set of double doors on the glass wall side. 'Your apartment is a corner suite,' she explains. 'It has seven rooms that I hope you'll find comfortable.' She then points down the corridor to another corner suite at the opposite end. 'Those doors lead to the king's suite, known as the royal apartment.'

'Oh. Well, thanks for that.' Counting four sets of doors on the opposite wall between his apartment and mine, I take small comfort from the knowledge that there are others on this floor. 'Who stays in those?'

'No one,' she says, a hint of pity in her voice. I catch her eye and it happens again, a sense of familiarity, this time stronger than before. Who is this woman? She's not an angel, I can see that, but neither is she ... 'King Luca doesn't like guests near his private rooms.'

'Oh, goodie, just him and me and an entire floor to

ourselves.' I point to a set of double doors midway along the glass wall.

'Balcony,' she says, raising my curiosity. 'It overlooks the main square.' And seeing my surprised face, she adds, 'It's not an escape route, Ebony.'

Not until I can fly, I correct her quietly.

Mela reaches past me to the gold door handles to my apartment, opening both doors simultaneously. 'Shall we go in?'

'I suppose you're coming too?'

She nods and withdraws her arm, her exposed skin inadvertently brushing the back of my wrist. My breath catches at her touch and my pulse skitters. Tingles hit the back of my neck with pinpricks sparking all over my scalp, as if the very air itself is electrocuting the cells at the roots of my hair, all sensations I would normally associate with my Guardian bond springing to life.

Zavier spoke highly of Mela. He must have known her before Luca banned him from Skade. He gave me the impression that I could trust this woman, and I'm starting to believe he was telling me the truth.

Oblivious to my reaction, she motions for me to enter. I take a deep breath before I step into the room that is going to be my prison for as long as I have to live here.

But any resemblance to a prison cell is laughable. It's large and light and airy, a contemporary designer style with a running theme of white, chocolate brown and red with elegant furnishings, including a dark leather sofa that could fit two of me lying head to toe. This sits at a right angle to a roaring fire contained behind glass, with two matching armchairs in front of it. Large protruding windows give extensive views over the city.

A hallway on the right leads to several more rooms. Mela opens the door to one she says is my bedroom. A great big window is the first thing I see, with another view across the city towards the river and mountains beyond.

The bed has a modern, glossy, white wood frame, a mattress covered by a luxurious white quilt, a stack of red, brown and white pillows laid perfectly across the head. Crystal lamps sit on bedside drawers of the same polished white wood and against the opposite wall there's a dressing table with a frameless mirror. A chocolate-coloured leather armchair sits in front. Jewellery boxes, hairbrushes, combs, clips, perfumes, all seemingly brand new, lie on the white wood top.

There's a fire in here too, also enclosed in glass. So now I know where the warmth is coming from and I pull off the cloak, which Mela takes and hangs in a wardrobe, which she enters by a door in the far wall.

I walk over to the dresser and run my fingers over the items spread along the top, catching my reflection in the mirror. My eyes are glassy and bloodshot, grey smudges underneath giving them a sunken look. My skin is pale, nothing like my normal bronze. My hair is a tangled dark red mess I'd like to forget. I hardly recognise myself. My mouth is hanging open so I shut it with what little energy I have left. And, yes, I'm tired. I'm exhausted, but part of this weariness is mood-related. And that's not going to go away with a few hours' sleep.

'Your wardrobe is full of new clothes you should find

adequate until …'

At her pause I catch her eye in the mirror. 'Until what?'

'I was just going to say until you settle in, but thought the remark a little insensitive for your first day.'

'You would be right.'

She points to the back wall. 'Your wardrobe and bathroom are through that door. There is another bathroom off the living room, and a kitchen.'

She pulls a dressing gown from my wardrobe and hands me two lilac towels. 'By the time you've showered, our meals will have arrived.'

'I'm not hungry, Mela. You go ahead and eat without me. I'll shower and go straight to bed.'

'As you wish. I'll see you after your shower then.'

When I've washed my hair and all traces of blood from my skin, I put on a pair of jeans and a jumper I find in the wardrobe. I want to be ready when Nathaneal breaks me out. Over my clothes I slip the dressing gown on, wrapping it tightly around my waist with the sash.

I spot the bottle of wine on a side table as soon as I walk into the living room. Mela goes over and pours me a glass. I take it from her hand and sip it, surprised to find it tastes really good. I gulp half of it down in one go, then the rest and put down the glass. 'I'm done in. I'm going to bed.'

She holds out a bottle of pills but I shake my head. 'One glass of wine will be enough to put me to sleep today. You can leave, or stay, or do whatever you want now. I'm not waking for hours.'

She follows me into my bedroom and pulls back the quilt. My temper flares, not because she's fussing, but because

31

I'm tired, my heart is broken and I want to cry in private, not in front of anyone who lives here and obeys Luca's commands. 'I can do that, Mela. Why don't you go and have your dinner?'

'I don't mind, Ebony. And our meals haven't arrived yet, so if you're feeling more like you can eat something –'

'Stop!' I don't mean to yell at Mela. She's only doing her job, and so far she's been nothing but thoughtful and kind. 'Look, um, can you just go for a walk until the meals arrive. I really need to be alone right now.'

She sighs. 'I'm sorry, Ebony, but I'm not allowed to leave you unattended.'

'What?'

'I'm under orders.'

'Ah, so you're really not a *handmaiden* but a *prison guard* who happens to be good at making beds and untangling knotted hair. Are you packing a weapon somewhere under that dress?'

'My role is to keep you company,' she explains calmly, 'and to ensure you have everything you need at any time.'

'Will you be sleeping with me too?'

Her face goes red.

Damn it.

'No, my lady, I didn't mean to infer –'

'Mela, you seem like a lovely person, but as my good friend would say, this is bullshit.'

'Ebony, two highly trained soldiers are outside your doors right now, guarding this apartment.'

'I have guards outside my door? They weren't there when we arrived.'

'They are there now, and I guarantee neither of them can untangle hair, or do any number of other things I will be doing for you. Would you rather one of them was in here attending your needs and helping you adjust to your new environment?'

I stride up to the front doors and throw them open, both at once. Two Throne soldiers in their full black armour, helmets on, weapons at the ready, swing round to face me, their movements lightning fast and deathly silent. I look up, and up, to silver eyes peering at me. Mela comes and stands beside me, and when I don't say anything but just gawp and stare, the guard shifts his gaze to Mela. 'Is there something we can do to assist, my ladies?'

With an open palm Mela points to the guard who just spoke. 'Ebony, this is Captain Elijah.'

'At your service,' he says, bowing his head.

Mela points to the other one. 'This is Captain Lhiam.'

'It is an honour to serve you both, my ladies.'

'Uh-huh.' They stare at me with slightly puzzled expressions, as if they're trying to get a read on me. I point to one, then the other. 'You two look alike.'

'We're brothers,' Captain Elijah says.

'Oh. Well, thank you, captains, but, ah, Mela is looking after my needs adequately.'

The meals arrive. Mela wheels the trolley inside and closes the doors with some murmured words to the guards, but I'm not listening. My head is spinning. *How do I get out of here now? How is Nathaneal going to find me? I'm eight floors above the ground, with Throne guards everywhere, even outside my door.*

A sense of desperation is making me nauseous. I need to

rest. I'll think about it all tomorrow. I start moving towards the bedroom when Mela points with her elbow to a door on the other side of the living room. 'My room,' she says, carrying her tray of hot food. 'In case you need me.'

'Fine,' I mutter, lifting a limp hand and giving her a weary wave, noticing how it's growing darker outside. Night is falling quickly.

I walk into my room, curl up in the foetal position on my bed and watch Mela through the narrow gap of my open door. She puts the tray on the edge of a low table in the living room. When she stands up, she bumps it with her knee and it falls to the ground. Food spills out as china breaks. I would get up and help her clean the mess, but I'm bone weary and call out instead, 'Are you OK, Mela?'

'Clumsy, that's all. I suppose it's just as well you didn't want a meal.'

Her joke is lame but still helps me to crack a small smile. 'I don't want to be disturbed tonight, Mela. Can you do that for me?'

She comes to my door. 'Ebony, I can't stop him. If he wants, he will just walk in.'

Which is exactly what he does, and the first thing he sees is the mess in the living room. He turns on Mela, who's still standing at my bedroom door. 'What happened? Did *you* do this? After you convinced me you were the best choice for this position? Are you going to prove yourself useless on the first day?' He lifts his hand as if he wants to slap her. Mela flinches to the side as if bracing for it. The slap doesn't come, but the fear in her eyes tells me that if it had it wouldn't be the first time.

34

'Stop yelling at my maid, Luca. *I* made that mess.' I pull myself into a sitting position. 'Mela was about to clean it up, but helped me into bed first to make sure I was all right.'

Mela slowly turns her face to me, and while she doesn't say a word, and neither do I, in that moment we make a connection. The Guardian bond springs into life and I realise, now that I've figured out exactly who Mela is, that the feelings of familiarity I've been getting around her have nothing to do with Zavier. His trust in Mela, his belief that I will be safe in her care, is not what has generated this powerful sense of kinship. Apparently a Guardian automatically connects to members of their Charge's family. In this case, being Jordan's Guardian has linked me to his mother.

Luca looks at Mela, then at me. He probes the outer ridges of my thoughts, trying to get in. I don't let him. I can't, or he'll know I just lied to him. Angels can't lie, but here I am lying with ease. What's with that? I hazard a guess it has something to do with my Guardian bond and the connection to my Charge's closest family member. Protecting her gives me licence to do what is necessary to keep her safe.

Dismissing Mela, Luca steps into my room. 'Your training will begin only once I decide you've had enough time to settle in,' he says.

'My training?'

'You want your wings to develop, don't you?'

So I can fly away, straight out of this world, as soon as no one is looking. 'Sure.'

'I have placed guards at your door. But since you've met them already, I can dispense with introductions.'

Good. Now you can leave so I can dream I'm in Nathaneal's arms.

'For now you will not leave this apartment. When the time comes that I allow you to venture outside the palace, you will have a team to protect you. Do not speak to them. They will have a job to do, and distracting them will only work to your detriment. Do you understand, Princess?'

'Sure. I have prison guards that I can't talk to, I get it.' Tears are starting to well in my eyes. It's the reality of my new life sinking in a little bit further. 'Mind if I sleep now?'

'I thought you might have a few questions.'

I drag myself into a straighter sitting-up position to feel less vulnerable. 'Yeah, actually I do.'

He pulls up the closer of the two armchairs and sits. 'Go ahead.'

'When do I get to go home? It's not like you can keep me here against my will. Clearly soldiers at my door indicate I'm not here of my own volition. And I happen to know the Free Will code is one that angels live by. In fact, it's a universal law.'

'The guards are for your protection. They will attest to that under oath if they have to. Ebony, laws are open to interpretation no matter where you live. Coming from Earth, you should know that.'

'And you would manipulate the law to suit yourself.'

'I do what is necessary.'

'Just wait until Nathaneal gets here. You should start running now, Luca, faster than you have ever run before. You won't have one unbroken bone left in your body by the time he's finished with you.'

He puffs hot air out through his nostrils as if he's bored. It's something the beast would do. How much of Luca is angel, how much beast? I shake the vile image from my head and try to refocus.

'You can't go back to Earth, Ebony. You will have to get used to living here.'

'Be assured, Luca, I will be leaving any minute now. There's no way Nathaneal will leave me here with you for even one night.'

He opens the door and calls Mela over. She stands awkwardly in the doorway, avoiding eye contact.

'What is it? Luca, what aren't you telling me?' Panic begins to make me breathe faster. 'Luca, what have you done?'

'I have sealed the gates, Princess, so even *I* cannot open them. No one can. Not your shining white knight. Not even the highest king of all the realms can get in or out of Skade.'

'*What?* Is that even possible?'

'It's more than possible. It's done.'

'No. *No!* For how long?'

'One hundred years.'

His declaration throws me into turmoil. Inside, everything is spinning. *Oh, Nathaneal, when will I see you again?* I close my eyes, my head falls back and I take in a deep, deep breath while I sink into a dark swirling vortex inside. A glimmer of light I recognise as the core of my soul flickers like the flame of a candle, reminding me of my immortality. *You're still thinking like a human, where a hundred years equates a lifetime*, the flame reminds me. And that's true. I'm an angel. A hundred years will pass and I won't be any older.

Nathaneal will find a way. I know he will because I believe in him, and I believe in our love.

I lift my head, open my eyes and pretend I'm not concerned. 'You don't know Nathaneal if you think sealed gates will stop him.'

'Oh, he'll try. For a while. A month. A year. Perhaps even two. Eventually duty will call him away. And he'll go and return. Try again. Fail. Try again. Three years will pass like that.' He lifts his hand and clicks his fingers. 'But by this time doubts will be taking hold. He may continue to fight them. Until …'

I hate myself for asking. He's just so convincing. 'Until what?'

'The rumours.'

'What rumours?'

'That you are carrying my child.'

And suddenly I can't breathe. It's as if Luca has sucked all the air out of the room with his poisonous words. 'Nathaneal won't believe any rumours started by you.'

He smiles without parting his lips. 'Perhaps not at first.'

My eyes flick to Mela. She can't hold my connection, and her glistening eyes tell me she's buying into this. She can see it happening.

'Then he'll hear that you've had a boy who looks just like his father.'

'No. No, Luca, he won't believe that. Nathaneal knows your tricks.'

'But, Princess, it won't be a trick. That's the day he will give up trying. By then he'll know that you love me, and why would he want you then?'

6

Jordan

Ever since Amber found me sitting outside the entrance to the Crossing, waiting for Thane to bring Ebony back, she won't leave. It's been hours. I've given up the soft approach. I've had enough of being nice. I don't want her company. I don't want any company until Ebony is home safe.

But like me, Amber is prepared to camp overnight. She nestles in beside me on the moist forest floor, resting her back on the same blackbutt tree. She's not going to miss that first glimpse of Ebony coming home. Since that's what I want too, I guess I can't blame her. So I tell her what I know. 'They had a battle.'

'What?' She sits up straighter.

'Skinner told me. He reckons Prince Luca won the battle and took Ebony to Skade, but I don't believe him. Thane won't let anything happen to Ebony. It's just that ...'

'Just that what?'

'Skinner sounded so sure we wouldn't see her again.'

'Adam's full of crap. There's no way Nathaneal will lose Ebony. No. Way.'

I shove my hair back from my face with both hands, and my jacket sleeves ride up. She sees my burnt wrists and shrieks. 'Oh my God, what happened to your wrists?'

She reaches for them but I lower them to my lap, tugging the sleeves down, then tell her how Prince Luca had me chained to a rock wall inside the cave where they had Ebony stashed. 'They drugged her, put her inside something called a *lamorak,* to protect her in the Crossing because she can't fly, and took off, leaving me for dead.'

'How did you get out?'

I can't tell her Adam Skinner seared the cuffs off my wrists with his bare hands. Besides making me promise not to tell anyone, the fact that he rescued me might elevate Skinner to hero status in Amber's eyes. The less she knows of him, the more likely she'll stay away from him. The dude works for Prince Luca. I don't want him anywhere near Amber.

She pats my hand. 'It's OK. You don't have to tell me.' Her hand lingers like she's giving me a moment to figure out if I wanna hold it. Her eyes tell me she wants me to take it, to keep it warm. When I don't, she pulls it away in awkward little movements.

So we wait and the forest floor grows moist, releasing the smells of fungi and mould into the air as the afternoon wears on.

Hours pass. It grows dark. We get hungry and I share a protein bar Skinner shoved in my pocket before he dropped me off. Amber breaks out a chocolate bar, giving me half. Food never tasted so good. Night arrives and brings the cold with it. Just how cold takes us both by surprise. Eventually Amber falls asleep on my shoulder. The stupid girl didn't even bring a jacket. I slip mine off and she grumbles under her breath as I move her around to wrap us both inside it. She settles then, snuggling into my shoulder. I get a whiff of her perfume. Man, how can she still smell so good after being in a damp forest all day and half the night?

Eventually I must have nodded off, because when I open my eyes the stars are fading. Soon the sun is painting the sky a crisp, clear shade of blue and birds take to the air.

Amber stirs, causing the coat to slip off her shoulders. She shivers and I make her put it on properly, despite her obstinate protests.

She pulls the sides together over her – um – ample chest and settles back against the rough bark. Drowsy, with eyes half open, she looks up at me. I can't stop staring at her face. It's like a kids' picture book, open, honest, and so interesting you wanna keep reading because you know you're gonna find something new. Her honey-brown eyes have a navy-blue ring round the outside edge that I never noticed before. Staring up at me through dark lashes, her face framed by messy blonde hair, her pink mouth parting with each breath she draws in and blows out in her dreamy state, she's like sweet and sexy at the same time.

'Jordan?'

'Yeah?'

'Can I ask you something?'

'Sure. Anything.'

Sudden noises from inside the portal interrupt whatever's on her mind. But it's not until a gust of icy wind blasts over us that I drag my focus from her eyes.

Three soldier angels, glowing and moving in such perfect

sync they appear as one, burst from the entrance. They don't see us. They don't stop. They weave through the trees like a speeding train. By the time I've got to my feet they're already gone.

Amber stretches up on her toes for a better look as the group heads in a south-easterly direction. 'Was that them?'

'I couldn't tell. They were too fast.'

'Did you recognise any of them?'

'They looked like soldiers from Gabe's unit.'

'Should we follow them to see what they know?'

I return to the blackbutt tree, shoving a dead log up against it to sit on. 'I'm gonna stay right here until I see Ebony.'

She joins me on the log, and after sipping from our water bottles we go back to waiting.

Hours pass before we hear noises again. We scramble to our feet fast, determined not to miss whoever comes through the portal this time.

Isaac staggers out first. I hardly recognise him for the grime he's wearing like a second skin. His clothes are all torn; hair matted, and while it's usually bright copper, now it's streaked dull red from congealed blood.

He walks past us, and then stops and slowly turns. 'Jordan? Jordan, you're safe!' He glances up at the canopy with a look on his face like finally something's going right. 'Are you well, lad?'

'Where's Ebony?' I ask.

Silence stretches between the three of us. There's not even a twitter from the flock of Aracals sleeping in the trees. Everything seems uncannily still. The only movement

42

comes from the flick of Isaac's silver eyes to the portal, once, then again.

Others are coming. They're not far behind him. Maybe they got separated. It easily happens in the Crossing. *Oh, God, let this be good news.* Amber squeezes my hand and immediately lets go.

Thane walks out. He looks even more haggard than Isaac. His eyes are glazed and surrounded by dark smudges. It's as if he's not inside his body, that he's somewhere else and this is only his shadow.

He looks exhausted and tortured and empty.

And I know: he doesn't have her.

He glances around as if searching for something he expected to be here, and looks disappointed that it's not. But beneath this momentary disappointment is a face I hardly recognise. I look at the portal again, waiting for a miracle. Panic swirls inside me. Amber catches my eye. She's verging on panic too. To see Thane here without Ebony destroys the last morsel of hope we were carrying. I nod and lift my open palm at Amber as if to say, *Leave this to me.* I start walking towards Thane with one thought in my head. I blast it straight at him. *Where is she?*

But Michael runs out of the portal right in front of me. He sees Thane and turns to him, missing me even though he's only a step away.

'What's going on?' I ask.

Michael jumps at the sound of my voice. 'Jordan. I didn't see you.' He runs a hand, discoloured with dried blood and dirt, down his shirt as if he's about to offer it to me to shake. 'Good to see you're all right. You had us worried.'

Thane says, 'The contingent is not far behind us. And Gabe says the cages will arrive any minute.'

Michael exhales. Something weird is going on. Not that I care. There's only one thing I want. 'Where is Ebony?'

Thane's eyes go black, his irises opening and closing. He's struggling to maintain control over his emotions. Shit. Shit! This is not good.

Michael glances at Thane without answering. So that's three of them who won't tell me where Ebony is. Is it guilt that's struck them mute? Thane swallows deep in his throat, licks his parched cracked lips, opens his mouth to say something but closes it again. It *is* guilt. It's on his face. It's in his body language. But by now I don't care how choked up he is, how shaken or caked in blood or … or anything.

Because now I'm scared. 'Where is she? Somebody tell me!'

Michael says softly, 'She's gone, Jordan.'

'*What?*' It's Amber, screeching. 'What do you mean, gone? Gone where?'

Isaac says, 'The Dark Prince took Ebony to Skade.'

'Nathaneal, are they saying you don't have her? That *we* don't have Ebony any more?' Tears well in Amber's eyes as this news chokes her up. She brings her hands to her mouth. 'Oh my God! *Oh my God!*'

I take her hands and pull her close, wrapping my arms around her. Over her head I stare at Thane. 'What happened? Why couldn't you save her? Did you use your powers?'

'I used everything I have,' he says.

Michael explains. 'We walked into a trap. Nathaneal sheltered Ebony with a protective shield but they ambushed us, kept his team from reaching them in time.'

'He pulled her out of my wings,' Thane says, as if he can't believe it himself.

'Shit. Shit!'

'We gave chase, but the gates came down between us.'

'She's *really* gone?'

'Yes,' he says, his face bleak, eyes glassy and dazed.

'I still don't understand one thing. Why aren't you in Skade right now looking for her? What are you doing here?'

'Jordan,' he says in a voice that's so empty it doesn't even sound like his any more, 'I will explain everything soon, but for now there is work to be done.'

'*Work?* What work? What can be more important than rescuing Ebony? You know, as soon I heard that *you* were with her, I thought, That's it. She's safe now.' I hear the tremor in my voice and give myself a shake. 'I really believed that you would find a way to get her back. I thought you loved her enough to do *anything* to save her.'

'Jordan, I understand you're hurting. This is killing me too.'

I need him to stop talking. To stop giving me excuses. I run at him to punch him in the face as hard as I can, but he grabs both my wrists and holds them out to the sides, so I yell instead, 'But *you* don't get to die, do you?'

Behind me I hear Amber choking on sobs. I glance back and see Isaac helping her up from the ground where she must have tumbled after I let her go. I'd forgotten I was holding her. Damn! She draws in a trembling breath. Her eyes are liquid and draining out of her. She's swimming in pain. Ebony was Amber's best friend. They were like sisters. And now they will never see each other again. I understand

Amber's pain. It cuts into me, makes me even angrier with Thane. My lips curl and my voice makes a vicious snarling sound like an attack dog.

I step back and he releases my fists, and before thinking the thought, I charge at his gut with my head.

Before I make contact he grabs both of my shoulders. 'Are you *trying* to break your neck?'

'I hate you for being so strong I can't even hit you.'

'Listen to me, Jordan, you'll only hurt yourself if you try. Last time you hit me you broke five fingers. Remember?'

'I *hate* you! And d'you know why? Because you did this to me. You should have just let me die like I was supposed to that day Skinner bottled me in the gut. You promised that my life would get better, and all you've brought me since is pain and anguish. And if I hadn't found Ebony for you, she'd still be here!'

He grabs my arms. Looking me in the face, he pushes my jacket sleeves up above the burns. 'Who did this to you?'

Yanking my arms free, I stumble backwards. Thane probes my mind, but I scramble fiercely. He peers at me with a penetrating look of remorse. 'I'm sorry, Jordan.'

I hold my wrists up and yell, 'These are nothing. Just tell me why you bothered to come back here when you don't have her? Why aren't you in Skade right now rescuing her?'

He takes a deep breath. 'He sealed the gates … for … for …'

Isaac finishes when he can't, 'A hundred years.'

Amber gasps. 'Oh my *God*!' She bursts into tears and runs into the forest.

'Amber! Amber, wait up!' She doesn't stop. I turn back to

ask Thane, 'Can't you open them?'

He exchanges a look with Michael. 'I tried.'

'And failed? You fail her all the time.'

He glances at the ground.

'Can *anyone* open them?'

Michael says, 'We're not sure. That's one of the things we have to find out.'

Gabriel runs out of the portal with a bunch of soldiers. He assesses the scene in a flash but says nothing. He nods at me. At the same time the soldiers who passed through earlier, along with a dozen Brothers from the monastery arrive with open-backed trucks loaded with rattling cages that could fit elephants inside them. My eyes boggle as I wonder what they need *them* for. Inside the first cage are heavy chains, iron poles and hundreds of cuffs, similar to the ones in the cave that gave me my scars. The sight makes my stomach drop. 'W-what's all this for?'

Uriel, Sami and a host of other angels in armour burst through the portal followed by an army of enemy soldiers, some so big they gotta be those Thrones that Thane mentioned were crucial to Luca's plan to steal Ebony.

Gabe's soldiers and the Brothers herd the prisoners into the cages, ten in a row, ten rows per cage, with each prisoner cuffed and a pole driven through their chains and attached to both the top and bottom of the cage.

The whole process takes a while, but eventually they're on their way to the monastery.

Isaac and Michael tag on at the end of the convoy and cast a glance at Thane, who doesn't appear to want to move yet. 'I'll be there soon,' he tells them, and watches the last of the prisoners leave before he turns to me.

He runs his fingers through his tangled matted hair, shoving it off his face. Standing in front of me, he lifts my hands and studies my weeping blistered wrists. 'What happened, Jordan?'

'Luca had me chained to a wall in the cave where he was holding Ebony. You won't believe how close to your place and the monastery it was.'

Shifting his hands to the burns, he attempts to initiate healing, but I break away. 'I don't want your help.' I take a step backwards. 'Haven't you damaged my life enough already?'

What I don't tell him is that I *need* to feel this pain. This pain I can handle. But without it I would get the full brunt of the other pain, the pain of missing Ebony, and I'm not ready for that yet.

'Where are you going?' he asks as I step into the forest.

I keep my back to him. 'To find Amber. In case you didn't notice, she was shattered by your news.'

He's quiet for so long I think he has nothing more, but when I start walking he says, 'There's a meeting at the monastery in ninety minutes.'

Without turning, I ask, 'What for?'

'To plan how we're going to get Ebony back.'

I take this in for a moment. A small spark of hope ignites inside me. 'Don't start without me.'

7

Ebony

I wake in a strange bed, disoriented, not sure if it's morning or night, or even what day it is. But it doesn't take long for reality to sink in, for me to realise that Prince Luca kidnapping me didn't happen in a dream.

Last night I didn't notice how cold it is in Skade. I didn't notice much at all. My brain was full to capacity and couldn't take in any more. But now my heart is thudding in my chest, pounding against the palm of my hand as I look up at an unfamiliar ceiling inhaling frosty air.

Mela comes to my door and I instantly feel my heart rate slowing down. She has a sympathetic smile and a compassionate look in her eyes that resemble Jordan's so much that I know I'm right – Mela is Jordan's mother. But what is she doing here, in this palace, with *him*?

'Good morning, Ebony. Did you sleep well?'

'Like the dead,' I murmur, then gasp, 'Oh, I'm sorry, Mela, how tactless of me to say that when you're surrounded by death here.'

'It's all right. I'm used to the souls now,' she says. 'I admit, sometimes I've wished death for myself. I even begged him once.'

'Forgive my ignorance, Mela, but I thought only souls came to Skade, not the living.'

She comes closer, and I see that she's breathing, her skin has colour, her heart is beating at a regular human rate, pumping blood around her body, but it's the brief glance I catch into her eyes that reveals the burning flame of her soul and I know absolutely. 'You're alive.'

'Death is not the end, Ebony. But here —' she glances over her shoulder, checking the door behind her — 'dead or alive makes no difference.'

'Are there any other living human beings in Skade?'

'I've travelled to every province and haven't met one like me yet.'

'It must be horrible to be the only one of your kind.'

She smiles, placating me, trying to make *me* feel better about *her* plight. 'I've found my place here. And you have enough to deal with, so please, don't think of unpleasant things today.'

'I'll try not to.' Instead I'll think of ways to escape.

Even if it's true that Luca has sealed the gates for a hundred years, it doesn't mean I can't escape *him*. Or his palace. That will take some planning and perfecting of my powers, and hopefully my wings will appear soon. But I have time. It's more than a year until I turn eighteen, the golden age of maturity when angel law allows couples to marry.

Mela has a calming presence, and talking to her keeps the anxiety at bay. It's almost possible to imagine I'm in Jordan's company.

And since I'm still here, Nathaneal can't yet have found a

50

way through the gates. He would have come for me if he could. So maybe Luca is telling the truth.

The thought makes my stomach roll. And roll. 'Argh … Mela, I think I'm going to be …'

She runs off, returning quickly with a ceramic bowl she holds under my chin. In the most undignified way possible I bring up the contents of my stomach, which are mostly liquid. It hurts and I want to die, but since I can't do that either, I settle for crawling back under the quilt, curling into the foetal position and wishing I could sleep for the next hundred years.

Like they do in fairy tales.

Like my daydreams when I was eleven and twelve, when I used to ride Shadow into the wooded hills at the rear of our property and pretend I was meeting my beautiful prince.

Oh, Nathaneal, where are you? What are you thinking?

I take a deep breath and wipe away the tears soaking into the pillow. Crying will do me no good. I'm not giving up on Nathaneal finding a way into Skade, but escaping is going to be top of my agenda every minute of every day until I'm out of here.

Mela strokes my forehead as you would a child with a fever. I want to scream at her to leave me alone. But that's just because I'm angry and scared. And lashing out from my fears and frustrations will get me nowhere. I will have to be clever to get through this.

I drag myself into a sitting position and swing my legs to the floor. The bowl with my vomit is still in Mela's hand. 'Thank you.' I go to take it from her, but she moves it out of my reach and heads to the bathroom at the other end of the apartment.

Standing at the bedroom window, I draw the heavy curtains aside so I can see where, exactly, I'm living. It's morning, though nothing like those stunning mornings growing up in the Oakes Valley. The sky here is dull, bleaker than the cloudiest, coldest, most dismal winter's day on Earth.

Streaks of purple, bright pink and crimson light suddenly fall on my hand where it's leaning on the windowsill. Skade's sun is trying to show itself through a break in the clouds. The break widens, and the sun's rays ripple across my arm. Skade's sunlight is surprisingly beautiful. I stare at the vivid colours. It lasts about thirty seconds before clouds swallow it up.

Mela returns with a robe she puts around my shoulders. That's when I realise I'm wearing only my undies and a singlet. The thought of Luca walking in and catching me in my underwear turns my stomach. I quickly slide my arms into the robe.

'If you're wondering who helped you prepare for bed last night, that was me,' Mela says, securing the drapes back with a silver rope. 'I thought it would be more comfortable than sleeping in your jeans.'

I tie the sash around my waist. 'Thanks, Mela.'

'After you have breakfast I'll draw you a fragrant bath, then do your make-up and help you into your new dress. It's a special day today and I'm under orders ...' She glances down at the floor, shaking her head, clearly annoyed at herself. 'The king has asked that you wear a specific gown today he had made for you by his favourite designers.'

'So today he's going to show me to his people.'

I was expecting this, just not on my very first morning. I was hoping to be gone before I had to participate in anything official.

Mela confirms with a nod.

'And I have to be washed, dried and fluffed up like a fancy French poodle. Do I get to wear a ribbon with a bow around my neck, or is it to be a collar and leash?'

She gets that sympathetic, motherly look in her eyes again, and smoothly steers me to a different subject. 'The views are better from the living room.'

I follow her, tugging my hair out from my robe, and see why. Last night I noticed this window protruded outwards, but now I see how this large bay shape allows views in three different directions, and from this elevation that's a lot of area.

I look through the wide centre panel first. Soldiers in their now-familiar black armour and hideous horned helmets patrol the paved grounds and the top of the great white wall that surrounds the palace.

Shifting to the right side panel, I notice a set of heavily patrolled street gates are wide open, allowing angels inside the big palace square. There are souls too, but in smaller numbers.

I try to open the window but it doesn't budge.

'I'm afraid they're sealed.'

'Did Luca really think I would jump from up here?'

'Not jump exactly.'

She means when I get my wings. He thinks of

everything, even the future. 'I was just angling for a better view of whatever's going on in that courtyard over there.'

She looks at me with a funny close-mouthed smile.

'What have I missed?' My brain must be a little slow this morning, but it quickly tweaks. 'Oh. Right. The big intro.' My gaze roams over the crowd, with more pouring in through the gates. *So many.* 'Who are they all?'

'Most are local citizens from right here in Odisha. Others have come from faraway provinces. They all want that first glimpse of their future queen.'

'Really?'

'Their *first ever* queen.' She watches me carefully. 'They have waited a long time for you, Ebony. Some of them have been waiting for thousands of years.'

'Mela, that's intense. I'm only a schoolgirl. A few months ago I was thinking about exams and career possibilities and … who my biological parents were. I didn't know I was an angel. I didn't even know angels existed.'

She gasps and pats my shoulder. 'My goodness, Ebony, you have a lot of adjusting ahead of you. I'll guide you, but you will have to let me.'

Mela is growing on me. She has a positive attitude, and a caring nature that's undeniable; I see it when I look into her eyes, and I feel so bad for Jordan and the childhood he endured without her. Zavier told me I would be safe in Mela's hands. It sure would be good to have someone close I can trust.

But I still need to be careful, because I haven't known Mela long enough to make that kind of judgement yet. I will learn more about her when I tell her that I know her son. All I need is the right moment. There's just something I'm sensing, as if she's evaluating me as much as I'm evaluating her, but for what reason I can't put my finger on yet.

'How did you end up living in the palace, Mela?'

She makes a distasteful hissing sound as she draws in a sharp breath through clenched teeth. 'It's a long story.'

'Gee, I'm so busy I don't think I have the time to hear it.'

She laughs. Thank goodness she gets my humour. 'Whatever his reason, King Luca wanted me, and what he wants he goes after relentlessly. When I died, he fought my Guardian Angel for my soul and he won. His was the first face I saw when I started breathing again.'

'It's usually a Death Watcher's job to fight your Guardian for your soul. Do you know why he brought you to Skade himself? What his plans are?'

She shrugs. 'No idea. He has never mentioned my death or resuscitation.'

'I'm sorry, Mela.'

She frowns. 'Dear girl, what are you apologising for? You had nothing to do with my early life, the choices I made, or what happened when I died.'

I brace myself. 'I think you're here because of me.'

'I don't understand.'

'I'm almost positive you're part of Luca's grand plan to make me live here.'

'What makes you think this?'

Her frown deepens as she stares at me. She's clearly confused. She doesn't have any idea. Maybe my hunch is wrong, but Luca wanted Mela for a reason, and I remember

55

Zavier telling me how much planning went into my abductions.

'I'm a Guardian Angel,' I explain, 'for a boy my age.'

'What are you saying, Ebony?'

'I know your son, Jordan. I'm his Guardian.'

She gasps and looks round for somewhere to sit. I lead her to the sofa. She sinks into it and looks up at me. 'You know Jordan?'

'Yeah. I do.'

'Is he well?'

I close my eyes against the last image I have of him, chained to a cave wall. I had asked him to pass my message of love to Nathaneal. 'The last time we spoke,' I tell Mela with a smile, 'he was arguing with me.'

She laughs a little. 'Still stubborn, I see.'

'Uh-huh.'

'I worried so much about him – where he was, who was looking after him. I had no family. His father was in prison and Jordan was only nine when I –'

'Jordan told me how he found you.'

Her eyes pierce mine. 'He remembers?'

'Clearly. And sadly I wasn't around to protect him because at that time I didn't know who I was. I wish it had been different.'

She gets to her feet, takes my hand and folds her other over the top. 'That wasn't your fault. I'm grateful for any light you've brought to his life.'

I'm so moved by her graciousness that I drop her hand and embrace her, and the Guardian bond stretches and weaves into a net that wraps around us.

A shrieking scream through the closed window breaks the moment and we both turn to look.

'Over there.' Mela points and I follow her outstretched arm to see an angel kicking a human soul one-third his size. Another angel, a female, pulls the soul up by his armpits and holds him while the first angel punches the soul in the stomach, following it up with a slug to the soul's jaw. Meanwhile, angels and souls alike open a space around them, enjoying the show.

'Why doesn't someone stop that beating?' I ask, anxious for the soul, now bent over double on the ground as the female angel prepares to kick her pointed shoe into his gut.

'As you will come to see, the souls here are an oppressed species. They have hardly any rights, and that pair of angels are his owners, giving them licence to discipline where and whenever they choose.'

Two Throne soldiers fly over and talk to the pair of thugs. Heads nod and the thugs calm down.

I'm surprised to notice a few angels looking at the thugs with barely concealed disgust, yet many more are disappointed the fight is over.

Anger ignites inside me at the injustice. Only the soldiers on duty could act. Other angels who didn't like what they saw were clearly frightened or not allowed to interfere.

A red haze forms at the edges of my vision. I take a calming breath. When I use my powers again, it won't be in uncontrolled rage. 'If I could fly,' I mutter under my breath, 'I would wing myself over there and … well, I'm not sure what I'd do, but it would be something that would wipe the smirks off that angel couple's perfect faces.'

I feel Mela staring at me and turn my face from the window to her.

'You would do that for a soul?'

'Yeah, of course.'

'What if an angel were getting beaten by a soul?'

That there's bullying in Skade, with Luca as king, is no surprise. But it's wrong no matter who is doing the bullying or who is on the receiving end. Mela is still waiting for my answer. 'It would make no difference to me.'

She hugs me, though I'm not sure why. I ask, 'How does it work here? I mean, when a soul arrives, what happens?'

'They stand before the king for judgement. He hands down their sentence, where and who they will serve, and for how long. Some end up in a faraway province, others remain here in Odisha. This can depend on the skills they came here with, whether an angel has a need for those skills or simply wants labour for their farm, their business or a maid for their home.'

'OK, so the souls who live in the city are what?'

'The lucky ones.'

Not exactly what I meant. 'That man did not look too lucky to me.'

'City souls get to live in proper housing, have food in their bellies, warmth, clothes, may even find companionship if the household is soul-tolerant or appreciative of the skills they bring.'

'And they get to enjoy the occasional beating.'

'Only by their owners.'

'Ah, well, that makes it all right then.'

She doesn't miss my sarcasm. 'It's the law.'

'Are you telling me there's a law that encourages the torture of human souls?'

'Laws can be changed.' She eyes me carefully. 'It would take a strong angel in a high position, someone brave enough to stand up to –'

'The king.'

When I next glance at the square it's from the bedroom after I've had breakfast, a bath and Mela has combed and trimmed my wet tangled hair. Thousands more have gathered, and I stare as they keep filling the streets.

As I watch the crowds I start to notice things, like how souls feel the cold much more than angels. They hold coats, jackets and even blankets tightly around themselves, while the taller, bigger-built angels wear suits and stylish dresses with flowing cloaks and fancy hats. It could be a day at the races, except it's not horses they've come to see.

It's me. All those people, to see me.

A shiver runs down my spine as my thoughts shift to what's to come. My bottom lip trembles, as it does sometimes, and Mela catches sight of it. Compassion sweeps into her eyes. She leans towards me and says softly, 'Ebony, you have a choice, and you need to make it soon.'

'Escape is the only choice on my agenda.'

She looks at me sadly.

'What? Am I supposed to just accept what's happening to me? My natural instincts wouldn't allow it.'

Leaning closer, she mouths almost soundlessly, 'Whenever you talk of escape, you must be extremely careful of who might hear you. There are some here in the palace that you can trust, but many more you can't. I can guide you, but discretion will keep you safe.'

I nod, letting her know I get it and will be more careful in future.

She peers into my eyes. 'There are certain things you should know, about me, about the palace, about the king. We will talk. But for now I need to finish getting you ready.'

We move to the dressing table, where she holds out the chair, motioning for me to sit. She selects a make-up brush. Our eyes meet in the mirror and she says, 'Finishing touches.'

Mela applies my make-up using natural colours, except for my eyes, which she accentuates with extended liner in vibrant violet and matching mascara.

With my make-up and hair complete, Mela pulls out a gown from the wardrobe. I remove the robe and step into it. The bodice is tight-fitting black lace in an intricate swirling design. It sits lower at the front than I'm comfortable wearing. I try to tug it up, but it doesn't budge. It has tiny cap sleeves that hang loosely off the shoulder. And while the dress hugs my body tightly to the hips, the lace then falls away in soft folds of taupe and black tulle with a skirt of velvet satin underneath.

At any other time I'd feel like a princess wearing this.

I slip my bare feet into elegant taupe-coloured high-heeled shoes. Then Mela pins a diamond tiara to my head. I don't go for fancy jewellery, but I will admit, as tiaras go, this one is lovely.

She stands behind me so I can view myself in the mirror. Who is this person looking back at me? I hardly recognise her, and yet there is something in those eyes – *my eyes* – that feels right.

No. No way. I don't mean that I feel right being here. It's just a pretty dress. The fact that Prince Luca had it made to represent a role he sees me in doesn't change that.

We move to the living room, where there is more room for Mela to survey her handiwork. She's beaming, and looks at me expectantly.

'Thanks, Mela, you've done a great job. I'm sorry I'm not more appreciative, but … So … what happens now?'

'We wait.'

The wait feels excruciatingly long and yet when the double doors silently open and Luca is standing there, shadowed by three Throne guards, it's suddenly too short.

He looks powerful – impeccably dressed in a sleek black three-piece suit with a purple flower in the buttonhole of his long blazer. There's no sign of physical weakness. Returning home appears to have invigorated him. With his long caramel-coloured hair slicked back in a ponytail, he is the epitome of a prince.

Just not mine.

He walks in and stares at me in a way that is unnerving. Taking his time, he walks around *inspecting* me, as if I'm a slave he's considering purchasing and is checking for faults.

He flicks his eyes to Mela and nods approvingly. She beams. I don't like how pleased she looks to have pleased *him*. But then she catches my eye with a directness that reminds me of her earlier warning to be discreet. I know then she's acting and that she's really on my side.

Luca runs his fingertips down the length of my hair, tracing one long curl as it falls past my neck, over my chest and on to my waist. His touch is gentle, but wherever he lingers, my skin blisters and peels like sunburn on rapid release. He finds this phenomenon fascinating. It's not; it's repulsive.

He moves to my other side and does the same thing, apparently fascinated with how his touch makes my skin burn, peel and heal in a kind of accelerated rhythm of life, or something. I want to slap his hand away. I want to slap *him*.

Mela shoots me a warning look when he's not looking. But by now I'm so furious I can hardly see straight. The red haze is blurring my vision. I stare at him through it. He doesn't speak but just smiles at me, knowing exactly what he's doing. The urge to slap him becomes difficult to hold back. He walks behind me and leans down so his mouth is level with my ear, creating an intimacy that makes me loathe him impossibly more. As I clench and unclench my fingers, feeling my power whipping up my body, he breathes one word: '*Outstanding.*'

The heat coming off him carries his unmistakable scent, but today it also has an evocative quality that saturates my senses. Some might find it pleasant. I certainly don't. My instincts are screaming at me to step back, move away. *Run*.

Somehow he can tell I'm about to bolt and locks his fingers around my elbow. Lightning doesn't move as fast. *Steady*, he says in that husky tone, in a mind-link that feels invasive. I start to tremble and try hard to quench the shuddering tremors by biting down on my lower lip.

I don't want to simply slap or punch him any more; I want to strangle him with my bare hands, gouge out his probing green eyes with my fingernails, rip out his teeth one by one with a pair of –

Are you quite finished, Princess?

Damn it, Luca, stop invading my head space.

Stop inventing ways to debilitate me in your thoughts. You're not yet adept at selective projection.

To prove his point he glances at the middle one of the three guards he brought with him and raises his eyebrows. The guard nods with a slither of a smile appearing.

'OK, I get it.'

'Good,' Luca says. 'Now, do you like your apartment?'

'As prisons go, I suppose it's not bad.'

He growls and tightens his fingers on my elbow. 'In a moment, Ebony, I will introduce you to seven million citizens of Skade.'

My jaw drops open. *Seven million are out there?*

'You will remember that you are soon to be their queen. Should I choose to kiss you on that balcony, you will respond in a manner that will gratify and delight your adoring public. Do I make myself clear?'

'I hear you.'

'That's not what I asked.'

'I understand that you want me to comply, OK?'

His lips press together as he scrutinises my face. A sudden frown forms. 'You do know *how* to kiss, don't you? Be honest and save yourself embarrassment. Do you require a private lesson prior to our public exhibition?'

My breakfast swirls and threatens to eject. I swallow, forcing it down, and clear my throat. The heat from Luca's body isn't helping. I feel like I'm on fire. Isn't it enough that I have to kiss him in front of his people? Does he have to ridicule me as well? My heart lurches at the possibility that

Nathaneal will one day learn that I kissed his enemy in a way that gratifies and entertains seven million Skadean angels and their human-soul slaves.

My heart gallops faster, and faster. I try to slow it down with controlled breathing and distracting my thoughts. When I think I can manage to sound calm I reply, 'Thanks for your offer to instruct me in the art of kissing, my lord, and though I am only *sixteen*, no tuition is necessary because Prince Nathaneal was a superb teacher. We practised relentlessly.'

He growls viciously and loud enough that Mela's eyes bug out. 'A word of warning, Ebony, be careful you do not go too far or I may have your tongue removed.'

If he's after a reaction, he's going to be disappointed with my silent response.

'I'm not known for my patience,' he snarls. 'Dishonour me in public, and the next hundred years of your life will be a living hell. I promise you.'

'And the difference would be … ?'

'You will know the difference.'

'Really? I doubt that.'

He takes my hand and lifts it to his lips in a gesture that contradicts the cruelty in his eyes. But I know what he's capable of doing, so when he tilts my face up with his thumb under my chin and forges into my mind, *You apparently need a taste*, I should know better than continue to taunt him.

Do you seriously believe beating me up on the inside, where no one can see the bruises, will help your cause to make me love you?

His thoughts slam into my head along with his darkness.

I try to block him, to pull away, to shove his thoughts back at him, anything to sever the connection or at least lessen the impact his darkness is having on my soul. I reach for my power but can't feel a thing. I search for the haze, but I'm not angry, I'm afraid. I look into his eyes, searching for something I can use as a weapon to spear back at him, but find myself drowning in his river of misery. It disconnects me from everything that is good. All the things he once had and can never enjoy again have left his soul bitter and cursed with envy. He needs power to fulfil him and he sees *me* being able to provide this.

His irises glow bright yellow and I see the beast sitting in a chair of golden vines in a room with black walls lit by smokeless fires in ancient-style urns. Dark angels, bigger, scarier than Thrones, stand guard behind him and patrol the room, ordering souls in one at a time. The beast, slouching in his fiery chair, looking arrogant and bored, examines each soul brought before him before announcing their penalty. One soul, a giant of a man with massive biceps, skin inked from fingers to armpits, and who looks as if he's not used to taking orders, refuses to accept his punishment. The beast lifts the soul by the throat, and while he holds him easily with one hand, he makes fire with the other and shoves a handful of it into the soul's arguing mouth. The soul shrieks in agony as the fire travels down the inside of his throat, scorching his skin all the way to his abdomen.

Shock and anger generates my power. It whirls inside me, giving me an immediate lift as it spreads rapidly out from my core. *Yes.*

Prince Luca feels it too and instantly releases me.

Taking a step back, he acts as if nothing just passed between us. He offers me his elbow as if he were a courteous gentleman. My whole body shudders with the power I didn't use. What a shame. I would have liked to smash my still-throbbing fists into his arrogant, perfect face.

I take a deep breath, straighten my shoulders, raise my head and hook my arm through his.

With a look of surprise and amusement on his face, we walk out the doors together.

I could be walking to my death. The feeling of dread would be the same.

8

Jordan

Amber is late. At this rate we'll miss the meeting. I've called her twice and both times it's gone directly to voicemail. She's probably in a reception black spot on Mountain Way. I decide to wait five more minutes before leaving without her. In the meantime, I back the Lambo into the driveway, kicking myself because I should have gone and picked her up instead of sitting on my butt in my living room, waiting for her to go home and change her damp clothes. I knew she was upset. Shit! After I left Thane I found her sitting in her mum's car sobbing, angry at the world. I told her about the meeting tonight at the monastery, that it will do us good to see how the angels are planning to get Ebony back. She'd taken a deep breath at the thought of positive action and started to pull herself together, promising she would meet me at Thane's place in plenty of time.

Finally I spot her lights on the long driveway winding through the forest. She pulls up beside me, locks her mum's Honda and jumps into Thane's Lamborghini, full of apologies.

'Hey, you're here now, that's what matters,' I tell her, frowning when I see her eyes are still red, her nose still shiny. 'Are you OK?'

She stares out into the darkness. 'I miss her so much already. We did everything together since we were, like, little kids. I knew even then that Ebony was special. She didn't want to stand out, but she did, especially at high school.'

She turns to me, but still has that faraway look in her eyes. 'People are so ignorant of anyone who doesn't slot into their narrow idea of normal. Not me. I loved Ebony's differences. Like the time I found a small white feather in my bathroom.' She sniffs, drawing in a deep shuddering breath. 'And now she's not here and I'm … I'm … so alone.'

'She wanted you to take care of Shadow.'

Her eyes refocus and light up like a sparkler. 'She told you that?'

'Yep. In the cave before they took her. She said you were her family and she loved you.'

She sighs. 'For as long as I've known Ebony, this is the first time she *really* needs help, and no one, not even the angels, can do anything.'

'I know.' *Man, do I get it.* I point to the seat belt. 'We should get moving.'

She starts latching it on, but before she finishes she spots my wrists and shrieks, 'Oh hell, Jordan, your burns are so much worse! Those blisters will get infected if you don't protect them.' She pulls out her mobile phone. 'I'm finding you a doctor up here.'

'I'm not going to a doctor tonight.'

'Yes, you are.'

'Amber, listen. We're running late for the meeting, and I'm not missing that for anything.'

She stares off into the darkness ahead, thrumming her

fingers on the dashboard. 'Will you let Nathaneal heal them?'

'No freakin' way.'

'What about Jezelle?'

Through clenched teeth I explain. 'I don't want a quick fix.'

She gets me right away. She always does. Where Ebony can see images in my mind, Amber is hyper-aware of my voice and facial expressions. 'You *don't* deserve this.' She slides her fingers beneath mine, linking our hands together. 'What's happened to Ebony is not your fault.'

As good as her hand feels in mine, I pull away. 'You don't understand. The things I did were reprehensible.'

'That's impossible. You love her too much.'

'I had my reasons.'

'Like what?'

If I tell her she'll hate me. But if she finds out from someone else, there'll be no coming back from that amount of hate. 'Prince Luca wanted Ebony to break up with Thane so no one could accuse him of committing the angelic crime of stealing another prince's fiancée. He blackmailed me into making it happen, so I told Ebony lies and planted her head with doubts, amongst other things.'

Amber's look is intense. She stays silent, listening as I tell her about my covenant with the Dark Prince, how he told me the lie that my mother was alive and I was the only one who could save her. 'If I could break up the lovebirds, Luca would release Mum. He said he'd bring her home. And for a while I believed him.'

When I finish she peers up at the stars and the only sound in the Lambo is our breathing.

'Follow me, Jordan,' she suddenly says.

She heads to the house, waits for me to open the door, then goes straight to the downstairs bathroom and hunts around in cabinets until she finds some non-stick dressings, crêpe bandages and tape. 'I also need sterile water and cling film.'

'Cling film's in the kitchen. I don't know about sterile water, but there's always boiled water left in the kettle.'

She runs out, returning with cling film and a glass bottle half full of water. She starts with my left wrist, rinsing it with the water, patting the wounds dry with the non-stick dressings.

'Looks like you've done this before.'

She flicks me a dubious look. 'Kind of.' She wraps the cling film next, and tapes it.

'What does that mean?'

'Remember those bad fires from a few years back?'

'Yeah.'

'Our old stables burned down. We got all the horses out, but a couple of the mares sustained some minor burns. I watched the vet treat them.'

'Horses?'

'Uh-huh.'

'How old were you?'

'I don't know, maybe eleven.' She looks up at me with a crafty smile. 'Still don't want a doctor?'

The crêpe bandages are secured now and I can tell she's done a good job; both wrists feel supported, protected. 'I'll take my chances with you.'

'Oh, will you now?' She smiles, the teasing spark in her eyes subsiding the longer she holds my gaze. 'She trusted you, Jordan.'

'That's what makes it so hard.'

Inside the car I lift up my one of my bandaged arms. 'Thanks for this.'

Our eyes connect. Inside my gut is churning. She smiles sadly. A tear oozes out, rolls down her face. 'You're welcome,' she says, and I start driving.

At the monastery Brother Bernard is waiting for us. He takes us down a few stone flights of stairs to a corridor with a steel door at the end.

The conference room has no windows, but fluorescent globes in the ceiling provide ample light. The walls are white, and a long polished timber table sits in the centre with a dozen or so angels around it on high-backed chairs.

I take a quick headcount.

Thane is at the table's head. He looks ragged and beaten but still has an air of authority about him. Michael is on his left, with Isaac, Jez and Solomon next along. On the opposite side are Gabe, and the two married couples, Jerome and Sami and Uriel and Tash, with their backs to the door. Three Brothers sit at the opposite end to Thane.

Amber and I make fifteen.

Everything stops when we enter. Those with their backs to us turn. Thane stands and comes over to greet us, but I pretend not to see him and sit myself down in the vacant seat next to Brother Tim, who introduces Monsignor Lawrence and Brother Alex in whispers.

Amber moves silently round to the other side and sits beside Brother Alex.

As Thane returns to his seat he glances at my wrists. He notices the bandages and his eyes move to Amber. He nods and silently mouths the words, 'Thank you.'

She smiles back. Realising I'm watching, she shrugs as she catches my eye.

'Jordan, Amber, welcome, and thank you for coming,' Thane says. 'These last two days have been trying for you both.' He opens his hands to indicate the others. 'And for everyone here.'

'*You* most of all,' Isaac declares, like a puppy yapping at his master's heels. I snort air out through my nostrils, louder than I mean to.

Everyone except Amber and the three Brothers turns their heads and looks at me with animosity shooting out of their eyes like double-barrel machine gunfire.

Holy shit, where is a hole in the floor when you need one? The longer they stare, the hotter my face grows. They've heard my thoughts. But I'm not backing down and apologising. No way. Thane's let Ebony down too many times. I can't just forget that.

To his credit, Thane calms everyone down. 'We can all appreciate Jordan's concern, considering the close bond he shares with Ebony. What's happening is particularly hard on him.'

Isaac nods and shifts his death stare away from me.

'As you all know, Prince Luca has locked the gates of Skade for a hundred years,' Thane begins, 'and he's not going to open them, even if he can, for as long as it suits him. Opening an area wide enough for a team to pass through is our first priority. Michael believes there is a tool that could puncture a hole in the gate. It's called a *hanival*. Some of you may remember it.'

Uriel says, 'I remember the *hanival* being used in the First War, but I thought the High King destroyed it.'

Michael clarifies. 'During my time on Empyrean, I learned otherwise.'

Jez asks, 'Everyone knows how vital time is in these circumstances, so how do we get our hands on it and do we know it still works?'

Michael explains, 'The *hanival* is secured in the High King's vault under the guardianship of the Twelve Sentinels.'

A collective sigh of relief eases the tension in the room. It's the knowledge that there's a weapon that can blast through Skade's gates – and probably anything. It's exactly what we need. I wonder who these 'Twelve Sentinels' are, and if they have the potential to get in our way.

'The *hanival* will function correctly in the right hands, but there are complications,' Michael adds.

'Such as?' Isaac asks.

Even I can think of one. 'If the Dark Prince gets his dirty hands on it, we may as well kiss the Earth goodbye.'

This time when their heads turn to me there's no hostility, and Michael says, 'That is essentially correct, Jordan.'

They start murmuring, but as soon as the Monsignor clears his throat, the room goes silent. 'Our purpose in being here is to facilitate Avena's angels of light in their promise to protect humanity, but we are also Guardians of Earth.'

Thane says, 'As the home of humans, Earth is our concern too, Monsignor. We share a common goal.'

The Monsignor nods but squirms uncomfortably. 'My desire is not to offend anyone in this room, but the question must be asked: is the life of one angel worth the price of possibly billions of human beings?'

I can't believe what the Monsignor just said. I jump out of my seat. 'Well, I'm a human being, and I say she is!'

'Jordan.' Thane lifts his hand and motions at me to sit down, his eyes clearly telling me he's gonna wait until my ass is back in the chair. 'Monsignor, let me put it this way – should Ebony remain in Skade for a hundred years, the risk to Earth would be immeasurable.'

'How so?'

'Prince Luca plans to build an army of Soul Readers from the combination of his and Ebony's bloodlines. When he has enough descendants they will infiltrate Earth and place an invisible mark that only the Soul Readers can see on every child who has the potential for dark acts. These Luca plans to take young, train and build his armies in secret locations in preparation to invade Earth.'

'I did not know this,' the Monsignor murmurs, his face turning as white as his robe.

And from the gasps and sudden chatter, neither did most of the others around the table. Amber catches my eye. Horror fills hers. Like me, she would be thinking of Ebony being forced to bear Luca's children.

The Monsignor shakes his head. 'This changes everything. We will assist you in any way we can.'

Thane releases a deep sigh. 'Thank you, Lawrence.'

'How soon can you get your hands on this weapon?' I ask.

Thane looks straight at me. 'Immediately after this meeting, Michael and I will travel to Empyrean to see the Sentinels.'

Gabe says, 'There's a certain protocol that has to be followed, Jordan.'

'But this is an emergency.'

'Yes,' Thane says, 'and I will ensure the Sentinels appreciate the urgency.'

Gabe scoffs at his brother. 'You can't just knock on the Sentinels' chamber door, Thane, and expect an immediate audience with the High King. An audience could take weeks to arrange. Some have waited months, even years.'

'*What?*' Amber gasps. 'Nathaneal, there must be a way to make this happen sooner.'

'We're trying our hardest to bring Ebony home,' Gabe yells, shifting his eyes from Amber to me, 'and you two are not helping. Can you do anything except complain that we're not fast enough, we don't do enough –'

I shoot to my feet, knocking my chair over backwards. 'Don't patronise us because we're humans and you have such a high opinion of yourself. This is just bullshit!'

'Mind your language, Jordan,' Isaac reprimands.

'OK! I'm just saying, it shouldn't be *that* hard to get our hands on a weapon to blast open a stupid gate. I suppose next you'll tell us you don't even know how to use the thing.'

Silence. Everyone turns to look at Thane. He says, 'I'm a quick learner, Jordan.'

'Oh, that's just brilliant. Why don't you have it already?' I look pointedly around the table. 'If that were my fiancée in Skade, I wouldn't be sitting around a table discussing what to do; I'd have done it by now.'

Amber hisses at me, 'Shut up, Jordan. Let him speak.'

'What? Are you on their side now?'

'We're all on the same side, Jordan, the side that gets Ebony back safely. Have you stopped to think that rushing

75

in bull-headed might fail, or worse, get Ebony killed?'

I open my mouth to say something but she doesn't give me a chance. 'The angels live in worlds we don't know anything about. They would know what rules they have to follow, and the ones they can break.'

'They make mistakes, Amber.' I turn to glare at Thane, 'How long is it gonna take? You gotta have some idea. You do know who she's with, don't you? Think about what that creep could be doing to her *right now*.'

'Young man!' Isaac bellows, his voice reverberating around the room, his dark eyes boring a hole in my skull. 'Your frustrations are only delaying what needs to be decided at this meeting. No one wanted you here. But Nathaneal insisted we let you hear our plans to help ease your anguish, and we obliged him. So, as our guest, I strongly *suggest* you sit down and shut up.'

I pick my chair up and thrust it down harder than I intended and now I don't know where to look.

'Jordan,' Jez addresses me, giving me somewhere to focus my eyes, 'we know how you feel about Ebony.'

I shake my head. They can't. No one can possibly understand this. *I* don't even get it.

'Jordan, your love for Ebony is intense. We see that. We *feel* it pounding away in your chest, pouring out of your skin, and we understand you better than you realise. But think about this – angels love *one* other for *all* eternity. Imagine how deep and passionate and powerful an angel's love has to be to endure thousands upon thousands of years. Sometimes that's why a partner is found for us.'

I glance at Thane, and this time I take in his red-streaked

eyes, the shadows around them, the sunken, skeletal cast of his face. I don't remember ever seeing him so carved up.

Amber's eyes fill with a fresh crop of tears, but she refuses to look at me.

Thane starts allocating jobs for the angels to do while he and Michael are away. Solomon is to keep trying to get in touch with his informant in Skade and find out whatever he can about Ebony, where Luca's keeping her, and how she's holding up. 'Anything, Sol. Anything at all, and wherever I am, you let me know.'

Solomon is huge, his hair black and all curls, skin like chocolate and sea-green eyes. Not only is he much bigger than the other angels, but he doesn't resemble them either, with his top-heavy build. He doesn't have the slender physique of the Seraphim. 'I have this covered, my prince. As soon as I hear anything I'll be in touch.' And when he says, 'I'll reach you,' I believe him.

'Thank you, Sol.' Thane glances at me. 'And when you do hear, inform Jordan and Amber immediately.'

'Sure thing, my prince.'

'Uri,' Thane says, moving around the table, 'check conditions in the Crossing and find us the fastest route to the island. Tash, supplies for three days. Isaac, you're in charge of weapons, and work with Gabe on the construction of the prison downstairs. Keep me informed. Jez, you're responsible for Ebony's parents, Heather and John. Let me know when they're well enough for a human hospital to take over their care.'

He goes on but he hasn't selected the rescue team yet, and that's what I'm waiting for, because there's no way

77

they're going to get Ebony without me. I don't want to argue in front of everyone now. I can do that later, after he and Michael return with the *hanival*. At least now I know I can travel through the Crossing, as long as I'm wearing a *lamorak*, and … one of them is willing to carry me.

Thane stops suddenly and tilts his head. *Shit*, did I slip up scrambling my thoughts? I brace myself for the straight-out rejection I'm expecting, but the other angels hear something too and flick curious glances at each other. Then Thane looks directly at Isaac and lifts his eyebrows. Isaac shrugs and heads to the door.

The door swings open with a bang before Isaac gets there. In the corridor, Brother Bernard throws his hands in the air as a female angel barges in, looking spectacular in skintight metallic bronze body armour. Her brown hair is up in a ponytail that reaches past her waist, with two deadly-looking swords crossed over at her back. She surveys the room, zeroing in on Thane.

Amber cups her mouth and whispers across the table, 'Who's that?'

'Ebony's sister Shaephira.'

Shae walks over to the table, where she takes the seat Isaac was sitting in. 'Whatever your plan is to retrieve my sister,' she says to Thane, with a look that dares him to argue, 'I'm going with you.'

Thane returns to his seat. Seeing the hurt she is feeling at the absence of her sister and knowing there are no words to soothe her, and that she is another person whose love for Ebony cannot be denied, he turns to Shae and simply says, 'Of course. Welcome to the team.'

9

Nathaneal

Finally the meeting nears its end. The plan is set and everyone knows what he or she is doing. There's just one more thing I have to do.

A few months ago, when I was forced to return to Avena to stand trial for revealing my powers to the enemy, the court handed me the punishment of repairing a forest destroyed by a cosmic storm. But that would have kept me away from Ebony for up to two hundred years and I couldn't stand the thought, so I suggested the alternative punishment of undergoing a dangerous mission into Skade to rescue two humans that Prince Luca had kidnapped and taken prisoner. The two humans were Ebony's adopted parents. Every team that had tried to locate John and Heather Hawkins thus far had failed, and so the court approved my request.

Unfortunately the mission took much longer than I had hoped.

Standing up, I indicate Gabe with my open palm. 'Before we finish up tonight, I want to thank my brother for looking out for Ebony and Jordan in my absence.'

Smiles and murmurs meet my heartfelt statement. I

motion to Gabe to stand. He does so reluctantly. 'I know your heart wasn't in it at first.'

He doesn't say anything, but shuts his eyes as I hail him with my praise. It's not like Gabe to shy away from adulation, but I have no idea what he underwent in those months of my absence. I never meant to be away so long. I told Ebony I would be a week. What struggles she must have endured when I didn't return and time marched on. But my brother was in my house, keeping her safe. And most importantly, he gave her my message so she understood why I loved her before I even saw her, and how I loved her even more once I had. *You and I will talk privately soon, Gabe.*

That we will, brother. We need to.

I hold out my hand. He looks at it for a moment that feels almost too long. Then he clasps it and I tug him forward into an embrace.

Cheers erupt with applause.

When we pull apart, he lingers while I turn to face those still sitting, more eager than ever now to bolt out the door and embark on their tasks. But Gabe clears his throat and says, 'Ah, brother, there's one more item that needs our attention.'

I catch a glance he shares with Jerome, and my throat tightens. 'What is it?'

Jerome forges a private link: *You're not going to like this, brother. You should probably sit.*

My heart screams, *No more delays! What more could go wrong?*

'I started out taking care of this issue on my own,' Gabe announces, 'but realising this problem was growing too big for me to handle alone, I enlisted a crew from my first unit to assist.'

Shae growls under her breath as Gabe explains how an unidentifiable entity with strength beyond anything he's encountered before on Earth now lives, breathes and slaughters livestock on human properties.

Everyone has questions but contains them, knowing I'm becoming agitated at this delay.

'We've come to refer to them as dark forces. It's what Ebony and Jordan called them the first night the entity chased them home, the night it made its first human kills.'

Michael asks, 'How did this dark force come into being?'

Jerome looks at me with something like pity.

Shae catches it and her condemning eyes soften.

Gabe explains, 'It exists because of how my brother's powers practically annihilated Prince Luca and his twelve Prodigies. In their severely weakened conditions they couldn't return to their own portal. They didn't even make it off the mountain.'

Murmurs start up around the table. They will be thinking the same as I am. How could I have overlooked such a basic rule of battle? *Bury your dead. Collect your injured. Clean up your mess.*

'And while Prince Luca and his Prodigies lay helpless on the forest floor, evil leached from them, like the sludge that oozes from the bottom of a sewage pit. And somehow the energy and matter came together, creating a powerful and dangerous entity.'

Is it my imagination, Michael asks in a private mind-link, *or is Gabriel enjoying this a little too much?*

He loves a good story, Michael.

And is that what this is? It seems too serious to be telling it like a horror story round a campfire to a group of Cherubs, but then he is your brother. You would know.

You have known him longer. Right now, I just want him to get on with it.

'The teacher Zavier came across the prince and his Prodigies in their dire condition and helped them into an underground cave, where they remained for several weeks while their bodies healed.'

'Where was the dark force during these weeks?' Isaac asks.

Jerome explains that they don't know. 'But once it was able to move, it instinctively sought nourishment. It picked up Ebony's scent and, drawn to her as Luca is, hid by day inside caves in deserted outback areas, returning at night to feed and be near her.'

'What is the situation now?' I ask, wondering, bizarrely, if this dark force misses her as much as I do.

With his flair for dramatics and a captive audience, Gabriel announces, 'After it *split in two*, it began taking shape. First the two appeared as if they were becoming angels, but ever since Ebony's been gone, the two have become *four* and taken human shape.'

'Oh my God!' Amber's shriek pierces through stunned silence.

Monsignor Lawrence says, 'Can you imagine what would happen if they ingratiated themselves into human society?'

It's a frightening thought that Jordan takes a step further. 'If they breed with humans, will they create a new species?'

No one answers. No one knows. And no one wants to imagine *that* happening.

The Monsignor asks, 'Where are they now? Can they be captured?'

Jerome explains, 'They have found refuge in the Cedar Oakes hinterland, up in the rocky hills where there are caves and dense forests.'

'Why there?' Jez asks. 'What's the attraction?'

From the opposite end of the table Jordan calls out, 'It's the closest they can get to Ebony.'

My eyes shoot back to Jerome. 'Is he right? They're hiding out on the Hawkins' property?'

Jerome nods. 'We think the dark forces are so attached to Ebony they've taken to living where they can pick up her scent.'

Amber says, 'Ebony spent a lot of time in those hills, growing up.'

I almost feel sorry for them. The part of them that came from Luca must be what keeps them drawn to her. A plan begins to shape itself. 'How much damage have they caused since moving there?'

My brothers exchange glances before Jerome shrugs. 'Not much. Their feeding frenzy appears to have eased, though they're still ravaging some local crops. Why? You have a plan already?'

Shae says, 'How long will it delay us in retrieving Ebony?'

Nothing is coming before that mission, I assure her through a closed link.

I stand and thank my brothers for bringing this matter to my attention. 'But for now the dark forces will remain where they are.' Turning my attention to the Monsignor, I notice Gabe staring hard at Jerome. 'Can you keep them on your radar, Lawrence?'

The Monsignor nods. 'I'll inform the Watchtower immediately.'

To everyone I explain, 'As soon as we have Ebony home we'll deal with the dark forces. Meanwhile, Uri, set up a team to keep an eye on them. Instruct the team to remain out of sight but to repair any damage they cause.'

'Will do, my prince,' Uri responds.

By now everyone notices how agitated Gabe has become at me. 'So that's it?' he says. 'You're just going to ignore the problem?'

I glare back. 'That's it for now, Gabe.'

He gives a derisive laugh, slamming his fist down on the table. 'Are you mocking me, brother?'

'Why would I do that?'

'I spent months following the dark forces, cleaning up after it fed, resuscitating sheep and cattle and even a kangaroo. I brought my own soldiers in; at times there were forty of us. And now there are four dark forces and you sit there and tell me you intend to do nothing but have them watched?'

'Gabe, it's because you did such a good job of observing them and their habits that I believe we can let them remain where they are for a few days more.'

'Who says you get to make these decisions? You're not a king yet, brother!'

'Being a king is not a position I covet. May all the stars and planets in this universe align if this be a lie ... *brother*.'

In the awkward silence that stretches between us like a rubber band about to snap, I explain. 'Gabe, I can't spare the time or the manpower to go after these dark forces straight away. We don't know what Luca is doing to Ebony, but I guarantee that every moment she is with him is torture. I have to get her out of there *now*.'

Amber's soft whimpers reach him. He casts a piteous glance at her and finally nods. 'You're right. I don't know what I was thinking. Ebony comes first.'

10

Ebony

Outside the apartment Luca points to the wall of glass on my left. It's a sea of Skadean citizens as far as I can see. They fill the courtyards below and pack the streets surrounding the palace all the way to the city borders. They sit on roof-tops and fences and even hang off poles, striving for a view of the balcony. The square itself is overflowing. Angels with children raised high, standing shoulder to shoulder, spill over the walls and hang out of every building.

'They can't wait to meet you.'

I choke down a gasp. I don't want him to think I'm over-whelmed by this, or intimidated, or in any way impressed. But my legs are growing heavy, as if I'm walking through viscous cement. I struggle to keep pace with Luca. The effort makes me breathe in large gulps of air as if I've just finished a long run. And suddenly there isn't enough air and I start to tremble.

Stop! Don't let him feel you trembling. Concentrate on one thing, just one thing at a time. What am I doing right this second? OK. I'm walking … on … on … tiles, big square shiny tiles like marble. Luca has my elbow and his grip is forceful, his odour, waft-ing from him, makes me want to vomit, and run.

Focusing on the moment helps distract my mind, freeing my legs, helping my breathing return to something resembling normal. Most importantly, the one visible aspect, my trembling, settles down.

The apartments between his and my rooms have their double doors wide open. As we pass one, I glimpse lavish furnishings, flashy gold and crystal decor, masterpieces hanging on walls with marble floors and plush rugs. Luca notices my interest. 'I prefer to keep them vacant, but occasionally an event will draw dignitaries and royalty from outlying provinces that will fill the palace to overflowing. Do you like them?'

Why is he always asking my opinion?

I should probably cut down on my sarcasm but it just seems to occur so naturally when I'm around him. 'Is there such an event today?'

He stops, and his voice when he speaks is deep and low, with a definite dangerous edge. 'It would be a mistake to underestimate the event occurring today, Ebony. These apartments are open because they require airing, that's all. Now I've answered your question, you answer mine.'

We start walking again. 'Well, they're not what I would choose.' At his questioning look, I explain. 'They're extravagant. It's just not my thing.'

'We'll see if you still think the same way in a few years.'

'I don't plan to be here that long.' *Damn, I could bite my tongue off.*

'You're forgetting the sealed gates.'

'I'm not forgetting anything.'

He slips into my thoughts, prodding, poking and

searching around. I stop and yank my arm from his grasp, shoving him out of my head as I step away. 'I can walk on my own, thanks.'

He glares at me, but I don't buckle. I try my hardest not to allow him back in. Not touching him makes it easier. He seethes, his eyes flashing to black, and I know then it's only a matter of moments before he forces himself through my barriers and inside my head, filling my mind with darkness, hurting me to teach me a lesson.

A guard steps up. 'May I be of assistance, my lord?'

The guard's interruption is so timely it makes me wonder if he understood that Luca was about to hurt me.

'Thank you, Elijah, but all is well here.'

Moving again, we pass another lavish but vacant guest suite. 'Does anyone other than you live in this palace?'

'Over a thousand live within these walls. The royal guards sleep on the floor immediately below.'

I file this information for later use.

He indicates the corridor that's behind us now. 'This level will only ever house you and me. Even our children will sleep elsewhere.'

'You're going to be such a wonderful father,' I mutter sarcastically.

He laughs. 'You will like it when the nannies are waking at all hours to feed our hungry babies.'

The thought of babies with Luca makes me nauseous.

Conversation ends anyway as we come to a set of pearly glass doors with gold handles, guarded by another pair of Throne soldiers in their trademark black uniforms. Captain Elijah steps forward and pulls a key from a chain around his neck. He turns it in a silver lock, and the balcony guards open the doors wide. Sheer white curtains flutter and a hum of excited voices rolls towards me. When the guards spread the curtains aside, the crowds go insane. I'm so tense the muscles in my arms tighten and a tremor runs through them. I stop and shake them loose. Luca waits, then hooks my arm, and feeling my tension he asks, 'Do the Skadean citizens frighten you?'

'No. I'm not scared of them.'

'Of me then?'

I can see some of the crowd over the balcony rail, a mass of enthusiastic faces, bursting with excitement to see their future queen – *me*.

But it doesn't change how I feel towards Luca, about what he did and why he brought me here. 'To get a wife you planned her abduction for a hundred years, you had an infant killed to make human parents loyal to your plan and you maimed and killed countless soldiers, both your own and your enemy's. You used dark magic, bribery, blackmail, had my memories eradicated and used a trick to slink around the universal code of Free Will. And once you got me, you imprisoned me in your world with no way out for a hundred years. And this, King Luca, is the kicker: after all that, you expect me to fall in love with you. I'm not afraid of you. I pity you.'

The crowd can see the doors are open, the curtains pulled aside, and can probably see us standing in the doorway not moving. The cheering drops to a low murmur.

Beside me, Prince Luca breathes deeply, his chest hissing like a rattlesnake. We both know, no matter how much he wants to punish me right now, neither of us can escape this very public appearance. And in this moment I have the power. I'm going to pay for it later. His anger sears into my bones. But right now I take comfort in knowing I'm not the only one who's going to be doing something they don't feel like and have to smile and wave with false cheer on their face.

Without saying a word, his arm still hooked in mine, he moves the few paces forward to the balcony rail. The crowd goes ballistic. I look out at an ocean of faces. There's a certain look in their expressions that I try to identify. After all, that's my strength – seeing the true soul of people through their eyes.

Luca waves while I still try to comprehend the feeling of the citizens of Skade. It's strange because both dark angels and human souls are carrying the same look, as if they're united for a common cause, and for a moment I wish I were standing down on ground level so I could peer directly into their eyes.

Luca lifts his hands and silences the crowd. 'Citizens one and all, listen carefully, for today on this balcony stands a young angel who will soon become my wife.'

More cheering erupts, but Luca settles it quickly. 'And when that day arrives, history will be made and Skade's future assured as we work towards becoming the strongest of all the realms.'

He turns to face me, holds out both arms to present me. 'Citizens, I give you Princess Ebony, your future queen.'

Clapping and cheering follows.

Luca watches the crowd. He's working out the best

moment to make his move, to give them what they want. In the meantime he waves, casting me glances meant to nudge me into doing the same. As soon as he hears the cheering begin to taper off, he reaches for my hands and moves closer. The crowd's expectations shoot to the sky. Their energy is so palpable it makes the air sizzle.

Luca peers down at me, letting me know that he finally has me where he wants me.

The flutters and spasms gripping my stomach intensify with the first touch of his hand at the small of my back, pulling me in close. He lifts my face with his thumb under my chin and with agonisingly slow movements his head lowers down, down, down, until his mouth touches mine.

The first thing I feel is heat, the heat that always seems to radiate from inside him. Fractionally after this, it's the pressure of his lips, strangely, unexpectedly soft. They brush mine with the unobtrusive feel of lush silk pillows.

But now the heat from his face is like an inferno, smothering me. It takes all my self-control not to shove him away and splash cold water over my head. He increases the pressure and his lips grow firmer and more demanding against my closed mouth.

If Luca deepens this kiss, I will gag. If he pushes my lips apart, I'll … I'll … I'm not sure exactly, but biting his lip comes to mind. So it's just as well for his sake that he doesn't, but his mouth stays on mine for what feels like a very long time, growing firmer and hotter. So hot that blisters form, quickly heal and form again.

It's not that he's a bad kisser. There's gentleness, and that surprises me. He's definitely skilled in the art of seduction, there's no doubting that, and that scares me more than a little.

But he's not Nathaneal. When Nathaneal kisses me, his tender warmth spreads through my whole body and I want nothing more than to melt into him.

Nathaneal's lips are the *only* ones I want on mine, certainly not his archenemy's.

When Luca finally lifts his mouth off mine, he does it slowly while watching me like a hawk, as if he's seeking the precise moment to pounce. My mouth is tinder dry, and without thinking of consequences, only my basic need, I whip my tongue tip out and moisten my lips.

But this is what Luca is watching for. He swoops back down, his tongue poised between his lips, catching me unawares. The intimacy shocks me and I gasp, shooting my breath around his tongue and into his mouth. Without giving me a chance to inhale much-needed air, he fastens his mouth over mine again, this time taking full advantage of his surprise tactic. He scalds the inside of my mouth with his tongue as he pushes into sensitive areas. I try to pull away, but his hand snakes into my hair, locking my face to his like a prisoner inside a jail cell.

The crowd goes insane, hooting and whistling and cheering wildly, while my stomach rolls over on itself and my head spins with oxygen withdrawal. I try to draw air in through my nose but the state of my nerves doesn't allow me nearly enough.

I'm almost out of air, but I would rather pass out in front of billions of people than draw from *his* lungs. I smack my palms against his shoulders repeatedly, until he finally gets it and lifts his head.

I gulp in air as if I've been drowning. Luca watches me, his chest rising and falling with his own deep breaths, an unreadable expression on his face.

Meanwhile, the tumultuous applause of the massive crowd seeps into my head. Dazed by the lack of oxygen, I allow Luca to turn me towards them. I grip the balustrade in front of me with both hands.

Slowly the faces below become clearer, and that look in their eyes I've been trying to decipher finally dawns on me. The knowledge of what it is makes me go weak at the knees.

Thinking I might faint, Luca swings his arm around my waist and pulls me against him.

The crowd's cheers incredibly grow louder, and that look in their eyes intensifies, which only makes me feel sicker in the stomach.

I hate Luca for putting me in this position, even more than I did already. What am I supposed to do now? But this ... this shouldn't make any difference. I don't have any obligation to these people. It won't change my plans. I won't let it.

I raise my hand, wave and even offer a small smile, something I never dreamed I would do.

But how can I ignore that look in their eyes?

That poignant, pitiful expression of hope.

11

Jordan

It's just as well I don't have far to drive. In my mood I'd probably take a sharp bend too fast, hit a few trees before soaring into open air to crash head first into rocks on the valley floor.

Probably explode.

Nothing left to bury.

Shit! I gotta get myself outta this dark space my head is in.

'Jordy, are you OK?'

For a moment it's Ebony I'm hearing and my heart flips over. She's the only one who knows how to pull me outta this hole. She has the right words, the perfect touch. Her warm hand on my shoulder always calms me. Those violet eyes hold so much compassion for me. And the way she says my name, shortened like a pet name for a puppy, is so damn cute.

'Jordan?'

I turn towards the voice, a heartbeat away from whispering her name. It's lucky I don't, cos it's not Ebony in my passenger seat like so many times before. This is *Amber*. And Luca didn't kidnap *Amber*. No, Luca took *my* girl, the girl I love.

'Drop me off here, thanks,' Amber snaps.

I glance out of my side window into what is arguably the darkest stretch of road between the monastery and Thane's place.

'Stop the car!'

I pull up on the shoulder as soon as I find a strip wide enough. 'What's your problem?'

She's in a hurry to get out. 'Unlock my door.' Her voice could be a sword. It sounds so deadly she could kill me with it. 'Do it, Jordan, *now*.'

'Not until you tell me why you want to walk on this deserted mountain road in the middle of the night, alone.'

There's something fierce in her eyes when she turns them on me. A flash of awareness ripples through my gut.

'Of course I don't *want* to walk out there in the dark alone, but it beats being in this car with you ignoring me or lamenting that I'm not the one who got kidnapped!'

'I didn't say that!'

'Not aloud!'

What do I say to that? Admit it and hurt her more?

'It's in your eyes, Jordan, every time you look *through* me. And I can't stand to be near you when you're wishing it were me in her place.'

'Amber, no –'

'I love her too, but I wouldn't want you to take her place. You really are a moron.'

Amber has to know I don't really mean it. 'I miss her *so* much, Amber, you've got no idea.'

'So much that you'd rather the Prince of Darkness had taken me in her place.'

'Don't say that. I would never want that for you.'

Tears are swimming in her eyes as I take her hands in mine. 'Please believe me, Amber, no matter what fleeting signs you might read on my face, I DO NOT want you harmed by *anyone* or *anything*.'

She hiccups and scrunches her nose. I try not to smile at how cute she looks when she does that. She sniffs again. 'Do you mean that? I mean, really, *really* mean that?'

I glance up at the stars to gather the strength I need to convince her I'm telling the truth. Then I collect her tear-soaked face in my hands and look into her eyes. 'As God is my witness, Amber Lang, I swear to you that I would kill anyone who even thought about hurting you.'

12

Nathaneal

Twelve Sentinels sit at one time, with each Sentinel serving between seven years and a hundred. It's a sacrifice and an honour to serve the High King on such a personal level, to deal out his directives, to be the instigators of his law and, along with the Archangels, to protect him.

Avena has no higher honour.

We fly night and day across three provinces, past the River of Twin Tunnels and over the Sea of Seven Winds, before reaching the shimmering white sands of Empyrean Island. Michael, Shae and I make our way on foot along a path that cuts through thick tropical growth that resembles a jungle more than a forest.

Since Michael has been here before, he leads the way. Empyrean was the best place for him after Luca slaughtered his wife, Thereziel, in a vindictive rage, destroying her body and soul. After three years in the Temple, meditating, studying and writing chronicles, he was able to return to his life again.

We reach a vast field covered in wild flowers. Glancing at each other in silent signal, we discharge our wings and fly low over the carpet of silk and velvet. Ebony would be in awe seeing this, running her fingers over the soft furry petals as I am now. One day I will bring her here.

'I have heard that Peridis is like this,' Shae remarks.

'Perhaps you should ask our High King yourself,' Michael suggests teasingly.

'I don't think so, in case he decides to send me there!' she jokes, but her voice turns serious as she shifts her gaze to me. 'I can't risk not being there when you bring Ebrielle home.'

'You will be there. And, Shae, the only name she knows is Ebony. It's her identity and we can't take that from her, not without her permission.'

She nods, and as the landscape grows rocky, we land on terra firma, finding we're closer than we thought. We tilt our heads back and look up at Avena's highest mountain, where, at the summit, the High King's Temple sits permanently concealed in mist.

Michael leads the way through a cleverly concealed path between rocks to stairs that will take us to the walled city.

'Any thoughts before we start the climb?' I ask.

Shae frowns, purses her lips. 'How many steps are there? I can only see the first three hundred and six.'

'In all the time I spent here,' Michael says as we start to climb, 'I never thought to count them.'

'Weren't you even curious?'

He shrugs. 'Not really, Shae. I didn't have the mind for counting stairs in those days.'

I close my eyes as a wave of grief flows out of him and slams into me, which, coupled with my own despair, takes me to a point of bleakness I can barely fathom. I double over, my hands on my thighs, unable to go on.

'Forgive me, cousin,' he says, rushing to my side. 'You didn't need that.'

'It's all right, Michael. It's passing.' He helps me straighten up and I take a deep breath.

'Sometimes it feels like only yesterday that I lost Theze.'

'I wish I had known her.'

Losing a partner is rare among angels. The emptiness left behind can devastate the one who remains, the heartache can consume them, rip the angel apart like an incendiary exploding on the inside. The trigger might be a memory, a familiar scent, the voice they hear in their dreams.

For me, without Ebony, it feels as if there are a million triggers: the memory of her face as the gates thundered down between us, the way her eyes clung to mine when Michael pulled me from her arms at my arrest; I miss her gentle, selfless ways, her struggle to rekindle her angelic ancestry, the touch of her fingers on my face. How can I go on without her?

The answer is simple.

I can't.

'Are we ready to begin?' Shae asks, practically jumping up and down. Her excitement at being this near the source of our power, the creator of everything, with the possibility of freeing her sister becoming reality, catches Michael and me by surprise. And as joy is meant to do, it spreads into us and lifts us both to a level where we can function.

Many stairs later, but with many more to go, we enter thickening mist. Shae pauses, stretches, arching her back.

Her enthusiasm waning slightly, she asks Michael, 'Are you sure we can't fly?'

'Not if you wish to enter the city.'

'So for those that come here, this is like a pilgrimage,' she ponders, 'for what more can one do when climbing stairs shrouded in mist except to think, reflect and wonder.'

We reach a platform with a railing and a bench. But no one is interested in the view, no matter how astonishing, and there is no time to rest. We push on, and several hundred steps later we reach the summit, where a colossal white wall protects the city, stretching so high its top fuses into the mist.

'They will be expecting us,' Michael says.

'They?' Shae asks.

Walking to the gates, he peers over his shoulder. 'The Sentinels. They will know by now that we're here and what we're coming for. But we'll still need their approval for an audience with the High King.'

An Archangel wearing a long white dress and matching cloak with a deep hood opens a door in the towering gate; her graceful, feathered wings sway slightly behind her. She greets us with a warm smile from pale lips, leaning down to kiss the air either side of each of our faces. 'Welcome to Empyrean.' Her voice is low and strong, her whitish skin flawless, her eyes amethyst in colour. 'I am Teeliah, and I'm to escort you directly to the Temple. Please follow me.'

Teeliah slips into the air on silent wingbeats, glancing back once to ensure we're following.

There is an aura of serenity in this place. It's tangible even from this height. And by the peaceful look on Shae's face, and ease by which she's moving, she's feeling it too.

Following Teeliah, we touch down on the Temple's front steps, moving inside through a spectacular glass atrium where plants thrive alongside a waterfall and a shimmering stream leaping with colourful fish. A corridor takes us to an area called the Centre, where a lift waits for us with its doors open. Teeliah takes us up to level twelve but doesn't get out. 'Someone will come for you soon.'

We thank her and the doors close behind us.

Only a moment passes before footsteps approach and another Archangel in similar dress greets us and leads us to the Sentinels' chamber. I can see that she is talking with Michael and Shae, but all I can hear is the sound of my heart pounding. This is it. I have to convince them to help us. I cannot fail Ebony at this first hurdle.

The room is round. The Sentinels – six male, six female – sit up on a raised semicircular platform, with Prince Cassiel from the Order of Powers at the centre, ready to judge whether our petition to see the High King is deserving.

It's all up to them.

Michael and Shae stand on either side of me. We are brief, to the point, as practised on our way here, taking turns explaining our cause, how important it is to retrieve Ebony and the situation that will occur should we not be successful. How Luca will create an unbeatable army to invade Earth, and how, in our capacity as Guardians, we will have failed.

The Sentinels don't ask us to leave. They're quiet for a few moments, undoubtedly conversing through a private mind-link.

Prince Cassiel stands. My mouth goes dry. This is it. He says, 'Prince Nathaneal, Prince Michael and my lady Shaephira, you make a strong case. You have our unanimous support.'

They will let us meet the High King.

Shae squeals, gripping my arm, and her joy slams into me, but Prince Cassiel has more to say, so I keep my emotions in check to listen to his instructions with a clear head.

'You are about to meet our glorious High King,' he says. 'Forget everything you know about him, all that you have been taught or told or imagined. Control your temper in his presence and do not waste his time. There will be no need for lengthy explanations. He knows your needs before you enter his chamber, your questions before you ask them, the limitations you yourself are unaware of having. Our High King is powerful beyond what we are capable of understanding.'

The other Sentinels nod when he says this. But telling me the High King is powerful beyond comprehension doesn't frighten me, but gives me hope.

'He could squash you like an insect,' Prince Cassiel says. 'He could burn you where you stand, and when he is glowing, whatever you do, don't look into his eyes.'

13

Ebony

On my second night in Skade I dream of Prince Luca dancing a Viennese waltz with me in an ivory ballroom with
crystal chandeliers, white candles in sconces over tables and
glass hurricane lamps on marble and gold stands. The room
is brimming with angels in fancy dress, costumes from
Earth's various historical eras, except everyone is wearing
a mask resembling an animal, bird or reptile. Prince Luca's
mask is a lion's head. Mine is a peacock.

It's like something out of a fairy tale but with a dark
twist.

Prince Luca is so tall I have to lean my head back to see
his face. The dream-me wonders if he's always this tall. His
eyes are mesmerising, glowing a deep golden yellow. He
twirls me confidently around the polished floor, clearly an
experienced dancer. He picks up the pace, spinning me
faster. The other dancers step back, making room for us.
They nod and smile at their king as we waltz past them.
Thoughtfully today Luca is wearing black gloves that stop
his heat from burning my hands. He makes a joke about it
and I laugh. He is charismatic and charming.

The dream-me feels safe in his arms. But the sleeping-me

knows something isn't right and squirms uncomfortably between the sheets. A red and fuzzy edge develops around my vision. It's the haze I get when I'm angry. But I'm not angry. Well, not the dream-me. I'm dancing to perfectly pitched violins, turning left and right as Luca spins me around the dance floor at an astonishing pace, almost like we're flying.

But the haze grows stronger, as if I'm trying to pull myself from the dream, as if the sleeping-me knows I'm in danger. I become aware of my body jerking. It shocks the dream-me and I miss a step.

My subconscious mind, which never sleeps, is working hard at waking me up.

But then Luca brings his mouth down to my ear and whispers, 'They're watching you, Princess.' His gloved fingers trace circular patterns on my bare arm. His soft touch surprises me. But more surprising is my physical reaction. In the one breath I both desire and hate him. 'You intrigue them,' he says.

I see angels smiling and clapping, faces I don't recognise cheering us on.

'You intrigue *me* most of all,' he whispers.

My mind stops fighting and Prince Luca smiles at the devoted crowd. 'Wave, Princess. They're waiting for you to acknowledge them.'

Like a machine designed to respond automatically to the sound of Luca's voice, I do what he says.

The music stops and Luca steps back, keeping his eyes fixed on me, more magnetic and compelling than ever. With an elegant sweeping movement he whisks off his mask and tosses it to the excited onlookers. Smiling and confident, he leans down and gently removes my mask, again tossing it to the cheering angels.

When his eyes return to me, they're a bright scalding green. My stomach flips, my fingers tingle, my pulse accelerates. Prince Luca is going to kiss me. Everyone can feel it. He tilts his head slightly, draws in a soft breath and slowly begins to lower his mouth.

'You are mine, Princess,' he whispers, closing the space between us.

'Forever,' he adds.

His mouth presses into mine, and my lips burst into flames.

I wake with a start and sit straight up in bed, my heart pounding. I breathe deeply, the pulse in my neck jumping. 'What was that?' I ask myself in a whisper that sounds loud in the dark silence. I lift my fingers to check my lips have not really exploded into fire. It's a relief to find them still intact.

Going to the window, I find my bearings and force myself to shake off the disturbing dream. I promise to find a way out of this palace before Luca has a chance to slip into my dreams and try again to make me fall in love with him.

14

Nathaneal

Prince Cassiel walks the three of us to the lift but doesn't enter the chamber with us. 'Good luck, Prince Nathaneal. I mean that on behalf of all the Sentinels.'

'Thank you.'

In the enclosed cabin, Shae asks Michael, 'When you were here thirty-four years ago, did you meet our High King?'

'He asked to see me once. We talked. He told me about Nathaneal. He gave my life purpose again.'

Shae flicks her gaze over me. 'But ... Nathaneal wasn't born for years to come.'

Michael scoffs. 'I know.' He looks at me. 'And as with the rest of us, we had to wait until he was ready.'

I need to change the subject. Keep a clear head. Thankfully the lift starts rising. And rising. The higher the altitude, the faster the gears grind and the sound of rushing wind takes on a shrill whistle as the decrease in air pressure forces trapped air in my ears to push outwards and pop. How fast and what elevation is anyone's guess.

When the lift begins to slow Michael reels off advice, 'Keep your heads lowered, your eyes sheltered, and no matter how shocking or surprised or painful it might become in there, remember to keep breathing.'

'Right,' I murmur through suddenly soaring nerves.

Shae's eyes widen as she catches mine. 'Anything else we should know?'

'He will appear first to us as light, then in either angel or human form. Only then can we look at him, though still not into his eyes if he is glowing, OK?'

'Affirmative.'

'Shae?'

'I've got it, Michael.'

'Good.'

We stand still, hardly breathing, as the elevator winds down to a smooth stop. In the instant before the doors open we glance at each other, and an unspoken understanding passes between us. This is it. If it doesn't go well, if we don't walk out with the *hanival* in our possession, it will be over.

I will have failed her. And eventually the entire human race.

Completely. Utterly. Failed.

My hands are shaking. *You're OK. Breathe. A few nerves won't hurt. Total collapse from holding my breath will. Remember why you're here.*

Ebony's face appears as I last saw her, as colossal Dark Thrones, their faces concealed beneath grotesque black helmets, pull her from my wings, her eyes weeping sorrow as she comprehends the horrors that lie ahead for us.

The memory is precisely what I need as I face the unknown and uncertain. The doors open and we step into a profound black void.

A flicker of light in the distance appears as a white dot.

It grows exponentially, rushing at us with the eerie sound of typhoon winds, though there is not even the hint of a zephyr. The light swells, building in an instant to a blinding dazzle. It surrounds us. As we lift our arms to shield our eyes, a radiant male figure appears in the light's bright centre. In a deep, strong, compelling voice, he commands us to approach.

Already I can see that this light – *his* light – is extraordinary. It bursts forth like the Sun's first explosive rays breaking over the finely arched horizon of Earth. Resplendent, it glistens as if every photon is – *impossibly* – a molecule, or less, an atom, each with the uniqueness of a snowflake.

The source of this light – the radiant man – speaks to me. *Come closer, my sweet prince of light.*

The nearer I draw to the source, the brighter, the more densely packed, the radioactive photons become. They're all around me. I lift my hand and notice – *again impossibly* – intricate details with individual photon strings, or 'rays' as humans call them. They move between my fingers, flashing with each lithe movement as they dance around, bumping into each other.

I soon realise this light is making its own radiance, its own energy. This is why it feels warm on my skin. The atoms are in constant motion, moving in all different directions, making heat, and even music. Every note is a unique sound. It's breathtaking. *Magical.*

I also realise there is nothing in this light to fear, so I lower my arm and allow the light to wholly embrace me.

Millions of photons attach themselves to my skin. Their

warmth feels like the embraces of butterflies. I hear their sounds, their harmonious ever-changing melodies. They mould around my body, sink into my pores and fill me with an all-encompassing sense of peace, contentment, trust and absolute …

It's love, Shae. In its purest form, untainted by angel or human minds. The light will not harm us.

She nods, while Michael stares. I open my mouth and inhale. Millions of photons tumble inside me, filling me, spreading into my lungs, my blood, enriching my organs; even my brain feels more alive, more … empowered.

Awareness like never before enriches my senses, energises my brain, settling in the pit of my stomach as I grasp an understanding of … *everything* – how vital the Earth is, how every human and every angel, including the excommunicated, the fallen and their innocent descendants who have no alternative, are all connected.

And how that connection is *this* light.

I reach for an understanding of how, why. *Open your eyes, prince of my heart, and see.*

I do as the High King commands and the light draws me in closer, closer, *closer*. I'm not moving physically, but my mind feels opened, enlarged with knowledge and love, always *love*, and I keep moving until it's as if I'm *inside* the source, and then I *see*. This is where all things once came. I see the explosion of creation, the generation of universes, stars and planets and –

I hear Michael call my name as if through a deep fog. He wants me to pull away, but I can't leave yet. He grabs my arm, but I slip from the physical contact as if my limbs were malleable. I'm seeing and feeling and hearing something never before seen or felt or heard. It's truth, the truth in its original, untainted form. And above everything I understand in this utopic sensory experience is the sense that the High King knows, and is pleased with me, and … somewhat amused.

I whisper to Michael and Shae, *Are you feeling this?*

Not as abundantly as I suspect you are, cousin.

And suddenly a compulsion comes over me, not only to *see*, but also to become one with the light. *Enough, Thane*, Michael calls. *You will go too far for me to pull you out.*

I take a step forward.

Stop!

I hear the voice. It's not Michael, and I do exactly as *he* says.

My eager prince, you must learn to listen to your minder. Prince Michael's wealth of experience is what you lack, and his advice is more golden than the sun.

I give myself a mental shake. What am I doing? Ebony's face immediately appears and I exhale a long sigh.

You come for the hanival, the High King states as he steps out of the light in the form of a tall dark-haired man with glittering eyes and honey-coloured skin, a glowing pale gold aura surrounding him. Armchairs appear, and by the time he motions to them and we all sit, his aura has softened to a dim, humming glow, and a room with white walls and a window into deep space has formed around us.

In a beautifully crafted speaking voice, with perfect enunciation, the High King says, 'The *hanival* is not a weapon, but when held in the hands of one who can wield it, it will multiply the energy of the holder many times over.' His head tilts to the side like a bird examining a ripe piece of fruit. 'But I cannot let you have it.'

'My lord, will you explain why you will not allow me the one item vital to freeing Ebony from the tyrant of all tyrants?'

'Prince Nathaneal, you must know by now that you are exquisitely dear to my heart and saying no to you is difficult. The world has waited long for your presence. And now that you are here, your heart breaks for your beloved and this clouds your sharp mind. The ramifications of using the *hanival* are too dangerous for all of Earth.'

'W-h-what ramifications, my lord?' Shae asks, close to breaking point.

'Sweet Shaephira, once a hole is forged, you will not be able to close it again. None of you will.' He looks pointedly at Michael, then me. 'Nor I, for that matter. Not even Lucian himself.'

This is crushing news. I truly thought Luca could open his own gates but it suited him for everyone to think he couldn't. Now I learn that he can't even repair them.

'I have no instrument that can close a damaged gate,' the High King continues. 'No such tool exists. The hole would act as a vortex, pulling out dark souls, demons and beasts. They will infiltrate the Crossing, locate the entrances to Peridis, Avena and Earth and tear apart the barriers I set in place to protect the worlds from one another. Imagine Earth with no protective barriers.' He shudders, distorting his aura so that the air around us ripples.

Michael says, 'Over time, the human soul would alter

from the contamination of evil.'

'Imagine the hysteria,' the High King says, 'when human beings see battalions of angels darkening their skies with their black armour and horned helmets, carrying shields, and weapons humans know nothing of, blowing trumpets declaring war. It would not be long before Prince Lucian's threat to control all the realms comes to pass.'

He suddenly stands and morphs into an angel taller than any other, his aura strengthening and emanating in glowing waves of colour. 'I cannot risk Earth becoming the Dark Prince's dominion.'

My mouth goes tinder dry as he glances down at the three of us. 'And nor should you. It is the oath you have sworn to live by.'

He focuses directly at me. 'Nathaneal, you are vital to the salvation of humankind and the existence of eternal life.' He inhales deeply, his massive chest rising and expanding, his colossal wings opening out to their full mind-blowing span, an expression of acute agony on his face. Retracting his wings, he softens his voice and adds, 'But so too is Ebrielle, whom we shall call Ebony, for that is how she knows herself at present. Together you make an unbeatable force.'

'My lord, I will block the way of *every* soul, demon or beast that would attempt to pass through a hole I puncture in the gates of Skade. I promise this. I make this vow before you, the High King of Avena and Earth, and in the presence of –'

'Tell me, Nathaneal, how long are you prepared to guard the punctured gate – a hundred years, a thousand?'

'If a thousand years was the price to free Ebony, my lord, I would guard it gladly. I would install rotating shifts of the best soldiers Avena has.'

'And will you also promise to stop the Dark Prince?'

'My lord?'

'If you do not stop the cause, the battles between light and dark angelic forces will continue to escalate until human life is enslaved under Lucien's complete control. The Dark Prince has found a deep power source within himself and the closer he draws to his heart's desire, the stronger he becomes, and the more dangerous. He is a real threat to human life and once he physically consummates with the object of his obsession he will transmogrify into the power force within him.'

He waits for my answer, watching me, giving me time to take it all in. And while I think about what he is asking of me, he says, 'There is no guarantee that over time the breach you create will not widen as its edges deteriorate. As dark souls force their way through it, rips can occur that might cause the entire gate to tear apart. Dark angels and beasts, sensing freedom, could widen the perforation from the inside, compulsively picking away at it like a scabrous sore. You would not be able to stop that unless you entered Skade with the intention of destroying the offenders. And if you don't stop Lucian before you leave Skade, he would construe this as an invasion, and he would be within his rights as king to declare war on Avena.'

He has made his point. I don't need time to think. 'My lord, I will do whatever is necessary. And I will be devastating.'

He falls silent. And then he nods. 'There is a way a gate can regenerate itself.'

What? My heart wants to burst out of my chest at this news, but until I know more I contain this compulsion to soar to the ceiling.

'Nathaneal, I am willing to give you the *hanival* if, after you have fulfilled your promise, you agree to provide the gate with what it requires to regenerate itself.'

Shae grips my forearm, 'Yes! Yes, my lord, we promise to provide whatever it requires.'

He glances at Shae with a compassionate look. 'I must have confirmation from Nathaneal.'

She nods, swinging her gaze to me, and waits.

'Sire,' I ask, 'how does a gate regenerate itself?'

'I'm afraid a human is required, and not just any human, but one whose heart flows with love.'

Silence descends in the room as if we are in the presence of death. Michael's gaze joins Shae's, burning into each side of my face as they both reach for my mind. But I block them. I can't look at either of them in case I see what they might be thinking – *who* they might be thinking of. I can't let my thoughts move in that direction.

The High King explains, 'Find a human whose heart flows with love and who is willing to sacrifice his or her life for this cause, and the instrument is yours.' His eyes shift to a low table that appears at his side, where an instrument with a crystalline metal barrel lies in an open titanium case.

'How does the act of regeneration occur?' Michael asks, dragging his eyes from my face.

'The gates are an infinitesimal assembly of microscopic

singular cells that radiate to each other, forming strings of living organisms. The strings are able to regenerate themselves from a particularly rich source of human blood and tissue. The beating of a human heart will create the unique environment required for the regeneration process to occur. Human tissue and blood are reorganised into the impenetrable solid mass that forms the gates.'

'How long would the process take?' he asks.

'A few minutes, but that would depend on the heart – how full of love it is, how strongly it beats, and how willing the human is to give to this cause.'

'Must the human be sacrificed?'

'Blood is required, the heart must be beating to pump it or the gate's fabric will not knit together. The gate will rebuild itself around the human, consuming all flesh, bones, organs, teeth, hair. Even clothes.'

I try not to show my repulsion, but shock is something I can't disguise. There's a roaring in my ears, the thunder of a waterfall, drowning my ability to make sense of this.

I hear Shae's voice, gentle as a meek lamb's. 'Will it hurt the human?'

How can she think so clinically? How can either of them contemplate such disturbing details?

The High King pauses so long it forces me from the temporary refuge of my dazed disbelief back into reality. There's a burning sensation in my throat now, along with the sound of rushing waters between my ears.

Will it hurt the human? Will it hurt the human?

I don't want to hear the answer.

Michael looks worried and gazes at me with concern.

He wants me to connect with him, let him know I'm OK. I can't yet because I'm far from OK. This is *not* what I came here to do.

Will it hurt the human? Will it hurt the human?

I came for a tool to help me open a gate of Skade, not to take the life of a human, and not just *any* human, but one whose heart flows with love, a heart that is beating while the body is being consumed!

But now even the High King is waiting for me to open my eyes. I have to get this over with so I can leave. Taking a deep breath, I open my eyes and wait.

Will it hurt the human?

Mercifully he doesn't make me wait long.

'Yes,' he says. 'The pain will be excruciating. The gate will not only consume everything, it will take the human's soul.'

15

Ebony

I can't go back to sleep. The dream was so vivid it felt real. I pull myself into a sitting position, swinging my feet to the floor. I'm afraid that if I slip back into the dream Luca will pick up where he left off. I can still feel the heat from his lips on mine, the flames that erupted as if my mouth were on fire. I wipe it with the back of my hand, but it doesn't help.

I turn my bedside lamp on and walk into my wardrobe, scratching my head at the sight of so many outfits. Wow, it's like a department store. I pick out a pair of blue skinny jeans with a label I've heard celebrities wear. They fit like a second skin. I pull on a white top and turn round in front of the mirror, peering at my shoulders. Angels make clothing from a special fibre. When wings push on it, cells inside the fibre reorganise, separating and returning to form naturally when wings retract. I assume it's the same here.

I brush my hair into a high ponytail and head down the small hallway to the living room, grateful Mela keeps the fires lit well into the night. The remaining embers are still keeping the room nice and toasty. I check the curtains are closed, go to the middle of the room and practise pulling up my power.

Nothing happens at first, but I keep trying, working simultaneously on slowing my breathing. I know my power comes from the centre of my core, that part of my mind that no one can reach. Nathaneal told me once to imagine a small room with a door only I can open. I do it now and a glimmering golden bud sprouts and draws me inside.

Containing my excitement at seeing my essence in its purest form, I focus on nurturing the tiny shoot, feeding it with love from my heart, coaxing it to open like a flower in bloom. Surprising me, it bursts into a bright flame and a rush of heat spreads throughout my body.

I smile as it sinks in: *this* is my power. It's thrumming through my veins, in every cell of my body. It's strong too, though just how strong, or how it compares to others', I can't say. Is it too strong? I don't know. But it's invigorating, as if it wants to burst through my skin.

From what I've learned so far, my power has the potential to be highly destructive. I've smashed vases, shifted furniture and thrown angels twice my size away from me.

Could I destroy this palace and still have enough strength left to walk out of the rubble? It's a heady thought.

I will practise every night, every day, every chance I get.

About an hour into the session a noise from Mela's room catches me off guard. I listen and hear her footsteps approaching. I'm starting to make progress and don't want to stop yet, but, while my instinct says I can trust Mela, I don't know how much Luca forces her to report, or simply reads through her mind.

She walks in and stops when she sees me standing in the middle of the living room with a weird expression on my face.

'What are you doing up so early?' she asks.

I sit down on the sofa. 'Do you always sneak around in the early hours checking up on me?'

'That's not what I was doing, Ebony. Couldn't you sleep?'

'Since Luca abducted me I don't sleep like I used to, so I have to do something to stop from lying in bed thinking too much.' I try to make this sound light because I like Mela and have a really good feeling when I'm near her, but my heart is too broken and I can't raise a smile to soften the hard edge to my voice.

'I'm sorry, Ebony. I didn't mean to startle you.'

'I'm sorry too, Mela. I shouldn't have had a go at you just for getting up.'

She sits beside me. 'I heard a noise and thought I'd check it out.'

'Ah, looking out for me. Now I should really be mad at you.'

She smiles. 'I have sleeping tablets, remember? Anytime, just ask.'

'Thanks, but it was just a bad dream so I thought I'd get up and exercise. Who knows when Luca will let me go outside?' I drop the hint.

She sighs. 'You're right. It could be a while.'

Not what I was hoping to hear. 'Do you know how long he plans to keep me locked up in this apartment?'

'Until he can trust you won't try to run, or …' She

presses her lips together as if she were thinking about something.

'What is it, Mela?'

She gets up and heads to the front doors, calling out in a weird loud voice, 'Would you like a cup of hot chocolate, my lady, to help you sleep?'

Not exactly what I was thinking, but I can't help a grin at her subtle-as-cement clue that the guards could be listening, so I continue the charade. 'There's hot chocolate in the palace?'

'He brought it over for you himself.'

'He? You don't mean … ?'

'The king? Yes, on one of his trips before he sealed the gates.'

Mela opens the front doors. Over her head I see two Throne soldiers I haven't seen before soundlessly turn on their heels. She asks them if they would like a hot chocolate drink and they politely decline.

Closing the doors, she turns to face me and runs a finger across her throat with a negative shake of her head. I get that she means the talk she wants to have with me will have to wait for a change of guards.

While Mela is in the kitchen, I open the drapes on all the windows. Streaks of crimson, blue and purple light hint of dawn over the distant snow-covered mountains, while nearer the city there's a thick overcast sky. There's mist in the air, dew on the ground. No doubt it's going to be another cold day in Odisha.

Down in the streets, blinking lights draw my eye to a team of souls collecting garbage from in front of houses, dumping it into a truck with an open tray. Two female angels, both in fur-lined black cloaks, supervise with whips they crack across the legs of any worker they deem to be slow – as if whipping someone's legs will make them move faster. Someone should whip *their* legs, see how much faster *they* move with whip-burned calves.

Mela returns with mugs of steaming hot chocolate that makes my nose twitch and fills my head with memories of Mum bringing me a mug during a stormy night. 'You weren't kidding about the chocolate.'

'I wouldn't dream of it.'

'How did he even know I liked the stuff?' I whisper, quickly adding, 'Forget it. I know he has spies.'

'You've met his Aracals,' she says softly.

'Those birds told him I like hot chocolate?' Her nod gets me wondering what else the shape-shifting creatures have told him.

After a while of standing at the window together, sipping hot chocolate and watching the sanitation teams at work, I realise Mela is not looking at the garbage collectors any more, but at me. 'What is it, Mela?'

'Ebony, if you're contemplating running, then I need to warn you: there are far more dangerous places outside this palace than in.'

Escape is my hope. I can't have that taken away, no matter how good her intentions. So I clear my throat and change the subject. 'Is Luca coming to see me today?'

'Sorry, Ebony, he hasn't told me what he plans for you today.'

'I thought he told you everything.'

She laughs and takes my empty mug. 'I'd better fix you some breakfast.'

As she turns to leave, I grab her arm. 'Do *you* tell him everything?'

'I'm not sure I follow.'

'Mela, you know I can tell when someone is lying, right?'

'So I've been informed.'

'OK, so can you answer me this?' She waits and I ask, 'Do you report to Prince Luca?'

She tilts her head and narrows her eyes.

I make myself clearer, 'Do you tell him everything I do, every move I make, every word I say?'

Her eyes flick away, but I need to know whether my gut instinct is right or not. 'Look at me, Mela. Do you tell Luca everything?'

She exhales a long breath. 'Yes. And no.'

Could she be more ambiguous? 'Tell me the "Yes" part.'

'I can't risk the king suspecting me of keeping secrets from him,' she whispers, flicking a glance at the doors. Lifting a finger to her lips, she motions for me to follow her into her bedroom. Closing the door behind us, she turns to face me. 'This room is safe to talk in, but we still need to keep our voices low. It's swept for listening devices several times a day.'

'Really? By whom?'

'Certain trustworthy guards when they're on duty.'

'Oh.'

'Ebony, remember down in the foyer when I told you the province of Zurat has a rebel problem?'

'Uh-huh.'

'There are rebels in Odisha too.'

'Here in the city?'

'In almost every province and major city in Skade.'

'Wow! How many? How strong are they? What are their plans? Can you put me in touch with them?'

She holds her hands up between us, and smiles. 'You're talking to their general.'

I swallow down a gasp as my mind buzzes with possibilities. Mela begins explaining and I try to contain my thoughts of runaway schemes in order to listen. 'The rebel army is growing in numbers every day,' she says. 'Except for me, they are all angels. I'm grooming my highest-ranking lieutenants to take over when, well, my mortality expires. Those who live and work in this palace are most vulnerable. They depend on me to be strong and not make mistakes, so I must be very careful, especially in the king's presence. And now that I've told you –'

'Of course I'll be careful too, Mela. But how do you keep Luca out of your head?'

'An angel of light taught me how years ago, but I think he did something to me at the same time, because ever since that first meeting we've been able to communicate through the realms.'

This makes me raise my eyebrows.

She nods. 'But it's too risky to do so from the palace.'

'Yeah, of course.'

'Luca has the strongest mind of any angel I know. I haven't risked linking with anyone since Luca appointed me your handmaiden.'

'Thank you for telling me. You give me hope that I'm going to get out of here.'

'Ebony …' Mela's voice trails off into silence, but her eyes are telling me what I don't want to hear.

'He's not lying about the gates, is he?'

'No.' Her sad smile is back.

'So this is why you have to tell him everything, so he doesn't suspect who you really are and put the entire rebel army in jeopardy.'

'I knew you would understand.'

'So what you're saying is that I can't escape for a minimum of a hundred years, and your rebel army can't help me in case Luca discovers their identities. I'm on my own.'

'As long as I'm here, dear girl, you're not on your own.'

'No offence, Mela, but it doesn't sound like you have my back, not with an entire army to protect.'

'Ebony, for now I can guide you, give you purpose for being in Skade and make your life as queen as fulfilling as it can be.'

'Fulfilling? Mela, I don't want fulfilling, I want escape. Freedom. Home. I want my prince back in my arms. Nothing else matters.'

As tears threaten, I bite down on my fist, and suddenly I just want to crawl back into bed with my knees curled up to my chest and my pillow muffling my sobs. I move to the door, square my shoulders and turn halfway round. 'Thank you for your guidance offer. I'll let you know if I need it.'

'Ebony, please –'

'Don't worry, I'll keep your secret, but, Mela, tell me, if I plan an escape and you find out about it, will you tell Luca?

Will you warn him? I really need to know whether or not I can trust you.'

She comes over and stands in front of me with her eyes open and clear. 'Ebony, I would *never* reveal your secrets.'

I nod, taking a deep breath of relief as I stare down into her soul and see she's telling the truth.

16

Nathaneal

I walk straight out the atrium door without stopping.
Michael hurries to keep pace.

'Thane!' Shae goes to run after me but Michael stops her.
What do you want me to tell her? he links.

It's not Shae's fault rescuing her sister means the death of
a human. I stop and wait for them. 'Ebony would not want
this. She would choose to stay in Skade for the entire
hundred years if she knew a human death was the price to
release her.'

'She will never know from me,' Shae says.

I turn to face her. 'Really, Shae? You could be around her
every day and keep such a secret? And when she asks how
we got the gates to open and close, where will you be looking? Will it be into your sister's eyes? And if she asks you to
look at her, what will you do? Avoid her for the rest of your
life?'

Tears begin to flow down Shae's cheeks; I pull her into
my arms and soothe her with my power to bring comfort.
She doesn't resist.

'Secrets kill trust in relationships,' I explain once she is
feeling stronger. 'And when Ebony finds out, because for

sure she will, your sister would never forgive me. I would not be able to forgive myself. It would finish us.'

'I'll talk to her,' she says. 'I will make sure my sister understands it was the only way to free her.'

'Angels swear to protect humans.'

'I know that!'

A crowd of curious Archangels begins to gather around us. Michael gets us moving. 'Of course Prince Luca has *everything* to do with this,' he snarls. 'The gates to his world were created by the High King, but to Luca's specifications. He knew precisely how to make those cells regenerate only with human blood and tissue. So to break into Skade one would have to commit an act so heinous as to turn one's soul black.'

'I can't ask a human to do this,' I tell them.

'What if we found a human who is, say, terminally ill?' Shae suggests.

'Then we would try to heal them, or at least extend their time with their family.'

'What about a convict facing a death sentence?'

'Who also manages to have a heart full of love?'

'It's possible!' Shae is desperate. Rescuing her sister is slipping from her fingers. And mine.

As we stride through paved streets, glass-encased tunnels, gilded bridges, I barely notice my surroundings. All I want is to get out of here and talk to the best engineers Avena has.

The Archangel Teeliah meets us at the gate, where Michael thanks her and Shae runs off down the stairs.

'I'm not giving up, you know,' I tell Michael.

'I didn't think you were, cousin.'

'Ebony must be freed, for her sake and for all of humanity. There has to be another way, and I'll find it. I will.'

His hand comes down on my shoulder. 'And I will help you.'

Shae stops and blocks my passage with her hands splayed on my chest. 'Thane, I get how this is a harsh, unforgiving option, just don't discount it completely. Please.'

I breathe in. I breathe out.

'She's my *sister*, damn it! Tell me you will at least think about using the *hanival*.'

'I was so hopeful coming here.'

'As was I,' she whispers, fear etched in her eyes as they shift to the case Michael has tucked into his belt. 'He gave us permission to use the tool. He trusts we will do the right thing. If we puncture a hole in the gate, we must seal it or chaos and evil will run wild and free on the Earth.'

'We have to be careful when it comes to human life.'

'If we don't save Ebony, Luca will create an army that will destroy the world.'

'I'm not dismissing this outright, Shae, and that's why it's killing me inside.'

Michael raises the *hanival* case in his hands. 'What should we do with this?'

My eyes drift over Shae's face. Her tortured doe eyes, her long slender fingers across her mouth, are so like her sister's they turn my heart. How did it come to this? A choice I must make but cannot bear. 'We keep it. A last resort. Now I need to think.' I leap into the air, unfurling my wings over their heads, and I don't look back.

17

Nathaneal

The house is quiet when we touch down. I check the garage and find it vacant. This is a good indication that Jordan is still at school. Michael secures the *hanival* in the safe inside my study's secret storeroom while I check the rest of the house. It's impossible for angels to lie, and yet some have learned to mask the truth in such a way that a lie is the result. Occasionally the truth does more harm than good, but how does one differentiate between an act of kindness and one of deceit? I'm not sure yet what I will tell Jordan when I see him. Finding he's not home is a relief.

The *hanival* was Jordan's hope too. He will be devastated that I won't be using it unless I can come up with an alternative way to seal the gate.

I run up to the third floor to check on Ebony's parents. I put them in the suite down the hall from my bedroom to stay until they're well enough to make their appearance in the human community again. Their recent imprisonment in Skade, beneath the Mi'Ocra Mountain, left them traumatised and near death.

Jez is looking after them. I find her leaving their room, quietly closing the door. 'They're sleeping now, but recovering well considering what they've been through,' she says.

'How are they taking the news?'

'Hard at first, but recalling their own rescue from Skade helps to keep them positive.' I nod, and she continues, 'The good news is they're ready to take the next step.'

'Officials will grill them.'

'They understand to be vague on details and memory. For believability's sake, I've left purple bruises, a few scars and signs of head trauma. But they're longing to be home and start rebuilding their lives.'

It's what they told me too in our conversation before I left for Empyrean. I rub the back of my neck to ease the tension there.

'They plan to stay at their neighbours' place – Reuben and Dawn.'

'Amber's parents.'

'Yes, while they supervise construction of their new house. I'll look in on them regularly,' Jez volunteers. 'If they're not recovering sufficiently under human care, I'll speed their healing along, help keep flashbacks to a minimum. They're going to be fine.'

'Thanks for taking such good care of them, Jez.'

She shrugs. 'It's my job. We take care of humans.'

We hear Isaac, Solomon, Jerome and Sami arrive on the front deck and head downstairs to greet them, but slow our pace when Isaac runs in ahead and Shae leaps into his arms.

'Hold me tight,' she whispers.

He catches my eye over the top of her head. *How bad is the news?*

I'll brief everyone in my study as soon as the others arrive.

Uri and Tash walk in next. Michael directs them to my study. Jez follows Tash inside while I wait at the door.

'We should restore our energy,' Michael proposes.

'There's no time for food. Immediately after the briefing we leave for Skade.'

Michael nods slowly. He has something to say, but Solomon arrives at the front door and he goes to greet him.

Isaac hears and asks softly, 'When was the last time you ate anything, Thane?'

I glance at him from the doorway, making sure to include everyone sitting at the table. 'I don't need food. It's been three days already since he took her. It's as if time is on a spinning wheel that's accelerating exponentially.'

'But you need your strength for this mission, Thane. We all do.'

He's right. Of course he's right. But the thought of delaying going after Ebony for even a second longer than absolutely necessary is driving me crazy. 'OK. We can eat while we discuss our course of action.'

Uri and Tash volunteer and take off to the kitchen.

Everyone is eager to know how we got on at Empyrean and if we have the *hanival* with us, but they know we will wait for Uri and Tash to rejoin us and for Gabe to arrive. Meanwhile, I ask for an update on the tasks I left with them.

Isaac goes first. 'I've been helping Gabe with the new prison facility. It's almost finished.'

'No problems?'

'You'd be surprised how many rooms the Brothers had already constructed after the Prodigies' last attack. We've closed off all the tunnels leading to or from the monastery, except for those that now form the spine of the new prison. It's a labyrinth down there but completely escape-proof.'

'Have you started questioning the prisoners yet?'

'Affirmative.'

'Anything useful?'

'Some.'

'Brief me on the way to Skade. And the Thrones?'

'Nothing yet. They will be hardest to break.'

'Keep working on them. They'll talk eventually.'

Gabe arrives and pulls out a chair. 'Have I missed anything?'

Tash and Uri walk in with steaming platters of food. The scent is intoxicating, lifting the mood in the room, and while everyone digs in I ask Uriel for the engineers' report.

'They're not finished yet.'

Gabe groans. 'They've had three days.'

'Yes,' Uri says, 'but they've had to consult with specialist biochemists.'

'What for?' Gabe looks at me, while Uri shrugs and across the table Michael catches my eye. I nod and all eyes turn to him.

He starts from the beginning, explaining what happened when he, Shae and I put our petition before the High King. He holds nothing back; to do so would be disrespectful to our colleagues. Gathered around my table now are the angels who will help me formulate the plan to bring Ebony home. They need all the facts, including how the gates' composition is of living matter and what it would take to seal a puncture of the size we require.

When he finishes the only sound in the room is our breathing.

Until finally Tash asks, 'How many realistic options do we have?'

'That's what we need to discuss,' I tell everyone. 'We need a new plan other than the one the High King gave us.'

A few of them start talking simultaneously.

'Just in case anyone is thinking that a human sacrifice is an option, I'm telling you now it isn't.'

'There was once talk of a back door into Skade,' Isaac recalls.

Solomon says, 'Luca destroyed it about a thousand years ago, after rebels leaked the location.' He shifts his glance to me. 'My prince, forgive me for asking, but why aren't we discussing our High King's option?' He looks around the table, making the others suddenly squirm. Principals, the angelic order Sol belongs to, have a more pragmatic approach to solving problems than Seraphim, who are more aware of our own and others' emotions.

Tash explains. 'It's a lot to expect of a human, even if we did find one who fit the criteria.'

'Oh, come on, people,' Gabe says. 'There *is* one who might do it willingly, and you all know I'm talking about Jordan but are too scared to bring his name up in front of my youngest brother.'

'We're not scared of Thane, you fool,' Jerome hisses. 'We're respectful. We are in our brother's house, which just happens to be Jordan's home too. If anyone brings Jordan into this discussion, it shouldn't be any of us.'

Unfortunately Jordan is the one human who comes to

133

mind. But it's an abhorrent thought, and it sickens me that his name enters my thoughts just as easily as the thoughts of those who hardly know him.

I start to respond to Gabriel, but he rushes to defend himself. 'Brother, everyone is thinking of Jordan. We may as well deal with it now.'

'OK.' I glance round the table, meeting the eyes of everyone in turn. 'I can't stop you from thinking his name, but I implore you not to mention this option to Jordan. He cannot be a candidate for too many reasons to explain.'

'I object.'

It's Shae. Of course. I understand where she's coming from, but on this no one will sway me. The sooner they understand this, the sooner we can get on with rescuing Ebony.

Gabriel says, 'Thane, we all know how close you are to this boy and that you find the very thought of his sacrifice repugnant. I do too, as I'm sure does everyone here.' Nodding heads and murmurs around the table concur. 'But we must think logically because there are consequences to leaving Ebony in Skade, and besides that, Ebony is one of us.'

'And Jordan? What is he? An instrument to use at our will? He is a human being, the very species we are sworn to protect, the same species who will suffer the most should I fail in this endeavour. I know what's at stake, and I'm telling you – I will find another way.'

Gabe glares at me from under his dark-blond lashes, so thick they make a near-perfect screen, concealing what he is really thinking. How much could Ebony see when she looked into Gabriel's eyes?

'Tell us *you* didn't use Jordan when he died and you caught his soul,' he says. 'Tell us you didn't use him as an instrument of your will.'

'I gave him a chance at a better life than the one that Luca ruined when he kidnapped Jordan's Guardian. I didn't know it would turn out like this. I stand by my decision to give Jordan a second chance. But since he still doesn't have his Guardian, who will look out for him if *I* don't? If I have to, I will protect Jordan to the end of his days.'

'Brother, humans live and they die. Some die young. We can't stop that. And we all know how full of love Jordan's heart is for −'

I'm on my feet before he says her name. 'Jordan can't hear of this. Not one word. Do you understand, Gabe?' I glance over the others around the table. 'Do you all?'

'I do,' Jez says, quickly followed by assurances from Michael, Uriel, Tash and Sami.

I turn to Gabe. 'I respect your different view, but I need you to trust me that I will come up with another plan. In the meantime, I need you to promise you won't tell Jordan about this.'

He groans. 'Thane, you have to admit Jordan is perfect. He loves Ebony, and he hates his life. I think he'll sacrifice himself willingly if we give him the choice.'

I slam my hand down on the polished timber table with more pressure than I mean to and it opens a fissure halfway to the opposite end.

'Now look what you've done,' Gabe scolds.

'Really, Gabe? You're concerned about a table? Tables are expendable. Humans are not. Jordan could never be replaced.'

'What do you see in that boy?'

'Courage. Honour. A willingness to be a better person.' My eyes sweep to Tash's as a memory springs to mind of the night in Skade when we searched for Ebony's human parents. We'd set up camp in the icy paths that formed a maze on the outside of Mount Mi'Ocra. Tash had huddled down with the wild dogs she'd successfully made into her pack when she'd had a vision and a seizure. She'd murmured, '*Someone you trust will betray you*,' right before she passed out.

'What about lust?' Gabe asks. 'For your fiancée?'

'Show me a seventeen-year-old boy who would not lust over my fiancée.'

That catches him off guard, and amused sniggers break out around the conference table. Gabe opens his mouth to say something, and closes it again. 'Touché,' he grins, and in that moment I glimpse the brother I know and have always loved. 'I just think you should give Jordan the chance to make up his own mind.' He glances at the others. 'We should take a vote.'

'No, we shouldn't.' I have to stop this before momentum takes over. Voting is our favoured method to settle disputes between us. But this is not one of those kinds of disputes, not when a human's life is at stake. 'We don't vote whether a human lives or dies.'

'This is about choice, Thane, a human's basic right,' Gabe persists, and he turns to face the others. 'Let's do this quickly in a show of hands. Who thinks we should give Jordan the chance to make up his own mind?'

I stare into my brother's face, 'Given the choice, do you

really think Jordan *could* walk away? Can't you see that if he knew, he would have no choice? The part of him connected to Ebony through the Guardian bond would not allow him to make an objective decision. Turning away would destroy him. That's why he can't be told.'

'And what of the greater reason Ebony must be brought home? The children Luca will make with her, the army over time that puts the entire human species in danger?'

'I'm aware that the sooner we bring Ebony home …' But I can't finish. Just being apart is tearing me up inside, and these thoughts bring images with them. Seeing Luca with Ebony in his arms, his hands on her, forcing her to … to … 'Gabriel, believe me, I understand the ramifications should we fail to retrieve Ebony before Luca makes her Skade's Queen. I know how much harder it will be once …'

Heads nod and for now at least Gabriel goes silent. But arguing with him has taken my attention away from where it should be – listening for Jordan in case he arrives home. It's a school day so he should be down in the Oakes Valley. Or he could be at Amber's. I don't know, and I'm not concerned as long as he's not *here*. I listen for his thoughts and breathe a little easier. There's still nothing.

But the thought occurs that if Ebony kept training in my absence, chances are Jordan would have too. The last thing we worked on together was blocking angels from getting into his head. Circumstances, his anger for me, would have motivated him to work on improving this particular skill.

Stars almighty! I shouldn't be listening for Jordan's thoughts!

And when I shift my focus I hear Amber straight away, frantically deliberating what to tell Jordan to make him leave and go to her place.

'No. No, no.'

Not only is Jordan home, but he's also close. How much has he heard? I spin around looking for him.

'What is it?' Michael is already at my side.

Jordan is here.

Where?

Close.

I've been listening. I didn't hear him.

He's blocking his thoughts from us.

Then, how … ?

Tash looks up and says, 'Amber is with him.'

I yank the door open and see them, their backs against the wall. I glance into the study which is so close, and I know. The only question is, how much did he hear?

Amber shifts her head from side to side. Her eyes are streaked red, pupils dilated and filled with fear. And I know then, he's heard enough.

Jordan's nostrils flare as he draws in a strangled breath and says, 'I'll do it.'

Amber shrieks, '*No!*' It's a guttural cry for help. She looks at me. 'You can stop him, right?'

He gives her a harsh glance. 'Amber, you don't understand.'

With a sense of heaviness, my eyes close. Maybe if I open them slowly enough, Jordan will not be standing before me and this will all be a bad dream.

'Did you hear me, Thane? For God's sake, man, open your eyes and tell me you heard me!'

He pushes past me into the study, where Jez, Isaac, Sol

138

and Jerome are hurriedly clearing the table. 'Stop, everyone, you can clean up later. Right now I need someone to tell me exactly what I have to do to make this happen. How? When? Where? All of it. I don't want to stuff up the one good thing I can do with my lousy life.'

Amber leans on the door, clutching herself around the waist, a pleading look in her eyes. 'Jordan, come home with me. Jordan, please …'

But he ignores her as if she weren't there. 'Who's gonna help me do this?' His eyes go first to Michael, who gives him a small shake of refusal.

Jordan glances at Isaac next, who wordlessly looks away. From one after another he receives similar reactions. He shifts his eyes between Jerome and Sami, both of whom I assume he's come to know in my absence, but my brother's piteous look and my sister-in-law's compassionate one only make Jordan growl.

He looks at Shae next, recognising her, and hope makes his eyes widen. 'Will you help me save your sister?'

Shae's hand whips up to her mouth, her eyes flitting to mine. *I love my sister*, she links.

I know, Shae. I do too. And I'm asking you to trust me. I will find another way to bring Ebony home and keep humankind safe.

She sighs. 'Jordan, what you ask is impossible for an angel.'

'It shouldn't be for you. We're not talking about any angel, you know,' he hits back. 'I heard you lot talking about taking a vote. Well, I'm saving you the trouble.' He spots Gabriel. 'You!' he points. 'You want me to do this. I heard you. *You* are gonna help me.'

Jez taps the table to get Jordan's attention. As she's healed him in the past, the two have developed a certain rapport. She comes and stands in front of him. 'Jordan, let's talk about this.'

'No. You're not gonna change my mind.'

'There are things you should know.'

'Stop! I don't trust anything you tell me because you would do anything Thane says. You're like his pet groupie.'

She steps back as if he slapped her. With her pride stinging, she loads her arms with dishes and heads to the kitchen, murmuring to no one in particular, 'Maybe we should let him do it, the ungrateful insect.'

An instant of regret flits across Jordan's eyes, but Jez misses it.

He then turns to Gabriel. 'What's it gonna take to get you to help me? I'll do whatever you want. Anything. Just tell me. Come on, Gabe, you're my last hope.'

Gabriel remains silent. He peers over the top of Jordan's head to me, a distinct apology in his eyes.

Sensing defeat, Jordan picks up a chair and hurls it at the wall. 'What's the problem with you people? My life isn't worth shit anyway!' He points a finger at me. 'You know that. You gave me a second chance but I blew it. You should be the first to volunteer me.'

'You didn't blow anything, Jordan.'

'Yeah, I did. Our deal was that I help you find Ebony so you could take her back to her real home. I helped find her, sure. But I've done nothing to encourage her to return to Avena. I've tried to manipulate her into *not* going. You don't know the things I told her when you were away, how I played on her doubts to make her believe she wasn't an angel. I wanted her to stay on Earth and I tried to make her stop loving you.'

'Sacrificing your life is not the answer to helping Ebony – or to correcting any mistakes you've made for one reason or another.'

He drops into a chair. 'What about my contract with the Dark Prince? He owns my soul. He gets me when I die anyway, so before I go to the fiery pits of Skade I may as well do one good thing with my life.'

'Luca manipulated you in a dream. I will deal with that as soon as I –'

'Just quit it, Thane! You think you can fix everyone's problems. Shit, you even think you can fix the world! But that's not gonna happen. There are some things that even *you* can't fix.'

Jordan lowers his head into his hands and murmurs, 'It's my destiny.'

Amber clarifies: 'He thinks it's his destiny to always love Ebony but never have her.'

He peers at Amber, his eyes troubled and sunken into his face. It surprises me that he can't see how much this girl is hurting to see him suffering.

'He told me he'd rather be dead than spend his life in perpetual heartbreak.'

'He said that *before* he learned of this?' I ask Amber by way of confirmation. When she nods, my blood boils. 'Do you think Ebony will enjoy being free at the cost of your death?'

He lifts his head, his eyes wide and round, as if this has not occurred to him before.

'Ebony could never be happy knowing you gave your life so she could be free. She's *your* Guardian, not the other way round. I'm sorry that on the day of my arrest I made you responsible for her safety. I only meant until she came into her powers, or accepted who she was. And I'm sorry I was absent for so long. After Ebony returned to Avena she would begin watching over *you*, Jordan. You would have a Guardian for the first time and your life would improve. That was our deal.'

'Why are you the one making all my decisions? Who put you in charge of my life? Don't I have *Free Will*? If I want to do this, you can't stop me.'

'True, but if no one agrees to carry you to the gates, it would make your willing sacrifice impossible.'

He gets up and storms around the room. He hadn't considered how he was going to traverse the vast and changing landscape of the Crossing. 'How is that fair? I thought you angels were democratic. I say we take a vote like Gabe wanted before you realised I was listening, and as well as accepting my choice, I get transportation.' He notices Jez returning to the room and nods. 'Good, we're all here. Now we can vote.'

'What for?' she asks.

'Everyone in this room right now is going to vote – "Yes" for my freedom to choose, or "No", this ends here, I get no choice. And if it's "Yes", it includes transporting me through the Crossing.'

'I don't know about this, Jordan,' Jez says, quickly backed up by Tash and Jerome. Isaac goes to say something but Shae stops him with a razor-sharp look.

'Vote in secret, if that's your problem.'

Everyone in the room appears uncomfortable. 'Jordan,' Michael says, 'let Thane explain why a vote is not a good idea.'

'OK. So what's your problem with it?'

I lay my open palms on Jordan's shoulders as I try to explain, 'Because we will have to live with our decision for the rest of time.'

Sarcastic laughter rips out of him. 'You poor immortals, how tough you have it.'

Amber slices through his response. 'We're the ones who will have to face Ebony, you selfish moron.'

He spins around and confronts her. 'At least she'll be free and you *can* face her. Time will help her forgive you, and time will help her forget me.'

'Jordan −' I try again to talk him out of forcing this vote − 'you have many reasons to live; you just don't yet know what they are.'

He seems to think about this, but then looks at Shae for her vote. 'You first.'

'Wait,' I call out.

He spins round, looks into my eyes and pleads, 'Come on, Thane, let them speak.'

I take a deep breath and sit. 'All right, but I will go first.'

I glance around the conference table, where everyone has taken a seat again. 'No one can begin to measure how much I need to bring Ebony home. As long as Luca has her, he wins. Every moment we delay could make a difference to the final outcome, but I cannot willingly condone the cost of a mortal life. I will find another way. I have specialists gathering their recommendations on how best to proceed right now.'

'Yeah, yeah, I'm sure they'll be very helpful. So what's your vote?'

'No. My vote is NO.'

He looks at Shae. 'Well, this should even the score.'

Shae doesn't disappoint him. She casts a YES. Beside her, Isaac does too, forging a brief apology of sorts: *I can't vote against my wife's family, and Ebony needs to come home, whatever the cost.*

If it were me – my willing heart – *the gate required to rebuild itself, how would you vote?*

That's not fair, Thane.

I let it go. He has the right to make his own decision; I'm just not sure he has done that.

Tash votes NO, Uri YES. Michael, Jerome and Sami all vote NO. Good, five to three so far. But then Gabe gives Jordan a YES. Jez says NO, which leaves Solomon, the last of the angels. He votes YES. It's a good result, except Jordan calls out, 'My vote counts too, and it's YES.'

'Now it's even,' Shae says.

Everyone turns to Amber, sitting silently between Jordan and Jez. The moment she realises her vote is the decider, her head starts swinging from side to side. She drags her chair backwards, flicking glances at the door. 'Don't look at me,' she says with the eyes of a fox caught in a trap. 'I'm not voting.'

'Amber, come on,' Jordan coaxes. He points round the table. 'They did, and it wasn't easy for them. Now you have to do this.'

'But, Jordan, it's the deciding vote. It's all on me. I can't, OK?'

She gets up to leave, but Shae blocks her exit. 'Our votes mean nothing if you don't give yours.'

Amber searches the table for an ally. Jez smiles at her sadly. Jerome tries to reassure her with a wink and half a grin.

Tash says, 'You have already made up your mind, sweetie. It's all right to say it aloud. Whichever way this goes, we will accept the decision, right, Thane?' I nod, and she turns to Shae for her answer.

'Of course,' Shae says.

'Jordan?' Tash pierces him with her dark opal eyes.

He shrugs. 'That was the agreement, so if the vote goes against me, I'll have no choice but to accept it.'

Silent tears trickle down Amber's face. She snags her bottom lip into her mouth as she stares at Jordan with big eyes. 'Just so you know, I think you're a great guy. A moron. But great in many ways, like how you love Ebony so completely that you're willing to *die* for her ... Oh my God, Jordan, that's the stuff of epic love stories and poetry.' She looks away for a moment and mumbles under her breath, 'Damn you for putting me in this position.'

Tears are streaming now. 'I love Ebony too. Everyone knows we've been close friends all our lives. We're like sisters, always have been, always ... But I couldn't do what you're willing to do. Maybe it's because I have family and I know it would kill them to lose me. I don't know.' She inhales a shuddering breath and I find myself holding mine. So far, nothing Amber has said indicates with certainty which way she will vote. And her thoughts are a mess, floundering in a cesspool of raw emotion. 'I know you want this *so* much, but I can't be the one to send you to your death. I'm sorry, Jordan, but my vote is NO.'

I exhale the breath I'm holding in a big sigh of relief. Jordan gets out of his chair and stares at Amber, too angry and upset to block his thoughts.

Michael intercepts him with calming hands on his shoulders. 'You have your answer, Jordan. Now you must leave this to us to handle.'

He pulls away. 'This is bullshit! I wish I could take myself to those damn gates! I wish I didn't need help from any of you!' His eyes shift to Amber again. 'Why didn't you vote YES? What's the matter with you? Don't you want Ebony back?'

She runs out, her footsteps pounding the tiles from here to the front door. He goes after her and grabs her arm, but she pulls away.

'Stop!' he yells. 'Amber, come back, you gotta change your vote. Amber, *please*.'

On the outside deck she stops and calls over her shoulder, 'Just so there's no confusion, my vote is still NO.'

18

Jordan

Tomorrow in the early pre-dawn Thane will take three teams to Skade to get Ebony back, and I won't be going with them. It sucks, but it seems like there's nothing I can do now.

It's quiet and peaceful out here, lounging on chairs on the front deck with Thane. It's night-time, and the only sound is coming from the nocturnal critters going about their business in the surrounding rainforest. By the time summer comes, most of the forest will have grown back, probably thicker than before Thane destroyed it with his power.

The night sky is drenched with stars that I can't stop looking at, but it's cold and I shrug deeper into the blanket Thane brought out a few minutes ago when I started shivering.

Thane closes his eyes and sighs. I hear his disappointment. I *feel* it. It's reeking from his pores. He wanted the teams to leave for Skade straight after the meeting ended, but Gabe argued for waiting a few hours to give the engineers and biochemists time to finish their reports. He offered to get them himself and convinced enough of the angels to vote with him.

That's the reason we're sitting out here like a pair of losers, waiting for the hours to tick past while God only knows what Luca's doing to Ebony right now.

This is the first time Thane's been still since the abduction, since probably well before that. According to Tash, after they'd rescued Ebony's parents Thane had his crew flying round the clock across Skade to reach Ebony in time. Maybe a few hours' rest will be a good thing in the end, make him stronger for whatever's ahead.

I still hate Thane for keeping the truth from me, but if … what am I saying? Oh God, *WHEN* he brings Ebony back, I'll forgive him everything.

'You don't look so good, Jordan. How are your burns?' he asks without opening his eyes. 'Other than being chained to a wall, you still haven't told me how it happened.'

'Mate, it's not rocket science. The cuffs were metal and too tight – they dug into my flesh.'

He opens his eyes and raises his eyebrows like he's waiting for the rest. 'Your wrists have third-degree burns, Jordan. They may not heal by themselves. If you don't want me to take care of them, go to a doctor.' His eyes rove over my face. 'Of course, I won't ask you as many questions as a doctor might.'

Hint. Hint.

'I'm not sure how long I will be away,' he continues. 'Mind if I just check them to make sure infection isn't setting in?'

Jeez, I wish he would shut up about my burns. Since last night the pain has gone beyond hurting. They're killing me now.

'Jordan, the reason you're shivering is because you're running a temperature. That's not a good sign.'

I suppose he's right. The burns should be getting better by now, not worse. I slither my arms out from under the blanket. Surprise registers for a moment before he carefully pushes back my jacket sleeves and unravels the bandages.

The smell is the first thing that hits me. *Ugh, gross*, it's enough to make me puke. But Thane remains stoic as he takes in the raised red flesh with shiny black patches and squishy white areas of pus circling both my left and right wrists. He looks up, and bright blue daggers of steel pierce my eyes. He then opens his mouth to say something, but it's as if he sucks the words back into his mouth and shakes his head instead.

'Mate, you've got no right to be angry at me.'

'About this?' He points to my wrists with an open hand. 'Oh yes, I do.'

'I can see they're bad.'

'At least your eyes are working, unlike your brain. How is your sense of smell holding up?'

'You're not funny.'

'That's because I'm not joking. You couldn't smell this when you showered?'

He's starting to freak me out. 'Can you fix them or not?'

'Tonight, I believe I can, but by dawn the fever from your poisoned blood would be giving you seizures. One look at these hands in a hospital emergency department and you would be heading straight for surgery.'

'To clean them up?'

149

'To amputate.'

For a few seconds I can't say anything. He's gotta be exaggerating. But then I remember. 'Shit, you don't lie.'

His face softens.

'I didn't realise.'

He lowers his glowing hands to my wrists and spends the next twenty minutes or so drawing out the infection, detoxifying my poisoned blood and healing my wounds. When he finishes I hold my wrists up under the soft porch light. My skin is pink, smooth and as good as new. I glance at him. He looks tired, like healing me has drained him. 'Thanks. I really mean it.'

He nods and smiles with half his mouth and ruffles my hair in the way he used to when we were mates. He tilts his head suddenly and his smile turns to a frown as he stares into the starry sky.

'What's up?'

He walks to the deck railing and turns to look up over the house. 'Gabriel is coming.'

'What for?'

'I don't know.'

I soon hear the brisk swish-swish of Gabe's big wings as he flies over and touches down on the lawn. The look on his face is deadly serious and my stomach drops.

'Gabriel,' Thane says, not waiting, 'what's happened?'

'We need to talk.' He gives me a pointed look. 'You don't mind if I take my brother for a walk, Jordan?'

It's hard to tell if this is a question or not. 'I could just go to my room,' I volunteer.

But Gabe has other ideas. 'No need. Why spoil a pleasant

evening?' He shifts his eyes to Thane's. 'Walk with me, brother?'

I don't like the look of this. There's something in Gabe's eyes I haven't seen before. I can't help but wonder what it is. Thane gives me a tight smile before he walks down the few steps to where his brother is waiting.

'What is it that you can't say in front of Jordan?' I hear him ask as soon as they begin walking.

Gabe exhales a long shaky breath, making the hairs at the back of my neck stand on end. *Shit, what can be wrong now? It's gotta be about Ebony. He's learned something. The reports, they must be devastating. The look in his eyes – oh hell – it's fear.*

Keeping my thoughts scrambled, I follow at a distance that I can still hear from. Thane's voice is sharp, demanding, and growing more anxious. 'Gabe? Did you meet with the engineers? You're worrying me. Get to the point.'

'Yes, I have the report and a solution, but there's something more personal I need to talk to you about, something I should have mentioned before now.'

They reach the start of the forest when Thane stops. 'Go on.'

'You and I both need a clear head going into this mission, and that's why I have to tell you …'

My brain is racing at warp speed, trying to figure out what Gabe's confession is about.

'Remember the message you gave me for Ebony?' he says.

Message? There's only one message worthy of this conversation. *Holy shit!*

They start walking again. I run to keep up, stepping as

lightly as I can over the damp forest floor, madly scrambling my thoughts. I can't miss this. Has Thane caught on what message Gabe is talking about yet? What could have stopped Gabe from telling her? Ebony practically begged him for it. I get a mental image of sitting in the Lambo with Ebony scooting into my arms, both of us in shock after the dark force chased us home from Zavier's place that first time. We'd just seen two cops incinerated in their car. Unbeknown to us, Gabe was waiting in the garage, watching in the darkness while we held each other and our heart rates slowed down. Nothing happened, except in Gabe's creepy imagination. Did he withhold his brother's vital message over *that*?

The judgemental jerk!

It gets darker suddenly. I look up. Clouds, sizzling with electricity, are zooming across the sky, obscuring the stars, the moon and anything else as they gather above the forest.

Goosebumps break out all over me.

Nothing about this developing storm is natural.

It hits fast, with lightning illuminating the sky in silver and purple streaks. A bolt, as thick as a telegraph pole, shoots straight into the forest, splitting an ancient blackbutt tree down its centre. Debris scatters as if a bomb has exploded. The force knocks me off my feet.

In a pleading tone Gabe yells out something I can't understand. Brushing away chunk-sized splinters, I get up and run towards their voices. But the sky opens up again. Purple lightning sizzles close a split second before it smashes into the ground. Trees shed their bark as thunder booms and rolls, shaking the ground from one end of the forest to the other. The pounding is so penetrating my ears ache. I cover them with my hands and crawl across the forest floor towards the blinding light.

I find the two of them in full angelic glow. I throw an arm over my eyes and watch them, facing each other, legs apart, wings shifting uneasily from their backs. I can just make out who is whom. Thane is holding a branch up over his shoulder like a spear he's threatening to drive into Gabe's chest.

'You kept the message to *yourself*?' he accuses. 'The *whole* time I was absent?'

Gabe shrugs, his palms out in front of him in a gesture of peace. After what he did, it's pathetic. He hears something and looks up. A bolt of white lightning shoots straight down from the sky. It crackles and hisses through the canopy, setting branches on fire as it forks into two, sending unfathomable streams of energy into the ground either side of him.

The Earth shakes, tossing me backwards again. Falling hard, I scramble to a tree, then think better of it and huddle behind a boulder.

Gabe gets up, his hands now shaking. 'Brother, listen to me. I'm trying to apologise. But I need to explain my reasons.'

'You knew how much I needed Ebony to have that message. You were with her every day; you must have known her doubts, seen how hard it was for her to believe without her memories. I couldn't give her back her own, but I could give her mine, and that message was so much more.'

Thane shakes his head in utter disbelief. The poor bastard had no idea. Well, nobody did. With polished all-black eyes glinting, Thane lifts the branch higher.

'I found them together! I didn't want to tell you. I knew it would hurt.'

He stops moving. 'Who? Ebony and Jordan?'

'Yes!' Gabe squeals. 'I'll show you. Then tell me what you would have done.'

Oh shit.

'Continue,' Nathaneal's voice is like a chip of ice. What can he be thinking? What will he think when he sees *that* image. And who knows if Gabe will tamper with it? Show it to Thane the way he misunderstood it. Oh hell …

I can't let Gabe put *that* image in Thane's head the night before he leaves to bring her back! I get up and run as fast as I can, shoving branches out of my way, stumbling over a rock and landing with my face in the dirt between them. 'Don't believe a word he tells you,' I yell from the ground, scrambling to get up. 'He misunderstood everything, and no matter how hard Ebony and I tried to explain the situation, he wouldn't listen.'

Thane looks at me, then his brother. 'One of you had better explain.'

'Me first,' I say. Ebony deserves her side told before Gabe tarnishes Thane's mind with pathetic excuses to get his butt off the hook. 'Whatever he shows you, all you need to know is that Ebony and I didn't do anything. Nothing! Maybe I would have if she had let me,' I confess. Honesty is what Thane deserves now, more than anything else. 'But I couldn't sway her. She was committed to you the whole time you were away, even though she hadn't received your message and I fed her lies. But in the moment Gabe is talking about, being together was the last thing on our minds. Only a moron would misinterpret me and Ebony comforting each other after witnessing two innocent people die in our place.'

Thane glances at his brother, but I can't tell what he's thinking. I have to convince him. 'Thane, I swear I'm telling the truth. I swear it on my life.' *No, wait, that's not worth anything.* 'I swear it on my mother's soul.'

He looks at me for a long time. I swallow deep in my throat and clench my hands into fists to help me hold still under his full black-eyed scrutiny. I've got nothing to hide. Not any more.

Finally he shifts his focus to Gabe. 'Ebony protected you.'

Gabe frowns. 'What are you talking about?'

'When we saw each other in the tunnel and the battle raged around us, I asked Ebony if she had received my message. I now realise she was fishing for a name. She figured out it was you, and while she didn't lie, she implied she knew and went along with my relief that you had passed it to her successfully.'

'What? Why would she do that?' Gabe asks, his voice as weak as a little boy's.

'So I wouldn't be angry at my brother.'

'I misjudged her,' he murmurs. 'This whole time I thought …' His voice fades. 'Thane, if Ebony didn't want you angry at me then, it stands to reason she wouldn't want you angry at me now.'

Gabe is still using Ebony's selfless nature to get out of taking responsibility for what he did. He's worse than a jerk.

'Do you have any idea how different today would be if you *had* given Ebony Thane's message?'

He doesn't answer and I hear myself snarl like a wolf, 'She would still be here with us.' I wish I were a wolf right now, a wild grey one, with giant canines. I would take Gabe's jugular out in one bite. 'I was with Ebony all the time. She cried over that promised message, thought it meant Nathaneal had forgotten her.'

Nathaneal growls from deep in his chest, and the sky ignites with hundreds of thick lightning bolts that split into thousands of crackling fingers that race across the sky. Thunder detonates, shaking the mountain from top to bottom.

I drop to my knees, gripping my ears.

The next thing I know, angels are crashing through the canopy. First to arrive is Michael, who goes straight to Thane's side. They talk, but my head throbs, both ears ringing, and I can't hear a word they say.

Uriel, Tash and Jez drop down a few seconds later. Issac and Shae must have gone to the house first. They run in from the driveway, moving so fast they're just blurs of light skimming round the trees. Other angels come too, a dozen or so, their glowing bodies lighting up the forest like fireflies. I recognise a few as Gabe's soldiers that used to come help him locate the dark forces. They must be part of the crew leaving for Skade in the morning.

Thane sends Jez straight to me. She tugs my hands down. 'It's all right,' she says, though I can barely hear her. 'Your eardrums have perforated and you have a few broken ribs, but I can help you. Keep still.'

She lays glowing hands on my ears, then looks at me with raised eyebrows. 'What did you think you could do? Stop them from killing each other?'

'Nope. As long as Thane was winning I wasn't gonna do a thing.'

'I see. So what has Gabriel done to upset you and Nathaneal so much?'

'He didn't give Ebony Thane's message.'

Her hands go still. Her eyes freeze on mine.

'I was just making sure Thane heard the truth behind the reason Gabe gave him.'

Someone suggests we take this inside. I hear the words clearly, but Jez is still healing my ribs. When she's done, I thank her.

Everyone starts moving towards the house. Michael carefully plucks the branch from Thane's hands. Jez picks me up. I tell her I can walk. She takes no notice. Then Thane takes me from her arms and carries me himself.

'I can walk, you know. I look like a child when you do this.'

'I'm sorry I hurt you,' he says. 'I lost myself for a moment.'

'Not long enough, if you ask me,' I say. 'Your message would have changed everything. It would have cleared her doubts, removed her confusion and completely transformed how she saw her future. Not getting your message made her think stupid thoughts, do stupid things. It helped her believe my lies. Zavier would have had no power over us if Ebony had known positively who she was. His plan to deliver her to Luca wouldn't have worked and we wouldn't have fallen into his trap.'

He shakes his head. 'It pains me to think of what Ebony went through, and how it all could have been avoided.'

'And look where she is now,' I remind him.

He growls, low and deep. Lightning flashes overhead. Angels look at us, but he just keeps carrying me to the house.

'And you know what? She told me once she wanted to know the truth of her heritage for your sake.' At his questioning frown, I explain, 'To make sure you weren't wasting your time on the wrong girl.'

Isaac holds the front door open and Nathaneal lays me down on the sofa. But I'm feeling fine and I sit up and grab his arm. 'What are you going to do to him?'

Gabe plonks down in an armchair looking exhausted, and too pretty, as far as I'm concerned.

Thane sits opposite him. 'If I didn't need you tomorrow, I would lock you up in a cell with Dark Thrones. Tell me why I shouldn't lodge a report of this incident with the Courts?'

Gabe leans forward, elbows on his knees. 'I can make this up to you,' he tells Thane. 'I have something to offer that will benefit both you and Ebony.'

'Sure you do, Gabe.' Sarcasm pours out of my mouth. 'As long as it's self-serving, because you only care about yourself.'

Jerome gives me a look that's part sympathy, part warning. He stops his pacing in front of Gabe. 'Whatever you believed you saw pass between Jordan and Ebony that night – or on any night – you had no right breaking the agreement you made with our brother. You gave him your word.'

'I know. And I'm really sorry.'

'But I'm willing to hear you out for Ebony's sake.' Jerome glances at Thane. 'Will *you* listen to him too, in case he has come up with an idea that might help?'

Thane looks at me, his eyes asking if I agree.

I shrug. 'S'pose it can't hurt to listen.'

'It's a simple plan,' Gabe says, barely waiting for me to finish. 'Our scientists, engineers and biochemists have studied the Skade gates for centuries. I saw them myself tonight. I talked to a team of our best and they've helped me come up with a solution.'

OK, now he has my attention.

'We take the *hanival* and use it to open a passage through one of the gates, and as planned, our three teams work together to find Ebony and bring her back.'

So far, so good, but nothing new.

'And what *exactly* are you offering?' Thane asks, apparently thinking along the same lines.

'Once we have Ebony back safe, I begin constructing an impenetrable brick wall made to the specifications formulated by our specialists. The wall will run parallel to Skade's twelve gates and no creature will be able to pass through it.'

'A wall that size could take years to build,' Thane says, but I can tell his mind is thinking about the merits of Gabe's plan. An impenetrable wall is not a bad idea.

'I'm prepared for that,' Gabe says.

'How would this wall work?' Thane asks.

'I'll show you the report on the way.' He taps his skull. 'It's in here. But simply put, the wall will be constructed from a combination of two of the toughest substances in the universe – *adamene*, and diamonds.'

'What's *adamene*?' I ask and, glancing around, I can see there aren't many faces that look as if they know either.

Gabe explains. '*Adamene* is similar to *graphene* but where graphene is limited to one dimension, *adamene* can be combined with other substances to form three dimensions, like the bricks we need to build the wall.'

Someone whistles, heads nod, angels whisper to each other, but I still have no idea what he's talking about.

'And what do we do while the wall is being constructed?' Thane asks.

'I won't let anything through the gates, I promise you. No souls or angels – not even Prince Luca himself – will escape. Under my command, half of my troops will construct the wall while the other half will patrol the breached gate, ensuring nothing comes through.'

Michael asks, 'How long before you can begin construction?'

'Everything we require to make the bricks and construct the wall is already on its way. And I promise to maintain the wall and patrol the gates for as long as necessary.'

'For a hundred years, Gabriel? Can you do that?' Tash, sitting beside me, questions Gabe's staying power, but she seems to be the only sceptic in the room, other than me.

'Yes, Tash, I'm committed for a hundred years if that's what I must do. But the wall will be completed well before then.' He slides his elbows to his knees again, pinning Thane with focused eyes. 'My offer means you and Ebony will be free from having to do this yourselves. You could get on with your lives.' He glances at me. 'And you too, Jordan.'

Gabe reaches across the short distance from his chair to Thane's and pulls his brother up with him. 'Thane, before all these witnesses, tell me you accept my offer.'

'What of Rebecca?'

'Who?' I whisper to Tash.

'Gabriel's wife.'

'Or haven't you told her?'

'She knows. We talked earlier this evening. She agrees it's the only way I can make this right between us.'

Thane goes quiet. Nobody speaks while he contemplates his brother's offer: to construct a wall that will replace the damaged gate with a combination of elements that nothing can break through, while monitoring the wall himself with his own soldiers for as long as it takes.

Thane looks at me and raises his eyebrows.

I run my hands through my hair. 'Whatever it takes, we gotta get Ebony out.'

'And we must do it *quickly*,' Isaac says, emphasising the word, then adding softly under his breath, 'if it's not too late.'

Everyone knows what he means. The thought that Ebony might already be carrying the Dark Prince's child is too much, and Thane turns ghostly white. It seems to help him make up his mind. 'I hold the right to decide whether to submit a report to the Courts,' he says. 'But since I don't have a better alternative, and time is not on our side –' he holds out his hand – 'Gabriel, I accept your offer.'

19

Ebony

I'm dreaming that someone has their hand over my mouth and I can't breathe. The dream-me throws my own hands around my assailant's throat and squeezes.

Then two things happen simultaneously. I wake up, and I realise the small, warm hand on my mouth belongs to Mela.

I drop my hands immediately from around her throat.

Gasping, Mela stumbles back into the armchair against the wall. 'I didn't mean to frighten you,' she croaks, touching her throat tenderly.

By now I'm crawling across the bed after her, quickly reorienting from the mix of dream and reality that threw me for an instant.

'Why did you do that?' I whisper, tugging her fingers down and checking her neck gently. 'Nothing feels broken, but you'll probably bruise.' I sit back on my heels. 'You're lucky I don't have a knife tucked under my pillow.' *Yet*, I add silently.

She lights a small glass-encased lantern she brought with her and says so softly I can hardly hear her, 'I thought we could take a ride.'

'In the middle of the night?' I reply just as softly. 'Why

didn't you tell me at dinner? I wouldn't have tried to strangle you.'

She flicks a look at the door and puts a finger to her lips, whispering even more softly, 'There was a late change of guards and I wasn't sure if I was going to be able to arrange my little surprise. You've wanted to get out since you got here, and I just now received word that everything is arranged.'

She brings me an all-black riding outfit from my wardrobe, keeping her voice extremely low. 'We have to return before the next change of your guards, so dress quickly.' She grins. 'I have a lot to show you.'

My eyes dart around the room as I put on a long-sleeve polo shirt, jodhpurs and boots. 'Who else knows? Is anyone coming with us?'

'I have friends waiting outside.'

Friends? A midnight ride? Tingles trip down my spine. *Could Mela have reconsidered using her position as general of the rebel army to help me escape?*

She places a black cloak around my shoulders, bringing the fur-lined hood low over my forehead before doing the same to herself. She then stuffs pillows under the quilt to resemble my sleeping body. From the doorway it's not a bad disguise, but she must be counting on no one taking a close look.

We move into the small hallway, where my glance goes to the front doors. They remain closed. In the other direction, the amber glow of a candle flickers from within her bedroom, where the door is slightly ajar. My heart is starting to beat rapidly.

Once inside her room, with the door closed, I have to ask, 'Mela, are you helping me escape?'

She looks suddenly wretched.

'Hey, it's all right,' I reassure her. 'I'm glad to get out, see something different.' *Something that might help me escape as soon as I'm ready to make my run.*

Taking my hand, Mela leads me through a half-size door entrenched in a timber shelving unit that appears to be nothing more than the lower half of a wood-panelled wall.

You wouldn't know the door existed unless you knew where to look.

Mela brings the lantern with us and I follow her with blind faith through a pitch-black tunnel to a door that opens into a narrow space between the walls of a pair of guest suites she assures me are vacant. We exit into a dusky utility room, stepping carefully around buckets, brooms and mops before crawling through a hatch at the opposite end that leads to the top of a spiral stairwell. There is no lift here, and no guards like before when Mela showed me to my rooms.

Mela gives me a quick glance that asks how I'm holding up. I nod and she points to the stairs, clearly mouthing 'nine'. I nod again, letting her know I get that there are nine flights we have to descend, which would put us one floor below ground since there were eight floors up to my rooms on the top level.

Mela treads briskly and I follow, being careful not to trip on the floor-length cloak that insists on getting between the stairs and my boots.

It turns out there are more underground floors but this is where we get off.

Setting the lamp down on the floor, Mela leaps across a void about a metre square to a narrow ledge at the foot of a brick wall, then motions with her hand for me to follow. She makes it look easy. It likely is, but not so much for a human. Mela, I'm fast learning, is no ordinary human. I take a deep breath and follow. Her grin is my reward.

Removing a square panel of fake bricks from the wall, we step into a tunnel large enough to stand in. There's just enough light from the lamp we left behind coming through to see our way to the end, where Mela turns the handle on a door and opens it.

'Not locked?' I ask.

She shakes her head. 'Only because someone left it unlocked for us.'

And suddenly I'm outside on a dark night, the air a mix of odd rancid smells. Even knowing the air is toxic, I take a deep breath, content for the moment to savour a sense of being free.

I follow Mela through shrubs and clinging vines to a narrow cobbled lane, where, up ahead and tucked into a dark driveway, I spot the tails of four horses.

We make our way there, hugging fences and gates and trees for cover. Looking back over my shoulder, I see the massive white perimeter wall with soldiers in their creepy helmets patrolling the top.

I cover my mouth to stop from squealing with excitement.

There *is* a way out.

And my handmaiden just showed me it. Mela – connected to me through the Guardian bond I have with her son – is the key to my freedom from Luca. She just doesn't know it yet. She may not be willing to help me escape, and I won't do anything to jeopardise her army or her position at its head, but now I know how to escape the palace on my own. It's just a matter of time to build up my powers and get my wings working. I don't care if I have to live in a cave for a hundred years; as long as I'm not with Luca I have hope that one day Nathaneal and I will be reunited.

Keeping the horses quiet are two male Seraphim angels, wearing long coats with hats that keep their faces in shadow. They acknowledge us with a nod, stepping back as we each take a set of reins. They maintain their distance behind us as we walk the horses away from the palace, sticking to the shoulder where high fences and walls with trees and bushes give us cover.

It really is uplifting to be out of the apartment. I take in everything I can, from the shuttered shopfronts to the neat houses, contemporary apartment buildings, communal garages and even stables, all shrouded in darkness.

Suddenly the swish of beating wings and a cat-like screech rends the air. I drop down, tilting my head back, as a giant bird flies overhead with a snake at least a hundred metres long dangling from its claws.

Mela motions to pull my hood back into place, dismissing the shrieking bird carrying his midnight snack as too common an event to make a fuss over.

Walking by her side a few minutes later, I ask quietly, 'Why are there no lights in this part of the city?'

'There's a curfew in the sectors surrounding the palace,' she answers. 'It makes it easier for the patrols to spot uninvited guests.'

When Mela thinks we're far enough, she stops and offers me a leg up, but I'm already gripping the saddle bar and hoisting myself over as I have done thousands of times before. It's like I can breathe better up here than when my feet are on the ground.

The mare allocated to me is taller and broader than Shadow. A sturdy war horse comes to mind, or they just grow horses bigger here. I run my hand through her luscious mane down to her shoulder and try to ignore the sudden ache in my chest at the thought of Shadow at home waiting for me.

While we were looking out of my windows earlier today, Mela explained how to tell direction in Skade using the river to indicate south, the gates north, the cliffs west and the factories with the rolling mountains behind them east.

So with the river on our right and the shimmering gates high in the sky on our left, I figure we're riding ... 'Are you going to show me the factories?'

'Not this time, but one day soon. Ebony, I need to warn you that no matter what you see or hear tonight, for your own safety, stay on your horse.'

At this ominous warning we ride straight through the clean, quiet streets of the inner city, with their tall buildings of pristine darkened glass, into rowdy streets of stone and brick high-rise apartment buildings with broken windows, portions of walls missing, vacant lots piled with garbage and animals furrowing through it. I focus on the animals until shapes take form, and when they do I gasp. They're not animals. And my heart twists at the sight of the scavenging angelic children who have not yet reached school age.

Mela turns me gently away. 'Come on, we've more to see.'

'But, Mela –'

'Food is expensive. It can get scarce in these areas, even for angels.'

Mela's Seraphim friends move up close and I soon understand why, when drunk, cursing angels start fighting inside a pub on street level, while scantily clad souls, both male and female, hanging off the arms of angels in long tailored coats and shiny shoes, gather around to watch. These streets are where the stronger, wealthier angels get their kicks by slumming it with the poor, desperate souls, and apparently poor and desperate angels too.

A three-headed monkey scurries past, squealing, while another, bigger animal, the type of which I've never seen before, lumbers after it with such a heavy gait it could pass as an elephant seal but for its four stubby legs.

At a busy corner a nightclub flashes red and blue neon lights while pumping loud, suggestive dance music into the street. A huge bodyguard stares at us as we pass. I keep my eyes averted, but can still see the swathe of gyrating angels dancing with each other inside, near-naked souls serving drinks while both angels and souls perform impossible gymnastic moves inside suspended cages.

Mela whispers, 'Angels as well as souls live in these areas. Criminals, escapees, the homeless, the clinically depressed – and their lives are only marginally better than those of the souls sent here.'

An argument on the ground floor turns quickly into a vicious fight with swords and knives flashing. Blood splatters across a window and Mela's friends hurry us away, though not quite fast enough. The window smashes. As Mela's friends protect us with their wings, I spot a furry animal floating in a street trough nearby. By its stench, it's clear the animal has been decaying for days.

Why no one has removed it yet boggles the mind. Where are the sanitary workers I see through my windows every morning?

Mela's angel friends know a shortcut back to the palace, and once we pass the stinking trough with the dead carcass I move my mare up beside hers. 'OK, I've seen it now, the slum area where both angels and souls live in squalor and are preyed upon by wealthy angels. I assume the souls here are those Luca hasn't processed yet. And the angels are the socially disadvantaged for one reason or another. But what I don't see is why you brought me here. You could have just told me all this, pointed out my windows, and saved yourself a lot of trouble.'

She's quiet for so long that we reach the curfew sectors surrounding the palace before she turns to me and says, 'I needed you to *feel* the tragedy of their existence. Even in the wealthier areas there are still problems. The air is just as unclean. Over time their constantly self-healing lungs take longer to recover and they are more susceptible to illness. So they look for ways to escape, some turning to mind-numbing drugs and alcohol, some attempting to leave the city. When they're caught, their homes are confiscated and they end up in places like those I showed you tonight.'

'Why me?' Even as I ask, my stomach twists with the answer. I saw it in the eyes of both angels and souls that first morning on the balcony. They looked at me and saw *hope*.

'Ebony, there is much more of Skade for you to see. When King Luca is positive you won't try to escape, he will show you the best parts. The impressive parts that make him look good. But I will show you all of it over time, and you will be able to make your own, informed decisions.'

Over time? Make my own decisions? And here I am hoping, with this beautiful mare beneath me … I look up at the gates, a shimmering beacon of white light in the dark night sky, and I wonder if this mare can fly like Nathaneal told me horses do in Avena. But with the gates sealed, what is the point of even dreaming of escaping?

'Mela, what is it you think I can do for these people?'

'Until you are queen you can't do anything except get to know them, and how Skade functions. Just your presence uplifts them. But after your coronation, Ebony, you will have the power to change laws.'

Oh jeez, she's pinning her hopes on me too. But how is that fair? I don't belong here. I don't belong in Skade. And I'm not staying. 'Mela, I'm still sixteen, and I know the Code of Free Will is universal. He can't make me do anything I don't want …' The look on her face makes me freeze. 'What is it? What aren't you telling me?'

'The king is not going to wait until you turn eighteen to marry you and make you Skade's queen.'

'*What?*'

'Preparations are already under way. Dignitaries in all the provinces have been notified to prepare for their journeys to the palace. The ballroom is being refurbished, decorations trialled –'

'When? Mela, when?'

'Your next birthday.'

'He's going to crown me on my seventeenth birthday, and what? Hope everyone assumes it's my eighteenth? But that's only a matter of weeks away! Can he get away with this?'

Unable to maintain eye contact, her eyes lower, her lashes flutter downwards. I take that for a yes. And by the time the gates open again, who will care what happened a hundred years before?

'Mela, I understand how you want to make this place better for everyone that has to live here, but you must know I'm leaving at the first opportunity. Maybe I can't escape Skade outright – yet – but I will escape the palace.'

We continue riding in silence for a while. 'A hundred years is a long time, Ebony. People grow accustomed to their environment. Their perspectives change, their memories fade, and this can alter their priorities. Something might happen that could bind one's heart to a place – or a person – over such a length of time.'

'Are you talking about me now, or Nathaneal?'

She doesn't answer.

'You think my prince will move on, don't you?'

'Not from what I've heard, but … when reality sets in –'

She's thinking children. 'Please, don't say any more.'

She brings her lips together in a pitying grimace. She doesn't need to tell me how Luca has waited a long time for an heir. He's not even going to wait until I reach legal age.

The thought of being intimate with him makes me shudder. And suddenly the memory of his kiss returns, how he used it to exhibit his dominance over me in front of his people. How will I ever forget his hands clutching my scalp and his hot tongue filling my mouth, scalding the tender cells inside as he showed how easy it would be to possess me?

The invasion might not leave physical scars, but the ones he seared into my soul, how will they ever disappear?

'Ebony, are you all right?'

Tears come to my eyes that I fight to stop. When I don't answer, she says gently, 'I've made a mistake bringing you out so early. Oh, Ebony, I'm so sorry. Please forgive me.'

I wave my hand at her to forget it. She's only doing what she believes is right for struggling Skadeans. She's the general of a whole army of angels who want a better life.

'Hold on, Ebony, only a little further and I will prepare a warm relaxing bath for you.'

I won't show weakness here, but, *damn it*, tears don't mean I'm frail and pathetic, only that I'm unhappy.

More memories come, as sharp as if I'm reliving each moment on that balcony right now. I hear the crowd cheering; see Luca's eyes, smoky and filled with desire. I can even smell his skin as he stands over me, claiming dominance (or trying to) before his people.

As the tears flow down my face, I look around the dark street, searching for something to quench this unbearable heat in my mouth.

'What is it?' Mela asks with a deepening frown. She glances at the angels as if they would know, but they only

172

shrug. 'Ebony, what are you looking for?'

But this is one of those tidy streets. It's virtually empty, with doors closed, blinds drawn, gates locked. There are no public toilets, not even a drinking fountain in sight.

I spot a circular brick structure up ahead, and with relief I slip off the mare and run towards it, my hood flopping back, my cloak pulling apart. I remember Mela's warning not to get off my horse, but she brought this on me, she showed me these places, she sparked this vile memory or flashback, or whatever this is.

Mela runs after me, her boots click-clacking on the pavement. The angels follow behind her, tugging our horses with them. 'Tell me what you're looking for. I might be able to help.'

It's not a well. There's no water. Disappointment arcs through my spine like a lightning bolt splintering throughout my body. What now? Where to? With all those stairs back up to my room, I'm not sure I'll make it. My mouth is on fire, filled with blisters, too dry to speak.

Mela grabs my arms and spins me around. 'Tell me what you need!'

I force some moisture up and swallow. 'Water. I need water.'

One of the Seraphim reaches into his saddle pack and draws out a bottle. He goes to hand it to me, but Mela snatches it and shakes her head at him. I grab it and swig a long gulp, swish the fluid around my scalded mouth and spit it out. I nod my thanks at the angel and take another gulp, swish again, and down the rest.

Mela is watching me with a frown carving a deep V in

her forehead. Tears spring into her eyes and she shakes her head, sharing her worried glance with her angel friends. One says, 'I carry another bottle if my lady requires it.'

Mela points to the near-empty bottle in my hand. 'Do you need more?'

I take a deep breath. 'I don't know. I don't know if I will ever be rid of it.'

'Rid of what, Ebony?'

I hand her back the empty bottle, taking my horse's reins from the angel's hand. 'Just drop it, Mela. I'm all right now. Really I am.'

I don't know what triggered that flashback, only that it felt so damn real. I wish I could ask Nathaneal how to stop it coming back again.

A sigh escapes before I get a chance to contain it. Mela feels bad enough as it is. This is not her fault. None of it is really. She shouldn't even be in this world. She should be home with Jordan, watching him grow into a young man she can be proud of. 'We should go.'

'Are you sure you're ready?' Mela asks.

'I'm ready. Let's go before someone discovers we're missing.'

Mela doesn't want to drop it, but the angel jerks his head towards the white wall, where soldiers in full armour walk along the top watching over the surrounding neighbour-hoods. They could spot us at any moment. She nods and hands our horses' reins back to the angel. 'We'll walk from here.'

The angels leave with the horses while I follow Mela, keeping low and out of sight of the wall. We make it to the secret door behind the overgrown shrubs. As soon as we're inside the tunnel, I touch Mela's arm to make her stop. I really need to explain. 'You want me to stay and make this place better for the souls and angels who have no choice but to live here, but, Mela, where is my choice? If I were to live in Skade for a hundred, or even a thousand years, the one thing that will never change is my heart. Mela, if Nathaneal should somehow find a way to break into this horrid place, I'm going home with him. And if he can't break in, I don't care how long it takes, but I will find a way out myself. I know this is disappointing for you and I'm sorry. But you should know that I intend to be out of here before I turn seventeen and Luca makes me his wife, because I'm sure you're right – I would have a problem leaving my own children behind.'

20

Jordan

After Thane and Gabe seal the deal, the angels start leaving. I look for Shae and spot her and Isaac walking down the driveway hand in hand. I run to catch up. 'Shae, can we talk a minute?'

She exchanges a glance with her husband of a thousand years. Isaac gives me a searching look while probing my thoughts. I scramble them like crazy, and after a minute he glances at Shae and shrugs. 'Don't keep her up late,' he tells me. 'She needs her rest before tomorrow. Nathaneal has asked Shae to be in the front team.'

'That's great, Shae. You'll see Ebony first.'

She swings a big grin over at Isaac. She's excited, unaware that I'm drowning in envy. What I would give to be there, to see Ebony the moment she's free.

Isaac leans in and kisses Shae's cheek, his fingers climbing up inside her hair. The couples are always so passionate. Anyone would think I was taking his wife off to the other side of the moon. He winks at her and the look is so intimate I drop my gaze.

'I'll be right behind you,' she says.

He takes off, and only then does she take her sapphire

eyes off him and turn them on me, motioning towards the front-deck stairs. We go and sit on the bottom one.

'I won't keep you, Shae. I just need to ask you a favour.'

She stares at me with Ebony's questioning expression. It puts me off for a second and I have to shake my head to clear it. Life is bizarre. The first time I saw Shae I didn't see a resemblance. 'I never noticed before how much you and Ebony look alike.'

She smiles and looks more like Ebony than ever. 'And you have become very good at concealing your thoughts even when holding a conversation. That's quite extraordinary for a human being, Jordan. But surely Nathaneal has told you of another, easier way.'

'I don't have time to learn it. Besides, Thane's too busy to teach me.'

'Did *he* tell you that, or is this your assumption because you don't like him at the moment?'

I don't answer. I'm not sure what I think about Thane right now. I'm giving him a break from my hatred until he brings Ebony home.

'What is this favour? A message for Ebony?'

She's never going to guess so I just come out with it, 'Shae, will you carry me to the gates?'

Surprise registers in her eyes as she turns them on me, boring into my brain. I can *feel* her poking around, searching for my reason. Then she says the one word that brings my plans to a crashing end: 'No.'

'Come on, Shae, I just want to see her. What's gonna stop you guys from taking her straight to Avena?'

She looks directly into my eyes and says, 'Ebony.'

21

Ebony

A light is on in Mela's room, giving us the first indication that something is wrong. A sliver of this light shows under the half-size door. Mela turns with her eyes wide and filled with terror. She grips my arm, stopping me from moving closer. Switching the lantern off, she mouths the words, *Go back!*

But the door suddenly flies open, wrenched off its hinges, and a Throne guard I've never seen before reaches in and grabs Mela around the waist. Dragging her backwards, he gives her a grave look as he passes her to his partner. He then turns to me. 'Come with me, my lady.'

I start moving backwards, as Mela had urged, every cell in my body screaming to run.

'I won't touch you,' he says, his voice deep and low, 'but *he* will punish Mela.'

'Can't you help her?'

He shakes his head, a gut-wrenching sadness in his eyes.

The other guard bends down at the door and looks in. He glances at me with the same soft silver eyes as his partner. 'My lady, the king requests your presence immediately.'

Mela screams. I run past both guards, who back quickly out of my way, to find Luca dragging Mela across the room by her hair. He sees me and drops her with a smart-alec grin on his face.

She scrambles to her feet and rushes towards me, her heartbeat erratic, eyes bulging and horror-filled. But Luca intercepts her, grabbing her by the shoulders and distorting the air as he tosses her in the opposite direction.

When she gets to her feet again, Luca is standing in front of her. 'Look at me,' he demands, his words spoken with an eerie icy calm.

She lifts her eyes. They remind me of a terrified filly's and my stomach clenches.

'Explain yourself.'

Mela takes a deep breath and straightens her shoulders. 'I just wanted to show my lady the city.'

'At night? After curfew?'

'I see now that it was foolish.'

'Did you take anyone with you for protection?'

She freezes, flicking a micro-glance at me that says she's damned either way. 'No, my lord. No one.'

She chooses to protect her friends. It's going to be difficult to continue the lie. Luca might not be a Soul Reader, but he has ways of just knowing things.

'Then why were four sets of horse tracks found at the western district perimeter?'

Damn.

'Oh. I apologise, my lord. I ah ... arranged for two soldiers to accompany us and watch over Ebony –'

'It's "*Ebony*" now?'

'*I* asked her to call me that,' I tell him, worried where this is heading.

He gives me a potent look to butt out. But that's not going to happen. 'Whatever you think she's done, Mela is *my* handmaiden, *my* staff member. Tell me what rule she's broken and *I* will deal with her.'

'Not a chance, Princess. You will stay out of this one.'

'No, I won't.'

His eyes flash to all black. It's only for a second, but I get a blinding sting in my head as if he's slapped my unsheathed brain with an open palm. My head flops to the side and I blink hard several times to readjust my senses.

Luca shouts a string of commands. The two guards from outside run in and stand one on each side of Mela, while the other two close in around me. I give them each a hard stare and they take a step back.

Meanwhile, Luca has grabbed Mela's chin and is forcing her to look up into his face. 'I want their names, Mela.'

She glances at me with remorse and sorrow. Luca notices and kicks her legs out from under her. Knowing I'm going to retaliate, he turns and punches words into my head: *Stay out of this, Princess.*

I will, if you stop hurting her.

She broke my direct command. I cannot release her without punishment. Understand now?

Depends on the punishment.

His eyes narrow and linger on me a moment longer before he returns his attention to Mela. 'Their names. Now.' He leans over her and yells into her face, 'Give me their names!'

I've seen Luca in a rage before, and I can tell he's just about there now. It's like watching a storm build, one that you know has the capacity to wipe your house and all your belongings away.

'But, sire, they're innocent of any wrongdoing,' she says. 'I gave them minimum information. They didn't even know whom they were protecting.'

'This will not go well for you if you continue to lie.'

Slap!

His hand shoots out flames as it connects to Mela's face. Sparks in the air slowly disintegrate while Mela's body pitches to one side, falling into the arms of a guard, who pats out the fire that catches in her hair, setting her on to her feet with more care than I would expect from one of Luca's soldiers.

'*Let me explain,*' I say through clenched teeth.

Luca turns and raises his eyebrows. 'Not until Mela gives me their names.'

Reluctantly she gives Luca two names. 'May I go now, my lord?'

He looks down his nose at her. 'Why should I release you?'

'I gave you the names, and now I would like to run my lady a bath.' She touches her cheek gingerly, wiping at the blood trickling from the corner of her mouth.

'You disobeyed my orders. You brought strangers into contact with Skade's future queen. You broke my trust, Mela. That's unforgiveable.'

Her frantic eyes flick at me before she pleads, 'Sire, you can still trust me. I'll prove it. Set me a test. Tell me what to do. Please, my lord, just give me another chance.'

'Stop grovelling. It's disgusting. Without trust, you're worthless to me.'

'I'll earn it back. I'll do anything. Please, sire.'

This is terrible. I have to think of something.

Luca motions to the soldiers at her side to take her out, but she drops to her knees, 'Sire, *please* don't throw me into the streets.'

'You're not leaving the palace,' he says. 'With all your knowledge, that would be foolish. You would go straight to my enemies. No, Mela, you will stay where my soldiers can keep their eyes on you until you serve out your sentence.'

She sighs with relief as if she had been thinking he was going to kill her.

'Luca, before you decide on Mela's punishment, you need to know that all she was trying to do tonight was change my attitude about wanting to escape. Mela's intention was to show me that as queen I could be good for the Skadean people.'

Surprise registers as he searches first my face, then Mela's. 'Was this your intention, Mela?'

'Yes, my lord.'

'Why didn't you come to me first with your idea, instead of slinking off in the middle of the night like a rebel? I could have given you protection befitting a royal party.'

'I thought it best to take my lady out in a manner that did not draw attention to her status. My lord, people act differently around royals, and Princess Ebony has a kind heart. I thought if she could just see a future for herself here, she might adjust more quickly.'

Luca rubs his chin. I hope he's changing his mind about punishing Mela. I recall how he tortured and killed his Prodigy Sarakiel when he felt no option but to act 'on principal'.

'Mela,' he says, 'whether your intentions were for Skade's betterment or to serve your own agenda, you broke my trust tonight and for that you must still be punished.'

'Luca!'

Princess, what would you have me do with her?

Is he really asking me to choose Mela's punishment? I think quickly before he changes his mind. Clearly he's going to make an example out of her. He raises his eyebrows at me. I'm running out of time to come up with some kind of punishment, something that will keep her inside the palace, or Luca will dismiss it outright. *The kitchens!* I link back. He tilts his head with a look that says he might consider that a viable option.

His eyes go to his guards. He must be mind-linking with them as everything happens quickly then. The guards around Mela return to their post outside, while the other pair secures Mela's hands behind her back.

'Hey, what's going on?'

He groans, flashing me an impatient look before announcing, 'Melanie Blake, handmaiden to Princess Ebony, future Queen of Skade, you are hereby sentenced to sixty hours' kitchen duties, to be served until completed in twenty-hour shifts.' He nods at the soldiers. 'Take the prisoner to Dathien with instructions to chain her to her bed when she sleeps.'

'Is that necessary?'

He says casually, 'I am accommodating your wishes, Princess.'

'But I didn't say anything about chaining Mela to a bed.'

'No, that part was all me.'

'She's my servant, and I say she doesn't require chains.'

There's an electric pause where the two guards hesitate, looking as if they're not sure whose orders to follow.

'What are you waiting for?' Luca snaps at them. 'Take the maid to Dathien now.'

They leave immediately.

As the other guards hold open the doors, Luca snatches my hand and starts marching me out. 'Am I going to the kitchens too?'

He gives me a withering look, turning left, the opposite direction to Mela. 'You can't stay in your apartment on your own.'

'Ah, hate to spoil this for you, but I've been sleeping in my own room without consequences for nearly seventeen years.'

'Not here, you haven't.'

A few strides down the corridor I stop and refuse to take one more step. Lately I've been able to reduce the red haze that blurs my vision when I get angry. I'm seeing it now, so I spend a moment bringing it under control.

He glares at me, crossing his arms over his chest.

'Why can't I stay in my room until Mela returns? It's only for three days, and you have guards outside my door.'

'Look what happened tonight, Ebony. The guards didn't even notice there were pillows in your bed until I showed them.'

'You?'

'Yes.'

'OK, then double the guard. Triple it. I don't care; just let me stay in my rooms.'

'Your rooms are being examined for secret passageways. Anything else?'

I glance down the corridor to the first of the vacant guest suites. 'I could stay in one of those. You said yourself they're always empty.'

'My forensic specialists are checking every room in the castle. By sunrise they will destroy all internal tunnels. There is only one apartment I can be sure has no secrets, and that's where I'm taking you now.'

My spine prickles. He's talking about his own apartment.

'Will you come willingly, or must I drag you screaming?'

I glance at the two Throne guards following us, their faces as rigid as cement rods. Do I have a choice? If I use my power, what will happen? There are soldiers outside Luca's apartment, at the top and bottom of the stairs, at the lift doors on every floor. What am I thinking? There are soldiers everywhere. 'This is only until Mela serves her sixty hours, right? Then I get my room back?'

'If you still want to return to your apartment when Mela completes her punishment, I will not stop you.'

If I still want to? What's with that? Of course I'll want to.

He hooks his arm through mine and we start moving again.

'You *can* trust Mela, you know.'

'She kept a secret from me. And if she's kept one, how do

I know she's not keeping more? She needs to know what risks she runs when she attempts to hide something from her king.'

I look ahead and, seeing the doors to his apartment, the two soldiers guarding the entrance, the reality of where he's taking me hits and my legs grow heavier with each step.

'What's wrong, Princess? Are you unwell?' He leans around me. 'You've gone pale. Are you in need of a healer?'

'No. I'm just tired.'

'I'm not surprised, since you were gallivanting through the streets of Odisha for most of the night,' he says, scooping me up into his arms.

'How did you find out?'

'I'd been judging souls for hours and wanted a moment alone. I stepped out on to the balcony and saw an angel running down Empress Lane with flames leaping around her head. I thought I was seeing a vision until I realised the angel was you and the flames your hair. I went straight to your room and found the pillows.'

Two Throne soldiers standing guard in full military uniform hold open Luca's apartment doors as he walks in, carrying me. The doors close behind us, and he sets me down gently on my feet in a living room of massive proportions.

He disappears for a moment, returning with a glass of water. 'Here, drink this.'

I take the glass under the heavy gaze of his watchful eyes and drink it down. I didn't realise I was so thirsty. I would thank him if anything about this 'relationship' were normal. It's not. The fact that he can inflict pain on me through his mind, hurting me in places no one can see, puts whatever this is into a category of its own.

When he takes back the empty glass, I look around at an apartment that could be the penthouse suite in a high-end hotel in Sydney's Northern Suburbs or New York's East Side. Modern, elegant, spacious, with sleek leather furniture, highly polished timber floors, a fireplace set in glass across an entire wall. As if this weren't stunning enough, the window is a wall of glass with views across the city. The courtyard, directly below, is lit up like a fairy tale garden, while to the south-east are mountains dotted with the lights of the communities who live up there.

Luca returns and lifts me into his arms again.

'Hey, I can walk now.'

'You're exhausted. I don't mind. You weigh practically nothing.'

'I suppose it hasn't occurred to you that *I* mind.'

He pauses and glances down at me, frowning, but doesn't say anything. He walks through another spacious room, then a dining room with a smoky glass table and a sparsely furnished sitting room with artworks like you'd find in a museum.

He answers my question before I pose it. 'There are twenty-two rooms. You'll soon find your way around.'

'Since I'm here only a few days, I'm sure I'll manage.'

'Yes, I'm sure you will.' He gives me a look that makes my stomach clench.

He stops outside a set of double doors for a moment as if to catch his breath, or brace himself, the thought occurs. Turning the gold handle on the left door, he walks through to what is clearly his bedroom, where he sets me down on my feet and steps away to watch my reaction as I take it in.

It's large enough to be an apartment on its own, with a bed sitting up on a sweeping curved platform of two wide steps. A wall of glass in the same shapely curve as the platform gives another view of the city and mountains. The room is stylish, ultra-modern with cream walls, cinnamon and coffee furnishings and a dark-red quilt covering the huge bed.

'Breathe,' he says softly into my ear.

I swallow to bring moisture to my suddenly arid mouth. And why wouldn't I be nervous? I'm standing in Prince Luca's bedroom, for pity's sake. Maybe Luca is right; maybe I am exhausted, because I'm beginning to think that if Nathaneal *could* find a way to break the hundred-year seal, he would have by now.

I'm beginning to think he won't be coming after all. That maybe he can't.

Luca draws in a deep breath through flaring nostrils as he looks down at me. I don't need to inhale to smell him; his scent is all over the room, a heady mix of the finest vanilla, pine and sandalwood, with the freshness of a forest and the unpredictability of a wild ocean.

I stare back up at him. 'I'm sixteen. You can't do this. There are rules.'

He doesn't answer.

It infuriates me. 'When you're not looking, I'll use my powers and destroy your whole palace. I can. You know it. You saw what I did in the tunnel.'

He cackles. 'Go ahead, Princess. Your temper in full flight would be very entertaining to watch.'

His lowered voice sends chills down my spine. 'Ebony,

you don't know how to control your power yet. Using enough force to destroy this palace would destroy you at the same time.'

'That's not true.'

He shrugs. 'At the very least it would weaken you, and in your exhausted state ...' he lifts his open palms in the air, 'who will be there to stop me from taking advantage of you, stop me from sweeping you away to one of my many homes?' He raises an eyebrow and gives a crooked smile. 'Now *that* would be fun.'

'Don't laugh. You don't know what I'm capable of.'

He becomes serious. 'If you destroy the palace, you will kill Mela. She's not a soul, you know.'

'I figured that out for myself.' And he's right; I wouldn't want to hurt her for anything. Clearly Luca already knows this.

He smiles, but this time there's no sarcasm. 'It doesn't have to be this way.' He's almost tolerable like this, without the hard edges and snide remarks. 'Go to sleep, Ebony. You're extremely tired.' He tucks a lock of my hair behind my ear.

His tender voice and the light burning touch of his knuckles on my face blindside me. He pulls the quilt and satin sheets down. My heart skitters in mad panic. *No. Please, no, I don't have the strength to fight him yet.*

I watch as he walks to the other side of the room, kicks off his boots, and flops into a deeply cushioned armchair I didn't even notice was there. Pulling his feet on to an otto-man, he sinks down into it, crossing his feet at the ankles. 'Go to sleep,' he orders, 'before I change my mind.'

I slink down under the sheets, clothes and all, shut my eyes and try with all my might to fall asleep.

22

Jordan

A car is driving out of Amber's place as I drive in, a bronze late-model Subaru four-wheel-drive. It takes half a click to realise who it is. '*Bullshit!*'

I pull up out front and run up the porch steps. Amber opens the door on my first knock and jerks backwards when she sees me, her eyes scooting to the road and back. 'What are *you* doing here?'

'What am *I* doing here? How about, what was *Adam Skinner* doing here?'

She folds her arms over her chest. 'You don't get to tell me who I can or can't hang out with.'

'So you are seeing him?'

'I didn't say that. What's it to you anyway?'

'He's bad news, Amber, and you know it.'

'What I know is that you judge Adam too harshly.'

'No way, you can't be falling for him.'

'I can, if I want to.'

I don't have time for games, so I try to simmer down fast. 'Amber, listen to me. We haven't been getting along so much lately, and I get that I'm the last person you wanna take advice from, but I know Skinner. I knew him when we were kids and best friends. I was there when his little brother drowned because of our stupidity, and because Adam couldn't handle his guilt at not being able to protect Seth, he turned on me. I understood his grief. I'd lost my mother to a drug overdose only two years earlier, so I let him go for it. I never fought back. But since the angels came, something's happened to him. He's involved in some real dark, dangerous stuff.'

'Go on.' At least she's listening.

'An angel got to him. I don't know how, or when, or who, though I suspect in the hierarchy of dark angels this one's somewhere near the top. This angel played on Adam's weakness, gave him powers in exchange for working for him, and now Adam is in over his head.'

She flutters her lashes as if she's flicking tears, and I panic at the thought that her emotions are for Skinner and I'm losing her. 'You gotta listen to me, Amber. You can't let Skinner in. If he's showing interest in you, you can bet your life he has an ulterior motive. It won't be because he thinks you're beautiful and smart and sexy with that hair and those eyes and ...' I take a breath before I chop my rambling tongue off with my pocket knife. 'It's because he wants something from you, or ...' *he wants something from me*, I finish saying silently.

She starts sputtering unintelligible words, but manages to say clearly, 'Go home, Jordan.'

'Hey, are you listening?'

'Am I listening? Let's see ... Adam finds me as repulsive as you do, but since he wants something from me, he's pretending to be interested.'

'*Jeez*, Amber, that's not what I said.'

'Yeah, it is.'

'Well, maybe, but I didn't mean it that way. You don't know Skinner like I do. He's bad news for everyone.'

'Really? So he's never done anything good for you?'

Oh-ho, what's he been telling her to make himself look like a hero? He made me swear to tell no one what happened inside that cave.

Amber puts her hands on her hips and waits.

'OK, yep, once he, um, saved my life.'

She gives me her I-knew-it-all-along look, then closes the door in my face, but I stick my foot out at the last second. 'I don't know what Skinner's told you, or how much; I just know he will use you and hurt you. He knew Ebony was walking into a trap, but didn't warn any of us. He got reinstated into our school even though he tried to kill me. You remember *that*, don't you?'

She nods.

I run my hands through my hair. What game is Skinner playing with Amber? I really have to get through to her.

She looks over my shoulder into the dark shadows of her front yard. 'Why did you come here tonight, Jordan?'

'I didn't like the way we left things.'

'Neither did I, but there's always text … oh, my *God*.' Her eyes meet mine. She's figuring it out. 'You came to say goodbye.' Her bottom lip trembles and she snags it into her mouth. 'Oh hell,' she murmurs. 'You really don't give a damn about me. I'm such an idiot.'

'Don't say that, Amber. I do care about you.'

'Really? Then why are you intending to leave me alone

with this?'

'But I'm not. I'm gonna make things better for you. For everyone. Give the angels a few days and they'll bring your best friend back.'

She scoffs. 'Do you seriously think this time they'll leave Ebony on Earth where she's obviously not safe?'

She has a point, but … relying on Skinner for comfort will ultimately bring her more pain. 'Amber, promise me you won't hang around with Skinner any more.'

'Give me a reason why I shouldn't. You're not the only one hurting, Jordan. Tell me you won't go, that *you* will hang around with me when Ebony leaves for good, and I'll never speak to Adam again.'

My heart starts pounding, building speed like a freight train. Why is saying goodbye so hard? And why is Amber making me choose between her and Ebony?

She groans, making a really pissed-off sound while rolling her eyes. Then, with a grunt of frustration, she reaches out, grabs my face between her hands and kisses my mouth. Her lips are soft and supple and raising my temperature fast. In complete control, she slows the pace, tilting her head at different angles as if she's tasting something salty, and then sweet on my lips. Prising my lips apart with her tongue, she takes the kiss to an entirely new level. Exploring with her tongue inside my mouth makes the fire she lit with her first touch turn into a raging bonfire. We remain lip-locked until we're both gasping and lunging for air.

She steps back. There's hurt in her eyes, pain in the voice she doesn't use but clearly wants to. Instead she turns away, shutting the door in my face.

23

Nathaneal

We meet in the still, early dawn at the entrance to the Crossing, where the forest grows thickest and usually abounds with Aracals looking to report to their creator. But this morning there are only the lyrical whistles of crimson rosellas and king parrots.

We leave in groups – first the three teams, spread no more than two minutes apart from first soldier to last, vital to ensure the three main teams travel through the same landscape and arrive together. Gabriel and Uri have each brought eight of their best soldiers, making nine per team, called A and B. They will support Team One – my team of Michael, Isaac, Shae, Tash, Jez, Solomon and my brother Jerome and his wife Sami, the pair whose ability to become invisible will be invaluable on this mission.

Close behind the teams are the rest of Gabriel's soldiers. They will follow in staggered units of five hundred at a time, until eventually ten thousand will set up camp at the blue light, the only Crossing landscape that doesn't shift. There, they will split into two units. One will build the wall that will reinforce the gates once we bring Ebony through and I have fulfilled my promise to the High King, the other will patrol the gates before, during and after construction, no matter how long it takes, ensuring nothing leaves Skade for the next hundred years.

We enter the Crossing and find ourselves flying over hills of pine forests. The deep green foliage has a silvery tint, usually seen at dusk, but the light is still the kind normally seen in the mornings. As I try to assess what this means, a sudden human thought shoots into my head.

But that's … impossible.

It happens again, followed by a colourful string of profanity.

There is no human in the three teams, and my mind doesn't want to accept what I'm hearing.

Angry at the only possibility that makes sense, I turn to Tash, flying on my right, with the question in my eyes.

I heard him too, she forges in a private link, adding as an afterthought, *Nathaneal, I did not bring him.*

I move a little closer. *Do you know who did?*

Shae appears in her thoughts, but Tash quickly discards the image. *There's only one amongst us who would put his own desires before your needs, my prince.*

Uncomfortable with this thought, I forge an open link. *All teams regroup on the forest floor immediately.*

Dedicated soldiers all, no one disobeys, objects or questions my order.

The forest floor is an army of giant trunks with a canopy so high and thick above us the created darkness forces us to increase our glow.

As soldiers drop to the ground around me, I listen carefully. Two members of Team A land with a slightly heavier force than I would expect. I wade between dozens of tree trunks before I see their glow, dimmer than that of the rest of us. I adjust mine similarly while I watch them assist their human cargo on to his feet. Lowering the *lamorak* to his waist, the pair checks Jordan over carefully for injuries.

My anger burns, not just at the bruises blooming like flowers over the boy's torso and arms, but also at the soldiers' attempt to hide the human, dressed all in black, behind them when they become aware of my presence.

'Step aside, soldiers.'

They do as I say. I tug the beanie off Jordan's head. As his hair falls over his forehead, he runs his fingers through it, appearing as vulnerable as a misunderstood child.

'Do you *want* to die?'

'Don't answer that.' It's Gabe's voice. I search for him among a growing circle of soldiers around us. He steps up. 'Looking for me, brother?'

'Are you responsible for this?'

'The boy came to me,' Gabe explains, 'wanting to be among the first to see your fiancé.'

'Jordan's presence here doesn't happen to benefit *you* by any chance, does it?'

'That's not fair.'

'Oh, Gabriel, I think it is.'

'I made my offer to build the wall in good faith. You accepted. Jordan's plea came afterwards. There is nothing more to it.'

Scrutinising my brother, I point out, 'You could have said no. Why did you agree with his request?'

As Gabriel continues to explain his actions, Michael

moves up close to my left side. No one else dares move, in case it appears they're taking sides.

'You know I supported Jordan having a choice from the start,' Gabriel says, 'and while I happen to still support that, no one stopped to think that maybe Jordan deserves to be among the first to see her.'

I catch him flicking a look to Shae. She stares straight at me but doesn't say anything. I rub the back of my neck. Usually this helps me think more clearly. If only I knew for sure that seeing Ebony was Jordan's only reason for coming. 'Is that why you're here, Jordan?'

Gabe answers for him. 'He thinks we're going to take her straight home to Avena.'

'Is that what you think, Jordan?'

He nods and I ask, 'Why didn't you come to me?'

'He came to *me*,' Shae says. 'I told him Ebony wouldn't do that. Apparently he didn't believe me.'

'I've got a right to see her,' he proclaims. 'This could be my last time. The Dark Prince has control of my life. He even gets to say when I die. It could be tomorrow.'

'Jordan, listen to me. I'm not going to let Prince Luca hurt you. I would fight him myself before I let him take your life.'

'You would do that for me? F-for a mortal? A nobody?' Seeming to need convincing, he shifts his eyes first to Michael, who blinks slowly, then to Jez, Isaac and Shae, who all nod or smile grimly. 'Oh my *God*, you *would* do that for me.'

I ruffle his hair and he makes a gasping, half-choking sound in his throat. 'But why? What did I do to warrant this … this … blind faith you have in me?'

I slide my hand round the back of his neck and pull him into my embrace. 'Sometimes there is no reason for the things we do, Jordan. We just do them because in our heart we know they're right.'

24

Ebony

Dull purple light seeping through the drapes wakes me from a beautiful dream where I'm sleeping with Nathaneal spooning my body in a perfect fit. Sated and warm, I roll over and lift my hand to his chest ... but it drops to an empty cold sheet. Disappointment floods every cell of my body. I snatch the sheet and crumple it between my fingers to hold back my tears.

Still a bit disoriented, I pull myself into a sitting position and look straight into a pair of glowing yellow eyes. *Shit!*

Fully awake now, I remember that's where I left Luca sitting last night when he ordered me to sleep. I'm in Luca's bedroom with the beast staring at me from a chair across the room.

Screaming, on hands and knees, I scramble to the furthest corner of the room and hug my knees.

He wakes and swears one word, viciously, in English as he morphs back into his angel form and comes after me, murmuring softly spoken comforting phrases that bring no comfort at all.

How could they?

He hunkers down in front of me. 'It's all right now. You

can stop screaming. Look, Princess.'

I turn my face partially towards him, keeping my eyes half closed, as if that will somehow help shield me should he still be the beast. I'm afraid that if I glimpse the beast this close up I will start screaming again, and go entirely insane before I stop.

'Ebony, look at me.'

No. I can't.

He swears again. 'Ebony, I was tired. I forgot to switch back. That's all. Look at me.'

My eyes bug out as I take a peek. '*He's* not here?'

'Not any more.'

'I thought you were an angel from Avena who led a rebellion against the High King. And when no compromise satisfied either side, you took your followers and anointed yourself king of a new world. You're not supposed to look like *that* thing with the …' I outline the curved horns with my hands in the air. 'How did it happen?'

'Not overnight.'

'Do you like it more?'

'I'm comfortable in either form, but the beast has more power.'

'Is that what it's all about for you? Power?'

He breathes in my scent as if he were the beast again, testing the air for prey. I shudder from head to toe. He wraps a blanket around me. 'There is nothing else as satisfying.'

'You only think that because you haven't felt the strength of love.'

He takes an age to answer, his eyes remaining on me,

studying my face. 'I will control all the kingdoms with the power of the beast.'

'Including Earth?'

He nods.

'Without love, a part of your life will always be missing. I wouldn't swap anything for the love my mum and dad gave me, or my best friend. Or for that matter, even my horse.'

'Ah, but that's where you come into it, Princess. You will provide me with the love of a family.'

Before I realise what he's doing, his arms are around me and he's lifting me to the bed, where he sits beside me, our legs hanging over the same side. He readjusts the blanket around my shoulders, straightening a curl hanging down the side of my face. It springs back. He does it again, watching with a small smile tugging at the corner of his mouth.

He goes to do it again, but this time he uses his knuckle to trace the outline of my face and my skin blisters from the heat of his touch.

I jerk my head to the side.

He grips my chin, bringing my face back, and we eye each other. Maintaining his firm grip, he traces my bottom lip with his thumbnail.

I yank his arm down, hissing at him, 'Don't touch me, Luca.'

With abruptness that is more in line with the Luca I know, he gets up. 'Well, we'll see about that.' He points to the wall behind him. 'In there you will find everything you need. There are two doors, one to your bathroom and one to your wardrobe.'

'But I'm not moving in. You said three days.'

'I know what I said.'

'What's going on, Luça? Is Mela all right? I want to see her.'

'It's not punishment if she gets time out with friends,' he says. 'You will see her when she completes her sixty hours.'

'I want assurance that I'm not a prisoner in your apartment.'

'In three days I will give you a choice to stay or return to your room. If you stay, I will inform the guards you are free to go and come as you please, as long as you remain inside the palace.'

I don't like the sound of this. What is he offering exactly?

I get up, tossing the blanket on to the bed. 'Let me get this straight. You're giving me a choice to either stay here with you and have access to the palace, or return to my apartment and continue being a prisoner in isolation?'

'Correct.'

Some choice!

But he's such a consummate liar I don't know what to believe. Even when I look into his eyes to read his soul, there's no light, no flame, just blackness like dark matter, like a black hole.

He leaves and I take a bath to mull over my choices, escape always my first priority. Without the secret passage-ways, it's going to be harder. But when Mela completes her punishment and we're back in my rooms, I will ask for her help, though not in a way that will bring her to Luca's attention again. Mela knows the palace, the city, the outer provinces, the demons' habitat, maybe even secret caves and

202

underground safe houses, information I will need to know.

After my bath, I wind a towel around me and step into the wardrobe Luca said was mine. *Oh, wow, there are so many clothes!*

And not just *any* clothes. I pull out a hanger here and there and haute couture dresses fall into my arms. On the other side hang designer jeans, cheeky burlesque skirts and outfits in blends of casual, gothic and steampunk styles. Along the rear wall are jackets and coats. A corset bustle coat in emerald green catches my eye. It's adorable. I can't resist dropping the towel, slipping into it and twirling in front of the mirror.

'Breakfast is ready.'

Oh-ho. I turn slowly at the sound of Luca's voice. He's standing in the doorway, his light brown hair wet and slicked back against his scalp, his vivid eyes as green as ever. 'I take it you like the clothes, or is it just coats you have a penchant for?'

I refrain from touching my cheeks to see if they're burning. I know they are! I could fry an egg on my forehead! 'How long have you been – uh … ?'

'Watching you is fast becoming one of my favourite pastimes.'

I mumble incoherent syllables under my breath.

He laughs.

I push him outwards, closing the door in his face, and quickly rummage through drawers looking for underwear. Next I tug on a pair of jeans in a red-wine colour with a fitted black leather jacket that I zip up all the way to my neck and try not to think what animal died for it. Finally I step into a pair of lace-up ankle boots in cream I admired earlier on one of the shelves. Everything fits perfectly.

We eat breakfast in the dining room. And soon after that I go and stand at the living-room window and try to figure out how long it would take me to run to the city's border from here.

'Plotting your escape?'

I jump at the sound of his silken voice at my ear. 'Do you have to do that?'

At his confused expression I explain, 'Creep up on me.'

'You've been living in the human world for too long.'

'You would know. You put me there.'

He walks to the front entrance doors and stops. 'I'll return before nightfall.'

'You're going out?'

'Would you like me to stay?'

'No!' I practically scream the word. 'What am I supposed to do all day?'

'Take a look around. I'm sure you'll find something to amuse yourself until I return.'

After he's gone, I change my leather jacket for a black coat, count to sixty, and yank open both front doors.

Two Throne guards turn on silent feet and block my exit. Behind them, another two swing silently into position so that the entire width of the double-door frame is covered. I lean on the jamb and groan. 'I just want to go the kitchens and bring back some milk to make a cup of hot chocolate,' I explain, leaving out the part where I don't trust their king and what I'm really going to do is find Mela and make sure she's all right.

'Apologies, my lady,' the Throne opposite me says. 'We're under strict orders.'

'I'm going to the kitchen. You can come with me, or move out of my way.'

'My lady, I *cannot* allow you to leave the royal apartment.'

I spin round and slam the door shut. But something in the way the guard emphasised the word 'cannot' tugs at me and I open the door again. Just as before, two soldiers turn to face me, a second pair soundlessly following. I look up at the guard who spoke before. 'What would the king do to you if I slipped past?'

Looking surprised, the four guards share looks with each other. The Throne opposite me says, 'He would have us executed in the square for inadequately protecting Skade's future queen, my lady.'

I stare back at him with my mouth dropping open. Would Luca really murder these four angelic beings because I managed to outsmart them? Clearly they're his best soldiers, or they wouldn't be guarding his apartment in the first place. 'Well then, soldiers, you'd better get on with your job.'

'Yes, my lady.'

As I start to close the door, one of the soldiers at the rear, the one Mela introduced to me as Lhiam, says softly, 'Thank you, my lady.'

I nod, feeling sick to my stomach.

Inside the living room, I pour myself a glass of water from a crystal decanter, drain it in one go and stroll through Luca's apartment. He has more rooms than my entire house on Earth, with floor-to-ceiling windows overlooking wide areas of the city, including the factories, the mountains, the cliffs, the shimmering gates and the hot glowing area where earlier Mela had shown me where the demons have burrowed out underground caves.

When I open an inconspicuous white door at the end of a hallway, I can't help a slow grin forming at the sight of a fully outfitted gymnasium. I race back to 'my' wardrobe in Luca's bedroom to change into something more suitable and train for the next three hours. I work on building my fitness because I'm going to need to be physically fit, but I devote more time on strengthening my powers. By session's end I stop only because I need sustenance.

I train again in the afternoon, practising moving heavy objects with just my will, which is turning out to be one of my more honed powers. I imagine the objects are soldiers coming at me and wonder if my power extends to moving living beings. I have a way to go yet before I can make my escape, but every improvement brings me one step closer to being free of Luca.

Even if I have to live alone in a cave for a hundred years, I'll do it gladly if it means one day I'll get to Avena and I will see Nathaneal again. By then he might have moved on, and while it grows next to impossible to breathe if I so much as think about him being with someone else, I swear that whatever it costs me, I won't ruin it for him.

The idea of Nathaneal moving on without me is torture. I find a sparsely furnished sitting room on the east side of the apartment with a single window that looks out at the cliffs where Nathaneal and his team rested, the day they brought Mum and Dad home to Earth.

Staring out the window, a flash of reflected light catches my eye and I follow it back to a metallic door. It's copper, if I'm not mistaken. Intrigued, since none of the other doors is copper, I turn its gold handle. Finding it unlocked, I walk through.

Oh, wow!

The room is circular and three storeys high, with a spiral staircase leading to the second and third levels, with wall-to-wall, floor-to-ceiling shelving, and balconies all the way round, giving access to thousands of books.

I spend ages trawling through ancient texts, diagrams and manuscripts, bound and unbound, written in languages I can't read or don't recognise. I thumb through numerous volumes before finding one written by a Seraphim angel named Lucian, dating back to the beginning of Skade's occupancy. I settle into a comfortable lounge chair, fold my legs up and pull the book on to my lap.

As I begin turning pages I soon see that the historian Lucian is really Luca. His calligraphy in black ink is old school and quite beautiful. Though not written in English, it's easy enough to figure out what I'm reading. The sketches on almost every page help a great deal. It's the history of Skade's settlement, starting with Prince Lucian's official claim of ownership; his rounding up of the natives, the demons who lived here already; and the establishment of his provinces, cities and regional areas. Then, in a separate section, he records births, deaths and marriages.

I read for hours.

The sun has long set when Luca finds me asleep in the armchair, the heavy ancient book across my lap. I stir as he slides it from my hands.

'Have you been here all day?' he asks.

'Uh …' I give myself a quick mental shake, remembering the hours of training I did, and simply shrug.

'Did you eat something?'

'A little.'

'At least you found something to keep yourself amused in my absence.' He offers me his hand. I ignore it, getting up on my own to make sure he keeps his distance. 'Whatever questions you might have, Ebony, from now on you have no need to seek the answers in a book.'

'I like reading. Anyway, what do you mean, "from now on"?'

He just smiles with his lips pressed together. My patience snaps. 'What do you mean, Luca? What have you done?'

'I've cancelled judgments for the next few nights.'

I take a step back, then stop. I have nowhere to run. Whatever happens, it's time to stand my ground and, if I have to, fight like the Seraph I am and always will be.

Still, putting on a brave face doesn't stop a stutter escaping when I ask, 'Why would you d-do that?'

He steps closer, his eyes fixed on mine, only breaking contact to lean down and whisper in his silken voice against my ear, 'Really, Princess, do you need to ask? There is a beautiful angel in my bed. Where else would I be?'

A shiver, as cold as the winds blowing across Earth's Antarctic Peninsula, spreads out from my spine to every cell in my body.

25

Jordan

Gabe walks me deeper into the woods and starts putting me back in the *lamorak*. 'I'm sorry I brought you here for nothing, Jordan.'

'Well, it doesn't have to be, you know.'

His eyes meet mine. 'I don't like to cross my brother.'

'Are you sure, Gabe, cos you do it all the time?'

'I'm the eldest,' he declares, a sudden distant look in his eyes. *Has he forgotten I'm standing right in front of him?* '*I* should have been the Sentinels' choice. It should be *my* name inscribed on an ancient rock announcing *my* royal destiny.'

Prince Gabriel is jealous of his little brother. I wouldn't be surprised to learn that Gabe hated Thane from the day he was born. That was the same day the Sentinels passed on the High King's announcement of how special the infant was, how one day he would marry a Soul Reader and the two would become king and queen of their own realm.

Everything suddenly becomes clear.

I recall what Thane told me about Ebony's birthing chamber, how it was hidden deep within the Lavender Forest, and how, later, nobody could figure out how the enemy knew the precise instant to strike – the precise instant Ebony was born. Not three minutes earlier when Thane's vest caught in the chamber's silk strands. Thane blames himself for inadvertently alerting the enemy. But the enemy was there already, waiting for a predetermined secret signal that the infant was born and ready for taking.

I glare at Gabe now, unable to keep disgust from my voice. 'I know what you did the night Ebony was –'

A surge of energy in the form of a gleaming blue wave shoots out of his body and thrusts me back against a tree.

Oh God, I'm right!

He's in my head now, probing around, finding out how much I know. I bring the monastery to mind, show him that I know he was the one who made it possible for the Prodigies and Prince Luca to breach the wall.

Traitor!

My chest tightens. My jaw aches. I begin to sweat profusely as pain spikes down my left arm. It becomes hard to breathe. He's doing this with his power. He's giving me a heart attack, making it look like my human body couldn't handle the pressures of the Crossing.

Oh my God, he's gonna kill me – right here in this forest in no-man's-land.

I bring an idea to mind and shove it at him, *Killing me now accomplishes nothing. You would still be indebted to your brother and have to guard the gates and the wall you're gonna build for the next hundred years. Meanwhile, Prince Nathaneal goes off to be the hero everyone loves. With his beautiful princess by his side, they'll crown him king before you finish paying off your debt – even though you were …*

I lunge for breath, but he's closing my air passage and my

heart is slowing down. His usually bright blue eyes shine all black as he uses his power to finish me off. It's getting harder to put one thought ahead of another.

Spots appear before my eyes. I'm passing out.

No, I'm dying. *Oh God*, I'm dying!

But if I die now, what has my life been worth?

I have to try again, just once more … *Listen, Gabe, you kill me now, and while it looks like … ugh … ugh … there will always be suspicion … but, let me … do what I really came here to do … and … no one will suspect you killed … the human boy.*

26

Ebony

I'm starting to move like a robot, numb except for the pain in my heart where I ache for all that I've lost, the parents I may never see again, the parents I may never meet. For Amber, Shadow and Jordan. I miss Earth, the fresh air, the peaceful mountains, the blue sky. I miss the farm, the home Luca had destroyed as part of his intricate plan to bring me here.

But above all I miss Nathaneal. Dare I let myself think of him? For just a moment? Eyes that are so blue and intense it's as if they were created to look inside my heart. And his smile? So magnificent it brings the sunlight into my soul. It would make birds sing and flowers bloom. Rivers run.

My heartbreak grows deeper by the moment. It's relentless.

But I force myself to move because I have to. It's about hope. Without it, I have nothing.

Luca is sitting at right angles from me at the glass-top dining table slicing up a *turyep*, a spiky green fruit native to one of Skade's outlying provinces. It has blood-orange flesh with, he tells me, nutritious black edible seeds in its centre. Unfortunately, when sliced open, it smells of dead flesh, reminding me of a rotting carcass, such as I saw on my clandestine midnight excursion with Mela. But the taste is not bad, like kiwi fruit crossed with papaya. Almost tropical.

He lays three slices and a spoonful of seeds on my plate. I'm not hungry and lift my eyes to the window. After last night, I'm not sure I'll ever be hungry again.

The sun is up, but as usual it's hiding behind grey clouds. Smoke billows from factory chimneys, spiralling into the already poisonous atmosphere. A large flock of birds the size of cars fly past, hindering my view of the city, where a million angels with their soul-slaves pour into the streets, making their way to work.

I close my eyes, and images of last night sweep me back to the moment when, just as I had got out of a shower, Luca appeared behind me. I hear his heart thudding, faster than usual. His breath shifts the hairs on the top of my head. I have an instant to brace myself, knowing deep in my subconscious it will not be enough. Nothing will.

He spins me around and tries to control me with a kiss, but I turn my head just in time and his lips sear my neck instead. His hands swing to my back and he presses me against his body, half carrying, half dragging me from bathroom to bedroom. With nothing between us except my towel and pants he's wearing low on his hips, the heat is unbearable. It's suffocating.

Surprising him, and myself to be honest, I pull up my powers and shove them at him. He hurtles backwards, smashing into a wall. Without taking his eyes off me, he springs to his feet and walks back slowly and with purpose.

'Don't touch me,' I sneer at him. 'I'm sixteen. I know the

213

law angels live by. There's no way I will allow you to touch me, no matter how many days and nights you keep me imprisoned in your rooms.'

Standing over me again, he stares at me with green eyes flashing black, and I know he's going to punish me by punching his power into my head. It's the one way we both know he can control me. But since he brought me to Skade I've taken every opportunity to practise improving my powers, and in spite of trembling from head to toe, I block his mind from entering mine.

It turns into a battle between us. And angry that I could have become this strong under his own nose, Luca screams and rants and carries on. I hurt his pride and it stings. But so does the slap he gives me across my face, and the brutal kiss that follows.

I fight back with everything I have – all night long.

But in the end, just before dawn, both of us bruised, battered and broken, I'm the one who has nothing left. He stands over me while I lie at his feet and curse him, swearing as if I've lived on the streets my whole life. As if I've just stepped out of prison.

He hunkers down, gathers me in his arms and lays me on his bed with the first sign of gentleness all night. But he doesn't fool me. There isn't a gentle bone in his body. Greed and his own needs drive this king. What he wants, he gets. It's a simple equation.

'I don't want to fight you, Princess,' he says. 'You need to realise there's no rescue coming. Your shiny white prince can't break the gates I fortified with an impregnable seal. Nothing can get through. Absolutely nothing. I'm not even concerned.' He holds out his hands, palms up and empty. 'This is your life now. Accept it and we will get along better than you can imagine. You will have the adoration of your people, and if it's love you want, you will have that too. From me. And from our children. I don't *want* to hurt you. But I will. Don't be mistaken about that.'

I want to tell him how wrong he is about Nathaneal, that nothing will stop him from coming for me. That the love we share is eternal, an unbreakable joining of two hearts that belong together. No matter what happens. Even if the sky falls to the ground and the sun spins off into another galaxy.

We will always love each other!

I want to scream the words into Luca's smug face.

But if it takes Nathaneal some time to break the gates' seal, I can't let Luca touch me and possibly make me … I can't say it. Just thinking of … of … carrying Luca's child inside me – the binding to him that would occur as a result will ruin so much. It would jeopardise my future with Nathaneal. I can't bear to think of the consequences.

No. NO!

I open my eyes, reorienting myself into the present. The city of Odisha spreads out in all directions before me and I sigh, remembering it was *that* moment last night that I knew I had to think of something. I knew Luca liked to make deals, and I thought if I could just get him to agree to wait until … until … *the wedding.* It was a workable concept.

Mela said he planned to marry me on my seventeenth birthday. That's still weeks away. That would give me time to train more, to strengthen my powers more, to grow a pair of wings at last. And to escape.

And by the stars, I would escape.

And somehow he agreed. But, as with all deals, there has to be give and take on both sides, and I had to give him something in return. We struck the deal that other than a kiss he wouldn't touch me intimately, as long as … as … he could … and that I would let him … look.

Oh … the horror, the shame, the stain now lodged deep inside my memories! Will I ever be rid of it?

Damn him!

That's how I came to be seeing in the dawn with my eyes open wide, the pillow beneath my face wet with my tears as I lay on his bed, my towel in a heap on the floor.

27

Nathaneal

The walk along the crystal bridge reignites memories of the battle where Throne soldiers ripped Ebony from my wings. Anger rears its head but I drive it out, focusing on what lies ahead and not behind. By today's end I *will* be holding Ebony in my arms.

Standing before the bright pulsating gates, I close my eyes and bring my thoughts to the point of absolute stillness. Maintaining this sense of inner calm I hold my hands out for the *hanival*, which Michael lays across my palms. My fingers close around the handle. It adjusts itself to my size with a silver glow as it stretches and reshapes itself.

'I think it likes you,' Michael remarks, generating a few sniggers that help to ease some of the tension the presence of this unknown device gives us.

With the *hanival* in my right hand, I wrap my left around it and stretch both arms out to shoulder height. The *hanival* is heavier than it looks, the tube barrel made of an unfamiliar crystalline metal.

I close my eyes again and re-enter my quiet state, drawing power up from my core and directing it into my hands.

It builds faster than usual, thrumming through my body and making my hands glow, and grow hot and hotter and hotter.

'Michael,' I check, 'is everyone in position?'

'All three teams are ready and waiting.'

'And Gabe's soldiers?'

'In place along the length of the twelve gates.'

'Have more arrived?'

'Affirmative. The total now is six hundred.'

'Keep the first six hundred on the bridge. When the next unit arrives, direct them to begin constructing the wall.'

As sure as I can be that we're prepared should the enemy be waiting on the other side, I release a steady burst of power into the *hanival*, simultaneously squeezing the tool's trigger.

A beam of bright silver light shoots out, hits the gate, and causes a flurry of sparks and embers. It's chaotic and loud. I plant my feet firmly so recoil doesn't affect my aim as I begin to burn a circle into the gate large enough for my teams to pass through one soldier at a time.

I keep a rhythm going of drawing up my powers, channelling them through my outstretched arms into the *hanival*. With each throbbing surge that pulses from my hands, the *hanival* magnifies my energy.

It's not long before my arms ache and my hands shudder from the immense power the *hanival* is generating. I now understand why the High King insisted the device not fall into enemy hands.

The possibilities of what the enemy could do with it are endless.

Everyone is on edge, wondering what awaits us on the other side. Another legion of Luca's armed forces? Prodigies or Throne warriors?

There's a flash of white light as ignition occurs and the circumference ignites. Sparks shoot out like fireworks, and a subdued cheer erupts around me as we celebrate this first stage. I've come full circle and the gate is definitely aflame, so I stop squeezing the *hanival* and draw back my powers, watching as layers peel away along the circumference and inwards towards the centre, eventually burning through the layers of the gate's substance to the other side.

The breach is successful. The gate is penetrated. We've done it. The good news quickly spreads through the teams.

Michael catches my eye and smiles. *Good work, cousin.* He shifts his focus to the gate, where the chain reaction has left a completely circular opening in front and what appears to be a tunnel of flickering gold flames clean through to the other side.

What do you think? I ask him.

It's enough. Even Sol will get through that.

Michael holds out his hand and I give him the *hanival*. He places it into its titanium box and locks it. As arranged, he gives the box to a pre-assigned soldier to guard with her life. The key he gives to another officer after the first has left to return the tool to Empyrean.

Looking satisfied, Michael nods at me and I turn my attention back to the gate. There is apparently no sound, no lights, no action stirring on the other side. *Could Luca be that arrogant? Could he really believe his seal is so impregnable he has*

no need to defend his gates? Or is he hiding in wait until we are
exposed in the Skadean atmosphere, to then hit us with everything
he has?

I take a deep breath and make my first decision of the
mission. *Jerome and Sami, you're up first.*

28

Ebony

This is it. I've spent three days in Luca's apartment, and now it's the morning he's supposed to give me the choice of whether I want to stay or return to my rooms. But he hasn't brought the subject up yet. We're sitting at the dining table, having our 'usual' breakfast, and if he doesn't raise the topic soon, I will. I look forward to shouting my '*NO, THANKS*' into his too-perfect face. I would rather be a prisoner in my own apartment than his plaything with palace-walking privileges. Yes, it might afford a better opportunity to escape, but … No. As long as I'm here, I will fight him every step he drags me further towards adapting. I will fight him every chance I get.

'You're quiet this morning, dear.' The endearment comfortably slipping off his tongue has the same effect as if he took a knife and carved my heart up like a *turyep*.

But it gives me an interesting idea to ponder.

'When I'm queen, if I stabbed you in your sleep would you die?'

His stare burns my face as I keep gazing out the window.

'You would have to slice my head off and make sure no one stitches it back on.'

'So I would have to burn it. Then you'd be gone?'

'You would have to burn my body too in case my head grew back, but there's one problem with that.'

I glance at him. 'What?'

'I rarely sleep, and when my eyes close my other senses strengthen. You should remember that when you're breathing over me with a knife in your trembling hands.'

'And if I were holding my breath and my hands were not trembling?'

A knock at the dining-room door interrupts our insightful conversation. A guard announces that General Ithran requests an urgent interview. 'He is waiting in your study, sire.'

As if he's enjoying our conversation more than a visit from the head of his war department, Luca grinds out through his teeth, 'Fine, but not my study. Send him in here.'

The general strides in, only to stop suddenly when he sees me sitting at the dining table in my dressing gown. He clears his throat. 'Sire. Morning.' He angles his sharp face marginally towards me. 'My lady.'

'What could possibly be amiss in the world today, General, that you would interrupt my breakfast?'

The general forges a private mind-link with his king. Abruptly, Luca's entire demeanour changes. The message has put him on alert and on edge. He flicks his eyes at me more than once, his lips pressing together, his fingers thrumming an obscure tattoo on the tabletop. By the time their silent conversation ends, Luca is up and pacing, stabbing the floor with each pounding, jerking step. I follow his movements, interested to note how his hands repeatedly clench and unclench into fists by his sides.

Frowning, he returns to the table, pulls a chair round to face me and sits. 'Ebony, I apologise for this ...' he struggles to find words, settling on, '*untimely disturbance*. A matter of some urgency requires my attention.'

'What's happening, Luca?'

'It's nothing you need to worry about.'

He leans in and kisses my forehead, cupping my cheek with his hand. I think he's going to leave with the general now, but he slides his fingers round my neck and up into my hair, where he grips my head and brings his mouth down on mine in a hard, open, urgent kiss. It's sudden, unexpected, like a spur-of-the moment decision. I try to pull away but his fingers hold me still. He takes the kiss to a feverish level before he slowly withdraws. And even then he lingers, kissing my lips softly, clearly reluctant to let me go. When he finally lifts his head, his breath is coming in short gasps.

What was that?

Luca has just revealed a vulnerability I would never have believed.

Even the general is stunned. I catch him staring at me as if I'm a witch whose claws are too long and lodged too deeply inside his hero's heart.

Luca dabs at the corner of his mouth with the back of his hand. His eyes are glowing as if he's burning up inside, flickering between his own bright green and the golden yellow of the beast. He gives me a lingering look like he wants to say more before he turns and walks out the door. General Ithran follows like a good dog on his master's heels.

What news could have brought on such a frenetic reaction?

My heart does a little clenching flip at the possibility that this could be Nathaneal … but the instant the front door shuts behind the general I stop thinking, I run to the bathroom, vomit, wash my face, brush my teeth and rinse and rinse and rinse.

But I still feel dirty. The truth is, I'm not sure if I'll ever feel clean again.

And if this is Nathaneal …

I take a shower and scrub my skin raw under the scalding-hot water. Eventually I get out. Wrapping a towel around me, I pass a mirror, glad it's too steamed up to catch my reflection. I'm pretty sure I've scrubbed his scent off me, but no amount of scrubbing will remove my shame.

I hear the front door open and close and I groan. Either Luca is back already, or a guard is checking up on me.

'My lady?' By now I know this to be the voice of Captain Elijah. 'I need to speak with you. Are you decent?'

Slipping on black jeans and a red lace-up top, I walk out to the living area, surprised to find Captain Lhiam standing there too, both looking intimidating in their black armour. 'Guards, what's going on?'

Elijah says, 'We need you to come with us.'

'Where?'

He flicks a worried look at Lhiam. 'We'd rather not say.'

'Is your king aware of this?'

'No, my lady.'

Luca has so many enemies I'm not sure what to make of this. Could these soldiers be part of a rebel faction planning to hold me ransom to further their cause? 'Tell me why

224

you're doing this.'

Elijah steps closer and looks straight down at me with his silver eyes open wide. 'I need you to trust me, my lady,' he says softly.

Accepting his offer to search for the truth, I look inside Elijah's eyes and see kindness, dignity and honour, but also bitterness. He detests his life. But there's loyalty too, which his soul holds in higher regard than anything else. I just can't see who his loyalties is for.

'Give me *something*, Elijah.'

'Mela needs you.'

'*What?* Is she in trouble?'

They both nod, and Lhiam flicks a furtive look at the entrance doors.

'Are you taking me to her?'

'Yes, my lady,' Elijah says, disappearing into Luca's bedroom and returning with a floor-length black velvet cloak. He places it around my shoulders and pulls up the fur-lined hood carefully so not to touch me. 'My lady, please keep your head down and avoid eye contact even if someone stops us. The palace is filling up with soldiers.'

'Do you know why that is, Elijah?'

'No, my lady, but they're everywhere and we need to hurry.'

We pass the first pair of soldiers at the top of the stairs, two more on the platform outside the lift. Elijah wasn't kidding about soldiers being everywhere. They're on every floor in double the numbers I recall from my first day. In the massive entrance foyer we walk past too many to count, but we keep a steady pace, and with the king's own high-ranking Throne guards looking brisk and efficient on either side of me, no one stops us.

As we turn down the long corridor of busy offices, where angels and souls work at their various duties, Lhiam forges a link with me. *Not far now, my lady.*

I nod to let him know I 'heard', but don't risk a private reply. Though I'm working on this, I'm just not sure I'm accurate enough yet at directing where my links go.

The blue door at the end of the corridor is the same one Mela took me through to enter the palace on my first day. It leads to Luca's private courtyard. She'd said Luca lets no one see it, but Elijah has a key on the chain he wears around his neck that unlocks it. In a palace this size, with all the secret passageways now destroyed, we need to use every shortcut Lhiam and Elijah know, even if it's risky. Lhiam hangs back to ensure no one is following until Elijah has the door open. The three of us hurry through and Elijah locks up behind us.

The courtyard is still beautiful beneath the dome ceiling, but I don't get time to sight-see, or to work out where the dome's opening might be, we just keep running along the paved area beneath the arched columns to another door that opens with the same key. This one leads to a spiral stair-case. By now it's afternoon and we move as quickly as we can. I grip the central pole and my palm stings with cold. I peer downward but can only make out the next two levels.

Lhiam leans over my shoulder, but he too is careful not to touch me. 'We should hurry, my lady, if we're going to get you back before the king returns.'

We descend five or six flights of stairs. By now I'm losing

track of where we are, and even where we've been. But we're definitely deep underground. It's dark and damp and icy cold, and I'm thankful Elijah thought to bring my cloak.

We enter a tunnel so pitch dark the soldiers' glow has no more effect than candlelight. But they've been here before; their movements are quick and purposeful.

Elijah leads us to an iron door where he knocks in a rhythm that resonates like a code.

The angel who answers the door is female, over two metres tall and thin, with straight enamel-white hair and pale mauve eyes. 'Come, she's asking for you,' the angel says, her voice racked with emotion.

The moment I see Mela lying on a low bed and curled in the foetal position, I know that it's remarkable she's not dead yet. I also know it won't be long before she is.

Mela's eyes are twin slits in a face covered in red bruises and gashes recently stitched up. Her right cheek has swollen to twice its normal size, her jaw crushed inwards with black pus-filled holes above her brow and again below what's left of her mouth. There are more stitches for a gash in her throat. She's struggling to breathe, and her heart is beating too slowly for her to survive for long.

The angel peels the blanket back, revealing more bruises, a three-pronged claw mark from shoulder to mid-waist and several more open wounds. Blood seeps from Mela's injuries, and alarmingly from her right ear and mouth.

How is this woman still alive? 'Oh, Mela.'

I drop to my knees, swiping tears from my cheeks. Afraid to hurt her, I hover my hand above hers, lowering it only enough to give her the warmth from my palm. And suddenly my mind fills with images of her wounds, like her three broken ribs, two of which have punctured her right lung, which explains her trouble breathing.

'Mela?'

Her eyes flutter and struggle to open.

'Who did this? *What* did this?'

Her fingers crawl up my arm to pull on my cloak. I lean in as close as I can without touching. '*Beast,*' she whimpers.

I look up at the pale angel and the Throne Guards who brought me here. *They know.* 'A beast did this? How? Did she fall into a cage at feeding time?'

The angels glance at each other, and while they make their minds up on how much they should tell me, I grit my teeth and demand the answer. 'What kind of animal did this to her?'

Elijah reports: 'The beast was panther aspect with prehistoric bear upper torso and head.'

'What?' *What is he talking about?*

Lhiam explains. 'The king called it a "win–win" result.'

'I don't understand.'

'He punished Mela for breaking his trust, rewarding his favourite chimera-beast for learning a new killing technique.'

'*He did what!*' Outrage brings the red haze to the edges of my vision, along with a gust of wind so strong it knocks the pale angel off her feet and turns every loose item in the room into a projectile.

I take a deep breath and force my power to calm down, ridding myself of the haze at the same time. Luca lied to my face when he promised to reinstate Mela as my handmaiden.

He had no plans to do so.

None whatsoever.

Which means he has no plans to let me return to my room. Ever.

Why did I believe him? He's a manipulative compulsive liar and I know that. He doesn't care about anyone or anything except himself. He has no capacity to love. He can only lust. For power. And apparently for me.

I stare up at the pale angel. 'Who *are* you?'

'My name is Rachana and I am of the Order of Archangels.' Her voice is soft and low and sad.

'Rachana, where are the healers? Can you bring one down here right away, please?'

Rachana hunkers down beside me. 'All the healers in Skade are owned by the palace. I have pleaded with each one, but it appears they are banned from healing *this* human being.'

Can Luca really be that cruel?

'Are you saying that even though Mela somehow survived the attack of a beast, she's not allowed to be healed?'

It's in their silence, their lowered eyes, their *shame* that they live in a world that allows such a disgraceful thing to happen, that I hear the answer even though it remains unspoken.

Elijah moves to the door. 'I'll go check on the king's whereabouts.'

Just as he leaves, Mela gasps and starts spluttering up blood. Without help, these will be her last breaths. Rachana helps me hold her up so she doesn't choke on her own blood. It's then she notices my hands, glowing brighter now

229

than they ever have. 'My lady, you have the gift of healing.'

Lhiam comes round to see for himself. But I don't need to look; I can feel my hands throbbing and growing hotter by the second. He takes over holding Mela up while Rachana turns my hands over and lifts her eyes to mine. 'Did you know?'

I shake my head. 'But … it's not the first time my hands have glowed.'

I recall the night I met Jordan and how Adam Skinner stabbed him out the back of the nightclub. Covered in blood, Jordan lay on the gurney with paramedics rushing to get him to the hospital. I didn't know how or why my hands were glowing, only that I felt a compulsion to help him.

I lock eyes with the Archangel. 'Can you show me how to heal Mela?'

She explains the approach a healer might take. My subconscious reaches inside Mela's body, guiding me. Just like with my powers, acceptance is essential, so I stretch my glowing hands towards Mela's chest and start with her ribs, seeing in my mind the way their sharp angles pierce the pink flesh of her lung.

I can do this.

I begin with tugging gently, imagining the bones aligning and knitting together. And with a gentle puff I inflate her lung.

Mela's sharp intake of breath rewards me more than anything else could right now. And it might be the excitement of accomplishing my first real healing, or the thought of how much more there is before Mela is well again, but I start to tremble. My hands shake first, then all over.

'It's your power surging through your veins,' Rachana says. 'Don't be afraid. It's natural and will pass as you accept your discomfort.'

Knowing this helps me feel better right away. Conscious of too much time passing, I refocus on Mela, concentrating on drawing out the steaming, dark, pus-riddled infection from the beast's saliva, then rejoining torn muscles, ligaments, tendons and finally skin. Next I shift my focus to her shredded spleen.

I'm almost finished when Elijah returns. 'My lady, the king is back at the palace and is presently stabling his horse.'

'How much time do I have before he discovers I'm missing?'

'From the stables he will want to shower in his rooms before joining you for the evening meal. We should leave now.'

'Wait, that's not what I mean. I'm not going back to his apartment.'

Rachana lays a cool hand lightly on mine as I finish healing Mela's spleen. 'If you do not return –'

I interrupt. 'You don't understand, I can't return. Look what he did to Mela. I'm not inside the palace now, am I? You can't make me go back. There's a river above us and I'm betting if I follow it, it will take me out of this city.'

No one denies my theory.

'But, my lady,' Elijah says, 'there is nowhere you can hide in Skade that he won't find you, and if –'

'No! You don't know what you're asking, what that monster does to me …' Images I can't stop flood my vision, images of Luca's face so close I smell his skin while mine burns off like petals held too close to a fire, his eyes raking over my unclothed body, as our deal allows, and his lack of control as he tries but fails to stop his form from shifting in and out of the beast. And then of course the kiss that always follows, his mouth slamming into mine to feed his ravenous hunger to possess me.

Tears sting my eyes, trickle through my fingers. I lower my hands to my lap, and through a moist screen the faces of the three angels swim back into focus. Not one of them is willing to meet my eyes. I inhale sharply, dispersing the tears and, I hope, their pity. 'I can't return to Luca's rooms and wait for him like a lost puppy, OK? So tell me, do you have a better plan, or do I run?'

Rachana strokes my hair with feather-light touches. 'My lady, if you do not return, I will not blame you.'

But something's wrong. The air is too thick as it hangs between us. 'Tell me,' I whisper, my voice sounding hoarse to my own ears, 'what am I missing?'

Rachana sighs. 'If you do not return, King Luca will behead Elijah and Lhiam in the palace square as an example to all who betray him. And when he learns Mela lives because you healed her, he will kill her with his own hands and enslave her soul for eternity to the darkest of Skade's penal colonies, perhaps even the demons' pit of perpetual fire.'

My eyes close. My breaths become shallow. She's right. I have to return even though it kills me to do so. *Oh, Nathaneal, where are you? I miss you so much.*

'I fear it is too late already,' Lhiam says sadly. 'By now for sure the king will be on his way to his rooms.'

'No, there must be a shortcut. Are there any secret passageways left?'

Elijah's light eyes brighten with a glint of hope, 'My lady, can you fly?'

'No, my wings haven't emerged yet.' I jump to my feet in a panic. It's not fair that these two caring soldiers will lose their lives because of me.

They share a quick glance before Elijah stands before me with his hands held out. 'I know that to touch you will bring me a judgement of death, but we have come this far.'

'That we have, Elijah. If you can get me back by doing this, then you have my permission.'

He takes the cloak from my shoulders and hands it to Lhiam, then scoops me up. Lhiam wraps the cloak around Elijah's shoulders, concealing me beneath it. Behind us I hear Mela stir. I poke my eyes over the cloak edge to cast Rachana a pleading look. 'Keep her safe.'

'I will do my best,' she says.

'Will I see her again?'

She hesitates, but only for a blink. 'You will, my lady.'

29

Ebony

We get back to Luca's apartment with the soft echo of his footsteps ascending the stairs. The three of us look down the corridor at the same time and see Luca, trailed by two Throne guards, on the last of the stairs. I exchange a brief look of relief with Elijah and Lhiam even though I'm not entirely sure we made it without Luca noticing something.

He appears abruptly beside me, his look asking what I'm doing standing in the corridor.

Elijah freezes, a tick in his jaw twitching like crazy. I rub my own chin in sympathy. Lhiam is stoic-faced and silent, which is what he normally looks like, but his Adam's apple bobbing up and down is a dead giveaway.

Luca leans down to say something, his breath burning the tender skin behind my ear. But before he gets a word out, I pull away, turning on him with an angry, frustrated look on my face. 'Your guards are dogs,' I complain with, I hope, enough attitude to draw his attention entirely to me. 'I want to see Mela.' I notice Elijah still has my cloak and words dry up in my throat. I swallow and swallow to work up moisture quickly. 'She should be in my apartment by now, but these … these *bullies*, refuse to let me leave.'

Luca's eyes shift from one guard to the other. Somehow they manage to keep their steely expressions intact. The pair of guards accompanying Luca arrives and stands back to attention as if waiting for something.

'Captain, why do you have my lady's cloak?'

'I threw it at him when he refused my request for the third time,' I explain and, careful not to touch him, I snatch the cloak from Elijah's arm.

Finally Luca nods. 'Good work, soldiers. Your replacements are behind you. Return to your barracks. You've earned a break.'

They both nod and thank him curtly. The new arrivals step forward and the two pairs exchange places. Watching Elijah and Lhiam leave brings a rush of relief that I'm careful to keep concealed.

Gripping my elbow, Luca walks me into his apartment, closing the doors behind us.

'I'd like to return to my own room now.' I confront him right away, keeping up the pretence that I don't know what's happened to Mela.

'Not just yet, Princess.'

'But you said after three days –'

'Things have changed.'

Nathaneal.

The thought brings his image. I dispel it as quickly as I can, pulling up barriers so Luca can't get into my head.

'How?'

But he still notices the light in my eyes and inhales a sharp breath through his nostrils, straightens his shoulders and moves to the window, yanking the curtains closed. When he turns around he has his temper under control. 'Have you eaten yet?'

'No,' I answer absently, my mind still whirling with thoughts of Mela, the lies Luca doesn't stop telling me, and the possibility that Nathaneal is somewhere close enough to bring the troubled look in this king's eyes.

We eat dinner in silence, with Luca watching my every move. I force the food down, one small mouthful after another.

A knock at the door distracts him, at least for now. A guard pops his head in. 'The designers have arrived, my lord.'

Luca allows them entry and three girls walk in – souls in their late twenties – a brunette and two redheads. The redheads resemble each other and are probably sisters. One has shoulder-length hair; the other has short hair with blonde highlights.

The guard introduces them, reeling off their names, but by now I'm so exhausted they sound too similar, like Cherry, Berry or Kerry. They bring loads of stuff with them, laying rolls of fabric on a makeshift table – muslin, taffeta, tulle, black netting and a roll of sophisticated black lace, while the other guard wheels in a sewing machine.

Luca stokes the fire, then sinks into a leather armchair with his legs on an ottoman, feet crossed at the ankles. 'The girls are here to prepare you,' he tells me.

'For what? A fashion show?'

His voice tightens. 'If you don't fight this, Ebony, you might actually enjoy the process.'

'What are you talking about? What am I being prepared for?'

The girl whose name I think is Kerry, the short-haired redhead with highlights, rolls out metres of the muslin across the table.

'Our wedding.' Luca watches me carefully as he announces this. 'I thought that would be obvious for someone as astute as you are, Princess.'

My gut twists and drops. *Run! But with the secret tunnels destroyed, gates sealed and Mela unreachable, where can I run that he won't find me? Stop me? Punish me?*

Think. Why prepare for our wedding now? Does this explain his troubled look?

Luca sinks deeper into the armchair and watches while the girls get started, first stripping me down to my underpants, then taking more measurements than I'm sure they need. They work judiciously, conscious of Luca watching while they cut and pin the muslin, try the garment on me, adjusting the pins where necessary to create the fit and look they're after.

The fabric is itchy and I can't help but move a bit. Kerry accidentally pins me and I wince. Luca pulls her aside and slaps her; the imprint of his palm shines red on her left cheek. I stare at it with my mouth open and spend the next part of the fitting standing stock still while she sticks me with pins repeatedly from having trembling hands. Each time she freezes and looks up at me with me wide eyes. When I don't react after the fourth, her shaking settles and she doesn't prick me again.

After the girls make the muslin dress perfect on me, they

rip out the seams and use it as the pattern to cut out the taffeta and lace. They take turns sewing, but it's still a lengthy process, while I'm standing for all this time in the middle of the room with just undies on and my arms folded across my bare chest.

The girls are not immune to my increasing discomfort. They flick little worried glances at me constantly, and while they too are growing tired, they speed up their work-rate, urging each other on, until at last they're putting a long flowing gown over my head.

It's a perfect fit, soft and silky, with a low, shapely bodice of black lace with tiny off-the-shoulder sleeves over taupe taffeta that flows out from my hips to the floor with a layer of sheer black tulle over the skirt. It's a beautiful dress. The girls smile at me, happy with the finished product.

But Luca's not. He orders the bodice lowered and the waist taken in. It takes three more changes while he stands back and watches, his lips sporadically twitching in amusement at my fruitless attempts to cover myself each time the girls remove the garment for alteration.

It's humiliating and degrading and I hate him more each time his eyes devour my bare skin. And even though Luca keeps the fire blazing, it's now about three in the morning and I start to shiver.

The shivering grows quickly worse. I take a deep breath, close my eyes and imagine Nathaneal walking up behind me, folding his arms around me, his solid chest warming my back, his skin on mine, his breath tickling my neck as he leans forward, wrapping me inside his loving embrace. And my soul purrs.

Caught up in my fantasy, I jump when Luca suddenly appears in front of me. He has a blue dressing gown in his hands and begins to put it around my shoulders, but I'm seething at how long he waited and I take the robe from his hands, spin my back to him and put it on myself.

One more fitting and the dress is finally finished. And just as I think it's over and I can get an hour's sleep or maybe two before the sun starts to rise, the girls take me to the bathroom, where Kerry runs a bath and Terry or Cherry washes my hair.

Luca is pouring himself a drink when the girls bring me back to the lounge room. The sewing machine and all the other dress-making paraphernalia are gone. He sees me, raises his glass and watches as the girls work on my hair, drying and curling and sticking it with glittering stones they tell me are real rubies, sapphires and emeralds.

A knock on the door turns out to be General Ithran coming for Luca. 'I have to step out for a while,' Luca says.

Finally!

But he orders the girls not to stop working on me until I'm 'complete', whatever that means.

He hands me a glass box with a sparkling tiara and matching necklace inside, all glittering pink diamonds. It's spectacular, and easily worth enough to feed a Developing Nation on Earth for a thousand years. I want to throw the box at him, shove the jewellery down his throat and run for my life.

When is this nightmare going to end?

Tears threaten and I lift my shoulders and breathe in deeply, blinking them back. I can't fall apart now, not when

I have to find my way out of this palace before this farce of a wedding takes place. And once I'm in the streets, I'll get out of the city and make my way to another province, somehow disguising my appearance and hiding where Luca won't be able to find me. If I can't return home to Earth, or be with Nathaneal on Avena, then living alone, in a mud cabin or a cave deep inside a mountain, would be preferable to being Luca's wife.

The door is closing behind him when I call out, 'When?'

He glances over his shoulder, his green eyes seizing mine and instantly bringing visions of the last few nights in his bedroom, in his bed, the heat from his body burning my skin, his insistent sensual mouth, his eyes devouring me, changing to yellow, his body morphing to and from the beast.

Bringing up my power, I shove the images out of my head, breaking his hold with a shudder. And I know then that no matter how much I try, those memories will haunt me for the rest of my days. 'When is this farce of a wedding set to take place?'

His eyebrows lift and his smile is supreme and smug. 'Sunrise.'

30

Nathaneal

A sound at the breached gate has me spinning around. It's Jerome and Sami, breathing hard as they collapse on the bridge, shedding their invisibility.

Jez rushes to them, and I see why as their forms become clearer.

There is blood all over them.

But it turns out the blood on Jerome and Sami isn't theirs.

It's still dark, but not far from dawn, and the city is alive, Jerome links. *There are coloured lanterns, dancers in bawdy costumes, jugglers, fire-eaters, glass-walkers, laser lights criss-crossing the sky –*

Soldiers are all over the palace, Sami adds.

Michael asks, *What's all that blood on your clothes?*

They share a troubled glance before Sami explains. *We tried to get eyes inside the palace and tripped a silent alarm. Twelve soldiers surrounded us. They knew something was out there, but since we were invisible …*

We drove them crazy, Jerome crows with a cheeky grin.

I stare at their blood-soaked clothing. *How did you escape?*

He locks his gaze to mine. *Brother, if we had let one enemy soldier escape, Luca would attack you before we returned.*

But now he's wondering what slaughtered his twelve soldiers, Michael says.

In the silence that follows, Sami continues her report, *From what we overheard, Prince Luca is arrogantly confident you can't break through his sealed gates.*

This confirmation of our suspicion is excellent news, and my lips twitch with the makings of a smile. I rein it in. Not yet. Not until Ebony is in my arms. And then let the stars stop me, because nothing else in this universe will.

No one is watching the gates, Jerome elaborates, *but whatever is going on at the palace tonight has everyone's attention.*

Prince Luca's arrogance will be his undoing, Isaac remarks. *He's not guarding the gates, but it sounds as if he's guarding everywhere else. Something must have happened to warrant such high security.*

Just the size of that festival warrants heightened security, Sami says. *Dignitaries, royalty, and a multitude of entertainers are in that crowd.*

But Isaac is right, because something did happen. *Solomon's informant contacted him.* I motion to Solomon to brief them.

The pair nods as they listen to Sol explain about the rebel army and how a few members took Ebony out for a midnight ride.

How deep is your informant involved in this rebel army, Sol? Jerome asks.

She's their leader.

Jerome blows a silent whistle of appreciation.

But two nights ago Prince Luca fed her to a beast.

The pair glance at each other with wide eyes. *Sorry, Sol,* Jerome says. *So is she —*

Ebony healed her, and now my informant is waiting to take us to Ebony.

The sense of urgency I've carried with me since Ebony's abduction threatens to explode if I don't get into Skade now. I can't be this close and not with her.

It's time.

I order Gabriel to leave two soldiers behind to watch Jordan. *Nothing must happen to him in our absence.*

You have my word, brother, he confirms, and I give the command to move out.

31

Nathaneal

The rancid smell of decay hangs heavy in Skade's night air, its two moons hiding beneath thick cloud cover, while in contrast the eastern horizon breathes out fire like a living dragon, with volcanic lightning exploding high into the stratosphere.

I glance over my shoulder to Michael. He catches my eye and tweaks his nostrils. Flying in the formation of a flock of birds common to this realm, we're careful not to even mind-link unless imperative, now that we're inside enemy territory.

After a few minutes without sensing a threat, I accelerate our descent, banking south to avoid the hot geyser fields. The white palace soon appears and, though warned, seeing the festivities with my own eyes still shocks me. There's everything there, from street decorations to laser lights chasing each other across the palace skies. There are colourful dancers, acrobats and as well the disturbing sight of wondrous wild animals chained at the neck, paraded by their masters wielding whips.

Most worrying is the high security. Armed soldiers in full battle paraphernalia patrol the palace perimeter and are all over the wall, the spacious palace grounds and surrounding streets. In many places they stand shoulder to shoulder.

Still descending, I sweep wide to the east, carefully avoiding soldiers patrolling the air space between the palace walls and Skade's vital river, and land silently on the floor of a concrete drain. I motion Solomon forward to take us to his informant.

As the ceiling is too low for flying we wade with hunched shoulders through putrid-smelling liquid. Eventually the liquid drains away and we follow Solomon into a second tunnel, where a sliding door at the end opens on to a circular stairwell. We descend numerous flights, moving fast and silently into another tunnel, even more moist and foul-smelling than the first. Water drips from the ceiling. A colony of double-headed rats, startled by our presence, runs over our feet to scamper up the walls in their rush to avoid us.

I order the team to increase their glow.

Solomon's informant waits for us in the cold darkness with a cloak around her shoulders. The woman has fair skin, dark hair and blue eyes that look curiously familiar. As we approach, and my eyes remain fixed on her, the strings of my memory unfurl and begin to connect, forcing a sense of awareness that something isn't right.

He greets her with the affection and relief of finding a good friend unharmed. The two have communicated often over the years, and she just almost died in a horrific manner, so this I appreciate.

Solomon?

My prince, this is my informant, Mela.

245

Now I understand Jordan's agitation on the morning when Michael came to Earth and arrested me for revealing my powers to the enemy. He had just learned that his mother was alive, but couldn't bring himself to believe it. I see now it is true.

I nod at the woman, quickly softening my shocked stare. *Hello, Mela.* My eyes shift to the big angel. *Sol, how did Mela come to be in Skade, and alive?*

Michael and Isaac approach, but remain silent.

I was there when Mela took her last breath. I felt the presence of three Death Watchers in the room: two behind me, one further away. As I weighed up my options, Mela's soul ejected from her corporeal body and rose to the ceiling. I spun round and took out the two behind me first, Solomon explains. *When I looked for the third, I saw to my horror it was the Dark Prince himself, running off with Mela's soul in his arms. I gave chase but he threw fire and other obstacles in my way. He proved too fast. When I returned, Mela's empty body lay on her bed, Death Watchers gone.*

He planned it all, Michael says. *He exchanged Mela's body while Death Watchers distracted you, wrapping the replacement body in a dark glamour so anyone looking would still see Mela's image.*

The significance of this human's presence in Skade is not lost on any of us.

I offer Mela my hand. She takes it and I become aware of her warmth, her pulse, the thudding beat of her human heart. *I have come to take Ebony home.*

She smiles. *Yes, I knew you would try. I just didn't think you could get through the gates.*

Mela, I wasn't aware of Luca's devious plans for the night you

246

died. I'm sorry Solomon didn't receive assistance in time to save you. If it's any comfort, your son lives in my house on Mount Bungarra. I keep him as close as I can. You'll see him soon.

Choked up, she simply nods.

Mela, will you take us to Ebony now?

There's a secret passage directly into the king's apartment that even he doesn't know about. I'll give you directions.

You're not coming with us?

There are too many stairs. I'll only slow you down.

Would you allow a member of my team to carry you?

She glances past me at the others, her eyes stopping on Sol, and she nods.

Go ahead, Sol.

He gently lifts Mela into his arms and, under her directions, leads us back to the circular stairwell where we run up more levels than we descended until we reach the palace's top floor. Here Mela takes us inside a dark and narrow tunnel where she warns us to be silent.

But it's not long before we come to a door with many bolt heads. Mela turns one near the centre and the door opens soundlessly, revealing the narrowest corridor yet. Pausing, I try to figure out why the floor is shaking. I'm just about to warn of an approaching earthquake when Shae grabs my two hands in hers and nods at me several times, her eyes telling me it's all right. It's then I realise it's not the floor that's shaking. It's me.

The end draws near. Ebony is so close now I can almost – *almost* – hear her heart beating. I take a deep breath and steady myself. Shae releases my hands, and then I spot two Throne guards dressed in full armour, helmets in the crook of their elbows, waiting directly in front of a door as if to block it.

Mela?

Allies. Captains of his royal army, but my lieutenants, both of them.

I jerk my chin at the door. *Where does it lead?*

The royal bedroom.

I swallow hard. So that's where I'll find her. Unwanted images push into my mind. I squash them all as distraction could lead to a crucial error I can't afford to make. Not now. Not when we're so close.

As we approach, the Throne soldiers do nothing to raise the alarm. Weapons at their sides remain still. They open the door, nod at Mela and back out of our way.

Light floods in as Mela rushes through, and though there are other things I should be doing right now, when I step into the room the first thing I see – the *only* thing – is the bed. It's big and luxurious, more so than I imagined in my worst nightmares, raised up on a circular platform with a red quilt across it, pillows piled at one end. Is this where Ebony laid her head at night? Did her tears soak into the silk-covered pillows? Did *he* lie beside her? Cradle her in his arms?

Michael's calming hand on my shoulder helps pull my thoughts to where they should be. I drag my eyes away and continue moving through room after room until, there, looking ahead through an open doorway into a large living area, I see her. She's standing still, watching Mela dismiss three female souls and wearing a long formal dress in black and taupe. It clings to her upper body as if painted on her skin, flowing from her hips. Her hair spirals down her back in long red-gold curls with sparkling gems running through it.

My breath catches. It's not been a week, but Ebony has changed, become even lovelier. She's grown up by force, her last youthful year stolen from her by an obsessed monster. Now she carries the air of eloquence she was coming into. And, by the stars, she's arresting.

It takes a whole heartbeat for me to realise she's wearing a wedding dress.

And suddenly everything makes sense – the crowded streets, the gathered dignitaries, the festivities in the front courtyard, the extra security. Now I understand it all.

Prince Luca plans to marry Ebony today.

Mela turns to Ebony, and they embrace like close friends. Ebony is visibly relieved to see Mela again and touches the right side of the woman's face, her fingers timid as they travel lightly from Mela's right eyebrow to the bottom of her chin, looking at her with awe.

But suddenly Ebony becomes aware they are not alone.

She turns slowly round and sees me. Her eyes widen and her lips part as she draws in a large breath, releasing a gasp that reshapes her mouth into an amazing smile. Blinking several times rapidly, she does nothing to stop the tears starting to trickle down her face. Then her smile collapses, and her jaw begins to tremble. She lifts a hand as if to cover her mouth, but stops it in mid-air. There is so much in her changing expressions, her eyes especially. They speak of joy, of disbelief, of stunned excitement and … and of love. Oh, there is love in those eyes. Those same eyes that have loved me for more than three thousand years haven't changed, except, if possible, right now they hold more love in them than ever before.

Her image blurs suddenly and for a heartbeat I panic that something is happening and she's about to disappear. A drop of moisture falls on my hand and I realise that I'm looking at her through a haze of my own tears.

She starts to run at me. I hold open my arms. She leaps into them, her force so strong I stagger backwards, but we're together and it wouldn't matter if we tumbled off a cliff. But my back finds the support of a wall and I lean against it as her legs fold around my waist and she buries her tear-soaked face into my neck.

'Are you real? Am I dreaming?' she whispers.

'This is no dream, my love. I've got you now. And I'm taking you home.'

My hands reach for her legs to secure her higher, but flounder in folds of fabric. Trying again, I gather her bulky skirt up and slide my hands beneath her thighs. She moans, and her husky voice, her warm lips, her breathy, unintelligible murmuring sounds in my ear have me reeling with the need to get closer.

I smile to myself at her reaction, and hoist her up higher, shifting my hands to her back, where of their own accord they slide up to where the dress ends. Her bare skin is like silk and so warm, now I'm the one moaning in a voice I hardly recognise as my own. '*Ebony.*'

She lifts her head and our eyes connect, millimetres apart.

'I knew you would come.' Her words are soft as her gaze roves over my face like a drawing she's sketching from memory.

She stops at my mouth.

I draw in a sharp breath.

Her eyes lift back up to mine, devouring me, and I can do nothing but press my mouth into hers.

Ebony meets my kiss with a hunger all of her own. It's almost my undoing. If not for the others spilling out around us, and Michael's mind-link of *Steady, cousin*, as he passes, I'm not sure I would remember where we are, or how urgently I need to get Ebony out of here.

There is only Ebony. There always was, and now that I have her back in my arms, there is only ever going to be Ebony in my life.

32

Ebony

I'm still inside Luca's chambers, but in Nathaneal's arms I've finally come home. He broke the seal that Luca was so damn sure no one could, and I'm so proud of him I could burst.

I knew he would come for me. And in my heart I knew he would be successful. He had to make it happen. Our love is of the kind that can't be kept apart. The universe will somehow always find a way to ensure we're together or risk being thrown out of balance. It's a fact. I'm sure of it. And it's this thought, this *truth*, that's singing in my bones, in the strings of my DNA, that I cling to, because we still have to get out of Skade safely. But as long as I'm with Nathaneal, and he holds me with the assurance that he will never let anyone come between us again, I know we will prevail.

Together, we can face Luca.

We can face anything.

I'm in his arms for only a few minutes, but what minutes they are. His hands. The touch of his fingers on my back. His *mouth*. I may not have the memories of our time together in the spirit world like Nathaneal does, but it doesn't mean I love him any less. This beautiful angel is my partner for all time. He is my life, my safety, my home. He makes me laugh, and I cry because of him. He makes my cells tingle and he lights my passions into raging fires. Who knows what he's risked to be here. I only know how relieved I am, how grateful and humbled by his efforts, and those of his team.

My blood flows thick and fast with my love for him.

As the angels prepare to leave, it's with relief I learn Mela is coming with us. She's the rebel army's general, and they'll miss her, but she's been training her top captains and lieutenants to take over. She's done more than her fair share for the Skadean people. Her time here is over. Luca would destroy her if she stayed. And I'm so glad she's going home to be with her son.

I slide down from Nathaneal's hips and his fingers automatically lace through mine. He's keeping me close. It's what I want too. But my sister is waiting and I turn and throw myself into her waiting arms. She squeezes me, inhaling and exhaling deeply, and there's so much relief in her eyes that guilt cuts deep into me for not acknowledging her as my sister the first time we met.

'Sweetheart,' Nathaneal whispers in my ear, 'from here on I will need to carry you. Do I have your permission?'

Images of Luca, what he did to me the last few nights in his bed, fly into my thoughts. If only there was some way to scrub my memory clear like Zavier did to my inherited memories when I was an infant. But *these* images are too intense, too recent. I only have to close my eyes and they appear. Like now. *No. No! If Nathaneal must see them, let it be at a time when I can explain. What will happen if he finds them too disturbing to live with?*

But our love is strong and has endured so much already. It will endure this too.

'Of course,' I respond.

He scoops me up in his arms. Our eyes meet, and his overflow with compassion and pity and guilt. He *has* seen the images. I turn my face away, unable to hold the scrutiny of his intense blue gaze. He loosens an arm and tugs my face back with two fingers under my chin. 'I want you to know that whatever Luca did to you in his rooms or anywhere in this entire kingdom makes no difference to how I feel about you and it never will.'

Tears sting my eyes. He leans his head down and kisses my forehead softly, gently, leaving his lips against my skin while waves of his love wash through me.

33

Nathaneal

We follow the rebel soldier Elijah back into the secret passage that runs off Luca's bedroom. The other rebel, Lhiam, keeps watch inside the apartment and when he joins us he will hold the rear, destroying the entrances of each tunnel as we pass through. It's a good plan. But the sound of movement through the front doors, a scream that could only belong to the Dark Prince himself, and soldiers rushing into Luca's front rooms alert us that our plan is already in trouble. As Elijah urges us to hurry, in my arms Ebony stiffens.

The tunnel door, Shae links. *We have to destroy it, Thane, before it's too late.*

But destroying that door is effectively signing the rebel Lhiam's death warrant. I flick a glance at Elijah, whose frown is a deep V in his forehead. He glances at the door, then at me, his loyalties torn. *They are brothers*, Ebony shares with me in a link.

Go! I tell Elijah. He nods, and starts to make his way to the door when Lhiam bursts in, closing it behind him and urging everyone to stand back and be silent. Using the weapon at his side, he shoots blue flames, sealing the door shut.

Let's go, let's go! Elijah links, running to take the lead again while his brother lets me know it was Luca with General Ithran and six guards who came to escort Ebony to her nuptials but found an empty apartment instead. *They will tear down all the walls to locate the escape tunnel,* he says. *He knows you're here. He became incensed when he saw you had already taken Ebony. I've never seen him so angry.*

Ebony and I share a look. She's worried. But there's no time for reassurances, even if I had any to give her. In silence we follow Elijah, who takes us through a series of connecting passageways and tunnels.

This pair of rebel Thrones are putting their own lives at risk to help us escape, but it's still difficult to trust them and the reason is simple. I don't know them. I don't know Mela either – a human being who has lived with the Dark Prince for eight years.

I open a link with the team and Ebony, forging my doubts with Solomon first. He quickly vouches for all three.

But, Sol, how do you know they're not leading us into a trap?

He comes up alongside me. *They were part of the crew the king tasked with destroying all the internal passageways. On their own initiative, and at great personal risk, they secretly kept open one set of linking tunnels to provide an escape route should any of the rebel army find themselves compromised. And now, to help Mela and Ebony escape, they're destroying even those.*

Where does this passage lead?

To a quiet lane outside the perimeter wall on the city's eastern side.

Outside the wall? I check, as this would put us in a decid-
edly advantageous position.

Solomon nods and grins at me before moving back into
position.

I glance down at Ebony. *What do you think?*

*I had the chance to search Elijah's eyes for the truth. He is loyal
to the rebel cause and to his own soul. He detests having to live
under King Luca's rule. He's very close to his brother and I trust
them both.*

We come to a circular stairwell and descend to the lowest
level. With some of my team behind me, some in front,
Elijah stops at the exit and checks the lane through a pinhole
viewer in the door.

And then he swears viciously under his breath. The news
is not good.

*Prodigies and Dominion soldiers have set up outside in numbers
too large to count. There are troops on the ground, snipers on roof-
tops armed with all manner of weaponry*, he reports.

Is there another way out? I ask, setting Ebony down on her
feet for now, but keeping a firm grip on her hand.

Elijah remains quiet for a moment. *My prince, there is
another way, but it's risky.*

Explain, Captain.

*Lhiam and I walk you all straight out the front doors, into the
crowd and across the festivities to the perimeter wall, where you will
then fly to the gates.*

But that's insane, Jerome hisses. *It will never work.*

Shae says, *Prince Luca will have every street exit covered by
now, not just this one. Maybe descending into a courtyard of thousands of excited Skadean citizens is not such a bad idea.*

What of Luca's private courtyard? Ebony forges with slow careful direction of her thoughts.

Lhiam says, *He knows you've seen it, my lady. By now he will have it closely monitored.*

Elijah elaborates: *The king knows you're here. He'll have soldiers coming in from all around to find you. To stop you. There'll be soldiers in all the courtyards keeping watch for you too, but in Skade crowds can turn volatile at the flick of an eyebrow, a misconstrued passing look, a drink not poured to the brim. If needed, a distraction is something my brother and I can easily arrange.*

Isaac rubs his jaw. *To walk through the crowd in that front courtyard is brazen. But we're trapped if we stay here, and considering our precious cargo, it's certain annihilation if Luca catches us. We have to try something.*

Shae agrees. *Let's do it.*

Soloman shakes his head. *What's up with everyone? We've faced worse odds. At least we know what's waiting for us in the lane outside. And we have two back-up teams ready at our signal. We should go out fighting.*

Sami?

Stay and fight.

Tash, your thoughts?

Courtyard.

Elijah peers outside again and comes to stand on the step below me so we are face to face. *Flying is banned in airspace directly above the palace. You need to know this if you elect the front courtyard exit. You would have to make it undetected to the perimeter wall on foot before you take to the air, or risk a soldier shooting you down.*

Michael?

The front courtyard could work as long we appear to fit in.

I can take care of that, Elijah says.

I run my hand around the back of my neck. The decision to follow this rebel soldier's instructions carries enormous consequences should it be the wrong choice. I've made so many mistakes in these past few months; can I continue to trust instincts that have let me down so much? But, in retrospect, my decisions have not all had negative results.

I study Elijah standing before me with his eyes clear and open and waiting for my command. These rebel brothers were born and raised in Skade. Luca didn't give them a choice to live anywhere but here in the capital. If it were up to me, this would be reason enough to give someone a second chance, just as I did Jordan, who had no Guardian to help him find his way. But it's also reason not to trust them.

Elijah, your life is about to change forever.

Yes, my prince.

You and your brother cannot remain behind in Skade. Once you have led us through the palace front doors, you and Lhiam are to gather anyone who might be in danger due to your actions and come to the gates. I pledge you both your freedom as appreciation of your assistance today. Unfortunately I cannot promise you entrance to Avena, but I can assure you that I will try. Otherwise you may live quiet lives on Earth.

Th-thank you, my prince. My brother and I will be eternally grateful and honoured to serve under your command, or live a humble life on Earth.

And I know then, in the tremulous smile he gives Lhiam, that I've made the right decision.

34

Ebony

We leave the stairwell and follow Elijah into a tight passage-way between rooms. Everyone is moving so fast it's as if their feet are not touching the floor. We step through a panel Elijah opens in a wall and find ourselves in a small room with vacant racks, empty shelves and a marble coun-ter. It's a cloakroom, not very big. Nathaneal and I end up near a slightly open door where we glimpse souls in black and white uniforms rushing past. Something big is going on in the adjacent room.

Shae, who's sticking close by, glances through the open-ing and relays what she sees, *Glitzy ballroom with ivory walls, crystal chandeliers, tables and chairs draped in black satin, with plenty of room for dancing in the centre.*

My heart jumps a beat, catching Nathaneal's attention. He frowns, looking down at me.

I've seen this room in a dream.

What is it? Nathaneal asks.

A ballroom.

Shae raises her eyebrows. She knows there's more.

For my wedding reception.

Though they're my own words, they wrench all the

breath from my lungs, forcing me to inhale a deep shudder-ing breath. Nathaneal holds me tighter while Lhiam discreetly closes the door, lifting his hands in the air to remind us to remain quiet.

Meanwhile, Elijah unlocks a door behind the counter, returning a few seconds later bearing cloaks.

Nathaneal lowers me to the floor to collect our cloaks. His touch as he places a crimson floor-length cloak around my shoulders has my stomach doing somersaults. He lifts my hair to pull it out, and hundreds of strands wrap around his fingers.

Shae helps untangle them, so amused she's almost laugh-ing aloud.

Others come and stare in disbelief, but mostly find it amusing and make comments at Nathaneal's unusual 'predicament'. But when Jezelle sees them she starts tugging at the strands impatiently, spearing me disbelieving looks that clearly accuse me of performing a childish, attention-seeking, time-wasting act.

She's not doing it, Nathaneal snaps at her with a sharp look.

I lower my gaze to the floor until my cheeks, burning with mortification, start to cool off.

Finally we're ready to move again, but before we leave the cloakroom, Elijah gives each of us a once-over. He hands Michael a black ribbon, pointing to his head. Michael gathers his masses of golden curls and ties them at the base of his neck. Elijah then helps Solomon into a black chain-mail vest to conceal his silver armour, since his chest is so massive the cloak doesn't cover him completely.

He checks Mela next and simply nods and smiles at her, letting her know he's happy that she's leaving. He then stands in front of me and pulls my hood down low over my face. I can hardly see where I'm going but I get it, he needs to ensure my eyes don't show.

Do nothing that draws attention to yourself; someone might notice you don't belong, he advises as he moves between us. *Right outside this door are two soldiers. We will walk straight past them. To reach the courtyard, we have to cross a large reception area crowded with high-ranking visitors, who will all have their own security contingents watching. So be careful. Whatever happens, avoid eye contact. If I stop, you must stop and fan out into couples and small groups, but stay close, ready to move on. And look as if you're enjoying yourselves.*

Lhiam, watching the corridor, urges his brother to hurry. Elijah takes a deep breath and opens the door. We follow him, walking straight past the two soldiers he just mentioned, and another two further along, with several more in the lift area. That's at least three times as many as the day I arrived.

Elijah doesn't even pause when we enter the palace foyer. But I don't need to look to know where we are. The chatter of hundreds of angels, maybe even a thousand or more, talking simultaneously, gives it away. I tilt my head high enough to glimpse angels wearing impeccable formal dress, and my mouth goes instantly dry. There are soldiers in uniform at every turn.

We keep walking, past the first alabaster column, one of many that support the high ceiling, separating it into sections of sculpted or painted battle scenes from any number of wars. I catch sight of chandeliers with hundreds of candles hanging down at different levels. If I wasn't so focused on the exit doors, I might be impressed at how the designers have created a warm ambience in such a vast space with so little furniture.

At a small, intimate area created by long sofas positioned at right angles, an angel with long brown dreadlocks sits playing a baby grand piano to a crowd of at least twenty enraptured angels. His music is breathtaking, and just as we're passing he finishes his piece to boisterous applause.

Without thinking, I glance at the piano man as he's going down in a bow. He catches me looking and stops. *Crap.* I want to avert my eyes really quickly, but I make myself take the time to do it in a manner that doesn't seem rude and arouse his suspicions. Looking straight at me he gives a wide sweeping bow, so I nod with as much poise as my thumping heart can muster, and ease my focus away.

But now I'm terrified that he will recognise me. *What have I done?*

You handled that perfectly. Just keep walking, Nathaneal links. *By the time he puts it together, we'll be out of here.*

I hope Nathaneal is right. I force my eyes not to glance back.

Souls, both male and female, in stylish black outfits, walk around offering trays of canapés and glasses of wine. A tall couple, with midnight-blue cloaks, and lots of sparkling jewellery embedded like tattoos on their hands, feet and faces, stop in front of us, blocking our path as they take their time selecting a sweet from a slave's tray. Elijah nods at the pair and picks one for himself. While they chat with him, a nearby soldier glances our way, his eyes narrowing as they come to rest on me.

Nathaneal casually moves in front of me, blocking the soldier's view with his back.

I shoot my eyes to the floor and keep them there until I see the bejewelled couple walk away with the soldier following closely behind.

Our group regathers quickly. But no matter where I keep my gaze, it's impossible not to notice more soldiers piling in and walking among the guests with alert looks and searching eyes.

Doors straight ahead, Elijah links.

We're almost out of the palace. Dare I hope we're going to make it all the way to the Crossing? Hope is a powerful motivating emotion and I live by the possibilities it can generate inside me. If I hadn't had hope during my time here, I would have had nothing.

Nathaneal loops my arm through his. *See the soldiers?*

I nod, not trusting the accuracy of forging a closed mind-link here amongst so many.

I don't want you to worry, Ebony, because your safety is my main priority. It's just that the plan I had hoped I wouldn't need to use is starting to look like I might just have to.

I'm not sure where he's going with this yet, but I want to tell him I understand if he needs to let go of my hand.

And suddenly Shae is on my left and Michael is moving in on my right, and I find I'm not so OK with Nathaneal letting go of my hand. A knot in my stomach tells me I'm starting to over-breathe. Panic is rising, something I can't allow when we're so close to freedom, so I try to muster a smile as Nathaneal moves ahead to Elijah.

Michael takes his place, hooking his left arm through my right elbow. *Hello, little one, I told you I'd bring him back. I just hadn't counted on having to bring you back as well.*

He's trying to make me feel at ease. Nothing will. Not yet. But I nod and smile to let him think I'm OK. I will be. Once we're in the Crossing and on the way home.

Shae squeezes my hand. *We're almost out of here, sis, and then I will give you a big hug from Mum and Dad.* Her unconditional acceptance of me shatters any doubts my angelic family might not want me.

If I were anywhere else I would shout to the world that I have a sister. And that she loves me!

The front doors appear in my line of sight, bringing me back to the moment, and my breathing starts speeding up again as doubts strike like arrows at my chest. Am I really going to walk out the palace front doors, cross the court-yard and, without anyone noticing, be lifted up to the gates? Or are we walking into another of Luca's well-planned traps? Is he a step ahead of us again?

Concentrating on Michael and Shae, I carefully forge a mind-link with them. *What happens if someone recognises me in the courtyard?*

Don't go there, little one.

But, Michael, that man at the piano —

Is playing again. Listen.

Do you know where HE is? HE always knows where I am. He's probably on the other s-side of those doors with those s-same Throne soldiers he used last time to c-capture me.

Ebony, Shae says, *right now Gabe and Uri and their teams are keeping the king caught up in a battle on the east side of the palace.*

265

He *thinks you're still in the stairwell. And while he's otherwise occupied, we're going to lift you out of here.*

Really?

Really.

No one will get hurt in that east-side battle, will they?

That's not for you to worry about, Michael says. *Just remember to keep moving. Before you know it, you'll be in the Crossing.*

I still can't fly. What happens when we need to take to the air?

Shae glances over her shoulder and smiles at someone close behind us. *You will be safe, sister.*

Michael says, *Breathe, little one.*

I am, a-aren't I?

Slower, he says. *Ah, look who the doorman is today. This should calm your racing heart.*

Or make it race faster, Shae jokes, smiling inside her hood, appearing to anyone watching as if she's relaxed and enjoying herself.

It's what I need to do. Appearing scared puts us all in danger. I have to try harder.

Look ahead, little one.

I force my mouth into a small smile, and when I raise my face I meet Nathaneal's gaze head on. His blue eyes are as intense as ever. He's so beautiful. How lucky am I to have him in my corner, wanting *me*, loving *me*, fighting the odds and taking the biggest risks to rescue *me*.

As we draw close to the exit he holds open the door. When I walk past him it feels as if I'm floating in a cloud, moving in slow motion. My eyes remain glued to his and, unable to stop myself, I turn my head back to hold on to his gaze for as long as I can.

Shae's grip on my arm tightens as she tugs me forward. But Nathaneal is not looking away yet either. His eyes are emitting so much love I can't force myself to look elsewhere.

Eventually he releases his breath and blinks. *Eyes down now, sweetheart*, he forges with a spine-tingling smile. *We are almost home, and then we can look upon each other until the end of days.*

With difficulty I drag my eyes away from his, and to force myself into the present moment, I take note of my surroundings.

It's a carnival atmosphere outside, with hanging lanterns, dancers in bright costumes of silk and tulle, jugglers spinning balls high into the air, fire walkers, glass eaters, clowns performing acrobatics without nets and many more activities. A rocket launches into the sky with a hiss and a loud bang. Instinct has me ducking, but Isaac's voice sounds in my head: *Look up, Ebony.*

An explosion of pretty lights in the pattern of an emerging flower opens up in the dark sky, dissolving over thousands of angels who 'ooh' and 'ahh' as more colourful fireworks burst into life.

And while the spectacular fireworks display occupies my thoughts, I hardly realise the closeness of the white perimeter wall. Michael and Shae watch the patrolling soldiers intently, waiting patiently for the right moment. When the soldiers are distracted by the fireworks display, they calmly wing into the air.

It's that *time?* I ask Isaac.

Yes, my lady, but don't you worry; I've done this before.

I watch him watch the soldiers on the wall, making sure I'm ready for when his hands close around my waist. He flicks me a glance and I nod. Scooping me up in one seamless movement, he leaps into the air, clearing the wall before releasing immense white wings that lift us high really fast. He shoots into the sky like an arrow, his magnificent wings barely moving, making hardly any sound while shifting large volumes of air. And I can't help thinking he really is good at this.

Tash brings Mela up next, followed by the others, who catch up and fall into formation around us.

Between the angels' beating wings, fireworks setting off lights in the sky, and fingers of early dawn creeping up the distant horizon, I spot soldiers flying towards us from the palace's eastern side. My heart quickens as I'm sure it's Luca coming after us, only for me to realise in the next burst of red, white and pink that it's Prince Gabriel in front.

Some soldiers appear to have trouble flying on their own, but as I watch them help one another fly as hard as they can towards us I start to believe – *really believe* – that I'm going to make it out of Skade today, and so will all the angels who worked hard to make it happen.

Look ahead, Isaac links, indicating with his chin the gates shimmering like a waterfall in the northern sky. We're still a fair distance from them, but each wingbeat brings us closer to freedom. I spot a burning ring of fire in the centre gate. This must be what Nathaneal did to break into Skade. I swing my head round to catch Mela's eye, expecting to see joy or at least relief, certainly not the shocked look etched on her face.

I glance down towards the ground and my heart skids to a halt at the sight of a livid Prince Luca with his highest-ranked general – Ithran – at his side as always. The two deploy their shiny black wings and leap into the air. Soldiers in black armour follow not far behind.

He's coming for me. Isaac, this time he's never going to let me go. He's going to turn into the beast and –

Stay calm, Ebony, Isaac links.

You see them, don't you?

I see.

And those?

I point further afield to where more enemy soldiers are taking flight. Hundreds more. Commanders appear to be rallying their troops on the ground before sending them up in rows to give Luca air support. And yet still more soldiers are running out of apartment buildings and houses. At this rate there will soon be thousands pursuing us.

I squeeze my eyes shut and take a deep breath as the familiar unnerving sound of battle horns begins playing their warning tune across the land.

35

Nathaneal

Isaac is carrying Ebony because I trust him. In the years we journeyed from land to land searching for her, he protected me when I needed it, and he led the way when I was too young or inexperienced and couldn't. As my mentor and friend, he's never failed me. I trust Isaac with my life, and today I trust him with the one who is dearer to me than life itself.

I knew I wouldn't get Ebony out of Skade without a fight. Oh, I had hoped not to spill blood, but that was naive of me. It will be hard on her should even one life be lost as a result, but once I have her home again we will find a way to heal each other as we always did during our time together in the spirit world.

Anticipating I am about to become especially busy, I glance at Ebony in Isaac's arms one more time. She's anxious – understandably – but she's safe, and for now that will do.

So leaving her in Isaac's care, I turn my attention to the gates in the northern sky. So close, yet … those horns playing their tune tell me the battle is imminent. The enemy is gathering, forming ground units first as they prepare to come after us and after us and after us. Luca will not stop until he has Ebony back and has extinguished my life. He tried sealing the gates, but I broke through them. He has run out of tricks. There will be no next time. Today it is either him or me. By the end of this battle only one of us will still be breathing. Only one will still have their soul.

Dawn is filling the clouds above with crimson light. I'm counting on there being enough warmth in this Skadean sun to carry out my final battle plan, my own last trick. With help from my two most powerful members, Michael and Uriel, I will create a catastrophic event that will end the war between angels of light and of darkness here on this day, and hopefully forever.

Having ordered Gabe and Uri to retreat once Team One was in the air, I search for signs of them and their team members now. They're on the way, but catching too much fire and taking too many hits. *Everyone, maintain formation and close in tight. Jerome and Sami, your powers are needed down near the eastern wall. Go give Uri and Gabe a hand, and do some damage.*

They take off, leaving behind only a wisp of displaced air from their invisible wingbeats.

This is where we will make our stand, high in the northern sky where, should things not … go as planned, we can still intercept Luca's army and stall them long enough to give Isaac and Tash enough time to escape into the Crossing with their precious cargo.

It's not long before Gabe and Uri and their team members begin to arrive. They join our pyramid formation, taking their pre-assigned positions along our northern and southern lines, keeping Isaac and Tash protected in the virtual centre.

When Luca realises we escaped his palace by another means than the lane, and that he's just missed the chance to cut my numbers down by two-thirds, he growls a lion's roar, making the air between us shudder. But, consummate fighter that he is, he regains his composure and continues preparing for the battle of his life, a battle I promise he will have.

Michael catches my eye. *We could make a dash for it now that we're all together.*

True, but it would be a temporary solution. The wall my brother needs to build could take months or longer, and in that time harm will befall angels of both light and dark as battles rage over and over again. Some souls should never return to Earth. Nor can the demons and monsters Luca has created in his laboratories find a home there. We can't let them through our defences. If we should fail to stop Luca here, in his world, he will take this battle to the skies of Earth. And then everything will change. Human beings would live in constant fear and danger. Our High King has foreseen this. So, no, Michael, this battle must be conclusive, and we must fight it here. Now.

It's what I should have done when I had the chance, and maybe my Theze …

Hearing the pain in Michael's voice, I give Ebony another final glance. Michael lost his wife, Thereziel, in a battle with the Dark Prince, but I'm not going to lose Ebony. I can't let Luca get his hands on her again. I can't let him create an invincible army from their offspring. *Michael, Uriel, you know what I need you to do. Begin now.*

Both immediately start drawing up their powers.

Isaac and Tash, whatever transpires, hold your positions and do

*not involve yourselves except to defend your cargo. If, however, the
enemy breaks our lines, leave immediately and do whatever you
must to deliver your cargo home safely. Understood?*

Affirmative, they confirm simultaneously.

Nathaneal, Ebony calls out, her thoughts weighing heavy
with guilt, *I can help. Don't hide me away.*

It seems Ebony has begun to comprehend her
exceptional powers, but without wings the element of
unpredictability could prove too dangerous for the one
holding her.

I forge a private link between us. *Ebbie, for us to have a
future together – and for the sake of all mortals on Earth – I need
to know you will remain safe. Will you do this for me?*

She links back, *Yes. OK. But will you stay safe for me?*

Michael hears her and flicks me a worried glance. The
stakes have never been higher. But I can't lie. I wouldn't.
And I won't make a promise I'm not sure I can keep.
*Ebony, I will do whatever it takes to ensure the future is safe for
us both.*

Though she's shadowed by Isaac's glow, I still see her
blink hard and hold it long, and when she opens her eyes
again they're as resplendent as the elusive purple diamond.

It's not exactly what she wants to hear, and it takes an
effort for me to look away without pulling her from Isaac's
arms into mine. I want to kiss her tears away so much it
hurts. I want to plant kisses all over her face, then take my
time with her mouth.

They're gaining speed, brother. Where are you? Gabe demands
as he takes his front-row position between Uri and Sol.
Whatever you're going to do, you had better hurry.

Are your soldiers in position?

Yes, yes. Hurry, Thane, can't you see them?

Our enemy rockets towards us in units of a hundred by a hundred, with Prince Luca and General Ithran at the head.

All teams, arms ready and await my command.

Without a moment to spare, I reach into my core and summon my powers. They throb to life, pulsing through my veins, pushing against muscles and bones and skin. *Not yet.* I hold back while I build and build.

Pushing my arms out, palms forward, I release my power as a pulsing beam of green light. Michael and Uriel direct their power into mine, and combined we create a torrent of flashing fusion energy, a tunnel at the beam's centre shooting out rivulets similar to solar flares. More powerful than lightning, the beam resembles the sea-green colour of a fluorescent ocean, a barrel a surfer might dream about, but it's not water the three of us are creating, it's raw binding energy, enough to power a small star.

We reach capacity and separate our power-streams. I direct mine into the rising sun, and because it's travelling the furthest I dig deep into my core to propel it on with staggered bursts of more pure power. It rips through the upper atmosphere, tearing through the protective layers that surround this world, zooming into space at colossal speed until … until … *bang! Bang! BANG!* It hits. The shock wave distorts space, creating a shimmering green aurora far across the Skadean sky. On the ground buildings shake, windows explode, while angels and souls run screaming into the streets.

Michael directs his power-stream into the river, where it

makes a colossal splash, creating a tsunami that rolls into streets, enters low-lying buildings and floods outlying streams.

Uri sends his into the clouds. A bright flash of light spreads across the sky in ripples. Clouds move, gathering together, and as they fill with ice crystals they begin their anticlockwise swirl.

With my power still pulsing into the sun, molecules in the high atmosphere change, warming the same ice crystals Uri captures in his swelling storm clouds.

It comes together rapidly, lightning and thunder the first signs to alert the capital, throwing Odisha's inhabitants into disarray, including Luca and his general. They order their troops to slow down, to coast in position, as they attempt to work out what we're doing and how to counter whatever this is.

But them taking a few seconds to figure out what we're doing is precisely what I'm counting on.

Hurry! Gabe forges. *When Luca realises what you're doing, he's going to get out of there fast, and he's going to come straight for you, brother, and then the rest of us.*

I check on Uri's developing storm and watch as the thick black disc-shaped clouds expand, consuming more and more surrounding clouds as they drink in the moist air Michael is bringing up from the river.

The moment Luca figures out we have created a hurricane, the whole of Skade hears his animal shriek. I keep my eyes on him and notice something strange happening. The air blurs and stretches around him, and as it clears I see his shape has altered – considerably. He's taller, more so than an

275

Archangel. But what's more startling, is that Luca's upper body is now that of a beast with horns that curve round almost full circle, ending in pointed tips. He shakes his head, now larger and, shockingly, that of a bull with glowing yellow eyes, and the sound that comes from inside him raises goosebumps across my skin.

I draw up more power and thrust it into the main stream, where it pushes the storm to the point where it can now continue to build with a force of its own – a tropical cyclone of cosmic strength that grows and grows and covers the entire city from the western boundary cliffs to the river in the south and into the volcanic regions of wilderness far into the east.

Our job is complete – well, mostly. I lower my arms and sigh. I have not felt this weary before, and yet I will need more strength to finish this.

Gabe grips my shoulder and shakes his head, grinning with elation and gratitude. 'You did it, brother! You did it!'

Shae reaches down from above me and ruffles my hair. 'Well done, my prince.'

We grow serious again quickly when cries and shrieks from thousands of enemy soldiers caught in the storm reach us. They're fighting a losing battle with one of nature's most violent cataclysmic events. And as hurricane winds toss our enemy about like toys, something flashes red from inside the hurricane's silent eye.

'No. No-no-no.'

Shae asks, *What is he doing? What's going on, Thane?*

I can't let him escape, Shae, I can't.

It appears that Luca – still in the form of the beast – has

located the hurricane's eye and is utilising this calm air to retaliate. Using his four black wings, he maintains a steady position and stares at me through masses of whirling clouds, his glowing yellow irises revealing the fury of his obsessive insanity.

And even though he is clearly stronger in the beast's form, he ignores the cries of his soldiers and their outstretched arms reaching for him. His focus is on his hands, where he's moulding fire into two golden orbs. They darken as he intensifies their concentration. Fire is in Luca's blood, always has been, though no one knows why. And now he's using it to … what, exactly? Burn his way out?

Apparently not.

Luca hurls his two fireballs at our pyramid formation, his intention no doubt to scatter us like pins. They pass through the hurricane's eye wall first with ease, picking up speed as they continue zooming through the spiralling, wind-driven thunderstorms, rain bands and rotating cyclonic winds. And still the fireballs keep coming at us, straight through a hurricane that covers an entire city.

To the gates! I order, relieved to see Isaac and Tash are already on their way.

But the fiery orbs don't make it through the outer hurricane walls. The relentless winds are finally slowing them, catching them, and in the swirling mayhem the orbs split open. Fire spills out like wine tumbling from a pair of carafes. Crushed and battered debris catches alight, flames spreading through the entire hurricane from top to bottom.

It is a sight both spectacular and horrific. It has us

stopping to stare. The fires are changing the hurricane's balanced composition. Explosions erupt throughout, some with such force they fling Luca's soldiers screaming into the atmosphere or to the ground. More debris ignites, becoming a maelstrom with soldiers caught up in the blaze, which is fanned by the powerful churning winds.

The fire spares no one except Luca and General Ithran, still in the calm centre. I stare at Michael a moment, the taste of horror bitter in my mouth. *He's going to escape.*

Michael's grim frown gives way to a small smile of hope. *I'm not so sure, cousin. Look again.*

The tropical storm is collapsing in on itself, with masses of clouds, wind, ice crystals and fire rushing towards its centre – which Luca-the-beast and his general are now hurriedly attempting to vacate. But the pressure of all that internal condensing is keeping them trapped inside a dense whirlpool of blazing matter.

'What's going to happen to them?' Shae asks.

No one answers. No one knows.

In the end it happens so fast that if any of us watching had blinked, we would have missed it. The storm condenses so thoroughly that the energy produced wrenches apart, limb from limb, the bodies of the last two remaining angels – Prince Luca and General Ithran. Those of us left watching fall silent as extreme forces tear Luca and Ithran's heads from their torsos, then their arms, legs, feet and hands, and even fingers, toes, eyes, hair. Body parts thrash around the shrinking centre, smashing into each other, condensing further and further until there are only molecules and atoms left spinning.

When there is nothing left to condense, what remains is a black tube of energy no bigger than a matchstick, than a toothpick, than a string impossible to see with a human eye. Bright light begins shooting out from both ends as it suddenly erupts, sending clouds of gas and dust hissing and spitting into space.

36

Ebony

Isaac's wings slice through the air. With every massive beat he carries me closer to freedom. But what will my freedom cost this world? Odisha is a wreck, with high-rise buildings tumbling to the ground; debris floating in flooding streets; screaming soldiers dropping from the sky, burning alive.

'Ebony, nothing you did caused this. And there is nothing you can do to change the outcome.'

He whips off his cloak and drapes it around me. We're so near to the punctured gate but the heat is already becoming unbearable. Flickering shadows turn gold and brighter gold as we enter a tunnel of flames.

With no thought for himself, Isaac turns me one way and another, shielding me from the turbulent reaction occurring around us. I'm grateful that he's taking no chances with me, but I don't deserve his special treatment. One day I will return the courtesy.

Being this close to freedom has my excitement building, but until Nathaneal and every soldier he brought with him pass through the gate, I will be worried.

Then we are through and Isaac is unravelling his cloak from around me. I take my first deep breath of nontoxic air and look around. The tunnel is busy with soldiers preparing for battle. Well armed, and in Gabriel's colours, they're stationed along the twelve gates and on both sides of the bridge.

Tash and Mela come through behind us. The dome tunnel with its crystal bridge is new to her and her boggling eyes show her astonishment. She reaches out, her hand grasping my lower arm, and through a mixture of laughter and tears she whispers, 'I'm going home.'

Elijah and Lhiam come through next, and Mela turns and disappears in the embraces of her two leading rebel lieutenants.

Isaac glances over my head at something behind me. I spin round to see my sister running at me, her boots click-clacking on the crystal bricks, her elation emphasised by her glowing skin. 'She looks like the sun,' I mumble in awe under my breath.

'Easy, wife,' Isaac warns.

But the energy exuding from Shae's body is warm, and as we embrace her love folds over me. It's just what I need to help break an increasing sense of surrealism.

Skade is no longer my prison.

I'm not in Luca's apartment.

And though I still have the wedding dress on, I'm not becoming his wife before thousands of witnesses.

'Shae, I'm free.'

She doesn't say a word, and from the way her bottom lip is trembling I'm not sure she can right now. She puts her hands on my shoulders as if to steady herself. 'Ebony, you really are free. Completely. Utterly. Prince Luca, King of

Skade, monster, beast, whatever he was or whatever you want to call him, he will never harm you again.'

'Luca is dead?'

'That he is,' Michael confirms, coming through next. His golden eyes sparkling, he puts an arm around my shoulder. 'It's all over, little one. Luca no longer exists.' His smile fades as a distant look appears in his eyes, and in a faraway voice he says, 'You always knew this day would come. Go, and rest easy now, my love.'

I step back to search his eyes, suspecting he's remembering when Luca killed his wife. But he gives me another warm smile. 'I'm fine, little one. Thrilled that you're safe and my cousin doesn't have to go through what I did.'

I'm thrilled too, but I can't relax yet. 'Michael, where is Nathaneal?'

'He's not far behind.'

I nod, relieved but still on edge, as I will remain until I see Nathaneal with my own eyes. 'Who killed Luca?'

'No one exactly,' Michael says.

'Then how?'

'Luca was right in the hurricane's eye when the storm collapsed. His body – and General Ithran's – tore apart when internal pressures caused the storm to condense exponentially. In the end there was nothing left but extreme dense energy that erupted into gas and dust.'

I keep looking at him with my mouth open, so he spells it out clearly: 'Ebony, Luca is completely destroyed.'

While the reality of this news sinks in I look for Nathaneal among the group of soldiers just arriving. A few have burns and other injuries that Jezelle swiftly attends to, with Isaac and Tash helping to triage them, while Solomon, Shae, Mela and I move back to make room.

The bridge is already a hive of activity when a few hundred more soldiers fly in wearing Gabriel's colours and full armour. They march down the tunnel, bringing with them trunks filled with weapons they quickly distribute.

The sight, so much like preparations for war, sends a chill through me. 'Shae, why do we need all these weapons now? We're not invading Skade, are we?'

Isaac reacts to my concerned voice. 'Would that worry you, Ebony?'

'Any war would worry me, Isaac. An invasion by either side would destroy good and bad, aggressors and the innocent alike.'

He nods. 'Wise words, sister-in-law, but rest assured we're not invading Skade; we're protecting Earth.'

Shae explains. 'Even though Prince Luca doesn't exist any more, we still have to ensure that none of the creatures that live in Skade escape, such as his supporting angels who might rally and retaliate, the demons he created over thousands of years and dark souls that should never return to Earth.'

Mela asks, 'How long before the gate is repaired?'

Shae shrugs. 'That depends on how fast Gabriel's troops can build the wall.'

'A wall?' Mela's knees buckle. Elijah and Lhiam rush to hold her up. She hoists herself to her feet. 'How long will that take, because anything more than a few hours is too long?'

No one answers. And the words they're not saying give me a bad feeling.

Meanwhile, Mela is looking frantic. 'Doesn't your prince know there is only one way to seal a breached gate and it's not with a wall?'

He's through. I feel him though I can't see him yet. As my heartbeat goes into overdrive, I thank the stars and everything and everyone that helped to keep him safe.

Solomon says softly, 'He knows, Mela.'

'Then he must do it!'

'It's complicated,' Solomon says, his voice carrying a tight edge. She hears it and says no more.

I push through a dozen soldiers to get to Nathaneal and I can tell he's pushing through at the other end to get to me. I feel him getting closer and closer as soldiers fall left and right out of our way, until suddenly there's no one between us, and our eyes meet. 'Ebony,' he says breathlessly. 'Come here.'

He opens his arms and I jump into them. He lifts me above his head and swings me around. Whistling, clapping and cheering breaks out. Nathaneal lowers me slowly, and the way my body brushes his on the way down awakens my cells like nothing ever has before. Then his lips devour mine. I can't breathe, so I breathe him into me in great gasps and he moans and plants soft kisses all over my forehead.

His eyes meet mine. 'Are you hurt in any way?'

'No. I'm fine. And you?'

'I'm good *now*.' He smiles. 'Luca can never bother you again. Did they tell you?'

'Yes. Thank you, with all of my heart.'

'Unfortunately there's still work to do.'

'So I hear, but I'm going to help you now.' It's a statement not a question. He looks into my eyes, shifting his gaze from one to the other, then he nods.

And just like that, everything feels right with the world and I know I am exactly where I should be.

But something suddenly alerts my senses. I rub the back of my neck and look around as my mind spins in confusion. This is what it feels like when my Guardian alarm blasts into life. But that could only mean one thing. 'Jordan is here?'

He doesn't deny it.

'Where is he? Can I see him? Why did you bring him?'

'It's a long story. I'll explain as soon as I've checked with Gabriel that his soldiers are in place and have begun constructing the wall.'

'Everything is in order,' Gabriel says, coming up beside us.

'And the rest of your troops?'

'Are on their way.'

Mela touches my arm. 'Did you say Jordan is here?'

Nathaneal turns to Gabriel. 'Gabe, have Jordan brought down. He's lived without his mother for long enough.'

Gabriel flies up through the blue light and brings Jordan back himself. Jordan is looking for me before his feet touch the ground. When he sees me, his grin could paint the sky. We hold each other for a few very precious moments. 'I thought I'd never see you again.' He glances up at Nathaneal. 'All is forgiven. You got her back, and that's all that matters. The rest is —'

He sees Mela and freezes. 'Ebony, is that who I think it is?'

My voice is thick with emotion. 'Your mother is alive, Jordan. You're looking at her now.'

He walks over to Mela and they study each other.

'How can this be?' Jordan asks, still not quite allowing himself to believe it yet.

'Luca lied and manipulated us all,' Nathaneal explains. 'But it's over now, Jordan. Luca is dead, and you and your mother can be together.'

Mela struggles to hold back her emotions. 'You've grown so big!' She thrusts out her hand about waist high to indicate the height he was the last time she saw him.

Subtle laughter ripples through everyone. Some wipe tears away as mother and son embrace for the first time in eight years. It's a private moment, but impossible to look away from. When I glance up, Nathaneal's eyes are on me, glistening. He smiles and winks and my love for him swells and grows impossibly deeper.

Michael and Jerome are at the gate assessing the situation in Odisha. They return with worried faces.

'What's going on?' Isaac asks, getting our attention.

'It's anarchy down there,' Michael says. 'Troops are trying to take control of the looting. And there are souls massing that don't look anything like humans.'

'Up this high, at least the souls shouldn't bother us,' Jez says. Then she notices their troubled looks. 'What's different about those souls?'

'They have wings,' Michael says.

Everyone gasps. Even the soldiers stop what they're doing until Gabriel yells at them, ordering another newly arrived unit to begin laying the foundations for the wall.

Jerome touches Nathaneal's arm and says softly, 'Bro, we got a problem.' He jerks his head at the gate. 'The reaction is escalating. It's especially visible on the inside. We don't have long before the entire gate disintegrates.'

Nathaneal turns to Gabriel. 'The wall must be completed in the next few hours.'

'That's impossible!' Gabriel protests. 'There's a process to making these bricks. They have to be set in a high-temperature kiln.'

'Make it happen.'

'My warriors can hold back anything that comes at us for as long as we have to. The rest of my company will arrive soon, and I'll allocate half to construction, the other half to patrolling the gate.'

Jordan is so happy he's oblivious to the escalating tensions in the air, making my Guardian alarm hum contentedly. Keeping an arm around his mother and a big grin on his face, he asks whoever is listening, 'Does this mean you people have got this covered and we humans can leave now? I would really like to take my mother home now.' He looks over at Nathaneal. 'Will she be able to live with us?'

'Of course, Jordan.'

'Oh, man, that's great. Thanks, mate.' He squeezes Mela's shoulder. 'Did you hear that, Mum?'

She nods and gives him a big smile, but can't dispel the worry from her eyes. Jezelle sees it too and gently coaxes the pair to a safer distance along the bridge.

When she returns Michael gives her a quizzical look and she shrugs, 'I didn't want to burst their happy little reunion when the flying dark souls arrive and we enter battle mode.'

Michael quips, 'You're not getting soft and mushy on us, are you, Jez?'

'Not in your lifetime,' she returns. 'Just saving myself work for when the gate disappears and all the inhabitants of Skade decide to leave for a better world.' She turns to Gabriel. 'Seriously, do we have enough military power here, right now, to stop those other creatures Prince Luca kept hidden in his underground compounds? You know I'm not talking about dark souls with wings.'

Nathaneal calls Lhiam and Elijah over. 'What did Skade's king keep locked in those underground compounds?'

Elijah says, 'That would be the chimeras, my prince.'

A chorus of exclamations erupts but quickly dies down when Nathaneal lifts his hand. 'How many?'

The two rebel Thrones glance at each other uncomfortably before Lhiam quietly clears his throat. 'Five hundred thousand, give or take a few hundred. Their populations alter daily. Some kill each other, some breed together and have … *infant* chimeras, but the king's preferred method was genetic modification. He would pit teams of scientists against each other in a competition of who could create the deadliest, fastest abomination. Of those winning designs, he had thousands cloned.'

Chills slink deep into my bones and everyone else's by the gasps of shock and outrage that greet this news.

Gabriel allocates more soldiers to building the wall.

Nathaneal glances at the foundations already beginning to show, then asks Gabriel to show Lhiam and Elijah the wall plans and brick-making formula put together by a specialist team of scientists, engineers and biochemists. He asks the Throne rebels, 'When this wall is finished, knowing it has been constructed out of two of the strongest elements in the universe, in your opinion will it hold back the chimeras?'

They examine the plans, then the bricks and mortar already laid, referring back to the formula and talking amongst themselves. Lhiam even tastes the mortar mix before he turns back to Nathaneal and sighs, shaking his head. 'No, my prince, I'm afraid it won't.'

'Oh, come on!' Gabriel cries out. 'Of course it will.'

'Believe me, Prince Gabriel, my brother and I want your wall to hold too,' Lhiam says, 'but the chimeras were genetically engineered for strength. They will bust through this wall as if it were cobwebs.'

As overjoyed as Mela is to have her son back in her arms, she's too concerned with the gates to stay away. She hears what the lieutenant is saying, and approaches Nathaneal with tears in her eyes. 'My prince, you don't have enough soldiers here to stop what's coming. I've seen one of those creatures up close. I only survived because Ebony healed me. Those creatures could scare a human to death just from fright.'

Gabriel snaps at her, 'We get it. You're terrified. You have a lot to lose.' He flicks a pointed look at Jordan, who's still standing midway along the bridge, watching quietly.

My Guardian alarm tingles as I pick up Jordan's rising concern. Catching my eye, he gives me a small grim smile and starts walking back up to us.

Meanwhile, Gabriel continues to rant at Mela. 'Your mortality sees death knocking at your door at every opportunity. All humans do. It scares you. You can't help it. You're obsessed with the event. It's as if you suckled your fear of death in the womb and when you were born the taste remained in your mouths, and so each morning you wake and wonder if today is the day.' He looks at Mela with scorn. 'Lady, you have no concept of what my warriors are capable of achieving in battle.'

'That's enough!' Nathaneal yells. 'Isaac, Shae, Soloman, take Jordan, Mela and Ebony home to Mount Bungarra. Fly as fast as you can. Do not separate in the Crossing. Tash, you will go with them to assist with their rotations. Do not stop until you are through the portal. Go directly to the monastery and make report. Warn the Brothers of an impending attack … on Earth. Tell them to send word to the Archangels to mobilise full battalions immediately.'

'Wait!' I call out. My Guardian alarm is starting to sting. I'm going to see if I can allay Jordan's fears in a second, but before these angels waste their time on me I have to explain, 'Nathaneal, I did what you wanted earlier because I was in the air, but I'm not leaving this time until this is over and you're free to return home with me.'

Sami appears suddenly, panting and shedding her invisibility in front of our eyes. 'My prince, we have only minutes before the first wave of …' She glances at Lhiam. 'Soldier, you may call them chimeras, but from what I've just seen, they're *monsters.*'

Nathaneal looks around, mentally counting heads. It's chaotic with infantry moving into action and setting up weapons all over the place. He yells out, 'Gabe, pull your warriors off constructing the wall and ready them for battle.'

'Affirmative.' Gabriel takes off, bellowing orders as he flies to various points along the bridge. Soldiers, both male and female, move instantly at his commands.

My Guardian alarm is going crazy now and I look for Jordan but can't see him in the chaos. Meanwhile, Nathaneal asks Lhiam and Elijah how we can destroy the chimeras. 'Do you know of any weakness that will give us an edge?'

'No,' Lhiam says.

'None,' Elijah follows without hesitation.

The brothers glance at each other as if selecting which one of them is going to deliver the *really* bad news. Elijah loses. 'King Luca had the chimeras cloned from immortal cells.'

An eerie silence descends over us at this devastating news. Protecting all human life has just fallen on the shoulders of our relatively small group. Not quite a thousand soldiers against half a million undefeatable monsters. The Earth is doomed if we don't hold them back. Our chance of success is slim. But I'm glad of one thing, at least: should the worst happen and the monsters defeat us, Nathaneal and I will be together in the end.

Jerome offers Nathaneal an array of weapons. He selects two long knives, slotting one down each boot, two swords he crosses over his back and something I don't recognise with a long handle that flares bright blue when he takes it in his hand. He then nods at me. My Guardian alarm is still prickling intensely when I glimpse Jordan up ahead. Keen to speak with him to find out why my alarm is reacting so strangely, I quickly select a dagger with a small handle. It feels good and weighty in my hand. Jerome holds out another long-handle weapon like the one Nathaneal selected. I take it in my other hand and it instantly flares bright purple, making Nathaneal smile, though grimly. He whispers, 'No one will separate us again.'

Shae, who is supposed to be taking Jordan home, rushes up to me. 'Have you seen Jordan?'

'He went that way.' I point in the direction I saw him last. 'I want to talk to him too. What's going on, Shae?' I stretch up and spot him moving fast, slipping between angels left and right. 'There he is.' My heart accelerates erratically. Something is wrong. 'Why is he running? Where is he going?'

Solomon suddenly calls out, 'Hey, youngster, what are you doing over there? Come away before you get hurt.'

I lose sight of Jordan for a moment as soldiers come between us, but finally get a clear view of him – standing in front of the gaping hole in the gate, a halo of sizzling flames tearing at the air around him, flickering tendrils appearing to reach for his body.

Mela screams.

Nathaneal swings round, sees what's happening and starts running to the gate, yelling, 'Soldiers, stop that boy!'

Jordan turns to face us. 'I don't expect you to forgive me today,' he calls out, 'but one day, when the Earth is at peace and not destroyed by monsters, I think you will. I'm counting on it.' He flicks a look over his shoulder and now his words come out hurried and urgent. 'Sorry, Mum. I wish we had more time together, but it seems that's not to be for us. I haven't done many good things with my life, but I can do this, and then everyone can go home to

a safe world.' He sees Nathaneal and a pair of soldiers closing in and flicks his eyes to me, calling out in a rush,
'Ebony. Oh God, Ebony. I'm sorry for all the hurt. Please,
tell Amber I'm sorry for hurting her too, and that I … I
was an idiot.'

Then, to everyone's horror, Jordan opens his arms out
wide and simply allows his body to fall backwards.

For an instant I think he's going to drop right through
into Skade, but the gate catches him, holds him in the
empty space as if there's a net, then it goes crazy around
him, shooting out sparks and spiralling loops of fire in all
directions. The soldiers reach him first, but the burst
of flames round the circumference keeps them back. The
flames don't deter Nathaneal though, and he dives for
Jordan, but hits something invisible and hard that flings him
backwards.

The gate wants Jordan.

It knows Jordan is what it needs to repair itself, and it will
stop anyone who tries to take him away.

I look for Mela with the intention of both of us appeal-
ing to Jordan to dislodge himself from the gate. It might be
his only hope. But when I see her, she's staring at her rebel
captains with a mind-linking look. Elijah and Lhiam's
normally stoic faces suddenly crumple but they remain
upright and rigid as Mela turns from them to me. She
squeezes my hands, and with a heart-breaking look in her
eyes, she whispers, 'Ebony, remember what you did for me?
How you saved me?'

'Sure, but why are you telling me this?'

Mela runs, and as I set off after her two sets of powerful

arms wrap around my waist. '*Mela!*' I cry out, pushing against the strong Throne arms that only tighten, the more I try to get away.

Elijah says, 'I'm sorry to put my hands on you like this, my lady.'

'Then don't! Step away, soldier!'

'It was Mela's last command, and as our general and our friend we are duty-bound to honour it.'

'Why is she doing this? She has a chance to live and make up for all those years she had to live in Skade. She deserves to go home.'

'Please accept her parting gift. It's what she wants.'

I reach for my power. It comes instantly. I blast it out and the Thrones go flying. I start running to the gates, intent on stopping Mela, and doing whatever I need to set Jordan free. But the Thrones dive after me. By the time they reach me it's too late, and all any of us can do is watch in horror as Mela sinks into the space with her son.

It shocks Nathaneal, who is in the midst of hurling a ball of sizzling green energy to break whatever is keeping him from rescuing Jordan. It narrowly misses Mela, bounces off the gate and explodes in a shower of sparks.

Jordan screams, his face red raw and with burns on all his extremities. He's obviously in excruciating pain as sparks and tongues of fire slither around him and into him. It's harrowing to watch as he arches his back, jerks his head and screams, '*Arghhh-ghhhh-ghhhhh!*' Again. And again.

The chain reaction occurring around Jordan accelerates when Mela joins him. Two humans must be more potent than one, the cynical thought occurs. Is that why she did it?

To hasten Jordan's death to lessen his suffering?

My Guardian bond burns with rage and my powers push at my skin, needing to free Jordan, needing to free Mela, needing to explode.

I think I hear myself suddenly scream.

Chaos erupts as angels seem to come at me from everywhere. Isaac, Shae, Jezelle, Sami, Jerome and Michael jump on me. They hold me down, stopping me from getting near Jordan. I try to break free, screaming at them to let me go, '*That's my charge whose flesh is burning off his bones!*'

Shae grabs my face in both her hands and plants her forehead on mine. Tears pour down her face, mingle with mine. 'You can't stop him, little sister,' she says. 'It's his will. His right to choose.'

'But he's going to die! They both will!'

I reach for my power. It comes easy and fast and I blast all the angels off me in one thrust. They glance at each other with wide staring eyes and confused expressions, but quickly scramble back on with Solomon joining them.

I'm so angry and mixed up inside, my power runs wild and the red haze returns to blur my vision more than ever before.

'You need to calm your power down, sister, before you hurt yourself. *Really* hurt.'

The angels holding me increase their strength, shoving their power, or calm thoughts, or magical antidote into me. The red haze reduces. While my power still throbs under my skin, I start to focus again.

I find a small triangle of a window between Shae's shoulder and Jerome's torso. Mela is speaking to her son. It's such an effort for her, and there's so much pain between them, that I find I'm rocking and humming and howling.

And the angels holding me rock and hum and howl along.

Mother and son stare at each other for a moment more, before Jordan gives her a small nod and collapses into her arms. She soothes him by stroking his back while around her a tongue of fire lights up her hair. I hear the sizzle, smell the odour, and I rock harder and hum louder. I taste moisture and salt, but I don't know whose tears they are.

Nathaneal stays as close to the ring of fire as he can. His eyes connect to Mela's and the two appear to communicate. But Mela is struck again by a lick of fire that whips around her neck. She doesn't scream, but the sound of her gasping for air, the look of agony on her twisted, tortured face, will remain a vivid memory for all of my life.

Somehow Mela finds the strength to pull her son in closer as the fiery strings of the gate ebb and flow and knit together around them.

Nathaneal rakes his hands through his hair and calls out, 'Mela. Mela!' She opens her eyes and he points to Jordan and thumps his chest with his open palm.

A light of awareness appears in Mela's expression. This was her intention all along, but once inside the gate, the pain or shock or something stole her ability to think clearly. With her eyes locked on Nathaneal's, Mela draws up her strength. With enormous effort she squeezes her son so hard it's as if she's trying to inject him with all the love she couldn't give him since she died and Luca abducted her. She kisses the top of Jordan's head once more and shoves him as hard as she can towards Nathaneal's desperately clawing arms.

But the gate fights to hold on to Jordan. Mela screams out that her love as a mother deprived of her child through no fault of her own is stronger than anything Jordan has in his heart. 'Be satisfied with me!' she cries out before her eyes close and she mercifully passes out.

Nathaneal suddenly spots something and scrambles across the floor. Jordan's foot has come free. He grabs it and pulls, and pulls, prising at each of his limbs until Jordan's entire body is in his arms.

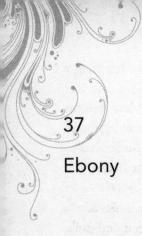

37

Ebony

Jordan dies in my arms.

I watch it happen as the gate seals around Mela, a puff of smoke the only indication that something catastrophic has occurred.

When Nathaneal carries his burnt, battered body from the gate and lays him gently before me, Jordan opens his eyes, stares up at us both, tries to speak but fails. It's then the light drops out of his eyes, like a blue sailing boat drifting into the murky shadows of an endless night. He loses his ability to see, takes one last shallow breath, and his heart stops.

Someone screams with such ear-piercing velocity the tunnel walls tremble. Angels cover their ears and stare at me with wide eyes as if I'm some sort of freak. I realise then that the screaming is coming from me.

Nathaneal takes my face in his hands. His eyes melt into me. Calming me. He lowers his forehead to mine. 'I will bring him back.'

Suddenly everyone swings into action. Isaac squats down beside me, and the next moment he's helping Nathaneal do something remarkable and really strange. Through my blurred vision I notice millions of infinitesimal blue bubbles rising from Jordan's chest. Then the two of them lift out a replica of Jordan coated with a glossy blue sheen. It's like watching someone being reborn. I stare, gobsmacked, as Nathaneal carries this pale, limp version of Jordan and passes him to Solomon. 'He is yours to guard.'

The big angel solemnly replies, 'With my life.'

Nathaneal then gets down alongside Jezelle to start healing.

Shae's hands come down on my shoulders, squeezing them so hard I glance up at her. She smiles encouragingly, indicating Jordan's lifeless body with her chin. 'He's in good hands.'

Nathaneal takes a deep breath and sighs. Jezelle gives him a concerned sideways glance. He looks exhausted. Of course he would be! He's used so much power perforating the gate, creating the hurricane and then pulling Jordan out of the gate, with nothing to eat and no rest in between. Does he have enough left inside to heal Jordan, whose wounds are horrific?

I remember then what Mela whispered before she dived into the gate and gave her life so her son could live. That I healed her. But she's the only person I have. These two healers have years of experience.

Midway along the bridge, a soldier yells out, 'Death Watchers coming!'

Jezelle looks at Nathaneal. 'Are you all right?'

It's then I notice Nathaneal's hands. They're glowing, but only dimly. And they're trembling. I jump down beside him. 'Go. Get out of here. You're all spent. But I'm fresh.' I hold out my hands – steady and glowing with such strength they look as if a fire is burning inside them.

When he doesn't move, I yell, 'Go! *I* will help heal Jordan!'

I flick Jezelle a glance. She studies me for a moment, then nods, and we work together, starting on the worst of Jordan's burns, the top of his shoulders, and his back, where flesh and muscle and sinew have burned completely away. The stench of his charred flesh stings my eyes and turns my stomach, but nothing will make me leave until Jordan is healed.

As soon as we are finished with his back and shoulders, I lay my hands on Jordan's chest, where his scalded lungs need healing from the smoke he breathed in.

Cradling Jordan's soul in his arms, Solomon paces back and forth until Nathaneal calms him. 'But they don't have much time left,' Sol argues.

'What's Solomon talking about?' I ask Shae with a brief look over my shoulder.

She flashes an uncomfortable look at Nathaneal and doesn't answer. I turn to Jezelle and raise my eyebrows. 'Tell me.'

'Jordan has to start breathing soon or his time will run out and his soul will not return to his mortal body.'

'And then what happens?'

Jezelle and the others around us all glance down the tunnel to where six tall angels in long black coats with hoods over their heads stand shoulder to shoulder. Facing them, and standing between them and us, are the angels Michael, Uriel, Jerome, Sami, Tash and Gabriel. 'Who are they?'

Nathaneal hunkers down beside me. 'They're Death Watchers, come for Jordan's soul as agreed in the contract Luca tricked him into making.'

My head shakes. 'No. No. They're not taking Jordan.

Don't let them. You cannot let them take him.'

Jezelle's fists clench and unclench. 'He should be breathing by now!'

'Was it something I didn't do right?' I ask.

'No,' Nathaneal says. 'I've been watching you. Your healing skills are remarkable.'

'So why isn't Jordan breathing yet?'

No one answers me. 'Has this ever happened before?' I'm starting to panic now. 'Should we try CPR or something?'

Jezelle says, 'He's your ward, Ebony.'

'Yeah, so what do you mean? I'm new at this. Someone spell it out for me.'

Nathaneal turns my face up to look into his eyes. 'Only *you* will know how to restart his heart.'

'Oh. OK.' *Shit!*

Jordan died for love. He made the biggest sacrifice any human can. He gave up his life so the world could remain a beautiful place for all those he loved. Whether his love for me was misguided because of the Guardian bond we shared doesn't matter. His heart constantly overflowed with love, and in the end what drove him to make the ultimate sacrifice was his love for mankind. Earth. The entire human race.

I lean over him, bringing my face down to his. 'Thank you, Jordy, for all the love you gave so freely from your heart. On behalf of your fellow human beings, thank you for the sacrifice you willingly made so they can live in freedom without threat or fear.'

I glance at Nathaneal, but I can't worry about what he will think. Not now. Returning my full attention to Jordan,

301

I lower my mouth on to his and kiss him, gently at first, then I prise his lips apart and blow air from my lungs into his.

Someone pulls me back fast, lifting me off Jordan just in time as his soul disappears from Solomon's arms and sinks into his mortal body. His eyes flutter open and he wakes with a gasp, looking dazed. Solomon lifts him to his feet for the Death Watchers to see. The one that appears to be in charge, a male with startling white hair and empty black eyes, steps forward and studies Jordan from head to foot. 'It appears we are not needed here today.'

Nathaneal tells him, 'Your king is dead. His soul, if he ever had one, exists no longer. When you speak with your new king, whoever that may be, make sure he knows that since Jordan died this day, he is now free of any contract Luca may have left behind.'

'A lifetime as measured in the mortal world is but a blink of an immortal's eye. We don't need a contract to claim this boy's soul. We'll return for him one day when he is old and feeble.'

'You will have no cause to return for Jordan, but if out of spite you do, you will have a battle on your hands like you've never faced before.'

Jordan stays quiet, casting a furtive glance between the two powerful angels glaring at each other. When the Death Watchers leave he turns, stares at the perfectly sealed gate for a long moment, then pulls me into his arms and sobs.

No one says a word. The angels discreetly gather their weapons and signal to me that they're leaving. Some blow me a kiss or pat my shoulders, or Jordan's. Gabriel gives Jordan an odd lingering look, a frown between his brows. He seems in a particular hurry to get moving, ordering his soldiers with silent commands that are nothing more than subtle jerks of his head and narrow-eyed glances. He sees me watching him and he gives me his usual salute, the two-finger tap to his forehead, before silently winging his way to the front of his troops and up through the blue light.

Still in my arms, Jordan's sobs reduce to shudders that gradually ebb away until he straightens his shoulders and inhales a deep breath.

Michael comes over and asks, 'Did you see Gabriel leave?'

'Yeah, a little while ago with his troops.'

He gives Jordan a quick but heartfelt goodbye and hurries off, taking Elijah and Lhiam with him, and the sight of the golden-feathered Seraphim flanked by two towering metallic-winged Thrones as they fly up through the blue light is nothing less than breathtaking. But what really astounds me is not their physical appearance, as beautiful as the sight of liquid gold between steel blue is, but how quickly and completely former enemies have come to trust each other.

By the time Jordan is feeling composed enough to tackle the trip home, only Solomon, Shae, Isaac, Jezelle and Nathaneal are left. They each hug him, telling him how sorry they are for the loss of his mother and what a brave and selfless thing she did.

And then it's time to leave.

38

Nathaneal

Solomon asks my permission to carry Jordan home and I approve, knowing it will do them both good to talk privately along the journey. Appointed Mela's Guardian at her birth, and in communication with her after her death and resurrection in Skade, no one knew Jordan's mother better than Sol.

I glance down at Ebony by my side, and almost have to pinch myself at the sight of her smiling face looking up at me. 'Ready, love?'

She nods, and I swing her into my arms and, with Sol, Isaac, Shae and Jez, head towards the blue light, and home.

'What was I like before?' Ebony asks, her eyes lowering as if she's concerned about what I'm going to say.

'You mean, when we lived in Peridis?'

'Yeah, in Peridis.' She lays her head on my shoulder and waits.

'Well, you were gentle with all the creatures there. Big or small, no matter how beautiful or odd-looking, you healed them all. Your compassion knew no end. And each day when the souls arrived, you moved through them looking for the injured.'

'Souls have injuries?'

'Some do, deep on the inside. Those were the ones you pulled aside and healed, removing all signs of their Earthly sufferings so they could live full, satisfying existences in paradise.'

'I did that?'

I nod, smiling down at her, and she shakes her head in contented disbelief.

'When our time to leave drew nearer,' I continue, 'and our soldier training intensified, you shone in the field. Before each session ended, you owned every weapon, apparatus or implement placed in your hands. But you couldn't kill – anything. And our trainer said you would obtain that ability once you came into contact with human beings.'

She lifts her head and studies me for a moment. 'Thank you.'

We then start forming a plan for our last few days on the mountain – on Earth, days where Ebony will be saying goodbye to the life she lived as a human, her friends and family, just about everything she has known, including her beloved Shadow.

But once we're through the blue light everything changes and our plans are scattered to the winds.

It begins with the sight of Michael arresting my brother some hundred or so metres along a tree-studded river. Gabriel's soldiers are gone, likely dismissed by Michael and sent back to their barracks. Elijah and Lhiam have Gabriel's wrists and ankles contained in chains, but my brother is not resisting. If he did, they would know it. We all would.

The five of us descend. Ebony slides from my arms to the

ground. 'What's happening over there, Nathaneal?'

'I'm not sure what Gabriel is doing with the rebel Thrones, but my brother is being –'

Ear-piercing sounds, too high-pitched for humans to hear, interrupt me. The sounds have us all looking up to the sky, where a slit directly above appears to be ripping the Crossing into two parts. Lightning flashes inside the dark void where twelve brilliant white orbs zoom out, punching through the atmosphere at phenomenal speeds, setting off twelve sonic booms across the landscape as the orbs fly faster than the speed of sound.

'Oh, wow, what are they?' Ebony asks.

'Archangels,' I murmur, making eye contact with Isaac over her head. *Did you know?* At his resounding no, I ask Shae, Jez and Sol. It seems no one knew that my brother was in trouble. Except Michael.

As the Archangels draw nearer, gale-force winds thrash around us, bending the trees by the river. Isaac and Sol hold Jordan between them until the Archangels touch down and the winds settle.

They wear long metallic-silver cloaks to the ground with hoods over their heads. One stands out in front – a male – while the other eleven touch down behind him in two rows. They look quite intimidating, especially as six of them are soldiers, wearing full armour under their cloaks. This row turns and marches on silent feet to where Michael, Elijah and Lhiam are holding my brother captive. They pull out a cage of linked chains and bind him with it. So now, even if he did resist, he won't be going anywhere but with his jailers.

Outraged at my brother's humiliation, I leap into the air, throwing my wings wide with the intention of reaching the Archangels and stopping them, or at the least taking Gabe in myself, but the lead Archangel meets me head on, wrapping his hands around my upper arms in mid-flight. 'Stop, Nathaneal,' he commands. 'You will have your chance to speak up for Gabriel later this day.'

Michael? I forge the link between us even though I know Archangels can't be thwarted. *Where are you taking Gabe?*

He looks at me with his golden eyes spilling sorrow. *Empyrean. For questioning.*

And what are you doing with the rebel Thrones? I made them a promise.

I know, cousin, and I'm keeping your promise. They are going for debriefing, after which the High King will reward them for their selfless assistance in Ebony's rescue with his permission to live in Avena.

At least this is good news and I'm happy for the rebel brothers, but what of my own brother?

As I return to the ground the six soldier Archangels shoot into the sky in the same manner they came down, except this time with passengers, Michael, Elijah, Lhiam and their prisoner.

Ebony links her fingers with mine. Her hand is icy cold. We watch in silence as the lead Archangel comes and stands before us. He lowers his hood, revealing long, straight ivory hair, skin as pale as an unripened peach, eyes the colour of polished steel. They graze over us with interest. When he realises Jordan is human, the Archangel tilts his head, peering at him as a bird might to decipher which fruit is the juiciest on a tree. Clearly this Archangel doesn't get out much.

Sol, take Jordan home and keep him safe until our return.

Solomon is in the air, on his way to Earth with Jordan held tight in his arms, before the Archangel grasps that the human is gone.

And beside me, Ebony sighs with relief.

'Greetings to you both, my prince, my lady,' the Archangel says. 'I am Prince Raphael, Captain of the Empyrean Army of the High King's First Guard. I have orders from our High King to return the two of you to Empyrean immediately.'

'Is this about my brother's arrest, Prince Raphael?'

'In part, yes, but not entirely.' He shifts his gaze to Ebony. 'Our High King would like to meet you, my lady.' He looks back at me. 'But we need to leave now.'

Ebony tugs on my hand. 'Don't let them put me in a *lamorak*. I don't need that any more.'

'Wings are not required for this journey, my lady. We will not be using the Crossing.'

'But we're *in* the Crossing,' Jez says.

'True, my lady, but there is a shorter … *method*, known only to Archangels who protect the High King, for obvious security purposes.'

Shae steps forward. 'Ebony is my sister. She's not yet eighteen and therefore I will accompany her.'

Isaac opens his mouth, but Raphael shuts him down. 'Your family ties are by marriage. You shall remain behind.'

Isaac is not about to back down and the two angels glare at each other. 'Prince Raphael, you are correct that my ties are by marriage, and that is the precise reason I will be going with them.'

With his eyes narrowing, the Archangel shifts his attention to Jez. But she's had time to prepare and is ready to state her case. 'I am Prince Nathaneal and Lady Ebony's healer. It is my privilege to travel with them wherever they go and I insist on continuing to do so.'

Raphael raises his eyebrows, evidently aware that both Ebony and I are healers in our own rights. My lips twitch at the audacity of my friends. Raphael, though, is less impressed. He growls under his breath and his remaining team members take a defensive stance.

'We mean no disrespect, Prince Raphael,' I quickly explain. 'We've just come from Skade, where –'

'Apology accepted,' he says, and at a near imperceptible nod from him, his team suddenly surrounds us.

39

Ebony

The Archangels have mesmerising eyes that are difficult to pull away from, especially Prince Raphael's. Standing a head taller than Nathaneal, he towers over us. Shae tries to stay close, but once one of the female Archangels wraps her arms around me it's like I disappear inside her cloak. And once we start moving, shooting straight up into the sky at a speed I can barely imagine, I stop thinking of what's ahead and concentrate simply on hanging on.

'I won't drop you,' the Archangel sniggers. 'Stars forbid, what would your prince do to me?'

A warm fuzzy feeling curls up inside me at her comment. How far has news of our love reached if Archangels concern themselves with what Nathaneal would do if confronted with the threat of losing me again?

Still, at this speed and with winds rushing around us, instinct won't let me relax until we're back on solid ground.

At least Raphael wasn't joking about knowing a shortcut. Actually, I can't imagine Raphael joking about anything. What feels like only a minute later we're landing inside their walled city of Empyrean, apparently right on the doorstep of the High King's Temple.

My Archangel unwinds her cloak and I step out with unsteady feet. For a moment I wonder if all that swirling wind has upset my equilibrium. I quickly realise that's not the case since Shae and Jezelle look fine as they walk around me, gasping at my altered appearance.

Hearing them, Isaac turns from Prince Raphael, takes in the situation in one glance and whistles appreciatively under his breath.

But by now Nathaneal also knows something is up and he walks away from Raphael mid-sentence, shifting Archangels out of his way until he's standing in front of me. His eyes rake over me from head to foot. He takes my hands and holds them out to the sides, then pulls me in close as if stepping up for a dance. 'Oh, Ebbie, you are more stunning than the stars.'

While I don't have a mirror handy, I'm acutely aware that I'm not wearing Prince Luca's wedding dress any more. It turns out I'm in a dress that hugs the upper half of my body in pastel lavender that darkens gradually to deep purple as it flows over my hips to about mid-calf in silky folds and a handkerchief hem. I lift the dress a little at the front and see a pair of strappy high-heeled silver shoes on my feet.

I glance at the Archangel who brought me here with questioning eyes. But all she says is, 'You can thank me later.'

Dismissing his team, Raphael leads us into the Temple, to an open central space where wide corridors spear off in seven directions. As we walk down one of these corridors, I find myself unwinding with a sense of serenity this place seems to be giving off.

The six of us enter a lift that rises to the top level, but instead of stopping there it continues ascending at a much faster pace through floors without numbers. I'm relieved when it eventually stops and Michael is waiting for us. Dressed in a white officer's uniform, he cuts a daunting figure. It's times like these I wish I had my memories back, not just the one or two that occasionally surface. Without memories of my life in the spirit world, or of my time in my mother's womb, and those that Seraphim Angels inherit from their ancestors, everything is new. It keeps me on the outside of this close-knit order. Each memory allows me a peek into the world where I belong. But it's not enough to feel that wonderful sense of belonging I can see they share. They get to belong without trying, and as I go forward into my life as an angel, I wish I could too.

'Hello, Ebony.' Michael smiles, his eyes widening at my appearance. 'You scrub up splendidly, little one.'

'Thank you, Michael. So do you.'

'This must seem like a baptism by fire to you.'

'I have no idea what's going on. I just hang around with you guys for the surprises.'

They laugh quietly, but everyone's mood is subdued. I understand that just being here is a big thing, and that whatever is about to happen could have serious consequences.

Raphael confirms this when he says, 'Ebony, I will escort you to a guest room until our High King is ready to see you.'

'What's this?' Nathaneal asks. 'You never mentioned –'

I squeeze Nathaneal's hand, making it clear I want to

handle this myself. 'Raphael, why do you want to separate me from my family?'

'You are new to our ways –'

'Actually I'm not. Through no fault of my own, I simply don't remember our ways.'

He glares down his very straight nose at me. 'The business we're about to attend to is far from pleasant, my lady.'

'I gather that, Raphael.'

'The High King wishes to spare you.'

'Oh. In that case, please tell the High King I can handle anything as long as I am …' I glance at the others, 'with my own kind.'

Raphael tilts his head for a second without losing eye contact with me. 'Very well,' he says. 'He will allow your presence.'

'Thank you, Raphael.'

He grumbles under his breath as he walks us into a room that's like the interior of an ancient amphitheatre. It's enormous and stunning, with a white tiled floor, high marble columns, intricate architecture and a semicircular arena where a thousand angels representing the nine different angelic orders are already sitting in the stands. Even the light here is different; bright, though the room appears to be windowless. And there is something about the air, as if it were a living organism that has the ability to deepen my sense of empathy, or, the thought occurs, awaken it.

It feels as if I have dived into an ocean of love.

I've never felt anything like this before.

Or maybe I have and I don't remember.

Soft murmurings from the stands die down when the

angels notice us. Heads turn to check out the newcomers. Raphael escorts us to the middle stand. Nathaneal wraps his arm around my waist in a protective gesture. He's keeping me close, and I don't mind in the slightest.

It's then I notice his clothes have changed too and I have to stifle a gasp. He looks incredibly *HOT* in an elegant, Armani-quality midnight-blue three-piece suit, with a white open-necked shirt. I force my jaw to shut and I touch his lapels, brushing an invisible thread from them. I want every angel in this room to know the Prince of Light belongs to me.

Shae, Jezelle and Isaac have changed too, and they look equally stylish and beautiful. They try to keep near us, but Raphael escorts them to the back row, before showing Nathaneal and me to the vacant front row, to the centre two seats directly in front of a round platform elevated by two steps all around.

Michael sits beside Nathaneal, and thankfully Raphael doesn't make him move away.

'Anything I should know?' I ask them both. 'Raphael wasn't exactly forthcoming with information.'

They both chuckle softly. Then Michael leans around Nathaneal and whispers, 'You only need remember that whenever the High King is glowing, don't look into his eyes.'

Just as I thank him a figure of a man manifests into solid form on the platform in front of us. At least eight feet tall, and wearing a white suit and matching long coat, he has a structured face that appears statuesque and yet also kind. His skin is not glowing, so I check out his eyes and find them hauntingly beautiful. Whenever he moves they change colours like the facets of an opal but with the shimmer of diamonds.

The High King walks down from the platform and comes straight over to Nathaneal and *me*. Wrapping his two long hands around ours clasped together, he welcomes us with a smile and the added words inside our heads, *Welcome, both of you. I'm glad you could come. We will talk soon.*

Not sure what I'm supposed to say or do, I just nod. He seems satisfied and walks back to address the entire semicircular arena from the platform. 'It is with great sadness that I have called you here to witness today's events.'

There's not a sound in the room.

'A traitor has been walking amongst you. A soldier of the Order of Seraphim. A captain and a prince.'

Gasps break out but the High King shuts everyone down with a sharp look. 'He was someone you have all welcomed into your homes. Who has drunk your wine and danced at your weddings. He mourned with you when you lost loved ones. Fought by your sides. Commanded your children in battle.'

The outrage is palpable, but so too is a deep sense of sadness. It's this sadness that pours out of the High King and fills the room. His eyes glisten. This is really hard for him. And I get it. He *loved* Gabriel. The thought occurs that he loves us all.

Angels turn and glance at our stand, their eyes roving up and down as if looking for the one who's missing. But no one is saying a word.

'I have gathered you here today to bear witness to this traitor's sentencing.'

Suddenly Nathaneal is on his feet. 'My lord, if I may examine the evidence I'm sure I could sort this out. I think a grave misunderstanding has occurred.'

The High King motions to someone out of sight, and the sound of rattling chains brings goosebumps out on my skin. Six Archangel soldiers in predominantly white uniforms, body armour, helmets, weapons hanging at their sides, walk in with Gabriel in a simple white tunic, his hands and ankles in chains, and force him to kneel before the High King.

Michael, are you sure? Nathaneal asks him in a link open to me too.

Michael's voice rings out like church bells in my head. *The proof is undeniable, as you will come to see soon. Don't let this get under your skin, cousin.*

The High King steps down to stand over the prisoner. 'Prince Gabriel, how do you plead?'

Gabriel turns his head to Nathaneal. 'Help me, brother. Only you can help me now.'

Still standing, Nathaneal frowns and rubs his neck. 'My lord, Prince Gabriel came to me. He confessed, and I forgave him.'

The High King looks at Nathaneal with eyes shimmering with empathy and remorse. 'Yes, prince of my heart, I saw that exchange and I was pleased.'

'He is my brother, and my parents have already lost one son because of the Dark Prince.'

'Nathaneal, listen carefully. Prince Gabriel did not act like your brother when he used a prearranged signal to alert our enemy to the precise moment Lady Elesha gave birth to a destined future queen.'

Nathaneal's head shakes. 'No, no, no, my lord, that was not Gabriel. That was my mistake. I tried to leave the birthing chamber in a hurry and my clothing caught in the protective webbing.'

His glittering eyes still pinned on Nathaneal, the High King is not finished. 'Prince Gabriel was no brother to you when he released the secret underground hatch to our blessed Holy Cross Monastery, allowing twelve Prodigies and Prince Luca himself to enter our Earthly sanctuary. Three Brothers died that day.'

Nathaneal hisses, running a hand round the back of his neck. 'That was you, Gabe? Really? Why?'

Gabriel drops his pleading eyes. Now the truth is out, he's no longer able to hold his brother's gaze.

'Nathaneal,' the High King's voice swells and fills the arena, 'Gabriel was no brother to *anyone* when he signed a pact with the Dark Prince.'

Nathaneal moans as if he's going to be sick. He drops down into his chair, his head in his hands.

My eyes meet Michael's. *This is killing him.*

The worst kind of deceit comes from the ones you trust the most, little one.

'Gabriel was no brother to you when he deliberately delayed investigating a powerful force that had attached itself to Ebony, allowing it time to strengthen and take form and multiply before he knew whether it was good or evil.'

The dark forces?

'Brother,' Gabriel pleads, 'the proof is circumstantial, taken from the imaginings of a human boy whose hormones were driving him crazy for his Guardian. Tell them how unreliable that is.'

Nathaneal turns to Michael. 'Is this true? Is Jordan a witness?'

'It's complicated,' Michael says. 'Jordan figured out that Gabriel was the traitor during his time in the Crossing. He put his life in danger by confronting Gabriel. But there are many more witnesses and documented evidence that I'll bring to your parents' house to explain to you and your brothers in detail in the coming weeks.'

I reach across and tap Michael's hand. 'Can I ask a question?'

But the High King answers before I even voice it. He knows I'm thinking about the dark forces he just mentioned. 'There are seven now. They will not harm you. To the contrary, sweet child, they came into existence already devoted to you. They live to serve and protect you. Earth is not their habitat. Before you leave the mortal realm they will come to you.'

He glances at Gabriel and frowns. 'Were it not for this traitor's sabotage, frightening those angels and forcing them to keep running, you would have learned of their devotion to you sooner and the seven would be trained by now.'

The dark forces are to be my personal guard? All that time they were just trying to get close to me? *The poor things.*

'What of my wife and children?' Gabriel pleads, bringing everyone's attention back to the drama still unfolding before us. 'Please, my lord, do not punish them, for they knew nothing of what I had chosen to do.' He flicks his eyes up to someone in the back row of the Seraphim stand and his eyes become glassy. His jaw is trembling when he lowers his gaze to Nathaneal. 'Brother, I'm truly sorry. I let my desire to be King of Avena overrule my senses. I was wrong. You will make a far better king.'

And there it is. His admission of guilt. Now what is the High King going to do with it?

The High King orders Gabriel to stand and the guards to remove his chains. 'We have seen what happens when angels are banished, and we must learn from the mistakes we made with Prince Lucian and not repeat them. Today Skade lies in ruins. It will take dedication, skill and hard work to rebuild it. Prince Gabriel, I am setting you that task.'

Shocked, the arena erupts in gasps and whisperings. The High King silences everyone with a glowing flash from his eyes and his voice booms out across the arena: 'Prince Gabriel, you will carry the title "Custodian of Skade".' Looking down at Gabriel, the High King's voice lowers but loses none of its intensity. 'This is not a reward. It will take patience, perseverance, humility and above all love. The people of Skade are broken and angry and lost. You have your work cut out. Do you believe you can do this?'

'I ... I don't know,' Gabriel says. 'But I'll try.' He looks up then with a glint of hope in his eyes. 'My lord, how long do I have?'

'The breached gate has been repaired, but the seal of a hundred years remains. This is how long you will have to rebuild the Kingdom of Skade and bring peace and a new way of living to its people. The rebel army has been informed and its soldiers will assist you, but the majority of the inhabitants are used to cruelty and know nothing else. You will need to show them that there is another way.'

The High King lowers a glowing hand over Gabriel's head. 'Prince Gabriel, you have not earned the right to have the power of such a position at your fingertips, so I will be watching carefully to see what kind of ruler you become. If, in a hundred years, I am satisfied with the result, I will crown you King of Skade, but if I am *not* satisfied, you will be stripped of your titles, your powers and your wings.'

'I will not fail you, my lord.'

The High King's eyes soften as he gives Gabriel a wry smile. 'It is not me you would fail, Gabriel. It would be you.'

40

Ebony

There was a time not so long ago when I looked into a mirror and didn't know who that person was looking back at me. Something inside me could tell that those eyes didn't belong to the life I was living. Now I understand why. My eyes see the truth.

And seeking the truth has led me here, to this magnificent arena surrounded by a thousand angels, a species that I now know I belong to, and a High King, a superior being who looks like a man but is not human, and maybe not even angel, but he's in charge of everything. He is the source, the light, the one.

And right now this all-empowering being is looking at me.

Noticing this, the angels fall into a quiet stillness. It's in this stillness that the High King opens his arms out, beckoning me. I get up and climb the two steps up to his platform on legs that feel like jelly. But he keeps his eyes on me, and somehow I can tell that I please him.

'Child of my heart, we have been waiting a long time for you.' He smiles gently down at me and I can't help but smile back.

'You are still a sweet child, I see. Well, you always were. But recently you have come face to face with evil, and though you didn't fully know who you were, evil could not defeat you. Abducted at birth, disguised as a human being, your memories eradicated so you could not know your identity, and raised not to recognise your own kind – no angel should suffer the anguish of such disconnection. This experience with the darker side has changed you. It has made you a child no more.'

He sighs, a troubled, frustrated sound, as if the loss of my youth and innocence is somehow his fault. 'Our enemy did everything possible to keep you from our sight, isolating you in a valley shielded by the walls of mountains, and even changing your name. But you grew into your strengths and became fearless in the face of a daunting enemy. One that exists no more and can hurt no one ever again.'

He looks up at the stands and announces, 'Prince Luca is dead.'

He holds still while the cheers and whistles settle, then turns to me. 'Close your eyes, Ebony.'

I do what he says, reminding myself to keep breathing.

'Ebony, it is now time to put the pain of your past away and look ahead to a future that promises infinite pleasure.' And with my eyes still shut, his joy pulses into me. 'Ebony, you please me greatly, and so I give you this gift.'

He lowers his hand to my head and his touch is electrifying. His long fingers fold down over my forehead, and his golden glow penetrates my closed lids.

Memories taken from me at birth begin to flash before my eyes. One after another, they roll in like a film. They're soon moving faster, a blur of images sliding into sections of my brain, finding their chronological order. Millions of images flicker back and forth at lightning speed.

Eventually he lifts his hand but otherwise doesn't move. The room is dead silent, but my mind is far from calm. It's feverishly processing all the imagery and associated information from my past.

When it's finally over and my mind quietens its frantic pace, I take a deep breath and savour the moment to absorb what just happened, to analyse what his gift will mean to me. The difference it will make.

I open my eyes to find the entire one thousand angels on their knees around the platform and looking up at me with anticipation on their faces.

But I only have eyes for one of them, and right now he's watching me, and weeping. I slip down beside him, wipe his tears away with my fingers, cup his face in my hands, and tell him the nature of our High King's extraordinary gift. 'My love, I remember *everything*. I even remember that my name is not Ebony.'

He clasps his hands over mine and brings them to his lips, where he kisses first one palm and then the other. He's trying to keep his emotions in check, but I can see how much this means to him. I *feel* it, and it makes me want to hold him and weep until I'm spent.

He looks up at our High King. 'Thank you for this great gift, my lord.'

The High King smiles and invites everyone to stay for a banquet. 'Today we celebrate the future,' he says, 'and we honour the return of an upcoming queen, who shall from this day forward hold the title "Princess of Hope".'

Everyone claps and cheers. The atmosphere is so buoyant in the amphitheatre that some angels begin to sing, while others take a partner and dance. Tables are brought in with platters of food and wine.

Nathe, as I now remember I always called him, pulls me into his arms and covers my face in butterfly kisses, exactly as I recall he used to do each morning to wake me up. When his lips meet mine, his kiss is so tender I could cry.

But his sweet tender kisses drive me insane with longing, and when he lifts his head I slide my hand around his neck and bring his mouth back down to mine, 'More,' I whisper. 'I want more. Remember, I have my memories back.'

He tosses his head back and laughs, but then he kisses me in the way I remember. My head spins as desire flares through my body. Shifting his mouth to my ear he murmurs three words, that up until this moment I didn't know I've been waiting almost seventeen years to hear him say: 'Welcome back, Ebrielle.'

41

Jordan

The first thing I do when I get home is take a shower. I peel my clothes off, leaving the pieces wherever they drop. They're rags now anyway. Maybe I'll have enough energy to throw them out tomorrow. Maybe after a long sleep I won't ache so much. Solomon held me so damn tight the whole way that I got bruises, and then bruises on my bruises.

I step under the hot jet, running my hand over the small scars Jez purposely left on my back, so that when time passes and it all seems like a dream, I'll have something to remind me that what happened was real.

Those scars will also remind me what my mother did for me. *As if I could ever forget that experience.* At least now I know the truth. She loved me all along.

I slide to the floor and let hot water hammer over my head and swirl down the drain. I don't move for ages. The heat soothes my thoughts as well as my aching muscles.

I should be ecstatic to know Ebony is out of Skade and safe for the rest of, well, eternity. And I'm happy for her. Of course I am. It's weird though. Part of me is thrilled, but the rest is … I don't know, in a crazy-sad place.

When I had Mum in my arms, all the old feelings from

when I was a kid came back, like her warmth, her smell, that sense of safety you get when your mum tells you everything is going to be all right.

I turn my face up to the hot spray. At least here, in the privacy of my room, in this clear glass cube, no one can see me cry.

42

Jordan

It's been a couple of days since they returned from Empyrean. I had just dropped Amber home after school and arrived back at the house. They walked in holding hands, Shae and Isaac right behind them. Somehow Ebony (as I still thought of her then) looked taller. It could have been the high-heeled boots and tight jeans that made her legs seem to go forever, or her long hair, redder than ever, tumbling to her waist, or the way she seemed at ease, comfortable in her own skin finally. I don't know. But even her eyes had changed. They'd become deeper, brighter violet, and her normally bronze skin, well, she glowed.

She was Ebrielle now. She had found herself.

And tonight we're celebrating her safe return.

By the time I throw on a pair of jeans and a white button-up shirt and head downstairs, the party's in full swing, with angels and Brothers taking up space in just about every downstairs room.

I step into the living room just as Amber arrives with her mum and dad. They've brought Ebony's parents with them, and when Ebony sees them walking in, she launches into her dad's arms, checking him out for injuries at the same time. Satisfied that he's OK, she moves on, taking her mum's face in her hands. They nod seriously at each other, and then they laugh and cry. Their emotions fuel the room so that even the Holy Cross Brothers tear up.

Amber spots me watching from the opposite side of the room and waves. Next thing I know, she's making her way over. I catch myself looking for her through groups of angels and Brothers and pieces of furniture. Something stirs in my gut. An awareness. A sense of something exciting. A perception of maybe ... pleasure? It happens every time I see her now.

And, according to Thane, I don't have to worry about Skinner hurting Amber any more. He won't be using her to make me do what his employer wants. Prince Luca is dead, giving Adam a second chance at a normal life, and he's promised Thane that a normal life is all he wants.

Amber arrives and smiles up at me. 'Hey.'

'Hey.'

'It's so wonderful to have her back,' she says, 'but I can't help wondering how long they'll be staying.'

I shrug. I don't know. I don't want to ask.

'Well,' she says, 'I'm just glad *you* got back in one piece. You'll be here with me now when ...'

I lean towards her, bumping her shoulder with mine. 'Feel like some fresh air?'

She nods. 'Sure.'

We head to the back door, but there's a line to get into the kitchen. Uriel and Tash, with three of their five daughters, who like their parents apparently love to cook, are serving dinner off the bench.

Someone lays their hands on my shoulders from behind and starts kneading my muscles. Without looking, I can tell it's Ebony. I would know those fierce fingers anywhere. I glance up at her, taking her fingers into my hand, and she smiles at me. Not so long ago I would have read this as a sign that she wanted me in a romantic way. But I get it now. I finally understand how the Guardian bond heightens my emotions and my senses when we're in close proximity.

And even though she's talking to me, her eyes are wandering off, seeking him out.

Thane must sense her. He comes out of his study with Michael in tow and stops, looks straight at her and winks. She kisses Amber's cheek, then mine and whispers, 'I'll catch you both later.'

As I watch her walk over to Thane there's a sense of freedom inside me I've never felt around her before. It's such a relief that I smile and sigh contentedly.

'Still can't take your eyes off her,' Amber remarks, her mouth drawn tight, her eyes unable to meet mine. And suddenly she's off, manoeuvring through the angels in the food line, pushing her way out the back door.

By the time I make it out she's halfway to the stables. 'Hey, wait up!'

She stops. I read this as a good sign and run over. But when I try to take her hand she turns and glances into the shadows around the barn.

I thrust my hands into my jeans pockets. 'I was smiling at Ebony walking away because, well, for the first time since I met her, I felt nothing. I had no obsessive thoughts. Amber, all I'm feeling around Ebony now is a sense of relief that I'm finally, *finally*, free.'

'*Free?*'

'Yep. You see, something happened between us that's hard to explain.'

'I heard about it. Everyone has. Ebony healed you and brought you back to life with her tongue in your mouth.'

'That's right and … wait … No, there was no –'

'Jordan, don't get me wrong, I'm really grateful Ebony saved your life.'

I try to take her hand again but she pulls away. 'Listen, Amber, please. There *was* something special about the kiss of life Ebony gave me, but not in the way you're thinking. It's as if she not only kick-started my heart but somehow freed me from my obsession with loving her.'

'*Really?*'

I nod. 'Ebony didn't just give me my life back that day, she gave me back my ability to love.'

Her eyes search mine. 'Jordan, what are you saying?'

'That I don't love Ebony any more. And I think … No, I mean I *know* that I'm … falling in love with you.'

She reaches for my hands. 'Stop talking,' she says. 'Don't say another word. Just come here and kiss me.'

And with a grin I can't keep off my face, I do exactly as she says.

43

Ebony

The party is fun, with lots of angels turning up and heaps of Brothers from the monastery. Some of the married angels, like Uriel and Tash, bring children, and since the three girls that came with them are all over eighteen they look more like their siblings. My natural parents will look young too, I suppose. I really need to get my head around this before I meet them. They decided to wait for me in Avena so our first meeting can be in a more intimate setting, where we can take our time getting to know each other. Shae assures me that I have nothing to be nervous about, and she would know. They're her parents too. It's just hard to imagine what meeting them will be like.

Since returning from Empyrean I've been trying to locate my uncle Zavier, who disappeared once Luca banished him from entering Skade with me. Apparently, he turned up at the monastery the day he returned to Earth, pleading to be taken in. To atone for his crimes he asked to serve his life out as a Brother. And since he's immortal, that will be a long, long time. Even though Zavier was pivotal in my abductions, in the end he did try to save Nathaneal from Luca's trap. I would like to thank him for that. But everyone is leaving now, and since he hasn't shown up, he either didn't accept my invitation or Monsignor Lawrence didn't allow him to attend.

I'm standing on the front deck with Nathaneal beside me, keeping me from falling asleep by tickling me under my ribs at regular intervals.

I might be falling asleep standing up, but I haven't enjoyed myself so much since ... well, I can't remember. I'm especially enjoying watching my best friends looking chummy and close and adorable.

'What are you smiling about?' Jordan asks when he catches me staring.

'Oh, nothing.'

'Are you sure about that?'

I look pointedly at their linked hands. They share a secret smile and Amber's eyes sparkle brighter than the stars. I can't remember when either of them looked this happy. Clearly it wasn't me Jordan needed in his life.

Nathaneal hurries to open the front door when he sees Amber's parents coming out, along with Mum and Dad behind them.

Dad comes straight over with a big hug for me. 'Promise to visit us before you leave.'

'Absolutely, Dad.' He's not asking for much, and this promise is easy to make, saying goodbye is going to be the hard part.

Reuben gives Amber permission to sleep over so the two of us can catch up, even though this is the first I'm hearing of these arrangements. As soon as our parents have driven off and we come back inside, Jordan and Amber wish us goodnight and head upstairs, their hands still locked together.

I can't help but giggle, while Nathaneal smiles and rolls his eyes.

We walk to my bedroom holding hands. At the door Nathaneal plants butterfly kisses all over my face. 'Goodnight, love,' he says with a moan of deep longing.

'Do you want to … come in?'

He snags his bottom lip and tilts his head slightly. 'You should sleep.'

'I could sleep in your arms?'

'Yeah, but then I wouldn't sleep.' With a last lingering kiss, he leaves.

In my room I change into a singlet top and a pair of pyjama pants, slide under the covers and feel my bones and muscles sigh in relief.

I drop straight off to sleep, only to wake with a jolt soon after with pain in my side. I hardly ever get sick, so I don't have much to compare this with, but the pain deepens quickly and before long I'm rolling over and curling my knees up into my chest. Unsure what to do, or how long this pain will last, I sit in my wicker chair for a while and contemplate making a hot chocolate or searching the house for a hot water bottle. But then …

Arghhh!

Shooting pain darts up both sides.

Slipping on my dressing gown, I head downstairs before I wake the others. It's probably something I ate at the party and will soon pass, or … dare I dream it could be …

At the back door, I swap my dressing gown for a jacket

333

and beanie hanging on a hook. Instinct and habit has me heading down to the stables to snuggle up with Shadow. I missed him terribly when I was away and I'm dreading the day I will be saying goodbye.

But midway to the stables the pain hits deeper, shooting under my ribcage, and I drop, gasping, to the ground, which is already moist with early dew. I try to crawl back to the house, but moving is impossible. So I curl up into a ball and do the only thing I can under the circumstances.

I scream.

Lights go on instantly on the top floor. A door bangs, and I'm comforted by the knowledge that help is coming.

Nathaneal arrives first as I expected; he probably leaped off his bedroom balcony. He tucks his wings away, hunkering down beside me. 'Talk to me, Ebbie.'

'I'm hurting.'

'Where? Here?' He cradles my head in his lap, carefully pulling off my beanie.

'No,' I answer. 'My ribs and … *argh*!'

'Your back?'

'Uh-huh.'

'OK. OK.'

'Do you know what this is?'

'I think I do.' A grin begins to form but swiftly disappears when I groan. 'It's all right, sweetheart.' He puts his arms around me. 'I've got you.'

'I heard her scream,' Amber says after a breathless run across the yard with Jordan close behind her.

'I peeked in her room but her bed was empty,' says Jordan. The pain eases a little, giving me a slight reprieve. But then my skin begins to glow and suddenly I'm lighting up the entire area around me. Amber and Jordan stagger backwards, throwing their arms across their eyes.

'Holy crap!' Jordan shrieks. 'What's happening to her?'

I'd like to know that too.

Still holding me, Nathaneal rocks gently. 'It's nothing you can't handle, but we need to get your jacket off.'

Getting my jacket off becomes a challenge when the pain intensifies and I stiffen all over. It grows hard to breathe, and harder to take. It's like I have a rocket under my ribs that wants to launch itself through my spine. I try not to scream when he peels the jacket off one arm.

Amber runs in and helps with the other sleeve. 'This will pass soon, hon,' she says. 'You'll see.'

'It's like … bones pushing against my skin. And … *ohh!* Something is happening. Everyone, you have to move back. Get back.' I lift up into a squat and notice they're all still standing around me. Somehow I have to make them understand they're going to get hurt. 'Something is building inside me.'

'You're not going to explode,' Jordan says, whispering to Nathe with a sideways glance, 'Is she?'

They're still not moving away, and I have no choice but to get up on my feet, shove my hands at them in a get-back motion and scream, 'Everyone, move! *Move! Move!*'

The three of them suddenly fly through the air, coming down hard on the moist grass some ten or so metres away.

'Sorry! Sorry!' I call out as they scramble back.

'It's all right,' Nathaneal says, reaching me first after checking Amber and Jordan are OK. 'We're all fine. How long have you been able to do that?' he asks with pride in his eyes.

'First time, but I've … *argh* … suspected I could for a while.' The pain changes, shifts down into my hips and my glowing body ignites into a lighthouse multiplied hundreds of times.

'Whoa, what's happening to her?' Jordan's frustrations soar. 'Are you gonna heal her now, or what? Look at her. Should we call an ambulance? Thane, do something or tell us what to do.'

'You're not helping by taking your fear out on Nathaneal,' Amber tells him gently as she plucks some grass bits off her top. He looks at her and she says, 'I'm scared too.'

'Nathe,' I ask, 'is this how it's supposed to happen?'

'I'm not entirely sure. You are unique, baby. But I can tell it will be over soon.'

'Good.'

He takes my hand and squeezes it. 'Remember, you've been waiting for this to happen. We all have.'

'What are you two talking about?' Amber asks.

I nod at Nathaneal and he tells them, 'Ebrielle is getting her wings.'

A ripping sound warns me their arrival is imminent. A sense of my insides stretching past where they should reach throws me off balance. Pinpoint electric shocks run up and down my arms and suddenly I'm jolted backwards and lifted into the air two, three metres. The ripping, jerking and tugging go on and on, lifting me a little higher each time. Finally everything stops – the tugging, the ripping, the pain – and I start to come down, floating at first, but then I drop, hitting the ground on all fours.

My wings are out. Nathaneal and Amber and Jordan come running to me even though I'm still glowing like a lighthouse. Nathaneal reaches up and touches the wing swaying above my right shoulder. He looks stunned, his eyes filled with awe. But all I can see is something huge and white and sparkling.

Sparkling?

'They're so *beautiful*,' Amber says.

Jordan simply stares with his mouth hanging open.

I twist round, angling my head this way and that to see them for myself. 'Oh, wow.'

When I was eight years old Mum took me to the village community centre to watch a performance by a local ballet ensemble. Taken with the dancers' beautiful costumes, Mum purchased the fabric and made me a similar one to wear at home. The dancers were dressed as fairies, their outfits created from a fabric called gossamer. This is what my wings resemble. They're delicate and transparent and they shimmer like gossamer.

I tug one down for a closer look.

Startled, Nathaneal cries out, 'Easy, babe.'

'Don't worry; I'll be gentler next time. That kind of really hurt.'

He grins and we all watch as a tiny white feather the size of my littlest fingernail falls into my palm.

While Nathaneal inspects the feather, Amber and Jordan examine my wings with gentle, inquisitive fingers. And it's so strange because I can feel their light touch. 'My wings are sensitive.'

After a few minutes of close examination, we agree there are eight wings in total, and they're all feathers – thousands, maybe even millions. Some are transparent, though most are white or opaque. The largest ones are as long as a pigeon or dove's tail feather, gradually decreasing in size all the way to the outside edge where miniature gold feathers appear seamless and so tiny I would need a microscope to pick out a single one.

Nathaneal is overwhelmed. He can't seem to stop staring, his eyes open wider than usual, his fingers trembling. Like now, as he holds his hand beneath a wing, he marvels at its sheer diaphanous texture.

And it strikes me then, somewhere deep inside, that these are *my* wings. They don't just belong to me. They're not simply a means to give me flight. They *are* me. Nathaneal stands still and silent, watching my expressions change as I take in my wings, so different from any others I've seen. 'They really are beautiful, aren't they?'

'That they are.' He smiles.

'How do I put them away? Can you teach me? Would now be a good time?'

He takes my hands and clasps them between his. 'Now is a perfect time, or you might find it hard to sleep with those wings in your bed.'

'Oh. Ha ha.'

He grins, enjoying teasing me. 'But first we should work on your glow.'

'Yep,' Jordan calls out, 'sleeping across the hall from a lighthouse could prove difficult too.'

Amber digs her fingers into his ribs playfully. We all laugh.

And everything is just how it should be.

Nathaneal tugs me down to sit cross-legged opposite him. 'Look at me.'

I do, and he says, 'Breathe.'

As if by example, he inhales deeply. I follow. He says, 'Again. In. Out.' He smiles. 'Good. Now shift your thoughts to your secret room in your inner core and search for that singular precious thought that's always there for you when you reach for your power, or need to calm down and centre yourself.'

I frown and he makes a fist around my hands, bringing it to his chest. 'In here.'

I close my eyes. 'OK, I'm there.'

'Good. Now, what do you see?'

'Is this a trick?'

I open my eyes and see his frown deepen. 'What do you see?' he asks.

'You.'

His mouth curves into an adorable sheepish grin. 'It's not a trick. I just had you shift your subconscious to something that makes you feel safe. Look at your arm.'

'Wow, it works.'

Jordan laughs. 'Yep, you're not a lighthouse any more.'

Gradually my skin goes back to normal. I glance over my shoulders. 'Will that work with my wings? There are so many. What will everyone think of them?'

'Ebrielle,' Nathaneal says in his calming voice, 'your wings are spectacular.'

Jordan turns to the house and cups his hands around his mouth to make a pretend loudspeaker, and even though no one is in there, he yells out, 'Someone bring this girl a mirror!'

Amber jokingly calls him a moron.

'I'll feel more confident when I know how to use them.'

Nathaneal swings straight into action, first helping me stand. 'Wings use muscles, ligaments and tendons that you control with your mind. With time the messages you send to launch and withdraw your wings will become subliminal and immediate. You don't tell your feet to move when you need to walk, or your hands to reach for a glass, when you want to drink from it, but for the first few attempts at moving your wings, you will need to do just that. It's called conscious concentration.'

'And this conscious concentration will control all eight of them simultaneously?'

'I believe so.'

'You don't sound so sure.'

'I have two sets, not four, but the principals should be the same.'

'What works for Nathaneal,' Amber says, 'will work for you too.' She takes my hand. 'You can do this. My God, if anyone can, honey, it's you.'

Jordan takes my other hand. 'I don't know how, but your time in the dark world has changed you.'

My pulse races in terror. My time in Skade was anything but pleasant. Is there a glimpse in my eyes of what the Dark Prince did to me?

'You have grown more beautiful, Ebrielle.'

Tears run out on to my lashes. I blink them away. It's the first time Jordan has used my true name.

'And your wings are like … butterflies and fairies all in one. They suit you.'

'I couldn't have put that better myself,' Amber says.

'Thanks, guys. OK, I'm ready, Nathe. Teach me how to use my wings.'

As the stars shine down with that crisp luminescent brightness you only seem to get on a cold night away from city lights, Nathaneal gives me my first lesson on operating my wings. It takes a few attempts. With eight wings it's not so easy, but eventually I grasp the concept and learn the skills needed to engage and withdraw my wings in a relatively smooth fashion.

But I'm soon struggling to keep my eyes open. Jordan yawns wider than the front door of a house, which sets the rest of us off and we unanimously decide that since it won't be dawn for a few hours yet, we should all head back inside and catch a few hours' sleep. Tomorrow will be soon enough to tackle the big step of actually flying.

Amber hooks her arm through mine and the boys walk ahead of us. Jordan says something funny and Nathaneal tousles his hair. The nightmare of the last few weeks fades a little as new, brighter memories begin to erase the dark ones.

44

Nathaneal

Ebbie is exhausted and I have no intention of leaving her to sleep on her own this time. Apparently, she has the same idea. She slips into bed, her hand reaching for me. 'Don't leave, Nathe.'

'I'm not. I'm going to hold you and make sure you sleep well.'

As I move to get in she flattens her palm on my chest. 'It's not sleep I need right now.' She locks her eyes on mine. 'It's you.'

'Ebbie ...'

'Come here, Nathe,' she says, her voice low and gravelly and spilling over with need. It pulls at my skin, slams my heart against my ribcage, makes my fingers clench and unclench. I brush my knuckles under her chin and she shudders, cupping my face with her hands. 'Even before the High King gave me back my memories I had remembered fragments here and there, but one especially lingered. It was the first time you sang to me.'

'Really? That's the memory that stayed with you?'

She nods and it takes me a moment to speak again. 'That was the night –'

'I know,' she says, and tenderly wipes away a tear trickling down my face. 'Nathe,' she says, 'before that memory I didn't understand why you were drawn to me. And every minute since we met in the school car park I wondered how … *why* such a beautiful being could possibly love me. It was beyond my comprehension. But the emotion that spilled from your voice in that memory showed me that the love I was seeing in your eyes then – and the love I see now – are real.'

She is so mesmerising, so vulnerable in her honesty that my eyes want to devour her. That night in the spirit world when I first sang to her ended in our first kiss, a kiss that had so much passion it left us speechless and gasping for breath. 'And now that you have all your memories back, do you understand why there could never be anyone else for me? Why I needed you back no matter what it took?'

She gets a teasing glint in her eyes, her head tilting to the side. 'Ah, well, you could remind me.' She slides her hands round the back of my neck and pulls me down so that my face and hers are only millimetres apart. Pliant and moving to her will as if I have none of my own, and to be honest I don't right now, my mouth hovers over hers.

She sinks deeper into the soft pillows, bringing me down with her. 'I need you to kiss me, Nathe. I need you to kiss me now.'

I lift myself on to my elbows and feel the flames of her desire whip out of her and meet the waves of mine washing into her.

'*Oh, wooohhh*,' she murmurs, closing her eyes, stretching her arms above her head, and breathing deeply of the heady atmosphere we're creating together. 'When you kiss me,' she says, her eyes still closed, her face turned up to the glass ceiling where the night stars look down on us, 'you lift me to heights I can normally only imagine. You make me feel as if I'm on the edge of a high cliff, breathing in purer-than-pure air, every cell in my body flourishing with life.' She opens her eyes and looks at me. 'Nathe, I need you to clear my memories of *him*. He only took me to dark places.'

'If I had the power to erase those memories, Ebrielle, I would have done so the moment I saw you in his palace. But I can give you new memories. We can make them together, ones you will never want to forget.'

She nods, accepting that this will do. Biting down playfully on her bottom lip and with a teasing glint in her eyes, she whispers, 'Nathe, let's start now.'

Shivers race down my spine and I shift on to my side, lift myself up on one elbow and put the palm of my free hand on the flat of her stomach. Sliding it under her top, I move my hand across her silky-smooth skin in unhurried circles. She gasps at my touch, and the whispery sound stops me thinking of reasons why I shouldn't be doing this and I move my hand with more purpose round her waist and up her side, and under her arm. She trembles and moans and arches her back to shorten the distance between her body and mine. 'Now, Nathe. Kiss me now.'

I lower my mouth to hers and slowly, gently, savour the texture of her soft, moist, hot, hot lips. She opens her mouth and breathes me in. Both of us sigh as our tongues meet. The way they fit together – always have – always will – makes us crave more of each other. More and more and more. She tugs on the hem of my shirt, releasing buttons as she runs her hands up and over my chest, pulling it off my shoulders.

'Ebbie,' I call out. 'Ebbie.'

Breathing hard, she looks into my eyes and waits, her own eyes now smoky, her body languid, her smile bewitching. She runs her tongue over her top teeth and murmurs in that low, ultra-husky voice, 'Your turn, my love.'

It is my undoing.

Oh, we had loved each other in the physical sense before in Peridis, but this … this is the first time in this reality, with these highly perceptive corporeal bodies.

My hands tremble and, noticing this, Ebrielle sits up. Facing me, she lifts her singlet top over her head, dropping it to the floor. I look at her with so much awe and love bursting out that I realise I could go on looking at her forever and never tire.

But she grows impatient. 'Come here,' she orders, and putty to her will, I do as she commands. Moving my hands through her hair, I cradle the back of her head and kiss her mouth. I kiss her hard and long and deep. Over and over and over.

Her lips move beneath mine and then mine beneath hers as we roll across the bed, our passions rising, our hands discovering secret places, touching, soothing, exploring, igniting fires that will undoubtedly prove impossible to put out.

'*Nathe* …'

Her voice. The urgency. Oh, stars!

I pull up for air and attempt to realign my senses. I shake

my head to try to adjust to reality. Soon there will be no going back, no control over anything we say or do or feel.

She sees. Of course she sees. And she frowns and starts to toss her head. 'No … Nathe …'

She pulls me down and we kiss. But then, with the greatest of reluctance, I disengage my mouth from hers, lift my head and in a hoarse whisper I gently remind her, 'You do know that we must –'

'Don't say "stop". I don't want to stop.'

Trembling with the effort, I gently lift off her. 'Then *I'll* have to. For as long as I can.'

As we lie side by side, our pulses having a difficult time slowing down, she curls under my shoulder, her bare skin igniting fires everywhere our bodies meet. 'You do know,' she says, teasing me, 'there is still a year and some weeks before I turn eighteen.'

'It will pass.'

'Oh, right. Easy, huh?'

'I didn't say it would be easy.'

She laughs, but her voice quickly turns serious, 'Nathe, if we can't wait until I'm eighteen, what do we do?'

'Ebbie, I have no idea.'

45

Ebony

I sleep soundly and well into the morning. I only stir when Nathaneal's arms unwind from around me. I watch him leave through heavy lids, waking again sometime later when he returns and sits on the edge of my bed holding a breakfast tray with one hand, stroking the side of my face with the other. 'Good morning,' he says with a smile. It warms my heart just to see him looking so contented.

'I missed my ride.'

'He'll forgive you.'

'Will he?'

He puts the tray at the foot of my bed, crawls in between the sheets and holds me. 'He will. There's only so long you can stay mad at someone you love.'

I'm always excited to see Shadow, but since I returned from Empyrean there's an added sense of desperation in our time together, as if we need to make every minute last twice as long.

After a shower, I go down to the stables. He picks up my scent from outside and makes unhappy noises until I'm in his stall and wrapping my arms around his long arched neck. When I release him, he prances round his stable in a circle, lifting his front legs like a dancing show pony.

Nathaneal grins from the stable door. 'He's certainly happy to see you.'

'He's trying to impress me so I'll take him with me.'

'Oh, babe.'

Wiping the tears from my face, I make a clicking noise and jerk my head. Shadow trots over, neighing and snorting like a frisky foal. I nuzzle into his neck and draw in a deep whiff of the scent that usually calms me. But not today.

How am I going to leave you behind?

I wipe away a fresh crop of tears and slide a glance at Nathaneal. 'He looks well. Who's been taking care of him?'

'That would be Amber.'

'Of course.'

'And Brothers Timothy and Colin, who pitched in with exercising and keeping the stalls raked out.'

'Please thank them from me.'

He nods with a small sad smile. I hold his gaze. 'Nathe, can I have a minute?'

His eyes soften. 'I'll be outside.'

Once I'm alone with Shadow, I stroke his face with one hand while he nibbles the fingers of my other. 'You know I love you, right?' He gives me a lovely soft nicker, moving his ears forward as he listens. 'We had fun together over the years, didn't we? All those exhilarating rides, I'll never forget them. You knew I needed to move fast, feel the wind in my face, and you gave that to me. It was the closest I came to flying. Thank you, baby. You brought comfort to a very confused little girl.'

He gives a tremulous high-pitched neigh, his ears

flickering back and forth, eyes roving. 'Shadow, one day soon I ... you know I have to go away. I would do anything to take you with me. I just can't, baby.'

He lifts his head and makes a shrill sound of distress. Nudging me backwards, he stomps around his stall.

'Whoa, boy, whoa, whoa down. It's not today. OK? Not today.'

I calm him and hold him, stroking his head, his neck, the shoulders that I love and know so well. I soothe him until his heart – and mine – slow to a more normal pace. Then I turn my head sideways and lay the left side of my face on his warm coat. Taking in all the scents and smells I can detect, I lock them into my memory.

When I go outside, Nathaneal watches me walk over to him. Frowning, he opens his arms. I walk into them and he holds me.

Amber turns her mum's Honda into the driveway, and by the time we walk back to the house Jordan is coming out the front door with a picnic basket in his hands. We decide to drive to the ridge together and we all pile in.

'Are you excited?' Amber asks, catching my eye in the mirror.

'I will be when I know it's possible to fly using all eight wings.'

'You'll be fine.'

'Hmm, I hope so.'

Beside me in the backseat, Nathaneal squeezes my hand.

'Well, whatever happens on the ridge today, whether I sail, or ... sink, I'm glad you're both going to be there watching.'

349

'You mean, you're glad you're gonna have witnesses,' Jordan teases.

'The only thing I'm going to witness today,' Amber says, 'is my best friend flying like a bird.'

I love her optimism. It helps to settle my nerves. I'm going to miss Amber. I could not have had a better friend.

There's no one on the ridge, no sightseers or hang-gliders or lovers looking for a secret place to be alone. It's a relief. And to give me a sense of the distances involved, the four of us walk around the edge together, starting with the cliffs facing west that overlook the Cedar Oakes Valley and a patchwork of farmlands stretching back for as far as the eye can see; then north to the abrupt drop over the Windhaven River; and lastly south to the mountains that hem the valley in like a box. It was in the south-west foothills that I grew up, knowing without understanding why I wasn't where I should be, neither in place nor in mind.

'OK, so where's the best viewing position?' Jordan asks as we move back from the edge.

They agree on a rocky area hugging the western cliffs.

'This isn't a show,' I remind him.

Jordan puts his arm around me. 'Good luck, Ebrielle.'

Amber gives me a hug before turning and giving Nathaneal a harsh glare. 'You do know what you're doing?'

Before he answers, Jordan tugs her away. 'He knows. She'll be fine.'

Unable to take my eyes off them, I watch with clenched fists as they climb over boulders. 'Be careful up there,' I call out.

Taking no notice, they leap across the boulders until they reach the one closest to the cliff edge. Amber goes straight to the outermost point, but Jordan brings her back to the safer side where they settle down together and share a quick but passionate kiss.

My lesson begins with simple warm-up stretches, moving quickly through exercises on controlling my wings' release and withdrawal, expanding on last night's session. But now, in the midday glare, I notice more things about my wings. Like their size when fully stretched out, and how little they weigh, how they hold themselves up with no conscious effort. Best of all, after a while, I start to think less about the steps and just *feel* how I want them to move.

We break for a short lunch and, thanks to Jordan, who packed enough food to feed a small army, we're still eating and sipping wine an hour or so later. It's so pleasant and relaxing that no one wants to move, and no one does for a while, content to pretend we're just two couples enjoying a picnic together one fine afternoon on the ridge. But eventually we all notice the sun has shifted over towards the western horizon. And since no one wants me making my first flight in darkness, Amber and Jordan pack up and return to the boulder on the cliff face, while Nathaneal returns to my lessons, explaining how my wings will work in pairs.

'Your smallest ones are at the top,' he explains. 'There's one on each side of your spine, graduating to the largest at the lower end of your ribs.'

Describing my wings helps me visualise the way they move. It's then I manage to maintain a steady rhythm of

351

running, jumping and getting the feeling of lifting about a metre off the ground. It's a start.

I spend the rest of the afternoon learning a technique called 'flapping flight'.

'This will keep you in the air,' Nathaneal explains, 'as long as you maintain a continuous fluid motion.'

I work steadily through the flapping exercises and pretty soon I'm moving all eight wings in a rhythm of six wing-beats interspersed with two-second pretend-glides.

'Breathe,' Nathaneal reminds me. And while running alongside me, he goes to straighten my posture, putting his hands on my sides, inadvertently brushing my sensitive ticklish areas and I collapse in a heap, laughing, wings fold-ing this way and that way over the top of me.

Parting my wings with gentle hands, he looks down at me, his blue eyes blazing with his love. 'Good news.'

Uh-oh.

'You're ready.'

'Really?' I've worked towards this moment all day, but now that it's here I get an instant sinking feeling in my stomach.

He reaches for my hand between the layers of feathers and I clasp it like a lifeline. 'Nathe …' I glance at the cliff edge and have to swallow.

'You'll be fine. I know you're ready.'

'Hmm, maybe I should request a second opinion.' I search the sky from one end to the other. 'Where is my sister when I need her?'

He takes my two hands in his. 'You don't need Shae. You're such a fast learner you hardly need me here.'

352

'Do not be ridiculous. Look, if you're just going to throw me off that cliff hoping my natural instincts will kick in, I have to tell you, that sort of thing doesn't happen with me. I don't have natural angel instincts yet.'

'I'm not going to throw you off the cliff.'

'Oh? Well, goodie, because for a second there I thought –'

'You're going to jump off it.'

'*What?*'

He puts his hands on my shoulders and pushes calm energy into me. I soak it up, absorbing it all. When he releases me I mutter, 'That's all? If I'm going to do this, I need a lot more of your calming magic than that.'

By now the sun is deep in the western sky, heading fast for the horizon. And it's colder now that the day is drawing to a close. A flock of Aracals flies overhead, preparing for their usual nightly jaunts. As long as they don't harm humans, we won't touch the flocks trapped on Earth when the gates sealed.

'May I suggest that what you're feeling is fear?'

'No, you may not. I'm not afraid. You heard our High King – he said I was fearless in the face of a daunting enemy. Nathe, I *want* to fly.'

His grin is lopsided. But I suppose he's right. Why wouldn't I be at least a little anxious? But fear has never stopped me moving forward before. 'OK. OK. So how far from the edge do you think I should stand?'

He walks me over to where the clearing begins at the base of a rock face. Then he turns me to face west and the cliffs that overlook the valley.

He can't be serious.

'You can do it!' Amber cries out.

I glance across the grassed area between where I'm standing and the cliff I'm going to jump off. Shadows are making it hard to tell where the ridge ends and the sheer vertical drop begins.

'*Ebrielle*,' Nathaneal says, his voice a soft plea as he steps in front of me and touches my cheek with his knuckles, 'trust me.' His eyes blaze bright blue, reminding me of his angelic heritage – *my* heritage. Flying is the last link I need in order to belong.

To *really* belong.

'I've got this.'

He smiles and slides his arms around me, lifting me off the ground. When he brings me down he whispers into my mind, *Thank you*, and kisses me long and hard and … oh so sweetly.

'More,' I whisper when we part.

'When you return.' He winks.

He steps back and opens his arms wide for me to pass. Amber pulls Jordan up on his feet, sensing that this time …

I psych myself up for the run. 'Nathe, if something goes wrong, you will catch me, right?'

'Every time.'

I take a deep breath, and as the sun sets fire to the splatter of low clouds on the horizon, I keep my eyes focused on the disappearing orange orb and run straight at it. Keeping my head and back upright, I ignore the urge to drop and roll to safety as I approach the cliff edge. Instead, I accelerate over it.

Oh shit, shit, shit.

I start to drop immediately. One second is all it takes for my feet to feel nothing but air and the knot in my gut explodes. I start over-breathing, a very human reaction to stress. But I'm not human.

I'm an angel.

And I have eight astonishing wings that only I can control.

With all my wings out and spread wide, I realise I'm not dropping but gliding.

'Look at her, Jordan,' I hear Amber say.

'She's like an eagle,' he replies, awe in both their voices.

But my wings aren't actually lifting me yet and the angle of the glide is heading pretty quickly towards the rocky ground and a narrow part of the river below.

I know how to do this, with six deep wingbeats interspersed with two seconds of –

Oh, forget that! Just flap those wings with strong purposeful beats. Move! Up. Down. Up …

I close my eyes and let myself go – *really* let go.

The sound of Nathaneal's wingbeats tells me he's not far away. I like the comfort that brings, but I don't need rescuing. I did it. I'm flying on my own.

He draws alongside me. 'Open your eyes, Ebbie, you're missing the view. It's spectacular up here.'

When I open them, the first things I see are *his* eyes, iridescent, brilliant blue, shimmering with love and pride. 'Wow, it sure is.'

His laughs, tossing his head back. 'Come on, let's go higher.'

Without calculating the degree I need to tilt my wings, I simply allow the notion of lifting to enter my thoughts and visualise *feeling* myself rising.

And my reward is a sense of being profoundly and uninhibitedly free.

As we swing round and fly past the western cliffs, Amber and Jordan jump up and down, cheering me on.

Beaming inside, I glance at Nathaneal. 'I could get used to this.'

'You were born to fly.'

'You know, I think you're right.'

We land on the ridge and Jordan and Amber run and jump down from their perch, still whistling and cheering. They hug me, then each other, and it's a rare moment of complete and utter elation. I savour it. I lock it away, adding it to all my other memories that I now get to keep forever.

46

Jordan

On Sunday morning I wake with a sick feeling of dread in my gut. Today is the day the angels leave. Today Thane will take the girl I knew as Ebony to make a home together in Avena.

'What time are they leaving?' Amber asks, waking up after a restless night.

I tighten my arms around her, pulling my quilt up over her shoulders. Some of her tousled blonde hair, damp with recent tears, falls over her eyes. I tuck it gently behind her ear. 'After we get up.'

She spins around in my arms and looks into my face. 'Then let's stay in bed all day.'

I'm not sure but I think she's serious. 'Great idea. On any other day I would take you up on that offer, but ...'

'Just not today.'

'I suppose we should get this over with. It won't be easy for Ebrielle either.'

'I know.' She sniffs and swallows down her tears.

Man, how are we gonna make it through the goodbyes? I'm glad Ebrielle saw her parents last night. Taking the opportunity to practise her flying, she and Thane flew down

357

into the valley after dinner to Amber's parents' house. And on their return they found the seven dark forces waiting on the front deck. One after the other, the small fierce-looking angels, glowing like shooting stars, fell to their knees and swore fealty to her, promising to protect her for eternity.

Who would have thought?

A knock at the door is Thane. He pokes his head in. 'Sorry, guys, but we need to get moving.'

'Yeah, OK. Give us ten minutes?'

'Sure. I thought it might be easier for Ebbie if you two were there when she says goodbye to Shadow.'

'Oh hell,' Amber says.

'If this is too hard for you, Amber —'

She doesn't let him finish. 'No. I'll be there. Wait for us.'

We dress without talking. I've felt sadness before. Jeez, my mother died — *twice*. But I don't remember ever feeling like this — sluggish inside, with heavy limbs, unwilling to move.

We meet at the back door where the girls hug and walk to the stables arm in arm. Beside me, Thane looks grim.

I haven't had much to do with horses, but when the girls stop about halfway from the barn and glance at each other with startled expressions, I get the feeling this is gonna be harder than anyone imagined.

The girls start running. Thane takes off after them.

'Hey, what's going on?' I call out. They're too busy opening gates and barn doors to answer, but then I hear it.

I've never heard a horse *cry*. It's a shock. It gets inside you. The shrieking, screaming noise Shadow is making leaves no doubt that the big guy knows exactly what's about to happen.

By the time I get there, Ebrielle and Amber are all over him, whispering, trying to stroke his head, but he's jumping around, lifting his front legs into the air, his eyes almost all white.

Thane moves into Shadow's stall. 'Hey, hey, hey, boy,' he croons, bringing the stallion's head down and holding him by sheer angelic force. Amber steps back for Thane to work his magic, and he does what he does best, pushes calmness into Shadow's chest through his glowing hands.

Ebrielle inhales a shuddering breath and glances at Thane. 'Thank you.'

He nods and moves out, leaving Ebrielle stroking Shadow's face with tender fingers and talking to him in a voice that's both calm like honey and soaked with sadness. 'My beautiful boy, I'm not going to draw this out because it will only hurt you more. You know that I love you. You know that, right?' He neighs a long trill sound and moves his head up and down. She pulls him back to her. 'Of course, I know. Don't worry, I know that too.'

She takes a deep breath. 'Shadow, even though we c-can't be together any more, I'll still be with you.' Her hand slides down to where Shadow's big heart is thumping away. 'Wherever you go, I'll be in here. Always. Remember that, OK?'

Shadow nickers and shakes his head. He understands her, but he's not happy. He starts kicking and pawing the ground, but then Ebrielle gathers her breath for one final goodbye. He senses this and, when she leans into him, putting her face flush against his neck, he holds still for her. 'Thank you for being there when I needed you, which was

359

a lot of times, I know,' she says with a wry smile, tears pouring out now. 'Be good to Amber, OK? And … ride fast, baby, ride as hard as your heart desires. Goodbye, Shadow. Goodbye, my beautiful boy.'

Thane motions to Amber, who hurries Ebrielle outside, then waves me over to help him hold Shadow down while he pushes his calm healing powers into the horse.

But we're not fast enough. We just get our arms around him when he lets out a wild primal scream that shakes me to my core.

47

Ebony

Leaving Cedar Oakes and everyone I love behind is crushing me. I said goodbye to Amber's parents and my mum and dad last night. It was hard and everyone cried. And now Shadow. Any more, and my soul will curl up and die.

Amber rushes me away, but I still hear his scream. I want to run back and comfort him, blanket him in my love, wrap him up inside it so tightly it will keep the two of us bound together forever – how we should be. I never thought I would have to part from him except in death. Not like this. To walk away feels so wrong.

But letting Shadow see me again would be cruel. Too cruel. So I stand here and let the shuddering sobs work through me, layer after layer.

'I'll take good care of him,' Amber says. 'How could I not love him? He's my link to you.'

'Thank you, Amber.' It occurs to me how hard this is for her too and I ask, 'But who's going to be there for you?'

Just then Jordan comes out. Amber catches my eye, lifts her eyebrows and shrugs.

'You know, Amber, it will be more like you taking care of him.'

'I know!' she says, carrying my joke a little further with a shaky smile.

'But only until I polish up my Guardian skills. Amber, Jordan's life is going to improve. It's going to be amazing.'

She smiles at this, but neither of us can hold a happy face for long, and when Jordan arrives he finds us in a tight embrace with Amber whimpering, 'I'm happy for you, hon. I really am. It's just that I'm going to miss you like crazy.'

'I'll miss you too, Amber. You have been more than a friend, especially this year with all that we learned about me and the Earth and its different worlds. Thank you for not simply assuming I was crazy and petitioning to have me locked away.'

She wants to laugh, but trying to be brave is stopping her. I press my forehead against hers. 'You don't have to say anything. I know. Thank you for being the best friend anyone could ever have.'

She bites down on her lower lip and nods.

Nathaneal joins us and we head to the portal, walking along the meandering paths through the forest that's growing back with lush, deep green foliage. At the portal we find Shae and Isaac waiting with my personal guard, the seven angels who were born of evil but now have sworn to protect me.

For the next few minutes everybody exchanges hugs and kisses. Then it's Nathaneal's turn to say goodbye to Jordan and they hug. Nathaneal gives Jordan encouragement and advice for the years ahead and hands him a set of keys, then as he steps back he musses Jordan's hair.

The keys puzzle Jordan and he holds them up. 'What are these for?'

'The house, everything inside it, the land it sits on – oh, and the car.'

'Are you serious?'

Nathaneal smiles. 'I've signed everything over to you. The house is in trust until the day you turn eighteen, but yours to live in from today. The paperwork is in one of two envelopes sitting on your new desk in your new study with the phone number of the solicitor who will lodge the documents with the courts as soon as you add your signature. There are also two financial accounts set up in your name. One is for your tertiary education, the other for living expenses. The details, account numbers, key cards are in the second envelope.'

'I-I-I don't know what to say.'

'Didn't I tell you that once you helped me find Ebrielle and she returns home to Avena your life would improve?'

'Yeah but, Thane, this … this is so much more.' He turns to me. 'Did you know?'

'Only this morning. Come here, Jordy.' He steps into my arms and I hold him tight.

'I'm not sure whether I thanked you for saving my life,' he says. 'I owe you both so much.' He glances at Nathaneal. 'I'll pay you back one day.'

'Jordan, you don't pay back a gift.'

'Thane, I won't let you down. I'll make something of my life.'

'Choose to be happy, Jordan.'

'Besides,' I tell him, 'you can't go wrong now that I'm

watching over you.'

'Yeah, about that, you haven't explained yet how the bond works. I don't have to look over my shoulder every time I take a —?'

Nathaneal cuts him off as gently as a brick through a store window. 'Ebbie, your uncle has been allowed to say goodbye.'

'Zavier is here? Now?'

He steps out from behind a thatch of trees, Brother Alex a pace behind him. He walks up to me with an uncertain smile. 'I've been under a code of silence since the acceptance of my plea to become a Brother of the Holy Cross. Brother Alexander is my mentor and he is allowing me to break my code for the purpose of saying goodbye to my niece, and to ask …' He pauses to gather his breath. 'Ebrielle, I'm sorry for all the harm and all the pain I brought down upon you. I know saying sorry isn't enough, but I want you to know that I regret it all.'

I hold out my hands and he takes them, and in his eyes I see a tortured soul so remorseful he is willing to do whatever he can to make amends. 'It's all right, Uncle, I forgive you.'

We embrace, and when we pull apart, the man who was once my teacher but really an angel, who betrayed me, saved me, and then warned me of Luca's trap, turns and walks back towards the monastery with Brother Alex patting his shoulder.

Shae and Isaac and my new security guard move closer to the portal. Nathaneal takes my hand. I wave at Jordan and Amber, but I can't just walk out of their lives like this. I run back and hug them both at the same time, squeezing them hard, but tenderly. 'I love you both. Take care of each other.'

I take Nathaneal's hand again and this time we walk into the portal, with me glancing over my shoulder and blowing kisses with trembling fingers and a racing heart. And suddenly there are no words left. Knowing this, Nathaneal releases his wings, sweeps me into his arms and lifts me into the skies of the ever-changing border realm. While he holds me, I rest my head on his shoulder and sob, for the end of my time on Earth, on the saddest day of my life.

But today is also the beginning of my new life, an eternal life with Nathaneal, living and breathing, learning and loving and growing amongst my own kind, with parents who have waited nearly seventeen years to meet me, and family and friends I've yet to meet but who will become integral members of my new world, the world where I know in the deepest parts of my heart and soul that I belong.

Avena

Standing before the great northern gates, I stop to catch my breath and absorb the reality of the moment. Today, I'm coming home.

While Nathaneal and Isaac have a chat with the Gatekeepers, two males of the Dominion Order, my own guard keep near and watchful with their large almond-shaped eyes.

Nathaneal and Isaac return with two towering Archangels, one male, the other, who appears to be in charge, female. He introduces them, explaining, 'They have orders to take your security guard to Empyrean for debriefing and training.'

'Is that necessary?' I ask. Since the High King told me the truth about the 'dark forces' I have felt a need to make up for the treatment Gabriel put them through. I can't do that if they're taken from me.

'They will be safe and return with invaluable skills,' she explains.

I ask her, 'How long will this process take?'

'That depends on their current skill levels, and how quickly they reach the standard considered adequate to protect you, Princess Ebrielle.'

My eyes fly to Nathaneal's, asking him why she just addressed me as Princess.

He laughs under his breath. Heads turn to him but he brushes away their questions, sending me the image of the High King bestowing me with the title 'Princess of Hope'.

Oh. That was for real?

Using mind-link imagery to communicate with my seven security guards, I explain that they have to go with the Archangels to Empyrean. They are unwilling to leave me, but I assure them I will be safe with Nathaneal until their return, and though they remain reluctant they go quietly, zooming into the sky via the Archangels' preferred method of transportation – straight up and very fast.

Linking his fingers with mine, Nathaneal squeezes my hand. He can't seem to stop grinning. He's so excited his heart is beating like a hummingbird's on a warm summer's day. He keeps looking for excuses to touch me, to whisper words, to suddenly pick me up and spin me around, or lift me into the air and gaze up at me with his blue eyes glazing over, shaking his head.

And now, as we stand before the gates, a few steps from entering Avenean territory, he leans down and whispers, 'Are you ready to come home, Ebbie?'

'As long as I'm with you, I'm ready for anything.'

The gates swing inwards, revealing the Arc of a Thousand Stairs, the bridge known throughout the universe for uniting one world to the next in spectacular style.

I watch with trembling knees as the stairs spiral downwards in their famous arc, appearing as if they're floating in air.

Shae's palms come down on my shoulders. 'Welcome home, sister.'

Overwhelmed with emotion, and still a little numb from all the goodbyes, I just nod, and wish that every time I close my eyes I could stop seeing Shadow and feeling my heart overflow with sadness. Leaving him behind has left a deep chasm inside me that's not going to be easy to fill.

Halfway down the glittering stairs, as my lungs gradually adjust to the subtle atmospheric changes, I get my first glimpse of the capital, Aarabyth. Its gleaming glass towers reflect the sunlight in a rainbow of colours that makes me sigh in wonder. 'It's beautiful.'

Nathaneal nods. 'Wait till you see the gardens in the Centre Square, the purple magnolia trees that surround it, and the Temple with all its pillars, and the towering cathedral where royalty is crowned, and –'

Isaac comes up behind us. Throwing an arm around each of us he looks at Nathaneal first. 'If your grin gets any wider I'm afraid your face will split into two, and Michael will have me hung and quartered.' He turns to me. 'There's plenty of time to see the city. It's hardly changed in three thousand years.'

I laugh. 'Wise words, Isaac. Let's go home.'

We reach the last stair and step on to the viewing plat-form. Apparently I'm going to be living on a property next door to my sister's in the Lavender Ranges, where she and Isaac live with their young daughter – my niece, whom I can't wait to meet.

A bubble of excitement tries to mushroom inside me, but just as quickly it deflates again. I stand still for a moment and just breathe. Underlying the flawless beauty of this land, there's also a sense of freedom. Of peace. It stirs inside my veins. And there's a scent in the breeze that's fresh and full of promise. I know I'm going to be happy here. It's just that now my heart is heavy with the friendships I've had to leave behind, my human parents, my best friends, and Shadow.

Nathaneal pulls up our linked hands and kisses my knuckles, one feather-light kiss after another. 'It will take time.'

I nod and manage a smile. He deserves to be happy.

Shae moves to the left of the platform, facing north. She glances at us over her shoulder. 'Ready, everyone?'

The four of us leap into the air, wings unfurling, beating, lifting us higher and moving us faster towards the Lavender Ranges, apparently named for their mass displays of lavender blossoms all year round.

'You *will* smile freely again, Ebbie,' Nathaneal says as he flies beside me. 'It won't be long.'

'I know. But, oh, Nathe, Shadow won't understand why I left him, why I'm not walking into his stable every morning and taking him out for our usual ride. I can't shake the image of him watching the door, and waiting. I know him. He will wait and watch every day. He will grow old watching that door. For the rest of his life he's going to think I abandoned him. And he will be right.'

He pulls me against him, wings and all. 'Let me hold you, Ebbie.'

I retract my wings and we fly facing each other, chest to chest, Nathe's strong arms folded around me, his hands on my hips keeping me secure.

I close my eyes, listen to his heart beating and let him take me home.

It's not long before we're landing on park-like grounds dotted with thatches of tall lavender trees, shady green willows, acacias with their carpet of gold foliage and exotic flowering gardens. We appear to be on a ridge overlooking a river hundreds of metres down a sloping embankment covered in colourful wild flowers. Shae smiles as she watches me take it all in, then turns me around and walks me up a gentle hill. Both of my hands fly up to cover my mouth as I gasp at the sight of my new home, a multi-level house of sand-coloured stone bricks with wide, clear glass windows, cute jutting balconies and a roof split into various levels, giving it the appearance that's it's about to fly away.

'Does this mean you like it?' Shae asks, her eyes flickering to Nathaneal and Isaac.

'Like it? Are you kidding?' I spread my arms out and twirl around. 'Look at this place.' My eyes find Nathaneal's. 'You did this?' His nod is slight, nervous, worried. 'It's downright stunning.'

Isaac whacks Nathaneal on the back. 'And you were afraid she wouldn't like it,' he teases, winking at me. 'Wait until you see what your fiancé has done with the inside.'

Nathaneal shrugs, and he's so adorable in his sudden vulnerability that I can't help but stretch up on my toes and kiss his mouth, thoroughly. He moans and wraps his arms around me and, lifting my feet off the ground, he kisses me back just as thoroughly. Immersed in each other, we forget where we are, who we're with, what we're supposed to be doing.

Isaac clears his throat several times before the sound penetrates our blissful fog. 'Plenty of time for that later,' he says, jerking his head towards the house with a cheeky grin and a wink.

In the end though, it's the sound of beating wings that eases us apart and has us staring up at a wondrous sight in the sky.

'Oh wow.'

I recall Nathaneal telling me once how the horses on Avena have wings, but to see one actually flying, a beautiful white stallion so similar to Shadow that tears gather behind my eyes ... Except for the big brown wings he's flapping, I could swear it *was* Shadow.

The angel riding him is Michael, accompanied by Jezelle, flying solo beside the pair. She lands in her usual elegant fashion on high-heeled boots, immediately retracting her striking turquoise wings as soon as her feet hit the ground. Meanwhile, Michael rides the horse all the way down, jumping off when the horse stumbles its landing and almost throws the prince clear across the field.

I stare in awe as the horse flicks his wings to their magnificent full width, then folds them down against his sides.

Isaac gives Michael a hand up while Jezelle comes over and kisses my cheek. 'How was your journey?'

'G-good,' I answer, stuttering a little, unable to stop myself from walking as if in a daze towards the horse. His wings look familiar. And even while they appear somewhat odd against the horse's snowy coat, I get the sense that I should know them.

Michael kisses my cheek. 'Welcome to Avena, little one.'

'Thank you, Michael. You have a beautiful horse,' I remark, still unable to take my eyes off it.

He flicks a glance at it over his shoulder. 'Yes, he is a beauty.' He hands me a gold card. 'But he doesn't belong to me.'

'Huh?'

He indicates the card by nodding his head at it. 'Could you read that for everyone to hear, Ebrielle?'

'Uh, sure.' I open the flaps at both ends and the first thing I notice is the calligraphy. Not only are the words written in flawless articulate strokes, it's as if the ink, if that's what I can call this gold lettering, is floating above the card, in its own dimension. 'Who wrote this?'

'The High King,' Michael says.

Closing my hanging jaw, I take a deep breath and start to read.

Dear Ebrielle,
The bond between a horse and owner can prove too deep to sever without consequence. It is the way with you, and it saddens me. I have therefore intervened with the laws of nature to set things right. The wings, donated by someone who no longer has use of them, come with glad tidings. Princess of Hope, please accept my personal gift to welcome you to Avena.
                                                                        His Highness.

I glance up, searching for Nathaneal, but he's already beside me, reading over my shoulder. 'Did you know?' I ask.

He shakes his head, speechless, his eyes glistening and brimming over with joy for me.

Shae asks for the card. I hand it to her and run the last few paces, melting into Shadow's warm, silky Arabian coat. 'Oh, baby, you're here. You're really here with me.' Tears flow down my face but I don't care who sees me crying this time. This isn't about being strong or weak; these tears are because I'm grateful and humbled and clearly overwhelmed.

With my arms around Shadow's neck, my face flush against his beating heart, I peer sideways at Nathaneal as he examines one of Shadow's new wings with awe, and suddenly my thoughts turn to Amber. How did she take the news of Shadow leaving? He was her link to me and now she's lost that. But knowing Amber as I do, she would want this for me.

I run my hand over Shadow's chest and across to his new wings, the rich dark colour so beautiful against his snowy coat. I touch his feathers with my fingertips. They're warm, silky and seem to welcome me with a sense of familiarity. I lift one wing and gently tug it part way out. *Wow. It extends from his body as if he were born with it.*

Catching Nathaneal's eye over Shadow's back, I ask, 'What will happen to Shadow, living here?'

Nathaneal says, 'I'm really not sure.'

But Michael is grinning. 'The king has bestowed Shadow with immortality.'

'*Really?*' My fingers start to tremble. 'Did you hear that, baby? You're going to live a long life here with me.'

Shae comes and checks out Shadow's wing which I'm still holding partly extended. 'This frame is more complex than is usual for a horse's wing.'

That's when it occurs to me. 'I know who these wings used to belong to. I know who gave them up for Shadow.'

Nathaneal raises his eyebrows while the others exchange questioning glances. 'My uncle,' I explain. 'Zavier.'

Shadow lifts his head up and down, flattens his ears and flaps his tail high in the air. Nathaneal shakes his head and smiles at me. 'I think the High King might have a soft spot for you. I hope this doesn't mean I have competition, because that could really get awkward.'

His remark has everyone laughing. But I roll my eyes and forge a private link. *There will only ever be you, my love.*

As Nathaneal continues to hold my gaze, Isaac coughs softly and suggests they should head inside. They all readily agree to wait for the others in the house.

And suddenly we're alone – not counting Shadow. And while I stroke Shadow's long neck, still in awe that he's here with me, I raise my eyebrows pointedly. 'Others?'

'A small gathering to welcome you home.' He shrugs with an adorable smile. 'I couldn't stop them.'

A noise from the house gets our attention. It's Tash tapping at a rear window. Considering that's Uriel I can see beside her, I'm guessing they're in the kitchen cooking up a feast. They see us looking and wave.

So while we've been out here with Shadow the house has filled up with guests. Solomon runs out and welcomes me to Avena with a kiss on my cheek before returning inside.

Meanwhile, a group of angels arrives that I don't recognise. Nathaneal watches them with interest and once they appear settled inside he slides his hand down my arm and links fingers with me. 'I have so much to show you, but the sun is setting soon and I believe it's time for …' He pauses to tuck a lock of my hair behind my ear. The strands wrap around his fingers. He gives a little shake and we both smile as they untangle instantly.

'You were saying? Time for what exactly?'

'It's time for you to meet Elesha and Rhamiel, your mother and father.'

'They're here? Now?'

'They're waiting inside, along with my parents and three of my brothers you haven't met yet.'

'Nathe, I'm not sure I'm ready for mothers and fathers and brothers yet. I've only just got Shadow back.'

He points to a barn and a series of stables connected to the house's southern end by a covered walkway. 'Shadow will be fine. We'll take him to the stables first, introduce him to his new friends.'

'Friends?'

He just flashes his stunning smile at me.

'I thought I was going to get a few days to unwind.'

He holds my face between his two hands and soothes me with a kiss that stops my pulse from skittering, a kiss so full of love it leaves no room for doubt. He draws back and looks into my eyes with his own a blaze of brilliant blue fire. 'Ebrielle, you have nothing to worry about. You're home now.'

He's right. I'm finally home. And I can't think of a more beautiful place to live.

The End

Acknowledgements

What a journey I've had with this series. It began as a thought in my hospital bed ten years ago that I shelved until I could write again. Chemotherapy for bone marrow cancer, and painkillers for a broken back, had the nasty side effects of damping down my concentration levels. Once I was home, my medications had me falling asleep on the computer, literally, every day for a few years after my transplant in 2004 until my health improved and my medication decreased. It was 2007 when I began to write the first draft of *Hidden*. By December the following year the first draft was completed and came in at a massive 140,000 words. After many revisions and trimmings the manuscript landed on my publisher's desk in 2010.

Ele Fountain, Bloomsbury Publishing's Senior Commissioning Editor, read it, saw how good this series could be and made me an offer for three books. It was like starting over again with my first publication. The joy was immeasurable.

My heartfelt thanks go to Ele, who pushed me to lift and lift until *Hidden* was right for the market that had changed so much in the eight years since my last book, *The Key*, had been published. Thank you, Ele. It was a pleasure working with you. I wish you all the best in your new adventures.

After fifteen years and five books together I will certainly miss you.

Zöe Griffiths, a lovely person and a brilliant editor, stepped in for Ele in editing *Fearless*. Zöe, I could not have been happier to land in your more-than-capable hands. Thank you for reading *Hidden* and *Broken* on your honeymoon and then pushing me into making *Fearless* the best of the series.

I also want to thank the staff of Bloomsbury's London, New York and Sydney offices for their tireless enthusiasm and dedication to the *Avena* series, with special mention of the beautiful covers, for which my many thanks go to the talented designers.

To my agents Geoffrey Radford and Janelle Andrew, I thank you both. Though you live and work on opposite sides of the world, I am grateful to have you both with me on this series and taking care of the million and one things that needed doing so I could get on with what I love best – writing.

I have a truckload of thanks for Sonia Palmisano from Bloomsbury's Sydney office. Sonia, I thoroughly appreciate your remarkable organisational skills and support at my author events. Thank you for smoothing the roads and clearing the paths.

Then there is my family. My sister Therese has been the fundamental driving force behind this series. I can't thank you enough, sis, for your encouragement and belief in me. You saved my life once with your abundant healthy stem cells, and now you have helped resurrect my career. What more can a big sister do? Wait, I'm sure I'll think of something.

Thank you also to my daughters, Amanda Canham and Danielle Curley, who have both embarked on their own writing careers. You are the first to read my stories, the first to critique them; you are my backstops, the jewels in my crown, and I am truly blessed to have you both in my life.

Finally, I want to thank *you*, my readers, for your support and encouragement, and for coming on this incredible journey with me. I am and always will be grateful.